GHOST WRITER

MARY LUDLAM SCUDDER:
Silent for 300 Years,
She Returns to Tell Her Story

GHOST WRITER

MARY LUDLAM SCUDDER:
Silent for 300 Years,
She Returns to Tell Her Story

by Phyllis Rowland

©2008 ISBN 978-0-557-03358-4
Library of Congress Control Number: 2009904237

The Bridge

The way I walk, I see my mother walking,
Her feet secure and firm upon the ground.
The way I talk, I hear my mother talking,
and hear my daughters echoing the sound.
The way she thought, I find myself now thinking,
The generations linking of the mind.
The bridge of immortality I'm walking,
the voice before me echoing behind.

Phyllis Rowland 1995

Acknowledgments

"Weft" and "warp" — weaving words — are the essential foundation or base of any structure or organization. The warp — threads that run lengthwise, and the woof — threads that run across, create the fabric.

In the following pages, the "warp" that runs lengthwise through this story supplies the factual threads documented in 17th Century history. Within these lines are the words of many record keepers, reporters, and writers whose works provide both primary and secondary sources. These are listed by chapter and number in end-notes following the conclusion of the book.

Across these vital strands of Colonial history, I have woven the somewhat fictional "weft" — the colorful threads of Mary Ludlam Scudder's own story.

Grand-Mary's memoir could never have come to fruition without the help of my faithful friends in Wichita River City Writers group; KWA's Thursday Critique group; and my creative friends and family — readers and tour guides — in particular Bill Geist, Kate Geist Stevens, Patsi Graham, Aleta Hastings, Esther Walker, Gina Ramsey, Shane and Cindy Geist, Susan Arnold, Pam King, Kristin Jessup, Heath Griffin, and Bill Ludlam. Thank you.

Much credit goes to my editor, Dave King, co-author of *Self-Editing for Fiction Writers*, whose lessons, advice, and critiques taught me nearly everything I know about writing. Thank you forever, Dave.

I appreciate the encouragement of Scudder Association members and others who are an integral part of God's promise to Grand-Mary: the grandchildren of myriad names who claim kinship with Thomas or Mary Ludlam Scudder or their Huntington minister, Reverend William Leverich.

I must also give credit to the spirit of Grand-Mary who visited me often throughout the writing of her memoirs, ever urging me to help her fulfill her God-given plan — to tell her story to descendants now scattered across the world, who are carrying out their own primary purposes.

MARY LUDLAM SCUDDER'S FAMILY TREE

WILLIAM LUDLAM+MARY UMN		PHILIP FORDHAM+ELIZABETH SHOTBOLT	
grandfather	grandmother	grandfather	grandmother
		Jamacia, b. 1603	
Anthony, b. 1607		Rev. Robert Fordham, b. 1605	
Obadiah, b. 1609		Philip, b. 1606	
		Ruth, b. 1608	
		FLORENCE, b. 1609	
		John, b. 1610	
		Mary, b. aft. 1611	
WILLIAM LUDLAM, II, b. 1605		CLEMENCE FORDHAM, b. 1607	
father		mother	

SCUDDER SIDE
HENRY SCUDDER, Sr. + ELIZABETH ? b. 1545

THOMAS SCUDDER, I. +ELIZABETH ?
         b. 1586   b. 1581

Ludlam Children:	Scudder Children:
Mary's Siblings:	Thomas II.'s siblings
John, b. 1626	Liam (William), b. about 1615
Luddie (William III), b. 1627	Elizabeth, b. about 1617, m. Bartholomew
Grace, b. 1630	John, b. abt. 1619
Anthony, b. 1631	Martha, b. about 1622
Hal (Henry), b. 1638	Henry, b. 1630
Abbie (Frances Abigail), b. 1641	
Joseph, b. 1646	
MARY LUDLAM, b. 1639 mar.	THOM SCUDDER II., b. 1625
Their	Children:
Isaac, b. 1657	Elizabeth, b. 1658
Maria (Mary), b. 1662	Sarah, b. 1665
BENJAMIN SCUDDER, b. 1668	Mercy, b. 1669
Timothy, b. 1670	Clemence, b. 1674

JACOB (BENJAMIN'S 7TH child), b. 1707 at Huntington, Long Island, NY
LEMUEL (JACOB'S 5th child), b. 1741 at Huntington, Long Island, NY
RICHARD (LEMUEL'S 6th child) b. 1774 at Princeton, Cumberland, New Jersey
LEMUEL (RICHARD'S 3rd child), b. 1797 at Somerset, New Jersey
JANE C. SCUDDER (child of LEMUEL) b. 1819 at Louisville, Jefferson, Kentucky
Married John Washington Heath
JOHN SYLVESTER HEATH (3rd child of JANE C. SCUDDER HEATH), b. 1844 at Alton,
Crawford Co., Indiana
GEORGE MILTON HEATH (5th child of JOHN SYLVESTER HEATH), b. 1878 at Fostoria,
Pottawatomie County, Kansas
BEULAH LILLIAN HEATH (2nd child of GEORGE M. HEATH), b. 1906,
Pottawatomie Co., KS
Married John Francis Wilson
PHYLLIS CARROL WILSON (1st child of BEULAH), b. 1932 in Wichita Co., Kansas

One

∾

My mind was running on several tracks Monday morning as I drove down Central Avenue. I had only two more clients' memoirs to finish—saving lives, one story at a time. Then I could retire to write my own story. A multi-tasker, I had one ear tuned in to my husband—spinning another WWII yarn.

"...I woke up with the incredible sensation that Betty Grable was kissing my face, all over my cheeks, my forehead, my lips. It was marvelous. And then it dawned on me—it was the dog slobbering all over my face, licking me. Wherever that dog was, generally speaking, that's where the commander was, and as far as he was concerned, sleeping on guard duty was next to treason. I leapt to my feet, grabbed the rifle that had been lying on the muddy ground just outside, assumed a sentry-like position, and just as the commander rounded the corner I called out, 'Halt! Who goes there?'

'Your commander,' he said crisply.

'Pass, Sir.'

His voice was clear, his tone approving. 'Very, very efficient! What's your name, sailor?'

'Rowland, Sir.'

'Very good,' he said as he scribbled my name down. 'Carry on.'

I watched as his dog trotted off behind him, and I could swear her tail wagged — twice."

With barely a pause, Ken began another of his stories. I loved hearing them. Certainly better than listening to Limbaugh on the radio. The light at Central and Rock Road turned red, and I slowed to a stop. I'd heard this story before, too, so with half my attention, I watched the giant electronic billboard at the corner rotate from one ad to another. First, the one with the grammar that always made me cringe: "Mommy and me go to...." I glanced down at the traffic light — still red — and missed the next change-over but caught a glimpse of the third, one I'd never noticed before — a solid, dark blue background with a bright glow of holographic words at least two feet high:

Phyllis, go to Grand-Mary.com.

I stared, blinked, then shook my head to clear my vision. "Ken, do you see that?"

"See what?"

The car behind me honked. I looked down to find the light green, and gunned my red Corsica right around the corner, heading south toward Circuit City on Kellogg Drive.

Writing my last client's memoir had left me with sleep deprivation, a dizzying spell of double vision, and a sizable check — more than enough to buy a big flat-screen TV.

I pulled into the parking lot and turned the key off. As we got out of the car, some old lady behind me called, "Hey, I've never seen a tag like that before. FLSRYTZ. What's that mean?"

I grinned. "Thanks for asking. It says, 'Phyllis writes.' Get it? I'm a writer." I handed her my business card, and with a quick wave goodbye, I hurried to catch up with Ken who, polite as always, was holding the door for me. In the store, we walked straight to the TV displays. "Can you really tell the difference between the picture on flat screens and non?" I asked the clerk.

"Sure, just look around. You'll see."

Ken paused to watch a bit of the TV's scenic channel supplied by corporate headquarters. He whistled. "Look at that!"

"Yeah, and look at the price." I moved on down the line of sets, all tuned to the same channel, and I swear something made me trip. Catching myself before falling flat, I ended up in front of the next screen as the picture changed to a dark blue stormy sky flashing an iridescent message:

PHYLLIS, GO TO GRAND-MARY.COM.

"Ken, look!"

"Look at what? Isn't that the same show I'm watching?"

Dizzying double vision hit again, and the message melted away into the original scenic shot. "I think I've had enough shopping for today." I touched Ken's arm. "Do you mind if we go on home?"

"Guess you want me to drive. Something wrong?"

"Just lack of sleep, I guess. I finally finished the Keyse memoir about 3a.m., then could not shut my mind down.

Dreams of editing kept spinning around in my head. Didn't get much rest."

Back at home, Ken settled himself in his lounge chair and flipped on the new KAKE-TV Channel 22. Across the bottom of the screen, a banner crawled to the left: WICHITA, KANSAS THUNDERSTORM WATCH UNTIL 11:00 P.M. MATLOCK, MATLOCK, ENGLAND COOL AND MISTY. FOR MORE INFORMATION — **GO TO GRAND-MARY.COM.**

"Ken, did you see that?" My voice trembled, but he didn't notice.

"Yeah, looks like it's going to storm again this afternoon," he said as he flipped to Regis and Kathy.

With both hands, I massaged my temples. If you don't believe in ghosts — and I do not — something like this can make you doubt your sanity. Sleep would help. "Hey, Ken, I think I'll go back to bed for a while."

"Mmm," he mumbled. He wouldn't miss me.

Unfortunately — or fortunately as the case may be — my office is next to the bedroom, and I couldn't resist the chance to stop and check....

I slid out the keyboard drawer, clicked the internet Explorer icon, and in the URL space, like an obedient robot, I typed "Grand-Mary.com." Suddenly thunder roared and the screen flickered and turned dark except for a strange request:

**I pray thee, Phyllis, dost thou yet edit and publish memoirs?
If that be true, I greatly desire thy help.
Thou wilt find here the first few lines of a chapter from
my memoir. If thou thinkest it worthy of thy time,
I would appreciate thine assistance setting my story right.**

I eagerly awaite thine answer.

REMEMBERINGS OF MARY LUDLAM SCUDDER[1]

Shrouded amidst luxuriant foliage, grotesque gargoyles scowl from the towering pinnacles of St. Giles Church. The ancient structure stands on the verge of a most romantic rock, overlooking our Derwent Valley farm and Matlock town below. In many parts of this English churchyard, graves are cut out of the solid rock. My fingers trace words chiseled into a weather-washed stone.

**Clemence Fordham Ludlam
Wife of William Ludlam
In ye 41st Year of her Age
Her Bleesed Soul Ascended Up To Heaven
August ye 4th AD 1646**

Mama's burial place. Time may someday wear away the graven letters, but the memories and the guilt I felt are forever carved in my heart.

～

Something about the woman's writing filled me with yearning, haunted me with its imagery, like a piece of the past bobbing to the surface of nearly forgotten memories.

But who was Mary Ludlam? Had she attended one of my writing classes? Or did the story ring a faint bell in the recesses of my own memories. My mother's funeral? No. Not the story. The name. My family history? Ludlam. Yes! I'd seen that name recently.

I checked the framed family tree that hangs in my office—Grandpa's research from 1927, all in his handwriting— Jane C. Scudder, married John Sylvester Heath. Jane C. was Grandpa's brick wall.

In the office light, I was startled by the reflection of a face in the framed glass, a pointy white collar, a white cap, and fringes of red hair peaking out at the forehead— not me at all. I'd kept my hair dyed blonde for years.

I turned to the computer and clicked "Index of Individuals" in my family tree program files. There it was! My seventh great-grandmother. Mary Ludlam, born August 4, 1639, in Matlock, Derbyshire, England, married to Thomas Scudder, 1656.

That's why the name was familiar—Mary Ludlam Scudder.

A message window opened on my computer screen:

"Phyllis, hast thou finished reading? Surely my story would be a better memorial than that weathered stone in Matlock Town, would it not?"

I typed my reply. "Yes, Mary. That is a great beginning! Are you one of my Ludlam cousins? Where do you live?"

"Well...I was born in Matlock, Derbyshire, England.

"Really! I spent a week in Derbyshire with a Friendship Force group in—"

"Yes, I know. I tried to get in touch with thee there. 'Twas in 1998."

Before I could respond, another line from Mary popped up.

"I was but a wee girl when we moved from England to Southampton, Long Island. Then when I grew up, I married Thom Scudder, & we moved to a farm near Huntington on the north side of the island."

"Up by Oyster Bay? I did some research in the museum library there a few years ago."

"Yes. I was hoping we'd meet then. I raised my family in Huntington just east of Oyster Bay. Dost thou not have all that information in thy family tree records? My husband was Thom Scudder, & the grandfather thou hast been searching for — the one born in 1797 — was my great-great-great grandson, Lemuel Scudder."

Great-great-great grandson? Preposterous! I opened my family tree program again. There. Mary Ludlam, birth date Thursday, Aug 04, 1639. The keys clattered as I typed my reply: "Mary, my math skills are nothing to brag about, but are you telling me you're from the 17th century? I don't think you'd be communicating by computer if you were 400 years old."

"Prithee, how else could I get thine attention? And henceforth, let us not be impertinent, my dear. I won't be 400 for another 36 years."

An electric icicle shivered up my spine.

"Oh, my child, I didn't mean to startle! Thou seemest so taken with the story of Mama's gravestone, I thought thee knew. Take a couple of deep breaths & relax. Light that bayberry candle sitting on thy desk, & I will teach thee how to listen with all thy God-given senses!"

A disquieting thought crept into my brain: Without a web cam on my computer, how can this woman see the bayberry candle on my desk?

Forcing myself to focus on Mary's instructions, with shaky fingers I struck a match and held it to the candle-wick before typing my response. "Listen, you say?"

"Yes, it's so much easier than reading printed words. Thou hast no idea the psychic energy it taketh for me to make these sentences pop up on thy computer screen. Just listen!"

I scrunched my eyes shut tight to make the phantom message go away. Sure enough, it worked. When I looked again, the screen was clear. Suddenly, my body felt limp. I hate to admit it, but sometimes my husband is right. I do need to get more sleep.

I flipped off the monitor and blew out the candle. The light woodsy aroma of bayberry followed me as I shakily made my way down the hall to my bedroom.

Even after I turned off the light and slipped under the blankets, sleep evaded me. Burrowing deeper under the covers, I closed my eyes, but the eerie feeling would not go away. I knew there were no monsters under the bed, but I wasn't so sure about the skeletons in the closet.

I tried to relax, to let sleep overtake me. A hazy image of a ship sailed across my brain... Mary's family sailing to... a new beginning...calm swaying...drifting toward....

Sleep prevailed, and I dreamed that someone gently tucked... a warm quilt....

ॐ

When the alarm went off at seven the next morning, I was already up and dressed. An eager, yet cautious curiosity propelled me to my office computer.

Mary's latest message had already arrived. "Art thou ready for thy first listening lesson, Phyllis?"

I placed my fingers on the keyboard, eager to begin. "Lesson?"

"The one Cousin Joshua taught me years ago," she replied. "Thou knowest Joshua Carman. Uncle John's son who went blind after the 1647 measles epidemic. He lost his eyesight, but he could listen better than anybody. He's the one who taught me how."

"Wait, Mary. If I'm going to—"

Her incoming message interrupted. "Phyllis! Art thou going to go on calling me by my first name?"

"You *are* Mary Ludlam Scudder?"

"Yes, we went o'er this last night."

"It wasn't a dream?"

"Not until after I tucked thee in."

I shook my head in disbelief. "So should I call you Mrs. Scudder?"

"It would have been 'Goody' Scudder in my day, but when we come right to it, I *am* your grandmother."[2]

I closed my eyes, and said a quick prayer for patience. "I suppose you like the sound of Great Grand-mother VII better? Sort of like Henry VIII? Did you know him?"

"Oh, come now. I'm not that old."

I paused for a moment. "Oh, I see. You want me to call you Grand-Mary? Like your website?"

"I'd like that. Sounds almost like royalty, does it not? Listen," she typed, and the writing turned into a whisper.

Listen.

Incredible! I could *hear* Grand-Mary's voice, velvety, melodic:

Now silence the clamor of thy spirit, and for this moment...

Still skeptical, I shook my head to clear it and reached for my little Sony recorder.

Thou needest a machine to do the listening? Tsk, tsk.

Grand-Mary's tongue tsking ricocheted across my mind, rousing early memories of my piano teacher. "Tsk, tsk, Phyllis. You are wasting your parents' money and your God-given talent. Are you just too lazy to practice your lesson?"

Grand-Mary's soft voice interrupted my reverie. If thou wilt diligently practice thy listening assignment, there will be no need for thy little gewgaw. Until thou becomest skilled at listening, though, I suppose thou canst turn it on.

Cautiously, I looked around. The idea of speaking directly with this apparition made me more than a little edgy, but I'd soon know the truth. If Grand-Mary didn't have answers to everything I asked, I'd know. Either I was hallucinating or she had channeled in on an astonishing wavelength. Frankly, neither of those options gave me even a smidgen of comfort.

I placed trembling fingers on the keyboard and glanced up at the monitor. From the flat screen, a misty vision took on shape and substance right before my eyes! A petite woman, certainly thinner than I. A bit of grey at her temples subdued the fiery red braid of hair that circled her head like a crown. A fringe of tousled ringlets lay across her forehead. Old, sea-blue eyes. Crinkled tissue-thin skin.

As if this were an everyday occurrence, Grand-Mary looked at me with a wide, playful smile and moved into the chair beside me. She began to speak, her voice soft, yet commanding. "Look at me! Attend to what I say as if, for this moment, I were the most important person in thy world." She leaned toward me and caressed my face, holding it between her soft hands.

I'm still in awe at the speed of email messages from here to Hanover, but from here to eternity? And in 3-D?

Though her touch was warm, I was shivering, but I could not look away. I didn't believe in ghosts, but if

Grand-Mary were—as she claimed—coming from not miles, but years away...?

I slipped a media card into the Sony recorder on my desk.

"Phyllis? How long doeth it take thee to turn on that gewgaw?"

I hit the ON button. "Okay, Grand-Mary." My voice quavered. "Let's begin with—"

"Relax. Light the candle—that will help thee. Then listen."

The flame flickered, casting an appropriately eerie glow. I inhaled deeply, filling my senses with its bayberry fragrance. "All right, Grand-Mary. Let's start at the very beginning."

"Thou soundest like Maria Von Trapp. Dost thou sing, too?" She raised an eyebrow. "Oh, never mind my feeble attempt at humor. We have a long, long way to go." Her grin widened.

Disbelieving my own eyes and ears, I shook my head. "For a woman who's been dead for over three centuries, you are certainly up on modern technology and 20th century personalities."

"Well, where dost thou think I have been all these years? Lying on a shelf somewhere, letting my mind rot?"

I plastered a look of acceptance and belief on my face, but I felt as if I were diving into unknown waters with this interview. And I'm no swimmer. Well, let's see how much she really knows about 17th century Mary Ludlam.

"In the graveyard scene," I said as I watched Grand-Mary's face, "when you're tracing the tombstone inscription, it sounds like you blamed yourself for your mother's death."

Grand-Mary nodded. Her eyes seemed scarred with remembered grief. "When I grew up, I understood that Mama was just one of hundreds of women in the 1600s who died in childbirth, but at the time, I thought she left because I had been so wicked. I was a wild child, always skipping out on my chores and running off to the Matlock hills, exploring the caves along Derwent River. Luddie was twelve years older than I, and he sometimes let Hal and me tag along when he looketh for arrowheads the Romans had left in the olden times.

"One summer day—a year or so before Mama died—I ran away to do a little digging on mine own. When my brothers finally found me and brought me home, Mama stood ready with a switch, chosen especially for her wayward daughter. In the wavering shrillness of Mama's voice, was it anger I heard, or fear? I will never forget her words...."

ANNO DOM 1646
MATLOCK, ENGLAND

"Mary, thou hast had this punishment coming for a long time. Now bend over!" Following the admonition of the Scriptures to spare not the rod, she applied the switch across my bottom, but I refused to weep.

"God's wounds! Wilt thou not even cry out in remorse?"

Grandmother Ludlam grabbed the cane from Mama. "Thou hast spared the rod over long, Clemence. I will show thee how to make her cry!" She pushed me down across the table, and lashed across my backside over and over. Her voice, too, made unforgettable marks. Angry welts rose on both body and soul, strengthening my stubborn determination to make no sound.

Panting, again and again Grandmother Ludlam flailed me with the cane. My chastisement continued as Grandmother added guilt and shame to her heavy hand. "Look to your sister! When Grace was of your age, she earned her keep knitting stockings and gloves for the family. but thou — thou art always roaming the hills, wasting thy God-given time. Thou wilt be the death of us all!"

Gasping for air, she loosed her hold on me and cast the switch at last into the corner. Tearless, I rose and saw her pale face contorted in a strange combination of sorrow and pain.

21st Century
Memory Catchers' Office

Grand-Mary paused, and when I looked in her face, I saw a similar mixture of sorrow and pain. My heart ached for the little girl who still remembered, and I covered her soft hand with my own. Grand-Mary resumed her story.

"Grandmother left us that very night, and Grandfather Ludlam's sad, lonely eyes were a constant reminder of my willful stubbornness. Such was my guilt. All winter I sat by the fire while Grace taught me the intricate stitches. At first, the yarn became knotted and tangled as I tried to hold it and the needles just so. But if my labor warmed my brother's hands while he herded cattle in the ice-coated hills next winter, surely God would forgive mine errant behavior."

"You were doing penance?"

"I was, and indeed, when the weather warmed and flowers appeared on the grazing land, my burden was lifted. God's blessing."

"So you never ran off to the Matlock hills again?"

"Oh, but I did. The temptation was too great." Grand-Mary turned her face away. She finally spoke, the lines on her face divulging deep-rooted emotions: "First Grandmother died, and then Mama, a year later.... Shall I tell the story to thee?"

AUGUST, ANNO DOM 1646
MATLOCK, ENGLAND

Like most other days on farms in Matlock, England, the day, August 4, 1646, began with early rising. Because Clemence Ludlam, heavy with her eighth pregnancy, was especially tired that summer morning, she awakened her oldest daughter, Grace, before dawn to help her knead the bread dough, rich with eggs, butter and spices. "Thy papa and brother Anthony need full nourishment today for their long hours at the mill, so pack the dough with fruits and nuts, Grace," she said. "Now that King Charles has Christianized hot cross buns, there be no reason to limit our enjoyment." The old queen had called the buns a Pagan custom, and limited their consumption. Ritualistic nonsense, Clemence Ludlam believed. Now she often blessed family celebrations with the yeasty treat. Nothing could equal the heavenly aroma wafting from the brick fireplace oven on such occasions.

On this day, while Clemence served each one a fragrant bun, straight from the oven, Will, her husband and head of the family, sat at the board scooping blobs of oatmeal for the children onto wooden trenchers—the middle hollowed out like a bowl.

Seven-year-old Mary wolfed down her breakfast and began stuffing bread, cheese, and a few leftover buns into a woven knapsack.

"Not so fast, young maiden. We have not yet asked God's blessings on the day." Will gathered his family around him, opened his worn Geneva Bible, and read:

Gather me the people together and I will cause them to hear my words, that they may learn to fear me all the days that they shall live upon the earth, and that they may teach their children.

Mary fidgeted, standing on first one foot and then on the other. Will smiled, remembering when he, too, was such an eager child. After a quick look at his family, he shut the book, closed his eyes, and bowed his head.

"Oh, Lord, we thank thee for our daughter Mary, with whom you saw fit to bless us but seven years ago today. Be with John, our elder son who is away, and go with each one of us as we depart to the tasks of the day. Disclose the brightness of thy face and be forever near. Amen."

Mary gave her father a quick hug and turned to her brother. "Comest thou, Luddie, today I get to go with thee to the pastures. Let us get started." She slung the knapsack over her shoulder and turned toward the door. "Come, now," she said. "Look. The sun is already up." She pointed out the kitchen window, and then looked again at her brother. "Art thou taking any tools to dig with? Dost thou think we shall find any Roman arrowheads or copper coins today?"

"Hold thy horses, Miss Priss." Luddie drained the last bit of ale from his cup, grabbed another hot cross bun, plopped a cap on his dark mop of hair, and headed out the door. "Come on, little slowcoach."

৵

Many a morning Luddie took his eight-year-old brother, Hal, along to help, but this August day was Mary's treat.

Driving the Ludlam herd of cattle before them, they followed the property boundary along the fast-flowing Derwent and crossed a little stone bridge, passing by the Ludlam mill where Papa and Anthony would spend their day.

Mary's legs began cramping with the climb, and when Luddie noticed the tears in her eyes, he took her onto his shoulders. Onward they climbed—nearly a half mile up the steep hills of Matlock over sun-browned heath and ragged stones. Onward to greener pastures from which the lofty limestone crags of High Tor rose nearly 400 feet above the valley.

After a brief rest, Mary was able to walk again, and encouraging a faster pace, she danced along beside the plodding cows while Luddie, assuring that no animal strayed, brought up the rear. Near the top of the hill, they veered back to the north, away from the miners' spoils where lead seeping through the soil might sicken a grazing herd.

The air was sweet and refreshing at this height, but the morning sun promised another scorching day. "This looketh like a good grazing spot," Luddie said.

"And a leafy bower where we can sit." Mary leaned the knapsack against a rough brown tree trunk. A straggling cow ambled toward a verge of rocks, snuffing the air. Luddie ran after her and headed her back to join the herd.

Climbing onto a bold outcropping of limestone, Mary stretched her arms upward, luxuriating in the promise of the day. She chanted a nursery rhyme she'd known forever, stopping with her special day.

Monday's child is fair of face,
Tuesday's child is full of grace,
Wednesday's child is full of woe,
Thursday's child has far to go.

"It means thou hast countless visions to achieve," Papa had told her as he nuzzled her cheek. "Thou wilt go far, my little princess."

From this height, except for the view blocked by the towering grey cliff at the south, it seemed she could see forever. Though tall for her age, she felt like a tiny, nestling redbird, not quite ready to fly.

In the distance below, the Derwent snaked its way through the deep valley, meandering its way through vast piles of rock and around a crazy quilt of fields and homesteads bordered by stone walls and dark-green hedgerows. To the west, across the river, the barren Peak Forest spread out for miles. "Luddie, canst we not see Haddon Hall from here?" she called.

He climbed onto the rock and stood beside her. "Well, perhaps that pinnacle thou seest on the horizon is the Tower of Haddon." He pointed toward a distant peak in the northwest.

"Tell me the story again, Luddie." She knew he could seldom resist her pleading. "Tell me about our cousin at Haddon Hall." Mary seated herself on a small ledge and patted a place beside her. "Please, Luddie, tell me the story."

"Of Benedicta Ludlow and Sir Richard?"

"No, no. I want to hear about the Princess Lady who ran away with the poor Earl."

He adjusted his lanky frame to a more comfortable position on the rock ledge. "Oh, that cousin was the great-great-great-granddaughter of Benedicta," he said, smoothing his little sister's tousled red tresses. Luddie was glad to have this diversion, for storytelling whiled away the hours. "How many times have I told thee this tale?" He grinned and began the story:

"Once upon a time, over a hundred years ago, there was a castle on the top of a high limestone outcrop overlooking the River Wye. There, Sir George Vernon, the fine-looking King of the Peak, lived with his two beautiful daughters — Margaret the elder and Dorothy the younger. The King loved to entertain, but when someone displeased him, he could be quite heavy-handed. More than once, he had condemned men to public hanging without a trial. The King loved his daughter Dorothy more than anyone else on earth and wanted to keep her forever safe in the castle.

"One day, a handsome young gentleman, John Manners, came to call. Sir John was quite smitten by the loveliness of the King's daughter as she was with him. But when the King heard of their friendship, he turned red with rage. 'He is nothing but the second son of a poor Earl,' he shouted. 'What maketh him think he's good enough for my daughter!'

"Soon a wedding was planned at the castle, but not for John and Princess Dorothy. Instead, it celebrated the marriage of her sister Margaret and Sir Thomas Stanley."

"Was Princess Dorothy sad?"

"Oh, yes." Luddie said. "So sad that she decideth to run away. During the wedding supper, it is said — "

"You forgot to tell what they ate at the supper. Did the King's wife make hot cross buns to celebrate?"

Luddie laughed. "I think it is only Mama who celebrates all special days with hot cross buns. At any rate, Dorothy did not eat any."

"Why not?"

"Because, it is said, she climbed to the castle tower and signaled her handsome suitor, and while her father was in the ballroom entertaining wedding guests, Princess Dorothy fled out the back door and through the gardens. She mounted her favorite mare and crossed over the little bridge spanning the River Wye, and there, at the foot of the bridge, she found Sir John Manners waiting for her. They rode through the night to far away Aylestone, in Leicestershire, and there they were married.

"Years later, when the King of the Peak died, Lady Dorothy Manners inherited Haddon estate, and forever after, the Manners family hath owned Haddon."

"And the castle is deserted now?"

Luddie nodded. "Yes. When thou wast just a toddler, the grandson of Lady Dorothy, who was also called Sir John, became the Duke of Rutland and moved his family to Belvoir Castle. From that time forth, Haddon Castle hath been empty except for a few servants who remain there yet today."

He looked across the green hills toward Haddon Hall. The summer landscape was alight with myriad colors — wild pansies and forget-me-nots, daisies and buttercups, violets and bluebells.

Mary was lost in her own fairy tale. "If I had a horse of mine own, I would call her Molly. And when the handsome prince came to call, I could run away with him."

Luddie laughed. "Please do not run away without thy dinner." He leaned to pluck a violet blooming at the base of the ledge, then with a flourish he bowed as he tucked it in his sister's red hair. "A princess must have violets to match her eyes," he said. Suddenly aware of his duties, he turned. "If the cattle are as thirsty as I, they must need a drink. Art thou coming with me?"

The herd, recognizing his call, followed them to a fresh water spring that bubbled from an outcrop in a shallow ravine not too far away.

Their thirst quenched, the cows returned to the grazing area to rest peacefully while chewing their cud.

In the shade of the tree, Mary opened the knapsack. "I know what let's do, Luddie. Let us pretend we are having a wedding feast. Thou canst be the handsome Prince Ludlam, and I wilt be Princess Mary Vernon of Haddon Hall. And thou wilt come after me, riding a white horse with a shiny red blanket where I canst sit." She offered her brother a crusty chunk of bread and a thick slab of yellow cheese.

When the last crumb was finished, Luddie leaned back against the tree trunk. "Look, Mary," he said, pointing. Far up in the sky a hawk with a reddish tail dipped and climbed in lazy circles. "Kree-eee-ar," came the faint call.

"I think she looketh for food for her children," Mary said.

For a while she was still.

"Art thou tired, Mary? Thou art so quiet."

"No, I'm listening.

"Listening? To what?"

"To God, I think. When I'm lying in the grass, I hear his heart beating. And I hear him in the breeze blowing through sun-dappled leaves and in the rain moving across the valley."

"A beautiful thought, little sister." Luddie smiled and then yawned. "This warm day makes me sleepy. Dost thou need a nap?"

Mary put her hands on her hips. "Luddie, I am not a toddler. And I will not waste a minute." She tossed her head, a determined gesture uniquely her own. "Look at all the pretty flowers, Luddie. I'm going to pick an apron full and weave a crown of glory, like the maiden's funeral garland hanging in St. Giles."

"Well, do not wander too far, Miss Priss. Thou might miss thy handsome prince if he cometh riding by."

To Mary's delight, each bloom she picked seemed surpassed by another and then another, and she filled the lap of her apron with the blossoms. A flat pebble glittered in the sun. Perchance a Roman coin? Holding her flower-filled apron with her left hand, she slipped the rock into her pocket with the right. She turned and waved to Luddie. Farther on she spied a bright feather, fiery red like her hair. That, too, she slipped into her pocket. When she turned again to see if Luddie was still watching, he and the leafy tree under which he rested— as well as the herd of cows—were nowhere in sight. Suddenly Mary stumbled, plunging headlong into some dark pit that seemed to have no bottom.

Startled by a distant cry, Luddie jumped to his feet. His sister had vanished. "Mary!" he called, running in the direction he'd last seen her. "Mary, where art thou?" The hills echoed his cry. Over the next rise, nearly at the foot of the High Tor, he spied a mound of color—blue and white and violet—splashed against a bed of green. It could not be Mary, lying so still. Fear bludgeoned his heart as he ran. Next to the blooms that had spilled from Mary's apron, he discovered the mineshaft, deep and dark. He called to his sister, but the only answer was the reverberating sound of his own voice. With no tools but the stick he'd brought for digging up Roman relics, there seemed little he could do. No lamp, no rope.

Papa, he cried silently. I need thee. It was nearly a half mile to the Ludlam mill, but that was his only hope. With tears blinding his eyes, he sprinted down the hillside to get his father and brother Anthony.

Far across the valley, a church bell began its evening toll.

≈

Will Ludlam, surprised to see his eight-year-old son, Hal, watched as the boy slid from his Shetland pony and hurried into the Ludlam mill. "Papa," he said, the lift of his chin matching the importance of his task, "Mama needs thee." He handed his father a note, written in a shaky hand.

> *Will, if thou wouldst attend the birth of thine eighth child,*
> *thou must come home at once. Hal will ride to bring Goody*
> *Morgan from Matlock. My time is near. C.*

Will Ludlam turned to Anthony. "The baby's early. Son, ride with thy brother to get the midwife. I will give instructions to the new apprentice for the order of Thomas Bowne before I leave. I will see you boys at home. Go with haste."

Anthony and Hal were barely out of sight when Luddie, gasping for breath, rushed into the mill. When Will heard Luddie's story, there was only one choice. Goody Morgan, the midwife, would care for his wife. He must go find Mary. "Get the rope, Luddie, and I will fill the lantern. We can both ride Nellie. She is a strong one." Will grabbed the tools they might need for Mary's rescue, saddled his mare, leapt onto her back, and pulled Luddie up behind him. Over the heather-covered hills they galloped toward the mine shaft near the base of the Big Tor.

℘

Mary awakened in a dark cavern. On her forehead a big knot had formed. No soft pile of hay had been there to cushion her fall as it had when she'd tumbled from the Ludlam barn loft last year. Her knees stung where she had scraped them, and her elbows hurt. She'd be in trouble again for disobedience. A sob welled up from the depths of her chest. Luddie must be worried. Perhaps it was night already, and Mama, too, would fret. From somewhere ahead, she heard the constant dripping of water. She was thirsty. Far away, there seemed to be a soft glowing form, like an angel with her mother's face, and on her head a garland of white flowers streaming down like a moonbeam through a foggy sky. Carefully Mary crept, feeling her way along the wall of an underground tunnel, moving toward the faint light. Gradually, the passageway turned and Mary found herself in a chamber even bigger than St. Giles Church. Through a crack in the rocky ceiling, light reflected on long, crystal columns. Perhaps this was heaven, but her head hurt, and the scripture she'd memorized at family devotions said in heaven there be no more sorrow or pain.

21st Century
Memory Catchers' Office

As if it still hurt, Grand-Mary rubbed her brow as she told me the rest of the story.

"The knot where I'd clonked my head was throbbing, but worse was the aching lump of remorse within my bosom. I had disobeyed Luddie, and now he'd be worried." Grand-Mary paused, holding forth her hands as if to grasp the memory.

"In front of me, the passageway seemed to be partially blocked by a long icicle. Water dripped from its tip, so I cupped my hand under it, then cautiously touched it with my tongue. The water was cool and refreshing, not freezing like the icicle I'd gotten my tongue stuck to the winter before. I held a corner of mine apron under the drip and pressed it to my forehead. The throbbing abated, and the sight of this amazing and wondrous underground palace diminished my heavy awareness of guilt. When Luddie came looking for me, mehaps we could explore the cavern together.

"I had not long to wait. When Papa saw the spot where I had dropped the flowers, he tied a rope around Luddie's waist and lowered him, with a lantern, into the hole. I was not very far down, and in minutes, Papa had pulled us both to the surface."

Grand-Mary sighed. "Luddie was begging Papa not to be angry with me. It was all his fault, he said. Papa shushed him and exhaled noisily, as if releasing a chest full of fear."

"I know how unmindful of danger Mary can be," Papa said. He hugged us both. "Now, I need to hurry home. Thy mother will be much concerned. Luddie, thou wilt see that the herd is safe, and bring them home in due time. We will ride on ahead." He mounted his mare, and Luddie lifted me up to sit behind Papa. I leaned forward against the back of my papa, put both arms around his waist, and held him close. The balm of Papa's forgiveness and affection soothed my pain and guilt, and I could hardly wait to share mine adventure with my brother Hal.

August, Anno Dom 1646
Matlock, England

A west wind had picked up by the time we arrived home, and storm clouds darkened the late afternoon sky. Cloud-covered hills above our valley rumbled ominously, and an occasional flash of lightning threatened the horizon.

At the barn, Papa threw his right leg forward over the saddle horn and dismounted. He took several steps toward the house before remembering I was still perched on the mare. He turned and helped me from my seat behind the saddle. "Daughter, go on to the house. Hal and Anthony have returned. I'll give them my horse to tend and then hasten in."

Our heavy, oak-paneled door was standing open, but as I entered the great room, no one gave me a glance. My sister Grace silently attended the iron pot of stew embedded in the hissing fireplace coals. Abbie sat on the wooden bench along the great room wall, clutching her rag doll. Mama was hunched over the table, her puffy face lined and grey as a ball of knitting yarn. I never remembered having seen her like that before. A frightening stillness pervaded the room.

"Mama?" I hardly recognized mine own voice, hesitant, high-pitched. I wanted to run to her, hug her, tell her how sorry I was to have caused her such worry.

"Shush, child!" Goody Morgan, the midwife, shook a long bony finger at me. "Canst thou not see thy mother is in travail? Leavest her be."

A piercing wail tore apart Mama's tightly clenched lips, and the midwife took her by the arm. Come now, Mistress Ludlam. Thee must lie down. She led Mama out of the room.

Soon Papa was there, pacing back and forth from fireplace to birthing room door. It was not seemly for him to be at his wife's bedside. Once he knocked lightly, but Goody Morgan only drove him away.

"Thee should know by now, Sir, that these things take time. What is this, number eight? And the last nearly killed her."

In the kitchen, Grace quietly ladled steaming nourishment into a wooden bowl. "Here, Mary, take Papa some stew."

I placed the bowl and a spoon at the head of the table. "Come, Papa. Eat."

He paused in his pacing, slowly turned, and took his place at the table, but he did not sup. Finally, he arose. "I'll be in the outer room," he said.

Later, when Goody Morgan handed my sister Grace the tiny bundle, her apron was splotched by great wet stains. "Mary," she said to me, "go get thy father."

I ran to the outer room where he was waiting. "Papa, thou must come quickly. Goody Morgan says—"

Wasting not a moment, he rushed into the great room.

The midwife shook her head. "Who canst understand the ways of the Lord?"

I saw Father's face contort as he hastened through the door to my mother's bedside. The sounds emanating from the birthing room pierced my heart. Never before had I heard my father cry.

August 4, 1646. My 7th birthday. The day my brother Joseph was born. The day my mama died.

ॐ

Three days later, the descending sun cast long shadows on the procession of mourners. My brothers—John, in his 21st year, Luddie, two years younger, and Anthony, younger than Luddie by three, helped Cousin Edmund, Uncle Obadiah, and Uncle Arthur[3] carry my mother's body up to St. Giles Church.[4]

The rest of our family followed—Grace, in her eighteenth year, with the infant Joseph in her arms; Hal, a year older than I; Grandfather Ludlam; and Papa carrying five-year-old Abbie.

Clinging to Papa's hand, I tried to keep pace, although my legs ached almost as much as my heart. A soft mist settled in, wrapping us in a shroud, white, like the wedding sheet wrapt round my mother's body. Save our footsteps on the stone-paved path, there wast no sound but the beating noise inside of me. Then, a distant cow bawled, a long, lamenting wail, breaking the stillness. The sound echoed the cry I had heard from my mother's room the day of baby Joseph's untimely birth.

Seated in the church at St. Giles for Mama's last service, I could not ponder the paintings of the four Evangelists[5] as I usually did at Sabbath worship. *Oh, Mama, I'm sorry I was disobedient last week. Come back. I'll never do it again.*

Rev. Thomas Shelmerdine,[6] the pudgy rector who had baptized me at the old Norman font in the rectory gardens, arose from his seat in the chancel and spoke to us.

"In the Book of Genesis, God said, 'I will greatly multiply thy sorrow and thy conception; in sorrow thou shalt bring forth children.' Mrs. William Ludlam was a daughter of our Lord who fulfilled the promise. Now she rests in peace without trouble. Blessed be the name of the Lord."

At last the rector raised his arms and we stood to sing the Psalm Mama loved most.

The Lord to me a shepherd is,
(The Lord to me a shepherd is,)
want therefore shall not I.
(want therefore shall not I.)

Line after line we repeated the tune set by our leader, the church clerk:

He in the folds of tender grass,
doth cause me down to lie:
To waters calm me gently leads,
restore my soul doth he:
he doth in paths of righteousness
for his name's sake lead me.
Yea though in valley of death's shade
I walk, none ill I'll fear:
because thou art with me, thy rod
and staff my comfort are.[7]

Sunshine broke through the fog, and a golden ray pierced the stained glass windows, as if God himself were reaching down to take my mother's hand.

Oh, Mama, come back!

21ST CENTURY
MEMORY CATCHERS' OFFICE

Grand-Mary's eyes mirrored a poignant sadness, but her petal-soft cheeks remained flushed with childlike eagerness. I waited for her to continue.

Grand-Mary sighed wearily. That is enough for today.

Quickly, I reached out to her. "Will I see you..." but Grand-Mary had vanished.

❧

Ken — my husband — says I'm compulsive. When I fill in one-down on a crossword puzzle, one-across calls to me like a salty potato chip: "Bet you can't stop with one." Until recently, I'd never realized I had a Ludlam grandmother. Now I was holding a bag full of cravings for just one more piece of her story, and I knew it wouldn't stop there. So many questions.

Except for vague images of Pilgrims and Puritans, I remembered very little from history classes covering the 17th Century. What had been happening in Mary's world when she was a child? Did she, as the middle child in her family, develop the same survival techniques as did my own middle child? What was it like to grow to womanhood, to give birth again and again, knowing that many a babe soon slept in satin-lined coffins, rather than in down-pillowed cradles. And in the 1600s, how did a motherless child like Mary get from England to America?

It occurred to me that I'd wasted my trip through England. I'd felt no sense of kinship there, no link with the past even though I must have passed very near the ancient High Tor where Grand-Mary had fallen into the cavern. Our tour group visited historic Haddon Hall and snapped pictures of the tombstones at old St Giles Church through our bus windows. Most of what I saw on that trip was so old it made English tea seem like a rank newcomer, and after a week, I'd had enough of dark, dingy castles. Along with souvenir boxes of Tetley's, a dozen bayberry candles—hand-dipped as they had been for centuries—and a stack of glossy picture postcards of all the antiquities I'd visited, I carried home a 14-day collection of illusive memories. Oh, if only I'd had eyes to see.

Noontime neared, and Ken, finding me engrossed in a British history internet site, slid a couple of Healthy Choice dinners into the microwave. I continued my reading, brushing up on my scanty knowledge of Grand-Mary's birthplace and time:

Civil War in England

...In the 17th century, Parliament was dominated by evangelical Christians such as Oliver Cromwell who wanted to "purify" the Church. In 1629, Parliament unilaterally condemned the actions of King Charles I. Revolution was in the air. Charles, exasperated by the politicians who refused to allow him to 'rule by divine right,' on the advice of his Catholic wife, Henrietta Maria, foolishly tried to arrest five mem-

bers of Parliament, which brought matters to a head. On the 22nd of August, 1642, with a small contingent of soldiers —

"Lunch is ready," Ken announced.

...King Charles raised his standard on a hill within the grounds of Nottingham Castle, commencing hostilities against his own people. The English Civil War —

"Your lunch is getting cold."

...The English Civil War had begun, with Oliver Cromwell leading the Parliamentarians against King Charles and the royalist supporters, called Cavaliers by Cromwell's men. At the start of the war, Wingfield Manor in Derbyshire was taken by a royalist force and used as a raiding post. Up to 200 men were garrisoned in the building. Mounted on swift horses, these men rode out to bring war to the surrounding country-side. In 1644 Sir John Gell, a Derbyshire local who owned lead mines in the High Peak area and had served as High Sheriff of Derbyshire, assumed control of Parliamentarian forces in Derbyshire. Two years into the War, Lord Grey of Groby and Sir John Gell — brave officers in the service of the Parliament — besieged Wingfield Manor, seven and a half miles across the valley from the Derbyshire village of Matlock...

Matlock. Grand-Mary's birthplace.

The alarm on my computer calendar beeped a re-minder — time to go cheer for my side — the WSU rowing team. I tore my fingers from the keyboard, grabbed a

quick bite of now-congealed TV dinner, and told Ken
goodbye.

$$\wp$$

When my illusory ancestor appeared that evening, I
had a pot of tea waiting for her, and I was bubbling with
questions.

"Grand-Mary, do you remember the battle at Wingfield
Manor? On my trip through England, I stood at the very
spot where John Gell's guns began firing on the manor.
It's just a shell of a building now. Look. I have a photo.
Were you old enough then to understand what was go-
ing on? Could you hear the guns during the attack?"

"Slow down, child." Grand-Mary lit the bayberry candle and then paused, as if she were sorting through a
trunk full of memories. She lifted her cup, then smiled.
"Thou thinkest this tea will help me recall my life in England, don't you? You know we had never heard of such a
beverage until after we came to the Colonies."

She took another sip and began her story. "I don't remember the beginning of the Wingfield battle at all. Even
though the first battle ended less than a half hour's ride
from our farm, I was too young to understand what was
going on. But I do remember when John Gell's forces
blasted a hole through the wall and captured Wingfield
Manor. I believe it was in…1644. I was almost five. Wingfield Manor sat high on a hilltop southeast of Matlock.
After the Roundheads moved their cannon to the wood
on the west side, its roar and the crack of gunfire echoed
across our valley. Sometimes we could even hear the soldiers yell."

"You called Parliament's troops Roundheads?"

Grand-Mary nodded. "Twas because of their haircuts." She put her hand over her mouth, suppressing a giggle. "In those days, the Puritans thought every species of vice and iniquity lurked in the long curly locks of the Cavaliers—royalist supporters of King Charles. A man's hair was the symbol of his creed, in both politics and religion. The more abundant the hair, the more scant the faith; and the balder the head, the more sincere the piety. No wonder the curly-haired King Charles felt that his head as well as his hair was in danger.

"I remember one afternoon after the boys who attended the new Matlock Grammar School were dismissed for the day, I joined them in playing Cavaliers and Roundheads—my brother Hal and Richard Shelmerdine, the Rector's son, and John Thomas Gell, and some other neighborhood children. Hal decided to climb a tree to get a better view of where the rogues were hiding, and I climbed up on the rock wall bordering Papa's field, swishing my broadsword—a Cavalier Lady joining the fray. From my vantage, I noticed my cousin Edward Ludlam sneaking along, a finger on each hand pointed like a pair of flintlock pistols, taking aim at Hal. I allowed him to move a little closer before giving him a whack with my sword."

Lost in the labyrinth of by-gone years, Grand-Mary's voice faded to a whisper as she told her story....

Two

❧

ANNO DOM 1644
MATLOCK, ENGLAND

"Ouch, Mary. Why did thou hit me? I'm on thy side."

"How can I tell which side thou art on, Edward? Dost thou have a plume in thy hat?"

Hal jumped from the tree. "The Duke hath been wounded!... Thou art supposed to fall down, Edward. That's the rules."

"Pow, Pow!" The shots came from John Thomas as he galloped up on his make-believe horse.

"Halt. Who goest there?" Edward squared his shoulders. "Art thou a Roundhead or a man of the King?"

"I'm hungry!" Richard said, loping up on his steed. He wiped the sweat from his chubby face and brushed back a long golden curl. Richard was always hungry. He enjoyed church dinners more than anyone else did, for there he could sample goodies to his heart's content. He turned to me. "Ho, yon maiden. Canst thou not bring us some bread and ale?"

"I am not thy maid, Richard. I am Mary Ludlam, a Cavalier Lady." But I was hungry too, so I dropped my sword and turned to go. "I'll see if Mama will give us some scones left over from breakfast. And while I'm gone, you Cavaliers had best look for feathers for thy hats so we can recognize the enemy."

No one was in the kitchen, so I eased Mama's big pewter bowl from the shelf. That would make a good helmet for a Roundhead. Then I helped myself to several scones and put them into the bowl. Now, what would a Cavalier Lady wear? On a wall hook I spied my Lord's Day bonnet with it's bright red ribbon ties. Just right. I slipped the ties into my pocket. I could carry only one bowl...so what else could I find to tell a Roundhead from a Cavalier? Hmm. Cautiously, I slipped Mama's scissors from her sewing basket and tucked them into my pocket.

℘

Hal and the neighbor boys were sprawled on the grass resting, but they quickly sat up when they saw me coming with Mama's sweet raisin scones. "Wait, Richard. Thy father is the Rector, so thou must say grace ere we eat." Whether we were Puritan or Church of England, we had all been taught to ask the Lord's blessing on our food.

Richard groaned, mumbled a short prayer, and stuffed a scone into his mouth.

After taking a few bites, I took the red ribbons from my pocket and tied them like a sash around my waist. The pewter bowl was empty now, so I placed it on my head. "Look, John Thomas, this will be just right for thee. Thine Uncle John wears a helmet like this. Sorry I don't have a yellow sash and red coat for thee like Cromwell's soldiers are wearing now."

Richard, with his mouth full, protested. "Where's a helmet for me? I want to be a Roundhead."

"I have a better idea for thee, Richard. I grabbed the bowl from John Thomas and plopped it on Richard's head. "Cromwell's men would never wear such long flowing tresses. 'Tis a sin." Quickly I withdrew the scissors from my pocket and began snipping away around the edge of the bowl.

Suddenly, a woman's voice called out. "Master Richard, where art thou? Thy father expected thee home an hour ago." Rev. Shelmerdine's plump wife came hurrying into view, then stopped suddenly and covered a high-pitched whine with her hand when she saw us.

On the ground lay my sin—masses of her son's long golden curls.

21st Century
Memory Catchers' Office

"So which side was your family on, Grand-Mary? Royalist Cavaliers or Roundheads?"

"Well, thou must understand that Grandfather—William Ludlam I—believed God Almighty had granted kings the right to rule as they saw fit. Still, there was a lawsuit—Ludlam vs. Matlock miners—for causing lead poisoning of Ludlam cattle. And since the King took a cut from mining profits—well, who can say?

"Grandfather Ludlam, a yeoman next in order to the gentry, cultivated his own land. In favor with the Crown, he often told of the time he loaned 40 shillings to Charles I.[8] I don't know if Grandfather was coerced as some of the neighbors were, or if he paid gladly. In spite of everything, I think Grandfather remained a Royalist."

"So you were Cavaliers?"

"Child, must everything be so black and white for thee? Life is not that simple, is it? We had family on all sides. Didst thou never read of the Padley Martyrs?"

Embarrassed at my lack of knowledge, I shook my head.

"No? Well, back in my great-grandfather's time, three Roman Catholic priests were hanged, drawn, and quartered, and their remains were draped over the chapel entrance at Derby, bloody entrails and all. One of the three be a Ludlam, Father Robert Ludlam, a Catholic cousin of ours who died a martyr.

"And there be Cousin Edmund Ludlam. He and his wife Elizabeth moved in with us after Mama died. Edmund was a Cromwell follower who fought against Charles I in the Civil War. Whenever his cot was empty, we knew he was either in hiding, or off fighting another battle."

Grand-Mary peered at me and raised an eyebrow. "So, what dost thou think? Were we Catholics? Anglicans? Presbyterians? Puritans? Families were often split by political and religious beliefs in my day, and I'll wager that hasn't changed."

Grand-Mary continued. "Now Mama's side of the family, the Fordhams, supported Parliament. Roundheads they were. At least her brother Robert was. About the time the Pilgrims boarded the Mayflower, he enrolled in Caius College at Cambridge, England, and after ordination, he preached at Flamstead's Church of England. Even so, he grew to favor the beliefs of the Puritans. Somewhat like thy religious fundamentalists, Puritans wanted to clean up the Church and society—purify them."

Grand-Mary leaned closer. "Now my dear child, I'm not telling thee that everyone who was against the King was ready to join the Puritans. Heaven forbid! Way before Oliver Cromwell started pushing Puritan ways, people complained about 'that crazy sect.' 'They're trying to stop our usual Sabbath amusements—dancing and archery!' one fellow said."

Grand-Mary chuckled, then in a gruff whisper she said, "Pious bastards, that's what he called 'em! And I once heard a young man claim he cared not a fart of his tail for any minister and swore all he heard in church was Puritan "bibble babble."[9] If he had been a Matlock boy, they might have threatened to clap him in the stocks, although I never saw that happen except in the colonies.

Her candid choice of words surprised and amused me, but with a straight face I said, "How did you learn so much about history? A lot of what you've told me happened before you were born."

"Well, it wasn't on the 6 o'clock news. Grandfather Ludlam and Papa, too, took great interest in political 'goings on.' Often at night, we'd gather around and listen to their stories again and again. I was too young to realize they were not merely entertaining us, but also teaching us history. I guess thou couldst say we Ludlam children were home-schooled. Papa mixed the events of our country with family stories, so we thought they were one and the same. Whatever question we asked would set him off on another story. His account didn't always answer the question, but we listened just the same.

"One night I said to Papa, 'Tell us about thy wedding to Mama. How didst ye meet? Didst ye elope, like Dorothy and Sir John Manners?'

Papa's face softened, and as he reached for Mama's hand, I caught a glimpse of the young man he had been.

"Thy mother and I published our marriage banns in 1625," he said. "This fair lass was little more than 17 summers, and I, a couple of years older." He paused as he revisited the days of his youth. "Yes, we wed the very year young Charles took the throne—a heavy mantle for one of barely 18 years. He insisted that almighty God had given him his rights, and he refused to call Parliament into session. Eleven years without meeting! King Charles ignored the very foundation of his rulership—the consent of his subjects."

With a vehement shake of his head, Papa continued. "When the Scots rebelled, Charles needed money and had to call on Parliament for help, but when they turned him down, Charles dissolved parliament again."

Papa's eyes were sad. "The poor harvest we had the next couple of years made the situation worse around here. Our family kept growing, but the crops did not. Even the cows grew thin. That was the year thy sister Grace was born, and then Anthony the next year—1631."

Papa lifted his Geneva Bible from the shelf. "About that time, thy mama's sister Florence, down at Sacombe, and her husband, John Carman, decided to sail off to the new world—the Massachusetts Bay Colony. They packed everything they might need— tools and supplies were hard to come by in the Colony—and then boarded the ship." Papa turned to the back cover of his Bible and took out a faded letter. Carefully he unfolded it and read:

8 June 1633
My Dear Cousins,

My wife has pressed me to sett pen to paper to tell you about our journey and our lives here in Massachusetts Bay Colony. After much difficultye, the ship Lyon with Captain William Peirce, landed on 4 November 1631. The wife of Gov. John Winthrop sailed on the same ship, and with us came also the teacher and pastor John Hardwick, young man of cheerfull spirit, who was ordained at Cambridge the year our brother, Robert Fordham, began his studies there.

We have settled about 4 miles from Boston Harbor, in Rocksberry, a Bay Colony settlement named for its distinctive outcropping of rock, somewhat like thy area of Matlock. The streetes are large, and some fayre houses, yet have they built their meeting house for church assemble, thirty-six feet long, twenty feet wide, and twelve feet high. Compared to our ship's quarters, it seems quite spacious. The meeting house is un-beautified without shingles or plaster, with a thatched roof, and without gallery, pew, or spire. The church is increased to about 120 persons now.

Having obtained proprietary grants for acreage suitable for farming, there be no end to the busyness at hand. There be much work to do, but we have faith that God himself shall give might to our labor, so that our travells and paines, our costs and sacrifices shall not be lost and in vaine, nor our hopes frustrated.

My beloved wife is well, though she be great with child. God has thus blest us. Lett me intreate and beseech thee to consider also coming to this land of opportunitye. There may be occasion to make composition with the Indians for more land and priviledges thereof. I am therefore the more confident that thee will not neglect any opportunitye to join us.

Sincerelye yours,
John Carman

Papa refolded the letter. "Your Carman cousins were the first of our kin to be born in the colonies." He went on with his story. "Your Uncle John Carman also wrote thy mama's brother, Robert Fordham, of the unlimited possibilities in the colonies—if one might endure the storms and bad crops, sickness, and conflicts with the Indians. Your Uncle Robert, preaching against the Articles of Faith of the Church of England as he did, was verging on a charge of heresy. It wasn't long before he began considering a move." Papa grinned, indulging in his usual bit of wry humor. "Perhaps it was a choice of what he'd rather risk, his head in England, or his scalp in the colonies," he said. "Whatever their reasons for the decision, Uncle Robert and Aunt Alice packed all their hussle-ments, even his large collection of books, and in May 1640, they and their four youngsters sailed for New England on the *Elizabeth*."

"Why don't I remember that, Papa? Be we not there to bid them goodbye?"

"Thou wert there, my little poppet, a babe in thy mother's arms. Ye would not remember." Papa patted my head and then continued. "After arriving in Boston Harbor, our Fordham kin settled in Cambridge, three miles inland. When the Archbishop of Canterbury—Laud was his name—procured a decree that ordered clergymen who had left without permission to come back to England, Uncle Robert gave up the ministry. Instead, he obtained land at Sudbury, Massachusetts, some 20 miles farther inland, and there he assumed the life he had known as a boy in Sacombe, husbandry—cultivating crops and raising cattle.

"Three years later, Uncle Robert Fordham wrote that he and Uncle John Carman had purchased from Chief

Tachapausha and six Indians whose tribe held it, a lengthy stretch of Long Island."

Papa turned the letter over to show us a map of Long Island. It looked like a big fish to me.

Papa continued. "Your Uncle Robert wrote that the part of the Great Plains he marked with a star was richly blessed with good loam soil, verdant woods and clear running streams. Safe harbors nestled in long white beaches. They called the place Hempstead." Papa paused, and his dark eyes gazed afar into the distance for a moment before he went on with his story. "Three of your Fordham cousins were born at Hempstead — over toward the west end of the long island. I'm sure their most exciting and terrifying event was the Indian assault on the Fordham plantation there. Thee were only five then, Mary, but you remember, do you not, when two of thy Carman cousins, Benjamin and Abigail, were almost carried away in that attack?"[10]

Laughing, I said, "Papa, ye always leave out the best of Ben and Abby's story! When we get to the colonies, I want to hear them tell it. They won't leave out the scary parts!"

I was eager to meet my cousins there. The spring after Mama died, Uncle Obadiah Ludlam sailed away to the tail of that big fish, and Papa could not wait to follow him. He settled his affairs in Matlock Parish, left the farm and mill in charge of Cousin Edmond and Grandfather Ludlam, made arrangements for Edmond and Elizabeth to share the house with us children and take responsibility for our care in his absence. All of us children prepared to follow him as soon as he was settled. All, that is, except John, my oldest brother. He was in a seven-year apprenticeship with a toolsmith, and could not go.

Papa attempted to comfort us as he prepared to leave, but mourning his beloved Clemence, he had little comfort to give. Sick he was. Sick of a broken heart, I think. His eyes were sad, and he never smiled nor called me his princess as once he did. Again I felt the guilt of disobedience that I could never undo. God's punishment was profound and unrelenting. I had not only lost Mama, but now Papa, too.

He gathered the eight of us around him to say farewell. "I'll find a better life and a home for us in the Promised Land," he said, "and then you will join me there."

He called the voyage a great adventure, but to me it felt as though he was running away, and it was all my fault. John was 21 and could very well take care of himself. Baby Joseph, barely weaned from his nurse's breast, would thrive. The rest of us seemed caught in the middle of a great void.

With Papa aboard the vessel, it began its charted course from Liverpool to Boston. A sob caught in my throat as I watched the big sails unfurl. Papa was standing on the deck, the fine spray kicked up by the moving vessel nearly obscuring his face. As the mist rose to an overcast sky, I watched as Papa removed something from his pocket. He waved his white handkerchief, and then wiped his eyes. When the ship began moving out into the waters, I called to him. "Papa!" But he had turned away and could not hear me. "Goodbye, Papa," I whispered.

I reached for Anthony's hand and looked up at him. His right arm was around the shoulders of our eldest brother. Tears streamed down John's face, and within my heart, a deep knowing tolled the reason. Until the judgment, John would not see Papa again.

Three

Anno Dom 1647
Papa at Sea

The sea and the vessel on Papa's first experience on such a large ship fascinated him so, he could not wait to add the story of his crossing to his repertoire of evening conversations with his family. When the ship arrived in Boston two months later, he sent a missive back to England. We read it over so many times that I soon knew every word by heart:

When we were out to sea and the sailing smooth, I made the acquaintance of Captain Nathaniel Starbucks of Wales.

Surprised I was to find, on such a far-off sea, a cousin of the Starbucks family we know in Derbyshire. A ruddy-skinned man like his kin, Captain Starbucks is strong and experienced.

"See here, Ludlam," Starbucks said to me, tracing his gnarled finger across the map, "here, is our charted course. A captain of a Nantucket whaler showed me the route. In the ocean there be a river," he said. "Its banks and bottom are of cold water, but its warm current creates a remarkable flow.[11] In a month or so, we'll pass the Isle of Sables, keeping two degrees

*south of St. George's Banks between the currents of the Gulph
stream and the places where the shoals bear their fearsome
teeth. After passing the banks, we'll steer the course southward
a degree to clear the shoals on the south of the Nantucket coast.
By taking advantage of the eddy stream that moves contrary to
the Gulph flow, the passage from Newfoundland to Boston
Harbor will be considerably shortened.[12]*

*About midway, a tempestuous wind blew up, bringing
with it gusts of rain and a vast heaving of the waves. Many
of the passengers became seasick, spewing, falling, and suffering contusions with the bucking of the ship. Fortunately, I
did not undergo these frailties and felt much at home on the
sea. Strangely, the storm brought me a fresh sense of exhilaration. Three days it was before the water quieted. With
much relief, we could again walk on the deck, away from the
stench of conditions below. The continuing rain brought to
me an immense renewal of spirit. Surprised I was to find
great pleasure in breathing the salt-sea air as if that were in
God's plan — his sign of approval for the new home I will establish for you. Somewhere, there be a plot of land situated by
the sea, waiting for us.*

Until then, God keep you in his care, I am

Sincerely, your Papa,

William Ludlam,

In England that fall, our Matlock garden was rich with
harvest. We prepared apple vinegar and ale, pickled pork
and salted bacon to take with us. We hung vegetables,
fruits, herbs, and beef to dry. We shelled peas and beans
and stored them in barrels in the dry barn loft. All winter
we worked to set in a store of bedding and clothing to

take with us: feather mattresses and bolsters, canvas
sheets, our spinning wheel; handkerchiefs, capes, shirts,
gowns, and yards of calico. Hats, caps, and waistcoats;
suits of frieze, cloth, and canvas. Wool stockings, shoes
and boots for the boys to last a year, and leather for
mending. All this store we accomplished and packed in
chests, ready for our journey. All would be needed our
first year in our new home.

Grace and Cousin Elizabeth taught me how to pluck
feathers from our geese, and showed me how to stuff
them in canvas bolsters. We carded wool from our sheep,
spun and knitted it into stockings and caps. When the
sewing was finished, we packed our tools: scissors, pins
and needles. In the woods gathering bayberries one day,
Abbie and I wandered into the St. Giles churchyard and
traced the words chiseled on Mama's stone.

"See, Abbie: C-L-E-M-E-N-C-E. That's Mama's name.
L-U-D-L-A-M. That's our name, too. 'A.D 1646.' That
was last summer. Now it is 1647, and then next year
when thou art seven...what comes after 47, Abbie?"

"I know. It is 48! Mary, dost thou think Mama can hear
me counting? I've almost forgotten her face, but sometimes in my dreams I see her smiling at me. And I think
her hair was red like thine."

I could not reply for a big lump in my throat, but I
nodded. We missed Mama, but all the hard work seemed
to lighten our sorrow.

Together, Abbie and I carried the baskets of bayberries
home where our sister Grace melted the waxy fruit. Then
she let us help her dip long wicks into the fragrant hot
wax. The candles were hung from the rafters of the
kitchen, like rows of shiny green icicles.

Baby Joseph, now a year old and learning to walk, was into everything, but Cousin Elizabeth had a child of her own and knew how to tend a small baby. Grace, too, knew the ways she had learned while helping Mama with Hal and me and Abbie. Sometimes when Joseph was fussy, Abbie let him hold the rag doll Mama had made for her when she was a baby.

From Mr. Greene, John was learning how to create the tools that yeoman found most necessary, as well as household utensils. He helped my brothers set in a store of tools: spades and hatchets, axes and hammers, hooks for fishing, and lead for bullets. John was so proud of learning his own trade. By working extra hours he added to the store an iron pot, a big copper kettle, a spit, and a frying pan.

The hours we worked were long, but each one brought us closer to being with Papa again. On the first day of May his missive arrived:

March 8, 1648
Dear Children,
I rejoice to hear that our old friends from Lime Tree Farms, Thomas Bowne and his children, John and Dorothy, are sailing to Boston in June, and praise be, they have offered to accompany you on the trip. I will meet your ship when it sails into the harbor. Are you ready? I know Cousin Edmund and Elizabeth will help you pack, and then will accompany you to Liverpool where the Bownes have booked passage for themselves and for the seven of you. I am sorry that John will not have completed his apprenticeship for yet another two years. Eager am I to see him once again, and this place could use a good toolsmith.

The mill here at Southampton does a good business, and I have talked with Mr. Edward Howell[13] about purchasing it from him. It is driven by water from a lively stream and pond that empties into a bay the Shinnecock Indians have called Mecox. It is out on the tail of the island, near Uncle Obadiah's land, and by boat less than three miles east of Uncle Robert's house.

I hope to contract with the town to be their millwright, agreeing to supply such necessities of the town as grinding of grain grown anywhere in the area and delivered to the mill. In return, they will furnish men to help me update the mill, a precious commodity in this Puritan community. Southampton Village, a farming community bordered on the south by the ocean, is supported also by whaling. These big sea creatures often are beached on the sand, a sight I am sure you will find fascinating and quite different from our inland region of Matlock. Each land is beautiful in its own way.[14]

By the time you arrive, we will have completed the addition to the Fordham house to make room for all of you, at least until, as a proprietor, I can provide our own acreage at the head of Mill Pond. When Southampton village was laid out, each head of family received three acres for a House lot; twelve acres for cultivating; and thirty-four acres for grazing lands plus shares in common woodlands. I look forward to obtaining a similar acreage for our family.

Thomas Bowne will see to helping you pack and will haul all the provisions to the ship. I believe your sailing vessel is called the Trial, and I fear you will find it well named. The trip across is indeed fraught with trials. I can only wish you Godspeed. My prayers will follow you, and I know the Lord will protect you on the journey. The Lord watch between me and thee, when we are absent one from another.[15]

Your Papa,
William Ludlam II

21st Century
Memory Catchers' Office

My computer date book reminder interrupted Grand-Mary with its incessant buzzing, and I hit the 90-minute snooze button to silence it. "So, was your sailing difficult?" I asked.

A light scent of bayberry remained in the room, but Grand-Mary had disappeared. I made a phone call, cancelled my appointment, cleared my calendar for the week, and began transcribing her voice into print. So many questions arose! A card I had once drawn from the *LifeStories* game said: "If you could ask any question of one of your ancestors, what would it be?" Any question? Only one? *Grand-Mary, when will I see you again?*

❧

The minute we came in the door from our usual breakfast outing the next morning, Ken sniffed suspiciously. "What's that I smell? You didn't leave a candle burning in your office, did you?" A former fire and safety chairman for his company, he's super cautious and hates candles with a passion.

"Hm, must be the new Glade scent I'm trying. Like it? It's bayberry."

He grunted in reply and plopped down in his lounge chair to finish reading the morning paper. I hurried into my office, knowing I'd find Grand-Mary there. A reddish wisp of hair strayed against the blush of her cheek as if she'd arrived in a scurry, eager as I to continue her story. I flipped on the Sony. My listening skills were improving, but I still relied on that little piece of technology to capture her words.

Grand-Mary nodded her approval. "I have read thy transcription," she said. "I like the way thou art turning the interview into a real story." Her sea-blue eyes sparkled. "Ready for more?" Without pause, Grand-Mary continued.

MAY, ANNO DOM 1648
MATLOCK, ENGLAND

Papa's missive spurred us on to work even harder, completing our collection of things to take to the colonies. At the end of May, in 1648, Uncle Edmund and my brothers finished building the last of five large wooden chests to carry our belongings. We had a long list of necessary items to include. Difficult it was to decide what we must leave behind. In the chests to be stowed in the hold, we crammed dried food stuffs, candles, seeds for planting the gardens at our new home, and tools and hardware for both kitchen and barn. In one end of a chest, we packed a change of clothing for each of us, Luddie's loom and yarn and other needful sewing supplies. Grace, always concerned for our good health, stuffed in at the other end fresh provisions for the crossing: prunes and raisins, spices, rice, and limes, along with a small pipkin and an iron skillet. In case any of us should be sick at sea, she made room for green ginger and conserve of wormwood. The ship would provide other foodstuffs and bedding.

In a special compartment, we stowed precious things that had belonged to Mama, poems and letters she received after her friend, Anne Dudley, had married Simon Bradstreet and sailed with her father to Boston. Mama treasured Anne's letters and shared them with us: "At Boston church I have met thy sister Florence and her husband John Carman," she wrote. "She reminds me of thee, dear Clemence."

Another time she wrote, "Life is rough and cold here. I have found a new world and new manners at which my heart rises up in protest. I vow women here have even less freedom than in England. My beloved Simon is often away on business, and I am homesick." At the end was a poem:

I am obnoxious to each carping tongue,
Who sayes, my hand a needle better fits,
A Poets Pen, all scorne, I should thus wrong;
For such despighte they cast on female wits:
If what I doe prove well, it wo'nt advance,
They'l say its stolen, or else, it was by chance.[16]

21st Century
Memory Catchers' Office

Grand-Mary pressed both hands over her chest, as if holding the memory to her heart.

"I saved that poem forever. Often the words could have come from my mouth. Chafing at man-made rules, how could I not rebel? If women were to be restrained from protests or questions, why then had God granted me a proper education and the wit to wonder?"

Grand-Mary paused. "I'm sorry," she said. "Sometimes I am distracted. Where were we? Oh yes, the special compartment. Along with Mama's papers we packed the Geneva Bible the Dudleys had given her when she left their employ, and the muslin-wrapped gown she wore when she and Papa took their vows—"

"A white satin gown?"

"Oh, no." Grand-Mary shook her head. "Brides didn't wear white in my day. Her dress was emerald green, to match her eyes, but in a practical fabric that could be worn as Sabbath best. Such a tiny waist it had that after her first baby was born, she could never again wear it. She wrapped it in muslin and saved it though, believing it would someday fit one of her daughters. But Grace inherited the big bones and height from the Ludlam side of the family, and the dress was yet too large for me the last I had tried it on. Remember, I was only nine the summer of our leaving."

"Your mother worked for the Dudley family? I thought in those days a girl's place was in the home."

"Yes, thou art right. However, the home they worked in often was not that of their parents. Girls served apprentice-ships, learning life skills to fulfill their God-given purpose, just as my brother John and other boys did. Sometime the apprenticeship began when they were no older than seven or eight. Nevertheless, Mama said she was fifteen when she went to live with Thomas and Dorothy Dudley and their six children.

"Mama sometimes called my sisters and me by the Dudley girls' names. 'An—Pai—Sar—Mer—oh, fiddle-sticks. Mary!' she'd say. Mama wasn't the story teller Papa was, but I remember her in the evenings, when I was only five or so, reminiscing about her life as a young maiden. After Mama's death, try as I might, I could naught call to mind everything she said. Somehow, talking about Mama lessened the loss we felt, so my older siblings repeated the stories, just as they'd heard Mama tell them. I can still picture her sitting by the fireplace, rocking Abbie's cradle with her foot. I see her long, lovely fingers entwined with bright colored yarn, knitting stockings for her family as she weaves her own fairy tale—the story of Clemence Fordham and the Good Knight William Ludlam of Matlock. In fancy, I hear her soft voice..."

Four
My Mother's Story

~

ANNO DOM 1620s
ENGLAND

Once upon a time, there was a young maiden named Clemence Fordham — not much older than thee, Grace, whose father and mother, afraid of spoiling their daughter by too great affection, placed her as an apprentice. They loved their daughter very much and wanted only the best for her, but as wise parents, they knew that a child learns better manners when she is brought up in a home other than her own. Hence, they made an agreement with the Goodwife Dorothy of Yardley Hastings that their daughter, Clemence, should stay with the Dudleys for six years, to be taught, instructed, and provided for as should be mete. She would receive clothing, food, lodging, and an education, especially in the art of housewifery. Clemence must not absent herself from the Dudley household neither day nor night without her employer's leave.

Now Dudley Manor was a three-or four-hour ride northeast from the Fordham manse in Sacombe, so no matter how Clemence longed to see her own family again, there was no going home.

Hal always interrupted her story. "Not even for Sabbath dinner?" he would ask his mother. "I'm glad John can come home on Sabbath days. I miss him."

"Yes, I'm glad, too," Mama would say. "But John works for the tool smith right here in Matlock. He hath not to ride three hours home and back."

"Please go on, Mama. Tell us more."

Well, the Dudley family was kind to Clemence and loved her almost as if she were their own. Clemence also learned to love the family: the boys, older than she — Yorke and Samuel, and the girls — Baby Mercy Mary, still nursing at her mother's breast; two-year-old Sarah; four-year-old Patience; and Anne, almost eleven.

When the tutor came to teach the Dudley children reading, writing, and Latin, and the spelling of 8000 English words from Mulcaster 's *Elementarie*, Clemence was included. And along with the everyday duties of a housewife, Mrs. Dudley taught Clemence how to do fancy stitchery, how to serve meals properly, and how to carry on a polite conversation. Clemence learned to garden and sew, and by example she learned the duties of a Christian mother. "Spare not the rod if the child is obstinate," advised Mrs. Dudley, "but for less grievous faults, let the child see thee astonished, hardly believing that he could do so base a thing, and believing he will never do it again."[17] Mrs. Dudley was wise as well as beautiful.

Knowing that our own mama was the most beautiful of all, we children would nod in agreement. "Tell us more, Mama."

As young Clemence joined in the children's studies, she helped the wee ones learn to read their primer and to write their letters. "A — In Adam's Fall We Sinned All; B — Thy life to mend, This Book attend."

In spite of the hard work and the long hours, there remained time for friendship and amusement. She made rag dolls for Patience, Sarah, and Mercy out of scraps left over from sewing. She played tag with the children, and "London Bridge" and "Ring around the Rosy."

Though she was older than Anne Dudley by five years, they were of a size. Anne, mature for her age and well educated from early childhood, was tall like her father. Clemence had inherited the small frame of the Fordham women. The two girls became fast friends, studying together and often sharing poems they had written. Anne confided in the other as if to an older sister, blushing rosy red when they spoke of Mr. Dudley's friend, Simon Bradstreet.

"Promise me," Anne would say, "promise me ye'll not forget me when ye return to thy home. We can send each other poems and missives, can we not?"

And Clemence would promise that she would always hold Anne in her heart, that indeed they could send missives, that she would never forget their friendship.

Clemence also knew she would never fail to remember Anne's brothers. Samuel, tall and broad like his father, was away in London, learning the law. Clemence's favorite was Yorke, smaller by far than Samuel, although the oldest of the children. Golden-haired Yorke had been a sickly child, and hence was quite spoiled. But he had the loveliest dark eyes Clemence had ever seen, and when he touched her hand, a shiver ran down her back.

"Come with me, my lovely little bird," he said to her one evening after working hours were over. "Come into the garden and I'll read to thee."

Clemence loved his deep voice and the way his full lips shaped the words.

> Come live with me and be my Love,
> And we will all the pleasures prove
> That hills and valleys, dale and field,
> And all the craggy mountains yield.
> The shepherd swains shall dance and sing
> For thy delight each Maymorning:
> If these delights thy mind may move,
> Then live with me and be my Love.[18]

Yorke's heavy breathing excited Clemence, but she thought more logically than did her suitor. She could never be his bride. They were ill suited. His rank in society was above hers, and his father would never agree to their union even if the Fordhams could offer a large dowry. It was part of God's orderly plan that there should be stations — the servant and the master, the child and the parent, the woman and her husband.

Still, as he pled his case with lute and an altered version of the song, his lovely lips shaped the words in *such* convincing tones:

> Come live with me, Clemence, my dove,
> And we will all the pleasures prove...

"My lovely bird, I must have thee," he whispered.

The look in his eyes made her weak with yearning, and his breath was warm and sweet upon her cheek. Tears ran down her cheeks as she struggled in his arms.

21st Century
Memory Catcher's Office

Grand-Mary paused in the recollection of her mother's story, and for a moment, I wondered if she would continue. I knew her father's name had been William, not Yorke, but after looking up Matlock on MapQuest, I still had no idea how Clemence, Mary's mother, could have been courted by a man from a shire six hours away. Bouncing along in a saddle for that long would be enough to give John Wayne blisters!

"Phyllis! Art thou listening? May we go on with the interview?"

"Sorry, Grand-Mary, I was just imagining the difficulties of travel in your day. Your mother did marry William of Matlock, didn't she? And wasn't—"

Without hearing the rest, Grand-Mary understood the question in my eyes. "You remind me of my brother Hal. "But Mama," he would say, "when is the Good Knight William coming?"

"Hush, Hal," I would say to him, nudging him with my skinny elbow. "You must be patient. They haven't gone to the fair yet."

When at last Hal leaned back to listen to the rest of the tale, Mama would say, as if for a moment it had slipped her mind, "Oh, yes, the fair…"

ANNO DOM 1656
ENGLAND

When Thomas Dudley announced that the whole family was taking a long-day's trip to Scarborough Fair, Clemence and her young charges were elated.

"We'll set out tomorrow morn," he decreed, then turned to Yorke. "Son, thou art nearly twenty years old now. I've brought thee up diligently in proper business, yet you play hooky at school and show no desire for a liberal education."

Yorke felt the sobering weight of his father's large hand heavy upon his shoulder. Mr. Dudley frowned and moved his head from side to side.

"Neither hast thou recognized thy calling in a skilled trade. It is time to free myself of my parental obligation to thee. We will share the gaiety of the fair whilst thou also givest attention to the various merchants and tradesmen displaying their wares. Mayhaps thou thus will find thy clear calling, else thou wilt spend thy future in servitude to thy younger brother when he takes over my affairs." With that, he posted the announcement of the fair on his son's chamber door where all could read.

Come ye, Come ye to Scarborough Faire
Come Ye Merchants and Tradesmen,
Gentlemen and Yeomen!
"The Theatre Troupe of Royal England
Announces that they will Entertain
Our Great and Future King Charles and his lady,
Princess Henrietta Maria
With a Jousting Tournament 15 August 1625,
in the Town Square.
The contest, as approved by King James,
will include full-gallop Jousts by Actors in Ancient Colors

portraying ye Knights of Olde.
Come ye, Come ye, to the Forty-Five Day Trading Event

Mrs. Dudley was not so enthusiastic about the trip. "There will be such crowds," she said. "People from all over England, and even some from the continent, come to Scarborough to do their business."

"Mother! Do not dampen our pleasure!" Anne, now in her fourteenth year often felt too keenly the bit of her mother's firm rein. "Wouldst thou not have us catch a glimpse of Prince Charles and his betrothed, the Princess Henrietta Maria?"

Yorke, mocking the art of the royal couple, began reciting his latest ditty:

When Summer warms Scarborough Fair,
And darkness flees in fear of sun,
Shall we not thank the Lady who
Inspires our music, and our fun?

The road to Scarborough was long, so the Dudley carriage stopped for the night at a way station with a tavern for food and drink and a stable for their horse. Early the next morning, after a breakfast of bread and cheese, they set out again. By the time the Dudleys stepped down from the carriage at the Scarborough Inn, Mercy, now almost four years old, had fallen back to sleep.

"Clemence," said Mrs. Dudley, weary from the ride and the constant chatter of her impatient children, "I need to rest, so I will keep Mercy with me. Prithee, Clemence, accompany the others to the fair across the way."

Clemence took the hands of her small charges. On one arm she carried a basket of frosted hot-cross buns she had baked to be sold at St. Andrew's Charity Booth. Anne dutifully stayed by her side while her brother ran on ahead, following the direction their father had taken.

So much to see! Jugglers and jesters jostled in and out around the rows of tradesmen's bazaars. Minstrels made music, merchants sold their wares and hawkers offered dubious holy relics. After finding St. Andrew's Booth and depositing their donation there, they heard the fair crier announcing the jousting match beginning in the arena across the way.

"Look," seven-year-old Patience shouted, pointing skyward. Overhead, birds of prey swooped and darted in the blue sky, showing off their hunting skills. Harris hawks and falcons. The display ended, and the blast of trumpeters announced the parade. Clemence and the Dudley children, edged forward into the waiting crowd and worked their way to the barricade separating the spectators from the stage—a three-hundred-foot arena. Crowds pushed in around them to cheer for their favorite knight. Clemence lifted five-year-old Sarah to her shoulders so the wee girl could see. Horses and riders paraded through the field—actors brightly costumed in full array, Sir Lancelots and Galahads and Black Knights of yore, plumes waving, chain-mail clanking, competing for the day's prizes. Their magnificent horses, groomed and gleaming in fine jousting harness, pranced majestically through the area.

Jousting combat had long been outlawed by king's decree, but this day's event, as originated by King James, was a compromise with the century-old ban. At one end, on the right side of the tilt barrier sat the knight mounted on a thundering steed. On the opposite side, at the center, was the quintain. Its weighty beam revolved on top of a post with a shield bolted to one end and a heavy bag of sand to the other. There would be no bloodshed here. Nevertheless, the tournament demonstrated an actor-knight's skill, for the dummy shields were much smaller to lance than was a man.

Speaking over the noise of eager spectators, the crier explained the rules: "Ye will charge the quintain at full gallop, aiming to hit the shield in the center without being unhorsed. Each of ye will have two tries. At the end of the event, the winning knight will be crowned champion and presented the prize."

The announcer turned to the crowd: "Choose ye thy favorite knight. Place thy bets on his admirable skill. 'Tis a merrie sport of pomp and chivalry!"

Seven knights lined up at the end of the arena. One by one they accepted the challenge, but few were successful. Often, the slit of their helmet left them little room to see, and they missed the shield entirely. Or, after hitting the shield with a glancing blow, they forgot the next crucial step and the sandbag came whirling around, slamming them in the head. Whop! And, unless their feet were firmly in the stirrups, the weight of their heavy costume dragged them to one side, and they were unhorsed. [19]

Only two successfully splintered their lances with a direct hit—the actor in the armor of the Black Knight, and Galahad who carried the legendary white shield with a blood-red cross.

The Black Knight arrogantly pranced around the field, hands raised, clasped in a self-congratulatory gesture. As he rode past his competitors, he jeered and made derisive motions with his fingers.

Once again, the announcer took center stage. "We have two winners! Be there another color who would challenge the Black and White? This game of sport is open to the public. Who wouldst yet venture into the fray?"

Suddenly appeared there a country boy, accompanied by two friends. He was dressed in cloth breeches and a plain shirt and jerkin. On his dark head he wore the brown felt hat of a yeoman; his horse, the rough-coated mare he traveled on, trained for pulling a farmer's plow or carrying the harvest to market.

"Look at the farmer boy's nag," the Black Knight said, pointing.

The young yeoman held his head high. "My name is Will Ludlam, and I will take the challenge," he vowed. The crowd cheered. Clemence and the Dudley children joined in their chanting: "Good Knight William, Good Knight William!"

"Where is thy helmet? Where is thine armor?" howled the Black Knight. "Thou canst not compete without the proper gear. 'Twould be an unfair advantage." With that, he grabbed the helmet of the actor with the white and red shield, and shoved it toward Will.

"We have a challenger," yelled the announcer.

The tall and broad-built Galahad stepped to the side of Will and his two country friends. "Help me out of mine armor, and thou canst wear it," he said. "We are of a size."

Will's friends, whom he called Nate Starbuck and Squire Bowne, stepped up to help Galahad unbuckle his armor. They slipped it over Will's shoulders and fastened it securely around his chest. Galahad handed him his lance and then his white shield. "Perhaps the blood of the cross will bring thee good fortune," he said.

Galahad then spoke quietly in Will's ear. "Sit firmly in the saddle, making sure thy feet are in the stirrups. Be prepared to use thy knees to cling to thy steed. Hold thy lance upright in thy right hand. At the signal, ride hard and straight ahead, with the tilt barrier to thy left. Lean slightly forward so thou canst see through the slit in the helmet. Keep thy lance upright. At the last possible moment, lower thy lance at an angle across thy horse's neck, couching it in thy right arm and pointing forward across the tilt barrier. Aim for the shield. Cling tightly to thy mount with thy legs, and be prepared to lean backward on impact. Otherwise the sand bag will swing around and knock thee out of the saddle."[20]

Will nodded. He clapped on the helmet, clanked the visor shut, seized the lance, and for luck, took the shield Galahad offered. While Starbuck checked the stirrups, Squire Bowne did a final check on the mare's bridle. Then Will rode to one end of the tilt-yard to start his run.

His stomach churned. To calm himself, he took a deep breath. Would his untrained mare know what to do?

Holding the lance upright, he spurred her into a trot. "Come on, Nell, old girl!" Finally, Will urged the mare into a gallop. He lowered the lance, angling it across his horse's neck to hit the quintain on his left—aiming the tip as best he could while squinting through the helmet visor.

Whack! The lance-point ricocheted off the shield's edge and Will slammed back against the saddle's high cantle. The shield swung around. Whop! The bag of sand hit him like a smithy's hammer. Spectators roared with laughter. Will's mare shied at the impact and nearly threw him from the saddle. He gasped for breath, barely able to hang onto the lance.[21]

Clemence's cheeks flushed, feeling the discomfiture of the yeoman knight. She watched as he removed the helmet, wiped his face on his sleeve, and then headed toward the beginning of the course to make a second try. As he was directly in front of the Dudley children, a sudden draft moved through the arena, and an errant gust whipped the emerald ribbon from Clemence's hair, unleashing a stream of long copper curls. The flash of the ribbon caught Will's eye, and when it alighted on the ground, with all the pomp and chivalry of ancient knights he dismounted and retrieved the colored band. Holding it up, he walked toward the barricade. "M'lady, doth this be thine?"

Clemence blushed and held out her hand. Before her, she beheld the face of the Good Knight—broad jaw, cleft chin below a wide mouth, a hank of dark hair sweeping across his forehead. His gaze was direct, and his eyes the color of dark green moss, suggesting the hidden depths of the sea. For a moment, her breath was quite taken away. Perhaps she should offer the ribbon to the Knight to tie around his arm, as did the knights of yore. But Will had remounted his mare and was riding off toward the starting line.

Again Starbuck handed him the lance. Again Will clapped the helmet on. "Yah!" he yelled. This time, he was no longer a yeoman's son, but a knight in armor with a ten-foot lance, galloping onto the field prepared to do battle for his lady's honor. His horse exploded forward, giving him the needed momentum. This time the lance hit the very center of the shield and exploded into pieces, the way it was supposed to do in a tournament. Sharp splinters rained back on his helmet and armor. He ducked to avoid the hurtling sandbag; the quintain, its hub squealing, kept spinning on its own momentum. The crowd broke into wild applause.

Game at an end, the three knights rode off with jingling pockets, two arm in arm, the other scowling as he pranced away.

"Girls," Clemence said to the Dudley children, "your mother will be expecting us in less than an hour. We had best be moving on." As they left the field, they stopped along the path to watch a dramatic entertainment per-formed by masked players. A banner flirted above them: *Staged by Inigo Jones and Ben Jonson to Dramatise the Ideals of the Stuart Monarchy,* it said. Suddenly trumpets announced the coming of Scarborough's most favored guests, and a carriage drew to a halt right before the eyes of the Dudley children and their caretaker. They stood opened mouthed as Prince Charles and his Lady, assisted by a palace steward, descended the steps. Most of the crowd was standing to watch the play, but they bowed and applauded when the Royal couple was escorted to comfortable chairs near the stage.

After cheers for the play died down, a troupe of musicians took the stage.. To the horror of Puritans in the audience, Princess Henrietta Maria rose and joined in the gaiety, singing and dancing along with the performers. Prince Charles, laughing and clapping with delight, added impetus to the Puritan scowls. 'Twas a sin to participate in such frivolity!

> Are you going to Scarborough Fair?
> Parsley, sage, rosemary and thyme
> Remember me to one who lives there
> For once she was a true love of mine

Tell her to make me a cambric shirt
Parsley, sage, rosemary and thyme
With no seam nor fine needle work
And then she'll be a true love of mine
Love imposes impossible tasks
Parsley, sage, rosemary and thyme
Though not more than any heart asks
And I must know she's a true love of mine

When the entertainment was over, Clemence took the hands of the younger girls, and she and Anne turned in the direction of the inn. A familiar voice caused Clemence to turn.

"Come live with me and be my love..."

Not ten feet away stood a flaxen-haired maiden, cheek-to-cheek with Yorke Dudley. His hand caressed her bosom, and the look in his eyes was one Clemence had thought belonged only to her. Suddenly an angry voice shouted, "Yorke!"

Clemence immediately stepped back into the crowd before either Yorke or Mr. Dudley could see her. Hot with shame and remorse for her easy gullibility, she hurriedly guided her charges down the road toward Scarborough Inn.

හ

After the Dudleys returned to their home in Yardley Hastings, Thomas Dudley's foul mood permeated the manor. Rubbing a hand over his flushed face, he reported that a brazen actor who called himself Galahad had inquired about his red-haired daughter. "Harrumph!" he had replied. "Refer ye to the maid Clemence, the care-taker of my children? Would that I had such a sensible daughter in place of my worthless son, but if she's taken up with thee, I am sadly disappointed. As he spoke, he glared at Clemence, but his arrow of outrage aimed directly at Yorke, no more inclined to a calling of hard work was he than before the trip to Scarborough.

When urged by his father to pray diligently, seeking God's counsel, Yorke insisted the inheritance left him by his grandfather would provide well enough "even for a bride and children."

"I want to go to London, Father. I've decided to become an actor—like the great Ben Jonson. He looked at his father with a sardonic grin. "I'm sure I can best serve the Lord by bringing pleasure to others—and along with my acting, I'll translate the Latin writings as did Kit Marlowe."

Thomas Dudley shook his graying head, disappointment in his eyes. Neither Ben Jonson nor the infamous Kit Marlowe was the role model he'd have chosen for his precious heir. Yorke seemed to enjoy the discomfit he brought. "Is not this translation beautiful, Father?"

> I snatcht her gowne: being thin, the harme was small,
> Yet strived she to be covered therewithall.
> And striving thus as one that would be cast,
> Betrayde her selfe, and yeelded at the last.[22]

The elder Dudley lowered his head, feeling great remorse at hearing Yorke's words. "Oh, my son, with our minister I have prayed that thou findest the path wherein God might turn thy weakness into strength." His voice grew more resolute as he spoke. "Now I know," he said, "the Rev. John Cotton[23] is correct. The church itself has taken the path of sinful pleasures and has fallen from God's grace. I, too, have fallen, and in so doing have been remiss in my duties to thee. I should have placed thee with a hard master long ago."

Yorke shrugged and turned away.

That night Clemence again heard Yorke's voice and the strumming of his lute. Tormented by his faithless behavior and uneasy about the argument she had heard between him and his father, she felt she must speak her mind. In the garden, she seated herself beside Yorke and gently took his hand. "Yorke, thy father's heart is heavy. Canst thou not reconcile your differences?

Yorke spoke harshly. "Methinks Father leans too closely to the Puritan way. He toddles after John Cotton like a lamb to the slaughter. Radicals! All of them! Wouldst thou have me follow them to the death? I would not!" He spat upon the ground. Then the harshness in his voice changed to one of mirth. "There is much marrow to be sucked from the bones of life. I will seize the pleasures of the moment!" He suddenly noticed the emerald ribbon woven within her plaited hair. "Ah hah," he said, snatching the ribbon from her tresses. I believe thee, too, may have seized a few pleasures at the fair." His upper lip twisting wickedly. "Phst, what a wench thou art." With that, he gave her a shove and spun on his heel, leaving her sprawled on the garden bench, cast away like spoiled milk.

At dawn the next morning, Clemence awakened to the sound of loud voices. Through her chamber window, she saw Yorke and his father loading bags into the Dudley carriage. The older man's angry words told her there would be no more forgiveness of his son's obstinacy. She dressed and set about her duties, working to forget her humiliation and sadness. The apprenticeship would bind her for yet another year.

Soon Mr. Dudley approached her. "Clemence," he said, I have received a request from one William Ludlam who art desirous of becoming thy suitor. He hath also approached thy father in Sacombe with the same request."

Mr. Dudley unfolded the page and handed it to Clemence to read:

Sir, I request permission to court the lovely Clemence Fordham who art now in your employ. Although I am no Knight, she may regard me as the rider who retrieved her ribbon at Scarborough Fair. My parents and I reside in Matlock Parish in Derbyshire where I am a freeholder, well established and ready to take a suitable wife. Although I am only in my 21st year, I have means to provide a home where we may safely abide and raise a family according to God's holy ordinance. With thy blessing and with encouragement from this fair maiden, I ask thy consent that I might call on her on Friday next.

Thy most sincere and honorable servant,

William Ludlam, II

Thomas Dudley not only approved the request, but also seemed eager for Clemence to find an industrious young man of her station who would love and honour her as his wife.

Mama paused in her story, and Hal could contain his impatience no longer. "So the Good Knight galloped across hill and dale until he came to Dudley Manor, right, Mama?"

"Yes, he did," Mama said as she smoothed Hal's dark hair.

"And Clemence and the Good Knight lived happily ever after?"

Mama's smile turned into a deep, throaty laugh. "Right thou art, my little lad." Leaning forward, she lifted baby Abbie from the cradle and placed her at her breast to nurse.

The tale of the Good Knight continued.

After the meeting with young Will Ludlam, Thomas Dudley released Clemence from her apprenticeship and presented her the gift of a dowry that she might contribute substantially to the union. Mrs. Dudley and her daughters, sad to think of Clemence leaving but rejoicing in her happiness, chose other gifts of remembrance — a Geneva Bible, a large pewter bowl and spoon for Clemence's kitchen, and a length of lovely emerald fabric and lace that she might fashion a bridal dress. Within the folds of the fabric, Anne tucked a poem she had written especially to honor her friend Clemence.

> Studious am I what I shall do
> to show my duty with delight;
> All I can give is but this poem
> and at the most a simple mite.
> Thou hast made my pilgrimage,
> Blessed me in childhood and in youth,
> Thou friend, so pleasant, good, and fair,
> I'll ne'er forget forsooth.[24]

Within a fortnight, William and his bride-to-be had published their banns. Before the October harvest festival, William and Clemence said goodbye to the Dudleys and to her father and mother in Sacombe, and moved, as husband and wife, into their Matlock Parish home."

Five

~

21ST CENTURY
MEMORY CATCHERS' OFFICE

Grand-Mary nodded her approval after reading the transcription of her mother's story, so I slipped another media card into the recorder and continued the interview. "You and your siblings were all born in Matlock Parish?"

"Yes, and all baptized at St. Giles Church. I believe our Ludlam kin still live in Matlock, but of course thou knowst our own family left in 1648. Joseph — my youngest brother — was nearly two by the time we boarded the ship. A hard journey for one so young. Grand-Mary's eyes seemed focused on a faraway time.

"That was the year of the King's defeat — an awful war, brother against brother. Parliament could find no law in all of England's history that dealt with the trial of a monarch, so Cromwell invoked an old Roman law. King Charles had not yet been executed when we sailed for the colonies."

I nodded. "I've read about the terrible conditions of early voyages. Was your ship anything like the *Mayflower* or the ships in Winthrop's fleet?"

"Oh, yes. Between the *Mayflower*'s crossing in 1620, and our journey in 1648, sailing ships changed very little — although we were better prepared than they. Much knowledge had been passed down from that first experience of the Pilgrim Separatists. Shall I tell thee now about our voyage?" Grand-Mary peered at me with raised eyebrows.

"On the *Triall*, your ship?"

"Yes, yes. I remember it vividly although I was not yet nine years old at the time. Perhaps the crossing was more difficult for most passengers than it was for me and my brothers and sisters. We would have borne any hardship to be united again with Papa."

With that, a shadow seemed to flit across Grand-Mary's face, but it was quickly gone.

"In my day, the word "Triall" meant departure, and we were Triallairs — travelers. Captain Hawk, a giant of a man, reminded me of Grandfather Ludlam — short curly hair, jolly smile, and sun-squint lines about his eyes. I felt safe in his care.

"We watched as sailors and servants loaded cargo — water and beer casks, barrels of flour, dried beans, peas and other food stuffs, bags of charcoal for cooking, crates of guns, swords, tools and other necessities — to stow them away in the hold. Next, they carried our trunks and chests on board — everything we could fit within them.

"The vessel looked wonderfully majestic with white sails unfurled and red flags flying. Even its figurehead — a hawk with crimson tail newly gilded — lent a spirit of courage and adventure."

As Grand-Mary revisited the day of their leaving, her eyes sparkled like sunlight on water and her pale cheeks took on a rosy hue.

"On 4 June 1648, the ship caught a fair breeze and set a westerly course," she said. "I was fair excited, though if the truth be told, a bit afraid to be traveling so far on such a large vessel. Nevertheless, its size diminished once the passengers boarded with their trunks and chests. There were perhaps a score of sailors and crew on the upper deck. The passengers lived 'tween decks where the space was so low that tall men like my brother Luddie could not stand erect. He counted eighteen travelers who slept in the aft cabin, and our smaller cabin, in front of the other, held six rows of bunks, three bunks high."

"Another eighteen passengers?"

"Oh, no! We each shared a bunk with another person—thirty-six travelers in one small cabin. When the ship had last returned from the Colonies, it carried tobacco to English buyers, so the sweet aroma permeated the ship, lessening the stale smell of our quarters. Even so, most passengers spent as much time as possible in the fresh sea air of the deck above us.

"For our little Joseph, the motion of the ship meant learning to walk all over again, but often at night, it was my own legs that mightily ached. 'Just growing pains,' Grand-mother Ludlam used to say when I cried in the night. Sometimes, especially when Joseph was ready for a nap, I stayed below with him, and we curled up in my bunk in a downy quilt—alone in a quiet nest with the rhythm of waves slapping the hull. Muted voices. Calm and lovely sounds. Best of all, the scent of tobacco reminding me of Papa smoking his evening pipe." Grand-Mary closed her eyes and inhaled deeply, her lips curved in a serene smile. She put a soft hand to her breast. "My heart beat a little faster as I pictured him meeting us at our Boston landing. He'd be laughing with joy and on his face the look of love I oft remembered from the time before Mama died. He'd hold out his arms in welcome, and I would run to him, and as he held me close, I'd brush back the dark lock of hair that was wont to fall over his forehead and I'd cover his sweet face with kisses. I imagined him holding me on his lap—as soon he would be—telling about his adventures on the long island."

The joy left Grand-Mary's voice, and again sorrow skittered across her face. With a deep sigh, she continued her story:

"Too often, my dreams were interrupted when rain and wind drove the others back to the cabin."

"Did you know the others in your quarters?"

"Only the Bowne family in the beginning. They attended St. Giles Church, so we knew them well—Dorothy and John, and their father who hauled our belongings and us to the ship, and Dobson, the apprentice who lived with them. They were in the bunks across the cabin from us.[25]

"My brother Luddie slept in our top bunk with that hateful Icarus, the stepson of Rev. Mather Cross. My little brother and I slept below them, and in the bottom bunk, my sisters—Abbie and Grace. Next to us, in the top bunk, were my brothers, Anthony and Hal. In the next row, Rev. Cross; Mather, Jr., a prudish little tattle tale; and below, his wife, Sara, and little Elijah."

"That's only twelve people," I said. "Twenty-four to go."

Grand-Mary paused, scanning each wall of my office, as if picturing the small cabin and inhabitants. "Yes, I still remember. The trunks holding our personal belongs and clothing were stacked at the end. Then, around the corner were the Royalls a family of five bent on avoiding contact as if in hiding. The first day aboard, only their fat, jolly cook, Peter LaRoux, spoke in anything above a whisper, and in French, with just a smattering of our tongue.

"Next to them, another family who at first seemed most unfriendly, the Kingsley brothers and their parents and sister, Joan Marie, about my age."

Grand-Mary turned to the right as she spoke— "and around the corner, in the bunk above John and Dorothy Bowne, was Joshua Prentice and his fey sister, Hannah." Grand-Mary nodded, the memory fixed in her mind. "The rest of the Prentice family filled the last stack of bunks—a small man with fearsome beady eyes and a nervous hand hiding his right cheek; his wife; their other children, Nicholas and Baby Anne; and in the top bunk their midwife, Polly, with Honour, the Kingsley servant." Grand-Mary spread her arms, in a gesture encompassing my small office. "All of us in a room no bigger than your workspace. Stifling it was, close and rank...."

ANNO DOM 1648
AT SEA

That first Sabbath we awoke to grey, threatening skies that soon became a pouring rain. Just imagine a breakfast of cold beans and beer by lantern light, followed by one of Rev. Cross's four-hour sermons in that crowded cabin. Praise be, the downpour stopped by noontime so with as much semblance of community as our oddly matched group would allow, we climbed to the upper deck's salt-sweet air and wedged ourselves amongst the chicken crates and water barrels to eat our hard biscuits and cheese.

As the Royall and Kingsley couples moved away from the rest of the group, I heard the fiery-eyed Prentice fellow say to his wife. "Stay away from them, Sarah. Their kind taketh pleasure in applying the brand." He adjusted his large white collar, concealing the scars on his cheek. "I think the Kingsley man was one of the ringleaders who committed atrocities in the name of the King at Naseby."

"Hush, Adam," She laid her hand on his arm. "The war is nearly over now." Tenderly, she teased her husband, "At least you escaped with both ears."

When the group had finished their biscuits, the preacher continued his lecture. Under the blue canopy of sky, the last hours of the sermon seemed less oppressive.

I remember my grandmother saying, "Small pitchers have wide ears," and how right she was. By the end of the day, I had collected a vast assortment of particulars about my cabin mates.

Matching the rhythmical slap of waves against the ship and the whipping sounds of the sails as wind gusts bellied them forward, Rev. Cross's strict application of the word of God took on a slow and tedious tempo, missing a beat only when he directed an occasional frown toward his wife. Mrs. Cross could not stop wee Elijah's constant crying. That, combined with the hullabaloo of the crew, made it difficult to attend the preacher's words, and the sailors' occasional derisive hooting gave Icarus Cross opportunity for sly mocking of his stepfather's mannerisms. Even though he had already achieved a place as least favored shipmate, difficult it was to refrain from laughing at his antics.

The activities of the sailors created a pleasant distraction, allowing the mismatched lot of worshipers to whisper among themselves or to fall asleep in the sunshine without fear of a rap on the head by some self-appointed churchman.

The Kingsley and Royall families, seated behind the others, were even less attentive to the message than others. "There's something strange about that Cross lad," I heard one of them say.

James Royall nodded. "Icarus, you mean? It's his bulging eyes and wicked grin," he said. "I trust that little fiend even less than the other bloody Puritans." James' eyes filled with anger, and when the golden haired child in front of him bumped the bandaged limb he had extended, he flinched mightily, sucking in his breath as he jerked his foot back. "Watch it, boy!" he hissed. Before anyone should notice, he swiped at welling tears.

It was clear my new friend Joshua Prentice did not carry his father's anger. He turned to James and ever so gently touched the young man's foot. "I'm sorry," he whispered, his wide blue eyes full of repentance. "I meant not to bump thee."

Quin Kingsley put a comforting hand on James Royall's shoulder. Then, turning to his left, Quin said to his brother, "Are you comfortable, Robbie?"

Watching closely, I saw Robbie Kingsley nod. He tried to speak, but a pitiful scar puckered one side of his mouth like the drawstrings of a money sack, contorting his words.

Was he one of the spies on Cromwell's rogues' list?

I saw Joshua's older brother, Nicholas Prentice, nudge one of the two girls sitting next to the Royall family.

Eavesdropping was much more interesting than the sermon, so I leaned closer to hear Nicholas' words.

"Polly," he said, "I think that angry fellow with the bandage is looking for trouble."

Polly put a hand to her mouth and leaned toward him. "I heard your father say he's a Cavalier."

"Yes," Dorothy Bowne murmured. "And now they're running from Cromwell. The Kingsley family too, I believe. Should they be caught, they will surely face execution."

Young Nicholas Prentice looked at his watch, then eased it back into his pocket and yawned. "Should the word of God be so boring as all this sermonizing? A glass of strong ale would be more to my liking."

The preacher's son, Mather, Jr., turned around and glared at the older youth. "I'm going to tell my father what you said. Thou art not a good Puritan, even if thy father does have S.S. burned on his cheek."

Nicholas raised an eyebrow. "A lot you know!" With barely a glance, he dismissed the young tattler. "Such a bother thou art. No wonder thy bug-eyed brother calls thee 'The Gnat.'"

Dorothy Bowne's eyes widened. "Thy father has the Sower of Sedition brand? What did he do to earn that?"

Nicholas leaned closer. "Thou wouldst not tell?" He put his lips to her ear. "Before he got caught, we distributed more Puritan pamphlets than anyone else in Cheshire."

Still standing at the head of his odd-lot congregation of saints and sinners, the Reverend Mather Cross looked toward the darkening clouds, raised his voice several decibels and began his ending diatribe.

"Surely the vengeance of the Lord shall be on this generation. With frivolity and iniquity, ye have brought forth bitter and poisonous fruit even in God's holy place. Let every one of ye flee from this wickedness." At that moment, the God of the eastern sky obliged with a flash of lightning.

Undaunted, the preacher continued. "Fly out of Sodom. Fly!" A clap of thunder punctuated his directive. "Look not behind ye! Escape to the mountain, lest ye be consumed!"

"Amen."

Geoffrey Royall stood and offered his wife a hand. "Elizabeth, let me help thee up."

She rose, and shook away his hand. With head held high, she turned to leave the deck, brushing past the timid Mrs. Kingsley. "Pardonnez-moi, s'il vous plait. We've heard quite enough from this 'purifier' of the church, est-ce que ce n'est pas vrai?" She fingered the rosary that graced her long neck. "I cannot wait to arrive in Virginia Colony[26] where we'll be free to worship as God intended. À mes oreilles, Latin will be a pleasant change from today's offensive tones."

Quietly, while attending the three-hour sermon, I had listened and observed those around me, pretending to walk in their shoes. As I struggled to rise, painful cramps knotted my legs. Deep within my young heart, an extraordinary empathy for my shipmates began to take root. They too suffered growing pains, each of their own kind. Branded and lame, bitter and frightened, Puritan, Catholic, and Church of England — all were fleeing Sodom, escaping to the mountain.

What a gathering of travelers we were — from the stoic and submissive, to stiff-necked authoritarians. From the healthy and strong to the ill and wounded, we were thirty-six sweating bodies with naught but salt water for washing. Too often rain kept us inside. Yet some found a calling within the bounds of our dimly lit cabin. Salt water became medicine in the hands of the Prentice midwife, Polly Durham. Skilled in knowledge of healing herbs, she could not long endure the stench of rotting bandages. With ne'er a by-your-leave, she carried a basin of seawater to James Royall. By lantern light I watched as she carefully removed the fetid wrap, revealing squirming maggots doing their work on the putrid wound. I could look no longer.

"Here, so'jer," she said, "soak your foot in this basin. 'Twill make it better."

While his foot was soaking, Polly moved to the next row of bunks and ministered to the wounds of Robbie and Richard Kingsley. She motioned to her bunk mate. "Come and help, Honour. I have no need for two petticoats. Tear this one into strips. This poultice of yarrow will speed their healing." She looked up at Honour with a wry smile. "Perchance 'tis good medicine for both sides."

Me thinks God had Polly in mind when he wrote, "Blessed are the merciful."

In fair weather, we escaped to the upper deck next to the galley. There be nothing like a cool breeze, the smell of the sea, and the sun on one's face to awaken an appetite.

The *Triall*'s quartermaster supplied each family a simple ration of food—beef, pork or salted cod, bread and butter, beans and peas, cheese, oatmeal, limes to prevent rickets, beer and water. Many passengers became ill at the beginning of our journey, so Peter LaRoux kindly volunteered his cooking skills and combined our ingredients in a large iron kettle that hung over the charcoal fire in the ship's galley. Unlike his sister, Mrs. Royall, Peter was warm and friendly and seemed not in the least intimidated by self-righteous authority. Nor was he biased toward one faction or another. He quickly took over the galley and with spices from his homeland, magically turned the most piteous stale provisions into fragrant ambrosia.

Peter sampled everything he cooked, and his belly was a great round ball, rounder even than that of Tommy Prentice's poor mother, who was great with child. When she could not navigate the ladder onto the upper deck, he freshened water with lime juice, or steeped caraway tea for her, guaranteed to soothe even the most upset stomach.

"It is my God-given talent," he said, when Joshua's father protested. "Please, Monsieur, allow me to serve in this way that I may earn my salvation."

Adam Prentice fingered the letters branded on his cheek, then shuddered. Drawing down the corners of his mouth, he made an odd strangling noise. One would have thought he'd swigged a sip of stale vinegar.

Rev. Cross pounded his back, and I heard him mutter, "I too retch at such profane ideas, Brother Prentice. Surely Catholics are not so corrupt as to believe salvation is earned. Ah, I fear we have yet much work to achieve among these rebels."

Even though Peter's *paner le pudding et la sauce de chaux sucré* and his *saler le porc et les haricots* cooked with ale was pottage fit for the King, 'twere those same two men who grumbled that they'd settle for a good old mess of fried fish and vinegar. Strict Puritans they were, but most unkind in their remarks. However, when the seamen decided to catch one of the porpoises that leaped and played around our ship, we all welcomed the change in menu. They hauled their catch on board and hung the big fish from a trestle, like the pigs we butchered back on our Matlock farm. Everyone seemed to think it was great sport.

While watching the butchering, even the stern Rev. Cross became quite jovial. "Tis God that affords us both entertainment and a refreshing meal," he said.

Even so, I could not help but think of the poor creature romping and playing in the sea with his companions, and in spite of the delicious aroma, the meat tasted bitter in my mouth.

Actually, I believe it was Peter's cooking that brought about my friendship with Joshua Prentice. Because Peter sang while he cooked, that got Joshua and me remembering all the nursery rhymes and songs we knew about eating: "Pease Porridge Hot," "Cockles and Mussels," "Three Ravens." It became a game to see who could think of another ditty to sing, and soon the others were playing.

Best of all was hearing Joshua sing by himself. Surprising it was that God could spare such a sweet voice from His angel choir even for a little while. Sometimes when little Elijah Cross cried with an earache, Joshua comforted him with "Hush-a-Bye Baby." And 'twas not only I who wiped away tears when he sang "Barbara Allen."

> All in the merry month of May,
> When green buds they were swellin'
> Young Willie Grove on his death-bed lay,
> For love of Barb'ra Allen.

Joshua was as good as he was fair, a sweet, gentle soul with a halo of curly blond hair and wide-with-wonder blue eyes. Often he entertained the younger children, playing "Ring around the Rosy," and "London Bridge" with them. Joshua's baby sister, Anne, toddled around after him wherever he went. One of her first sentences was, "Me, too, Josh," and he would wait patiently for her to catch up with him.

When Icarus taunted and mocked him, Joshua only smiled. But when Icarus called *me* a dirty woodlouse one day, Joshua pegged him with such an icy stare that Icarus went off howling.

"You're a cockroach, Joshua Prentice!" He stomped away, playing squash, his favorite game. Hordes of vermin inundated the ship, so it took no imagination to crush a bug with every step. "Squash, you cockroach! Squish, you woodlouse! Smash, you one-footed slug!" That was Icarus' name for James Royall, the Cavalier with the wounded foot. James' eyes were showing less pain than the previous week. Polly's medicine was working.

That night, when fey little Hannah Prentice slid between the covers of the second row bunk she shared with her brother Joshua, she suddenly screamed and jerked to a sitting position, bumping her elfin-featured head on the bunk above her. Nearly in hysterics, she threw back the quilt. Quin Kingsley, in the adjacent bunk, was watching. When he saw the dead rat, smashed and oozing blood in the middle of Hannah's bunk, he marched across the cabin, grabbed Icarus by the scruff of the neck, and with Anthony's help, dragged the sadistic young troublemaker back across the room. "Icarus Cross, you're one fine example of the Puritan way!" Quin's lips curled in disgust. "Shame on you! Treating a barmy child in such an ill manner. Now pick up that rat and dispose of it."

ഔ

The next evening, to escape the confines of the cabin, we carried our bedding to the upper deck to sleep under the stars. I cuddled up beside Grace and Abbie, but when I shut my eyes, I could still see the squirming maggots on the soldier's wound. Could it have been only last year when we children played Cavaliers and Roundheads after school, laughing and swinging at each other with make-believe swords? War was a game then, bright ribbons and feathery plumes and snacking together on Mama's raisin scones. Now it was all about bloody bandages and maggots, suffering and the loss of innocence. War was not a game!

Can people sleep with their eyes open? I decided to try. Above me, I found the North Star right where God had placed it, shining down toward four big stars, the "Wagon of King Charles." That's what Papa called it, but I heard Peter telling Joan Marie it was the Great Bear. I don't think that was a good thing to tell her. She just clutched her doll even tighter. So I told her what Papa said—that it was a wagon, and it was so huge it could hold King Charles and Princess Henrietta Marie, and his whole palace.

There must have been a hundred million stars out that night. Did God make all of them? And most puzzling of all – *Who made God?*

"Grace," I whispered, "if God is so great, and bigger than all the sea and the sky, why did He let Mama die?

And why does He not stop his children's fighting before anyone else gets hurt? Does He not love James and Quin and Robbie as much as He loves Joshua and thee and me?"

"You talk overmuch, little sister. The Bible says 'If you love to listen you will gain knowledge, and if you pay attention you will become wise.'[27] And when you do, you can answer *my* questions. Now go to sleep."

We sailed in good winds and fair weather for nearly a month, but one fateful morning we awoke to an ominous red dawn. Sailors on morning watch scurried about uneasily, keeping wary eyes on storm clouds gathering in the north. By midmorning, strong northeasterly winds had shifted to the north, tossing and rolling the ship. At the Captain's summoning whistle, a dozen or so sailors climbed aloft to furl the sails, their ladders pitching and jerking with the ship's wallowing motion. Crew members sounded their warning, "Laying on starboard!" "Laying on larboard!" before stepping out onto footropes looped horizontally under the spar. Bracing themselves, they bent their bellies over the wooden yardarm, straining to gather and restrain the great bulges of canvas sails that galloped in the fierce gale. During the approaching storm, there would be no steering the ship.

With the daring of carefree youth, fearless and fascinated by the sailors' actions, Joshua and I braced our backs 'gainst the ship's galley, too excited to finish our stale breakfast of hardtack.

"Mary! Did you not hear the captain's orders? Come now, thou must go below!" It was my brother Luddie, come looking for us. "Joshua, thy mother is worried. Come, you young rascals, make way to our cabin. 'Tis not safe on deck. All the others have taken refuge below." Luddie pulled us to our feet just as a huge wave washed over the deck, nearly knocking us to our knees. We reached the tween deck and darted into the bedlam of our crowded cabin. Grace was holding both Abbie and our little brother in her lower bunk. Joseph, whimpering, clung to Grace, so I left him with her, and Abbie and I climbed into the middle bunk.

In a nervous pool of light cast by an overhead lantern, across from us I could see Joshua's father, the brand on his cheek flaring red as he boosted his son up into the top bunk with his sister Elizabeth. But the clamor of sailors running to and fro on the deck above us, and the deafening roar of the sea blotted out his words.

Through the hatch we heard Captain Hawk's orders. "We want no fires on ship. Douse your lanterns!"

Light disappeared with a puff, and we heard the clanging sound of the hatch closing.

Fearful dark it was and the air hot and oppressive. The sounds of the crew running here and there on the upper deck, crying "Pull!" "Tighten that rope!" "Heave to!" made us more afraid. Sweat poured down my back.

That night, Peter managed to find cold biscuits and cheese in a trunk of supplies. Grasping bunk rails, he made his way 'round the cabin, distributing food stuffs to those who could eat. All day and on through the night, the storm tossed us one side to the other. Seasick and scared, tumbled and jostled, slammed we into each other. In the sweltering cabin, I reached for a basin, and shared it with Abbie. The ship bucked and rolled, sloshing the smelly contents of the basin all over our mattress. A terrible stench filled our throats and our nostrils—sweat drenched bodies and vomit, and urine-soaked bed clothes. In the corner the waste bucket tipped and its contents spilled over the floor.

With no respite, so great was the tossing of the ship, waves seemed to be rising like mad fearsome mountains, one after another. Rev. Cross cried out, praying God for our safety. Surely God could hear him o'er the roar of the storm, but I felt our Heavenly Father would sooner attend to the cries of the babies, Elijah and Ann, and our own little Joseph, or to piteous prayers of the mother of Joshua who cried out in pain with each toss of the ship. Had her birthing time come? Abruptly the ship wildly lurched to the starboard and I was tossed in a heap to the floor.

With panicking voices, my brothers called out. "Was that Mary? Oh, sister, how bad art thou hurt?" With the next violent toss of the ship, somebody across from my bunk was flung with force to the floor. An ominous thud!

I heard Hannah's screams. "Joshua! Mama, it be Joshua!" as he tumbled across to the spot where I lay. In the darkness I found him and lifted his curly head onto my lap.

Once more waves thrashed the ship. Then suddenly the storm stilled.

The hatch opened, and a chilly wind raced into the cabin as Captain Hawk, carrying a lantern, descended the stairs. "Is everyone here all right?"

Luddie and Anthony dashed to my side, checking to see if I was injured. Quin Kingsley and Mr. Prentice raced across the room, kneeling at the foot of my bunk, reaching out to Joshua.

"Oh, my son, art thou all right?"

I knew the answer, but I could only shake my head. Tears streamed down my face. Oblivious to the blood trickling across my fingers, blood that seeped from the huge gash on Joshua Prentice's forehead, I held my dearest friend close to my heart.

The deep blue of morning sky peeked through the open hatch. The storm was over.

Clutching Baby Anne, Mrs. Prentice stared straight ahead, then closed her eyes, shutting out the scene unfolding in our cabin. With gentle hands, Polly Durham brushed the hair from the empty eyes of her mistress, then straightened the woman's rumpled white cap and pointed collar gone sadly askew.

Grief was no respecter of divided loyalties. Quin Kingsley reached into his trunk, and from under a red Cavalier's cloak, he pulled a large bundle of white silk. When Mr. Prentice had finished washing his son's face, Quin carefully unfolded the bundle and handed it to Mr. Prentice. "We have no clean burial sheet," he said, "but I'd be honored, Sir, if thou would use this flag instead. It was given to me by my Grandfather LaRoux before he died. He was an honourable man."

Quin swallowed hard and wiped his eyes with his sleeve. "See, Sir, the blue of the field is a match for Joshua's eyes, and the golden arch glows like his fair hair."

Humbly, Joshua's father received the gift. Hands trembling, he placed his son's body between the silk folds. My sister Grace, with needle and thread from our trunk, stitched the sides of the flag, creating a soft cocoon around Joshua's body, and when she finished, Captain Hawk placed within the bundle heavy weights from the ship's store.

First Grandmother Ludlam left us. Then Mama. And now, Joshua. For the first time, I realized that even a child could die.

Soft were the voices that echoed the scripture, line by line. Unexpected compassion muted Rev. Cross's usual thundering tone as he committed Joshua's body to the deep.

I could not watch, yet even now the picture remains in my mind.

I slept fitfully that night, dreaming I was in a cavern so dark I could see nothing but my hands, pale and trembling. They felt sticky and I wiped them off. A bolt of lightning crisscrossed the sky, illuminating great crimson stains on the white apron Mama had just washed and ironed for me. Suddenly a huge bird began circling overhead, then darted toward me as if I were its prey. In the angry voice of my grandmother, it screamed, "Kree-eee-ar!" I cried out for my father, but he was far away and could not hear me. When I awoke, it was Grace who held me, not Papa.

"Mary, dear, art thou having a bad dream?"

The cabin was as dark as the cavern, and I could not quit sobbing.

"Hush, dear, everything will be all right." Grace climbed up into the bunk with Abbie and me and held me close, stroking my hair until my racing heart slowed its pounding. Finally I slept.

The weather for the remainder of our crossing was fair and calm, but a storm raged within me. I sat quietly on the sunny deck most days, shivering and cold. How could the sun shine so brightly, yet offer no warmth? How could a loving God take Joshua away? Perhaps He was not loving after all. Perhaps, like Rev. Cross said, He was a God of wrath and vengeance.

A week after Joshua's death, the sounds from his mother's bunk reminded me of Joseph's coming, the day Mama died. On that day, I stayed in my bed with the ague—chills and fever. To blot out the sounds, I pulled the covers over my head and closed my eyes. Later, I awoke to a baby's cry and Mrs. Prentice's soft, peaceful breathing.

After a time, I heard her say to her husband, "Please call Quin Kingsley." And when Quin came to her, she took his hand and said, "With thy blessing, Adam and I would like to name our baby after thee. We'll call him Joshua Quin Prentice."

Quin blushed and smiled. "I'd be honored."

Two months from the day we left England, we awoke to the music of seagulls circling overhead. A joyous cry came from the crow's nest. "Land ho!" From the deck in the dim light of an early dawn, we could see a thin line of land in the northwest.

"The Isle of Shoals," said Mr. Kingsley, who had visited the colonies once before, seeking a place where his family could find refuge.

As the sun rose, in the light of a pink and purple dawn, we spied a ship lying at anchor just off the isle, and three or four fishermen's boats, shallops with both sails and oars.

"Sir, how far are we from Boston?" someone asked when they saw Captain Hawk approaching.

"Twenty leagues, by my count," he said, smiling his crinkly-eyed smile. "With good wind, we should arrive there shortly after nightfall. Tomorrow we'll drop anchor in Boston Harbor."

A great cheer went up from the passengers as sunlight beat a clear path across the water, pointing our way through the shoals.

Never before had I seen such joy on my siblings' faces. All of us chattered at once, thoughts racing in time with the beating of our hearts. Even little Joseph began jumping up and down, singing, as if he, too, could hardly wait to see Papa. We Ludlam children joined hands and danced around Joseph, making up new words to his favorite song: "Ring around Joseph, Pocket full of posies, Papa, Papa, we're coming to town."

Enough water remained in the ship's barrel to clean our faces, preparing for our long-awaited arrival in Boston. From one of our chests, Grace pulled the only clean clothes we had. After Joshua's death, I had changed my bloody dress for a gingham Grace had sewn for me, and now I had nothing fresh left to wear. I tried to smooth my skirt, and with a wet cloth, I daubed at a spot of stew I had spilled on my bodice.

Giggling and nervous, we Ludlam girls took turns brushing each other's hair. Grace plaited my red tresses and wound the braid around my head like a crown. "Turn around, Mary," Grace said, laying down the brush. "Let me see how you look." Surprised I was to see tears in her eyes when I turned back to face her.

"Mary, you've grown so tall. You look just like Mama." Abbie nodded in agreement although I think she was too young to remember. When Grace put the hairbrush back in the trunk, she hesitated a moment and then reached for the compartment that held Mama's treasures. Unfastening the clasp and raising the lid with one hand, she withdrew Mama's emerald wedding dress with the other. "Here, Mary. I can't think of a happier day for thee to wear this."

In our joy, we forgot the stale smell of the cabin, and in its place, I imagined once more the aroma of Papa's tobacco. Soon, soon, we would be together again

Anno Dom 1648
Boston Harbor and on to Long Island

God gave us a favorable wind and by noon the next day, the *Triall* weighed anchor in the inward harbor of Boston. A fearful flickering traveled down my spine. Was Papa there waiting?

We scanned the wharf for his dark head — for a tall, lean body and slightly stooped shoulders. Surely he would be wearing the typical clothing of a Puritan yeoman — with a little extra polish for the occasion.

Papa was nowhere in sight.

Along with other passengers, the ship's crew carried us and our trunks from ship to long boat to wharf. In the lengthening shadows, my siblings found seats on the wharf, waiting for Papa. Too nervous to sit, I stood, first on one foot and then another. Waiting. Thomas Bowne and his children, eager to catch their boat to Huntington, asked if they could help, but Luddie assured him we would be all right. Papa would soon be there.

Suddenly there was a shout from a small sloop pulling into the inner harbor. "Haloo!" Papa bounded up wooden steps from sloop to wharf, worry lines between his dark eyes disappearing, pursed lips relaxing into a broad grin as he spied us standing there. "Oh, my children!" He reached for Luddie and Anthony, held them out where he could take a good look at them, and then gathered them in his arms.

My wobbly legs had given way, and I found myself sitting on one of our trunks, unable to move. The others ran to Papa. Hal and Abbie, and Grace, holding Joseph. Tears streamed down their glowing faces.

"Grace, how lovely you are. And surely this can't be my baby!" Papa shook his head in disbelief. "Come to Papa, Joseph. My, what a big boy you are!" He cuddled his youngest child. "Red-haired, like your mama," he whispered as he kissed the top of Joseph's curly head.

"Papa, Papa, remember me? I'm Hal!"

"Hal, my lad!" As if he knew his son was at that "no hugging" stage, he reached out and shook his hand. "How you've grown! How old are you now—ten?"

"Yes, Papa." Hal grinned, proud but shy.

"And Abbie! My little one! How pretty you look today! Have you forgotten your old Papa? Come give me a hug." He knelt beside her on the wharf.

Suddenly bashful in front of this man she barely remembered, she ducked her head, and then slowly came into his arms.

It seemed as though Papa had never been away. Same dark hair, a lock falling over his forehead, same gentle face and sparkling eyes. The mere sight of him satisfied my longing. Wearing Mama's emerald wedding dress, braided locks wound like a crown around my head, I waited breathlessly.

"Where's Mary? Where's your sister?" he asked. Abbie pointed toward the trunk where I was sitting with the lowering sun at my back.

At last, Papa turned to me with a broad smile. Eyes alight with joyous anticipation, he held out his arms. Abruptly he gasped. His mouth sagged, and the light I saw in his eyes flickered and vanished. "Mary?" His voice wavered and his erect posture wilted as it had after Mama died. In a gruff voice he said, "Come, child, it is growing late. The Scudder boys are waiting to take us home to Southampton. On one foot, he turned away.

Deeply wounded, the icy fingers of the guilt I felt when Mama died, again grabbed my heart and squeezed. Sorrow weighed me down like a stone, and I could neither speak nor move. Perhaps Papa was angry that I was wearing Mama's dress. Perhaps it was not me that Papa wished to see. It was Mama.

On the wharf, Papa motioned to the young men watching from their vantage point in the sloop. Quickly they bounded the steps to the wharf.

Luddie helped me up from my seat on the trunk, then Anthony and the three Scudders hoisted the chests full of our belongings, and we followed them down wooden steps to their two-masted boat, the Scudder family's sailing vessel. Luddie stepped down into the sloop and held out his hand to me. Suddenly my foot slipped and I lost my balance. Before I could grab Luddie's hand, I plunged headfirst into the dark sea.

In an instant, strong hands grasped my waist and lifted me out of the water. Gasping, I opened my eyes and looked up into a handsome, tanned face with solemn deep-green eyes. His wet shirt clung to broad shoulders and muscular arms.

"Child, you gave me a fright," he said as he hauled me into the sloop. "You all right?"

I nodded, but a raging blaze of embarrassment burned my cheeks. Everyone was staring at me, anxious looks on their faces. As soon as they saw I was not hurt, their concern turned to amusement, adding coals to the fire. I must have been a sight standing there on the deck, dripping wet, festooned with slimy-green swags of sea weed.

My brother Hal laughed and pointed at me. "Mary, you look like a big green frog hopping up out of the water!"

My hero, almost as drenched as I, was the only one who seemed sympathetic. "Oh, not a frog," he said. "Young Aphrodite rising from the sea." He smiled. "Somebody get a quilt to wrap her in. The breeze is getting chilly." He turned back to me. "Takes a while to learn to walk again, once you've been on board ship for so long. Those sea legs don't work so well on dry land."

Grace pulled a quilt from our chest, along with the blood-stained dress I'd worn on the ship. Wrapping the quilt around me, she said, "Master Scudder, would you please lead us to a cabin where Mary can change into dry clothing?"

My rescuer nodded. "I need to change also," he said. "Prithee take the cabin on the left, and I shall take the one on the right."

By the time I was dry and dressed, our trunks had been stowed and we were headed south out of the harbor. As soon as the sloop was underway, the Scudder brothers took time to introduce themselves.

"Just call me Thom—since my father is called Thomas." The man ran his fingers through his still wet hair, brushing it back from his forehead. With a gesture to his left, he said, "This fine looking chap is my older brother, John, and this one is my kid brother Henry."

"That's me." The youngest of the three laughed and doffed his hat in a humorous sweeping bow. "Guess we're all kin of some sort—fourth cousins or something there about, according to thine Aunt Florence."

"We ran into your Papa at his mill on Mecox Bay," John Scudder explained, "and since we'd planned to check on some land for purchase in Southold, we agreed to sail him to Boston to meet you, and then into Long Island's Peconic Bay to the harbor at North Sea.[28]

These newfound cousins were a friendly lot, and in no time, they were showing off their sloop to my brothers. John, quiet and shy, was the oldest. Henry and Thom were about Luddie's age, although Thom was taller. They had grown up in Salem, a few miles north of Boston, where their father, Goodman Scudder, was a respected and successful proprietor. The Scudders had settled in Salem in the Massachusetts Bay Colony, having left Kent, England, at the end of Charles I's first decade as king.

Both the Scudder and the Ludlam boys enjoyed swapping stories about the storms they'd survived at sea. "Only ten, just like you," Thom said to my brother Hal, "Can't forget the great hurricane of August 1635. Slammed into the coast and sank our consort ship, the *Angel Gabriel*."

John took up the story. "Terrible devastation," he said softly. "Several lives were lost."

Thom nodded. "Our ship, *The James*, had anchored at the Isle of Shoals where she dragged, then lost all other anchors. To avoid grounding and destruction, Captain Graves was obliged to get underway. *The James* arrived in Boston split nearly in two, her sails in rags and with many seasick passengers."[29]

Henry Scudder put his hand over his mouth and wrinkled up his nose. "I remember that. But it didn't take me long to get my appetite back." The brothers laughed. "I was plump for a nine-year-old. Haven't changed much either." He grinned and patted his rounded stomach. "Still hungry, and still as wide as—"

"Look!" Papa interrupted, pointing westward. Out of the summer haze, a strip of green stretched along the horizon. "Over there," he said. "Long Island." I stared across the water at the paradise my uncles had described in missives they wrote to Papa, the place where he would forgive me and love me as he did when I was a small child. I took a deep breath. Sweet was the salt wind and the sounds of seagulls. We were almost home.

21st Century
Memory Catchers' Office

Grand-Mary's eyes were shining when she looked at me, asking, I think, for the assurance that her story warmed my heart as it obviously did hers. Her cheeks were flushed with the remembered excitement of their landing in America. When I smiled, she patted my arm. "Be thou ready for a break?"

I nodded and clicked the recorder's off-button. "I'll transcribe what we've taped tonight, and be ready to hear more in the morning."

So vibrant was Grand-Mary's presence that when I turned to her, I was surprised to find only an empty chair where she had been sitting.

It was midnight before I finished the transcription. Too keyed up to sleep, I logged onto eBay where I found an original copy of a Geneva Bible, translated from the Greek and Hebrew:

"Offered is a beautiful copy of the last edition of the Geneva or 'Breeches' Bible (so named because Genesis III 7 describes Adam and Eve clothing themselves in breeches made from figs) printed with copious commentary, and illustrated with numerous woodcuts depicting maps, buildings and artifacts pertinent to Scripture."

The bidding had just closed, and the winning bid was US $2,499.00. Wow! What a treasure! Wonder whatever became of Grand-Mary's Bible. I made a note to ask her about it and to tell her about the one I saw on e-Bay.

Pleased with the progress we were making, I left a note and the transcription of her story open on the monitor, knowing that closed or not, my files were an open book to Grand-Mary. She'd be back for another session in the morning.

℘

Following a night of cryptic dreams, I awoke edgy, eager to begin the day. After a quick shower and a dash of lipstick, I bounded down the hall to my office. Half way there, the aroma of bayberry met me. Eager as a kid on Christmas morning, I was sure Grand-Mary was waiting.

The monitor screen was lighted but only a great emptiness loomed in the chair where she usually sat. Her absence left me bereft, hollow, as if Christmas had come and gone and I'd missed the whole celebration.

On the screen was a note from Grand-Mary:

I read the latest piece of the story this morning, Phyllis. Good work! Sorry I had to leave. There's something I must do before we continue. I figured out that Sony thing, and I've left a new chapter or two for you to edit in my absence – sailing from Boston into the Peconic Bay on the Scudder boys' sloop and then riding in Papa's ox cart on to Mecox and Southampton – and then my first year on Long Island.
Grand-Mary

True to her word, she took up the story right where my transcription left off. I sorely missed Grand-Mary's presence, but as I edited, I imagined her soft-as-silk voice, and the poignant loneliness I felt lessened.

Six
~

Perchance 'twas my eagerness to see our new home at Southampton that made the trip seem so long. As the sloop skimmed across the water, the sounds of the sea and the soft calling of the gulls finally lulled me to sleep. I awoke to the sound of welcoming voices, and felt strong masculine arms lifting me from shallot to pier.

"Hello, little one." A tall comely man about my father's age, with straight strong limbs, held me and peered into my face. Tanned and handsome, his warm, sea-blue eyes seemed oddly familiar.

His countenance was pleasant, especially when he smiled. "My, but you remind me of your mother when she was your age. Takes me back to my childhood years at Fordham manor in England," he said softly. "Welcome to the New World, Mary!"

"How do you know my name?"

"After I left England," he said, "thy mother used to write of thee in her letters. How proud she was of her lovely little red-head, her strong-willed daughter!"

My heart wanted to believe him. "She was proud?"

"Indeed she was! Just as she was of me when, in spite of dire consequences, I followed the inner voice of my heart."

A peaceful feeling flowed over me, sweet as warm honey. I lay my head against Uncle Robert's chest.

I heard Papa bidding the Scudders Godspeed as our Fordham kinfolk helped us into a wagon. A tall boy introduced as our cousin, Gideon Fordham, took the reins.

"Giddap!" he called to the horses.

"Where are we going, Uncle Robert?" I asked.

"Home," he said. "Tomorrow you'll be meeting all your Fordham cousins and the rest of your mother's family—Aunt Florence and Uncle John Carman and their children are there."

"Abigail and Benjamin? I can't wait to hear how they were almost captured by the Indians."

Uncle Robert laughed. "I'm sure they'll tell you about it. It makes a good story now, but that year was bad for both the Dutch and their Indian neighbors. There were killings on both sides and calls for war."

The wagon wheels groaned and squeaked as they bounced over the rutty road. "Squee-arr!" A sudden twinge of fear tweaked my heart, and I tightened my hold on Uncle Robert. "Are we safe here?"

With the back of one finger, my uncle brushed a strand of hair from my eyes. "The Indians who live in this region are Shinnecocks—a peace-loving people. Yes, my child, you are safe here." His solemn expression changed and his eyes sparkled. "The family is eager to greet you, but first, methinks, you all need a good night's rest."

The rhythmic clip-clop of the horses felt very much like the rhythm of the ship. I heard Uncle Robert say it was

six miles from our landing place on Peconic Bay to
Southampton. I could not keep my eyes open. In my
dreams, strong arms lifted me from the wagon and long,
sure steps carried me through an open door. Vaguely I
was aware of gentle hands tucking me into clean-
smelling quilts stretched out on a smooth oak floor. I
slept.

Happy voices and the heavenly aroma of bread fresh
from the oven awakened me. The Fordham house over-
flowed with people—Papa and the seven of us and all of
Mama's nieces and nephews, cousins I had never met before—the Fordham children—Gideon and John, Molly
and Hannah, Clemence, named after Mama, and three-
year-old Joseph. Then there was Abigail Carman and her
five brothers—baby Thomas, John, Benjamin, Caleb, and
Joshua. I could remember his name for he looked like a
younger version of my friend Joshua on the ship. Blonde
curly hair and large blue eyes fringed by long lashes. But
how would I ever keep the rest of them straight? Two
Abbies, two Johns, another little Joseph and another
named Mary but called Molly, six years older than me.
Never before had I been part of such a gladsome reunion!

Uncle Robert's wife, Alice, had risen before dawn to
wash our clothes and hang them on a line to dry in the
early breeze. I found her in the kitchen, taking fresh
loaves of bread out of the brick oven, and tending the
wild turkey roasting on a spit over the fire. Aunt Florence helped, but she was pale and weak and unable to
work for long without sitting down to rest on a stool by
the fire. She made herself useful, stirring a huge kettle of
oatmeal hung from the crane in the fireplace. Iron skil-
lets, one filled with eggs and another with fish, sat on
trivets over hot coals.

Aunt Alice smiled and greeted me. "Good morning, sleepyhead. Your sisters and brothers have already bathed in the tub down by the pond. Would you like Hannah to show you the way? I remember how eager I was to wash off the grime of that journey when our family came to America." She handed me a towel and a bar of sweet smelling bayberry soap. "Hannah, please get Mary's clean clothes from the line and show her to our bathing place."

Cousin Hannah led the way to a small shed at the back of their property, down by a pond that stretched as far as the eye could see. There a tub of clean water waited for me. What a wonderful feeling it was to sink into the water up to my neck and wash away the stench of our long, fitful journey!

"Here, it's your turn now," Hannah said as she picked up a fine-toothed ivory comb. "Let me help you with your hair." After undoing my braid, she lathered the foaming bubbles into my hair, tickling my scalp, and sending giggly little tremors over my head, but such smelly soap it was.

"You don't like it?" Hannah grinned. "Smells like hell, doth it not?"

I drew in my breath, shocked at the forbidden swearing that came from my cousin's mouth.

"No, no," she said when she saw the look on my face. "You've read the book of Revelation, haven't you? Remember it says in the end, the Devil will be cast into the lake of fire and brimstone. That's hell!"

"That is what hell smells like?"

"Well, this is flower of brimstone mixed with vinegar. The beasties in your hair don't like it either. They'll soon be gone. Now stand up," she said.

So relaxed I was that at first my wobbly legs refused to obey. She took my hand and pulled me to my feet. Pouring a pitcher of clean water over my head, she rinsed my hair and body clean.

Cousin Hannah set the pitcher down and handed me a towel. "I was only five when we came to America," she said, "but I still remember how pleasant it was to bathe after we arrived, as if the water cleansed my heart as well as my body, washing away all the fears and trepidations of the voyage." Hannah smiled. "You certainly smell better. Now get dressed and you can help me empty the tub into the pond. I think breakfast must be waiting for us by now."

Outside the Fordham manse,[30] the men had set up long planks for tables that soon were covered with bounteous platters and heaping bowls of food and accompaniments. A pitcher of fresh milk, warm and frothy, straight from the Fordham's cow. Mugs full of bubbly beer. Large woven baskets filled with wild blackberries, sweet and juicy. I shared a hollowed-out trencher with Cousin Hannah, and we heaped it full. After the scarcity of food on the ship, only joyous threads of conversation and storytelling kept me from the sin of gluttony.

The adults sat on benches at the table, my papa at the far end holding Joseph, while we cousins assembled in a big circle on the grass. Without overmuch coaxing, Benjamin and Abigail Carman told us about their narrow escape from the Indians' savage assault on their home at Hempstead.[31]

"'Twas four years ago, when Abigail was nine and I was ten," Benjamin began. "Just a year earlier, Uncle Robert and Father had bought land — two-thirds of the Great Plains we call Hempstead — from three Indian chiefs, the sachems of the Marsapeagues, Mericocks and the Rockaways.[32] The sachems had become our father's friends, so we really weren't afraid of them," Benjamin said.

In the morning sun, Abigail shivered and wrapped her arms around herself. "Well, maybe a little scared. The day of the attack we children were alone in the house while Mother and Aunt Alice worked in the garden of the Fordham plantation. And Father and Uncle Robert and our older brothers and cousins were working in the fields with the neighbors, going from one man's field to another. As was their custom, the men stacked their firearms on the edge of the field."

Benjamin continued. "I envied the older boys. Our brother John and Cousin John Fordham got to watch the weapons that day. Like sentries in a box, they stood on a stump, keeping a lookout for marauding Indians." Benjamin's eyes glittered as he spoke. "Couldn't wait 'til I was old enough to be a sentry." He stuck out his lower lip. "But I had to stay with Caleb and Joshua and our youngest Fordham cousins. While they played, Abigail and I went down to the spring for water. When she lifted the pail—"

Abigail interrupted. "Let me tell it, Ben." She took a deep breath. "When I lifted up the bucket of water, a terrifying black and yellow painted face with a big bone through his nose," she held her index fingers up to her nostrils, "was staring at me through the thicket on the edge of the clearing."

"You should have seen Abbie's eyes" Benjamin said. "Big and dark as skillet lids." He looked at his sister and gave her a lopsided grin. "She dropped the bucket and ran. I turned around to see what had frightened her, and when I spied those big ol' savages, I knew they were Canarsie Indians on the warpath. Fierce painted faces and bright feather headdresses," Ben explained. "I took off runnin' right behind her as fast as I could go." He swung his arms as if he were fleeing for his life. "If we could get to the house, we'd be safe behind the heavy door."

Breathless, Abigail continued. "When the men in the field heard us screaming, they dropped their scythes and grabbed their guns and came running."

"Those Canarsies were faster than Abigail and me. One of them grabbed Abbie, but when the taller one reached for me, I fought back." Benjamin demonstrated a swift kick.

"That ol' Indian raised his hatchet," Abigail said, "and if—"

"Yeah! Father came running and shot that Indian dead, right between the eyes!" Benjamin grinned. "If Father hadn't arrived when he did," he said as he patted the top of his head, "I'd have lost my curly locks!"[33]

"What happened then?" my brother Hal asked, eyes bright with anticipation.

"Well, the men caught seven of those savages, and Father arrested 'em and put 'em in our cellar 'til Governor Kieft's soldiers came to pick 'em up."

"The Indians really weren't after us," Abigail explained. "They were stealing pigs."

"And Abigail was so plump they thought they caught one for sure." Benjamin doubled over, slapping his leg and laughing at his old joke. His sister stuck out her tongue and when he continued heckling her, she jabbed him with her elbow.

"What happened when the Dutch soldiers came?" I asked, covering a giggle with my hand.

Benjamin straightened his face and continued. "Well, they killed three of the Indians in the cellar—there was blood all over—and then the men took the other Canarsies away. Later we heard two of the savages drowned when Kieft's men tied twine around their scrawny necks and towed them behind the boat. And at the Fort, the soldiers dispatched the other two with their knives."[34]

Straight from the civilized countryside of Matlock, England, my Ludlam siblings were wide-eyed at our Carman cousins' story. My heart drummed an excited ka-thump-a-ka-thump, but the story terrified my sister Grace. She seemed to have shrunk in stature, and her face was grey. "Savages?"

Aunt Florence's face was pale. "Well, what would you call a male animal, who lives in a dark hut in the wilderness with no claim of property and no title of ownership who supports his family by dragging home an occasional bloody beast he has shot with bow and arrow. Naked except for a loin cloth, around his neck hangs a necklace of teeth, and from his belt dangles a bloody scalp. He is waving a hatchet, smelling of smoke and smeared with bear grease. His chest and face are streaked with red and yellow paint, and making unintelligible grunts and shouts. Well, what would you call him?"

In a quavering voice, Grace asked, "How far away are those savages?"

Uncle Robert turned from the table and reached to pat Grace's dark head. "Don't worry, dear. Our Hempstead plantation is over 70 miles away, down toward the west end of the island." Uncle Robert's eyes were warm and calming. "And when we told the Dutch Governor Kieft that Penawitz, the sachem of the Canarsie Indians, had killed some people and set their houses on fire, he sent out three boats with over a hundred soldiers aboard. After landing in Cow Bay, they marched toward Hempstead.

"On the way," Benjamin blurted out, "they wiped out two Indian villages and killed a hun'ert and twen'y Indians, with only one Dutch soldier kilt and three wounded.[35]

"But you still live at Hempstead?" Grace frowned and shuddered. "Why?"

Uncle John answered. "Oh, yes! We feel quite safe there now. And it's so beautiful there! At the southern edge of the plains, Robert and I came upon two streams that occasionally broadened and formed little ponds. One stream winds pleasantly southward, and the one from the north crosses it at an angle, forming the ideal site for a town. A beautiful place! Long, waving grasses lie to the north where we could pasture cattle. We immediately began the construction of a palisade for protection from the Indians, and then built dwellings and a meeting house. It's beautiful there. Our own Garden of Eden. In the forest to the south are whole groves of walnut trees. Walnut oil or milk is worth £20 a ton in France. There are white cedars and red maples. Oak, chestnut, and hickory trees. Ponds of fresh water three or four miles across. Spring waters as good as cold beer. Deer and buffalo and flocks of wild turkeys feed on berries, chestnuts, and beechnuts. Sea and shell fish in abundance and plentiful supplies of oyster shells to make lime. Fowl and eggs of all sorts."

The color had returned to Aunt Florence's face. "The flowers there equal the gardens I remember in England," Aunt Florence added. "White dogwood blossoms and tulip trees, yellow with blooms."

Aunt Alice nodded. "An enchanting place. Sometimes I miss it, even now."

Uncle Robert joined the conversation. "Along every waterway, nights are loud with the clamor of ducks, too many kinds to name. Sky-darkening flights of birds move over the land in season, coming and going. Rivers filled with salmon, sturgeon and alewives, waiting to be plucked from the waters. Bays, inlets and narrow canals meandering through the uplands. Marsh meadows rich in marine life."[36]

To me, his words sounded like poetry.

"But Uncle Robert, if thou loved it so," Grace asked, "why then did thou move?"

"It was time," he said in a grave voice. "The townspeople of Southampton invited me to become their minister, and though I was happy with the church at Hempstead and my position as governor there, I could not refuse the benefits of Southampton. Although the salary was not great—£60 for the first year and £80 thereafter, I felt God's calling here, and I must heed His voice rather than our King's command." [37]

I rose to help wipe the trenchers and clear the table and soon discovered the Carman family had been just as surprised to meet us as we were to meet them. I heard Aunt Florence telling how the measles epidemic had swept through Hempstead, left her terribly weakened, and worse, had stolen away Joshua's sight.

"Thank goodness, Caleb and Abigail can help me," Aunt Florence said. "They feed the chickens and pigs, card and spin flax into yarn, make soap and candles, and tend the garden while the older boys help their father with the farming. But I still have my hands full nursing Thomas, our latest child, then preparing and preserving food, spinning yarn, making clothing, towels and sheets, and all the other duties of housewifery."

Aunt Florence, seeming embarrassed by her weakness, spoke softly. "Alice, John and I are hoping we might board Joshua here with you and Robert, and that your Gideon[38] might consider tutoring him along with your children. Joshua's five now..." she hesitated and then went on. "I must admit he's into everything, but he's bright and curious, eager to learn."

"But he can never see to read, Florence. How would Gideon teach him?"

"Joshua listens. You'll see. For a blind child, he amazes me. Sounds and noises and music mean much more to him than to the other children. And he has an astounding sense of touch and smell. He can name the trees in our garden by feeling their bark. He knows the wild flowers — lady slippers and columbine and lupines — by smell. He knows when the plum bushes bloom. On Sabbath last, he brought me a bluebell he had picked and asked what color it was. When I told him, he said, 'I remember blue. It's like the sky.'"

I ducked my head so Aunt Florence would not know I saw the tears in her tired eyes.

"Please, dear sister-in-law," she said to Alice, "can you make room for one more child in your home?"

Aunt Alice smiled and even though she was plump and placid and not at all like my own mother, right away I loved her. "Of course we can make room," she said, taking Aunt Florence's hand.

Uncle Robert had an allotment of land, similar to others who lived in the village, of 12 acres for farming and 34 acres for grazing land plus shares in common woodlands north of Southampton village. The Fordham house, with

the recent addition added, had two stories with six sleeping rooms upstairs; and on the main floor, a great room, a
study with shelves for all Uncle Robert's books, a bedroom, and a kitchen with a stone fireplace all the way
across one end.

The house sat on a three-acre lot next to a long stretch
of water they called Town Pond. After dinner, on the
way to the beach, passing the back lots of several
neighbors along the footpath, we children skipped stones
across the water of the pond, then made our way on
down to the Atlantic shore. What a pleasure it was to run
in the warm sand at the edge of the sea, waves lapping at
my feet. Pearly pink seashells were strewn along the
edge of the water and I could not resist stooping to
gather them. Soon my pocket was filled with these lovely
treasures.

Laughing gulls glided overhead, dipping and swirling
in the azure sky, echoing our laughter with a cacophony
of giggles as if they were enjoying the day as much as we
were. A lone killdeer scurried along the shore chitter-
chattering its staccato notes. Farther out into the water, a
great egret stood on one leg, adding its deep raspy notes
to the harmony of sounds. I stretched out on my stomach
on the warm sand, shaded my fair skin with the white
cap Aunt Alice had loaned me, and propped my head on
one hand. With the other, I scooped up handfuls of sand,
letting the sparkling grains slowly trickle through my
fingers. Luxuriating in the wide open spaces and fresh
air, I watched the waves hungrily lap their way toward
me, then peacefully retreat, washing my slate of old foot-
prints away and leaving new treasures for me to gather.

All too soon, it was time to bid my cousins goodbye.
My brothers and sisters and I climbed into Papa's small

boat to sail three miles east to Mecox Bay and north to the head of Mill Pond where Papa ground grain in Mr. Edward Howell's mill. While we had been sailing to the colonies, Papa had found time to build a small house near the mill with two small sleeping rooms upstairs, and below, a great room and a kitchen.[39] Certainly not as spacious as the Fordham house, but compared to our crowded quarters on ship, it was roomy indeed, and after we arranged our trunks and other possessions, our living quarters looked quite homey.

In expectation of our arrival, Papa had planted and tended a vegetable garden on the three-acre plot he rented and he was raising a few pigs and cows. Chickens supplied us with feathers for bedding, eggs, and meat. We had plenty to eat, but the work was hard and the hours were long.

Under Grace's direction, I struggled to learn the everyday duties of a colonial woman. Abbie and I helped bring in greens from the garden; we shelled peas, snapped beans, and husked corn outside the open door. In the fireplace, we cooked family meals, often stews or porridge, in the black iron pot that hung over the fire. The fireplace gaped like a hungry mouth, always demanding more fuel. The bricks of the hearth and chimney radiated heat, overmuch in summer, and seldom enough in winter. No matter the season, there was always wood to chop.

As three-year-old Joseph learned to run and climb, his care required watchful eyes to keep him out of mischief. Abbie let him help her feed the animals and chickens. She taught him to sing his ABCs and to set the table with the wooden trenchers we shared. He learned to count out spoons and pewter mugs for each person. A bright babe he was.

With the change of seasons, summer into fall, came harvest—time for gathering crops, drying and storing fruits and vegetables for the cold months ahead. Sometimes the neighbors gathered to butcher pigs and sometimes a calf, then together, they salted the meat for curing and drying.

We gathered bayberries as we did in England, and after melting the waxy coating from the fruit and leaves, we dipped the two ends of long candlewicks into the hot wax, and then hung them over rafters in the ceiling, dangling alongside bouquets of drying herbs—fragrant blessings to the senses.

After harvest was over, Luddie found other quarters. He met the beautiful and vivacious 16-year-old Elizabeth Smith,[40] and when he was offered an apprenticeship working with her stepfather's fine stock of cattle and many weaned calves at pasture, Luddie was eager to make the move to the Smith homestead.

Hal and Anthony chose to stay in Mecox and the milling business, working with Papa.

ॐ

In the winter, with no garden to tend, we had time to spin, pumping away on the pedal of the spinning wheel, creating thread from flax, and then strung the threads on a loom and wove them into fabric—often the men's job—. Towels and bedding we fashioned from the plain colored cloth.

With our fair share, besides using the meat for food, we boiled the fat skin—the blubber—to make oil for lamps.

We saved ashes from the fireplace, and after boiling blubber or rendering lard from animal fat, we made lye soap, stirring the bubbling mixture over the fire. The smell was most unpleasant, acrid and overpowering.

Papa built little Joseph a small wagon with wooden wheels, so on the Sabbath when the family walked the three miles to worship on Meeting House Lane[41] in Southampton Village, he rode in the wagon while Papa or my older brothers pulled it behind them.. Sometimes, after a short while walking, growing pains knotted my limbs, and Papa would say, "Mary, sweeting, hop in the wagon behind Joseph. Give thy limbs a rest."

When winter and freezing weather came, my sisters and I rode in the family cart, pulled by Papa's team of oxen. The men carried firearms, powder, shot and swords along with their psalm-books, lest Indians attacked.

The Puritan church based their tenets on the beliefs of John Calvin, like our old St. Giles Presbyterian church did, but there the similarity ended. These Puritans were self-governed congregationals. "Reverend Fordham does not claim to be a saint whose divine call sets him apart," members of the Southampton church often said. "He is one of us."

No bishops ruled. Puritan leaders had determined to purge the church of all Papist and Lutheran errors— ceremonies and holidays, especially those of pagan origin like Christmas.

We had delighted in the beauty of St. Giles, our church in England, built of lovely old stones and surrounded by stately gravestones and gardens. Inside, the sun shining through its stained glass windows cast its light on colorful paintings and ornate furnishings.

The meeting house in Southampton was barren in comparison. Freed from the "fripperies" of England's churches, few windows graced its rough pine walls, emitting very little light. Having neither the light nor the warmth of a fireplace, while seated on hard wooden benches, we used heated stones as foot warmers, carried with us from home each Sabbath.

Although the Southampton meeting house was cold that first winter, we met many warm, like-minded people who became our friends. Although Reverend. Abraham Pierson, the first minister of Southampton had devoted much time to instructing the Indians in Christian religion, we soon learned how pleased the people were to have a minister like Uncle Robert who did not insist on the church managing local affairs as the previous minister had done.

Southampton, they explained, was not ruled by religious authority like most Puritan settlements. Here, one did not need to be a church member in order to have full rights of citizenship, the right to speak and vote at town meetings. I was too young to grasp the importance of this decision at the time, but I understood that was what led to Uncle Robert being chosen as their new minister.

Because of the dissension over this decision, the church had split, and the Rev. Abraham Pierson had gone, taking part of his people with him.[42] However, the most influential townsmen remained and welcomed Uncle Robert. Southampton entered upon a new order of democracy, a new era of success. Uncle Robert, with a master's degree from Cambridge and ordination by Bishop Williams of Lincoln, England, was esteemed as a learned man of God. An astute businessman also, he fast became the richest man in Southampton, earning a double measure of respect.[43]

Because Puritans did not work on the Lord's Day, all labors had to be completed by sundown on Saturday. On Sunday morning, since the meeting house had no bell, to be sure no one overslept, Mr. Howell marched through town beating the drum a half hour before meetings, then stood at the door of the meeting house drumming the second reminder. After the three-hour morning services, we ate the cold lunch prepared the previous day and discussed the morning's scripture and sermon. Inattentive children were soon caught in their sins. It paid to listen.

In the new Southampton meeting house, the pulpit was high above the congregation, and under it the deacon's pew faced the people. Directly in front of it was the seat for the magistrates. The first year we attended meeting house at Southampton, men and women entered by separate doors. The women sat on one side, and the men sat together in rows on the other side with small boys in front of them where they might be boxed on the ears if they misbehaved. Older Puritan boys, regarded with suspicion and disapproval by elderly Puritan eyes, sat in a special section at the back of the meeting house, perhaps to isolate the distraction of their unruliness from the main body of the congregation. Reverend Pierson's tithing man still served as an officer elected to preserve order in the meeting house during service. A stickler for following Puritan rules of behavior and punishment, the tithing man spared not the rod, using such raps and blows as he deemed fitting when adults fell asleep during the sermon or when mischievous boys behaved like miscreant monkeys.

The boys, dressed like their grave and stern God-fearing fathers in knee breeches and homespun coats, wiggled, squirmed, and scraped their feet noisily on the sanded floor. It was difficult to sit still, and when the day was hot the afternoon sermon seemed especially long. When the beadle[44] looked the other way, sometimes one of the boys would sneak a kernel of corn out of his pocket, and with a furtive snicker, surreptitiously shoot it at an unsuspecting head. Laughter was not permitted on the Lord's Day, and I remember when one boy was brought before the magistrate, charged with making indecent faces and causing misbehavior and laughter during the sermon. He was fined three shillings and was soundly beaten by his father afterward.

Another time, Jacob and Isaac Smith, charged by the tithing man with smiling during the service, were found guilty and had to pay five shillings each.

At meeting house Papa introduced us to one of his customers at the mill, a man proud to be numbered among those who founded Southampton, the first English town in New York. Thomas Halsey and his family lived on Horse Mill Lane, not far from Town Pond where Uncle Robert lived. They soon proved to be good neighbors in midweek as well as on the Lord's Day.

When Grace was unable to accomplish a task by herself, Phebe Halsey, Thomas's kindly wife, offered advice, like a substitute mother, teaching us to cook with native herbs and berries that were sometimes unfamiliar to us.[45]

Elizabeth, her 14-year-old daughter, soon became my best friend. Four years older than I and a bit taller, when a bodice became too tight for her, she folded the garment neatly, and thoughtfully wrapped a bright bow around it, a special gift to me. I basked in her friendship. The only girl in their family, she preferred out-of-door activities with her five brothers to stuffy inside chores, so we had much in common. I shared with her the poems and letters my mother had left us, and showed her the pages of Mama's lovely Geneva Bible adorned with graceful scrolls and colorful flowers.

We looked forward to seeing them at meeting house each week, and when the congregation voted to change our seating to family pews, glad I was that the Halsey family pew adjoined ours.

When the shutters were open in summer, the sunlight streamed in the windows, but with the shutters closed, the congregation sat in darkness. Uncle Robert struggled to see the scriptures in this ill-lighted place and oft he relied on memory. Stuffy and close, the air with its dry, woody scent permeated the building, an odor I yet associate with church.

In either heat or cold, three hours is a long time to sit still. I must admit that Elizabeth and I, during the sermon, found diversion in imagining pictures in the grain and swirls of the wooden ceiling.

One Lord's Day during planting season, Uncle Robert read from the 8th chapter of Luke:

And some fell on good ground, and sprang up, and bare fruite, an hundreth folde.

At my left, Elizabeth nudged me. Hiding her mouth behind her hand, she whispered, "Look at his ears."

Uncle Robert finished the verse:

And as hee sayd these things, he cryed, He that hath eares to heare, let him heare.

As he paused, he turned in our direction. In the wall behind him, knots in the wood aligned on either side of his temples like very large ears. I had trouble stifling my giggles until Grace, on my right side, jabbed me with her elbow.

Would I be able to participate in the family discussion of the sermon, replying sensibly when, along with the other children, I was questioned about what we remembered and understood? To make up for my wickedness, I tried extra hard to attend to the rest of his message, although without much success. Soon a cunning spider caught my eye, spinning his web high in the corner back of the pulpit. A buzzing fly seemed doomed to entrapment. Was it predestined to fall into the evil snare? Or perhaps the web was a symbol of God's calling. Then could the fly not resist if it were chosen? Were there not many paths leading to the center?

Following the three-hour church service, the congregation adjourned for the midday meal where they discussed the sermon before returning to their benches for another three hours of preaching and further discussion. In spite of all my questions, this was not the place for a child such as I to voice the blasphemous ponderings about spider webs and such that ran through my mind. God's laws were not to be questioned.

ॐ

That fall, 'twas Elizabeth Halsey who taught me skills she had learned from her mother—how to create brightly colored dyes from plants we gathered in the forest. Saffron and snapdragons, bloodroot and bluebells, lily of the valley, bark of white birch, cedar and butternut. Mistress

Halsey showed us how to prepare them before adding to steaming kettles of water, heated over a fire pit in the yard. Dipping the woven fabric in the dye turned dull colors into brilliant hues. After drying, we cut and stitched these swatches into lovely garments. I liked making the dyes and cutting out the pieces of linen or wool — sleeves and bodices, collars and cuffs, skirts and breeches — but found needlework distressing and tedious.[46]

As soon as a garment was outgrown, we handed it down to the next child in line. In my day, baby boys and girls both wore long gowns. Not until they were nearing six years old did they follow the style of their parents, girls in skirts and petticoats, boys in long shirts and knee-length breeches like their fathers. However, so fast did my little brother grow, before Abbie was ready to give up her gown, Joseph needed a new one.

Most people in my day had but few items of apparel, and laundry day came only in warm months when we could wash our clothes in water from the bay, scrubbing them on a board with a bar cut from the solidified lye soap.

In early spring, my sisters and I planted fields and moved rocks from the garden area. We soaked reeds and made baskets, along with the daily chore of milking the cow, and carrying water from the stream.

I must admit that most of the responsibility of the household fell on Grace's shoulders. She seemed to take great pleasure in pleasing my father and brothers with her work, while I found the usual female duties dull and wearisome. Grace was often irritated with me, for often when the work was monotonous, my mind was far away. Dreaming… thinking…wondering…or asking the unanswerable questions that so frustrated Grace who preferred a narrower path of thought.

Expected to attend the words of the minister and participate in the weekly discussions that followed, I dared not speak out. 'Twould have been unforgivable to question God's word. But I could not reconcile the punishment of eternal hell fire with a loving God. How could I but ponder His ways? How could a God of love wreak vengeance on innocent children? How could He predestine some to perish forever while choosing others to live with Him in heaven? Even my nights were haunted with images I could not understand.

One afternoon when Elizabeth's brother Isaac brought grain to Papa's mill, she came with him, and the two of us trekked into the woods to gather colorful plants to use for dyeing cloth. Suddenly Elizabeth saw a shadow flicker across the path. "Sh-h." she said. "Methinks someone watchs us."

Abruptly, from a tall oak, a hawk flew into the air with a loud flutter of wings and its eerie cry. Kree-ar! Kree-ar!

Elizabeth's face went as white as her cap, and I tried to calm her. "Oh, look, the hawk has dropped one of its red tail feathers. And here's a plant with blooms almost the same color. Elizabeth, would this one be good for dyeing cloth?"

My friend reached to pluck the flower, but her hands were trembling so she could hardly grasp the plant. Nervously, I kept up my chatter as we finished filling our baskets.

"Dost thou think the Indians paint their faces with dyes from these plants?" I asked. "My Carman cousins said the ones that attacked them had red and yellow paint on their faces, and one had a bone in his nose."

Elizabeth's face turned pale. "Does that thought not frighten thee, Mary? What if an Indian is tracking us? Prithee, may we not hurry back to thy house?"

I, too, felt edgy, but I refused to listen to my fears. "Oh, Elizabeth, was not thy father one of the men who purchased the land from them? He said Shinnecocks welcomed the group and led them to this beautiful land by the sea."

Elizabeth only ducked her head.

"They even showed the Southampton settlers how to plant corn and fertilize it with fish, didn't they?"

Elizabeth nodded, but still her eyes were wide with fear.

"Did you not tell me they taught the settlers how to dig the clams and scallops from the bay? And remember the fun we had at the clambake with the Indians last summer?" I could hear the pitch of my voice growing higher and my words seemed to be racing with my heart, but I continued chattering as we meandered.

Elizabeth shuddered. "I oft have frightening dreams about the Pequots. Father says they are cruel savages."

"Don't worry, Elizabeth. The Shinnecocks are friendly. And anyway, Papa's mill is not far away. He would hear if we cried out."

Suddenly Elizabeth caught her breath—a loud gasp—and pointed. "Mary, look there in the bushes!" she whispered.

Elizabeth's fears were contagious. Carrying the baskets of plants we had gathered, we ran down the path to the mill.

As we neared the millpond, a horde of ducks rose like storm clouds into the sky, startling us with the noise of their sudden flight. Screaming, we reached the kitchen door at the back of the mill. By that time, my legs were knotted in painful cramps, and I grasped the door latch to keep from falling. The door swung open, spinning me around. In the west, I caught a glimpse of smoke silhouetted against the red sky, but that, as well as my pain and fear, was soon forgotten in the face of a more immediate problem.

When Grace saw me, she slammed down a skillet full of sizzling bacon, splashing hot grease on the table, burning her fingers in the process. "You've been out traipsing through the woods all day leaving me to do the housework," she screamed as she plunged her hand into the water bucket to cool the burns. "If you want anything for thee and thy friend to eat, thou canst cook it thyself!"

My friend lowered her eyes, as embarrassed as I was at Grace's outburst. "I'm sure Isaac must be finished grinding his grain by now," Elizabeth said quietly as she turned and slipped out the door.

Grace continued her tirade. "I'm tired of doing all the work, but it's easier to do everything myself than to get thee to do things correctly!" She grabbed my arms and began shaking me. Thou art a complete dunce when it comes to cooking and cleaning, and I am sick to death of trying to deal with thy piddling, off playing in the woods or daydreaming when thou should be working."

Her face reminded me of Grandma Ludlam's with her bitter slash of a mouth and harsh angry eyes. I felt guilty for letting Grace carry the heavy load in Mama's place, but she was my sister, not my mother, and I resented her telling me how to do everything. There was only one way to accomplish a task—her way, and there was no talking to her. She scoffed at my questions and dreams. I much preferred the company of Elizabeth Halsey or my brothers, working outdoors or playing in the woods or at the shore.

That night when Grace again complained to Papa that I did not heed her directions, I tried to tell him how I felt. Surely, if I could talk to him, he would understand. How I longed for the old days when he would take me in his arms and sooth my troubled heart. "Papa, I don't mean to be—"

Coldly, he stopped my words and reached for a small branch from the fireplace kindling. My heart froze. Surely, my beloved Papa would not deal with me so harshly.

The punishment hurt me deeply, not my backside, but my insides. Tears ran down my cheeks, and the pain was even greater when Papa laid down the switch and I saw that he too was crying, as he had the day Mama died.

"Go to bed, Mary," he said in a gruff voice.

For the first night since we moved into the mill house, my dreams were senseless images, a clamor of sounds and visions. Silent icons of angel faces and pale death masks. Red circles painted on Indian faces. Crimson-stained fingers pointing at me. Censuring eyes. Papa's eyes. Elizabeth Halsey and her mother, aprons splotched with great red stains, stirring steaming vats of bloodroot dye. The cry of the red-tailed hawk, its wings crashing like waves against my heart. Screams awakened me. "Elizabeth!" I cried out.

Surprised was I that it was Papa who came to comfort me. "It's just a bad dream, my little poppet," he whispered. He held me close, softly singing a lullaby I had not heard since I was a babe in his arms until the violent sobs that shook my body subsided. At last I drifted into a merciful sleep.

The owl that made its home in the mill awoke me to a grey foreboding dawn. Determined to shoulder my share of the responsibility, I arose and descended the ladder from my upper room. Stoking the embers in the fireplace, I added small chunks of wood. Then, in the firelight, I filled the porridge pot with water and stirred in a cup of ground oats and a sprinkle of salt from the box. Flickering flames cast eerie shadows across the hearth, then gradually disappeared as sunlight streamed into the kitchen window. As I worked, I could hear Papa, already in the mill, tapping and testing the working parts—a regular practice of maintenance. The clip clop of a horse's hooves sounded, and my chest tightened as I heard Papa call to its rider. "Thou art out bright and early, Thomas. What can I do for thee?"

Grace and our brothers were rising by then, coming into the kitchen, surprised to find me there preparing their breakfast. On the path outside the mill, a horse whinnied and then took off at a gallop. Anthony and Hal had just stepped across the threshold into the mill area when Papa met them.

"Your first customer has already gone?" Anthony said.

Papa shook his head and brushed past Anthony. Hesitantly, he looked my way as he came into the room. His face was drawn and pale. "Mary..." As he stopped to clear his throat, his lips trembled and he reached out to me. "Daughter..." he hesitated for a moment, his brow furrowed, "What disturbed you so in the night? Wast thou...wast thou dreaming of thy friend Elizabeth?"

My breath caught in my throat, and I could not speak. I knew I did not want to hear his forthcoming words.

"Children," he said as he looked around the room, "you all must hear what I have to say so that you may take every precaution. Our early morning caller was Thomas Halsey who came to tell us the painful news. Last evening, Pequot Indians crossed from the Massachusetts coast to attack Southampton. When Isaac and Elizabeth returned home from our mill at dusk yesterday, they found their mother lying dead with an Indian arrow through her chest. She is the first woman on Long Island to die by the hand of the Red man."[47]

My brothers and sisters stood with their mouths open, frozen in place by the paralyzing news. Finally Anthony spoke. "Mistress Halsey is the only one, Papa? They did not burn down Southampton?"

"No, thank God, it stands. Halsey's stacks of hay were destroyed, but their neighbors drove the marauders away and put out the fire on the Halsey roof before it had taken hold. As we speak, our friend Wyandanch, sachem of the Montauk, is preparing to lead an expedition to capture the murderers."

Out of this sorrowful calamity, a still small voice spoke within me, the voice of a ten-year-old, to be sure; but for the first time, I felt a sharpened discernment of duty. I was ready to put away childish things, to take my rightful share of responsibility. With a great sense of certainty, I looked at my father and said, "Elizabeth has no sister to share her sorrow, Papa. With thy permission, I must go to her. I know what it is to lose thy mother." I took my cape and cap from the peg, swung the wrap around my shoulders and put on my bonnet, tying its sash under my chin."

Papa nodded. "Anthony will drive thee there in the wagon, Mary. Until these savages are caught, it is not safe to walk in the woods alone." Papa took his musket down from the peg on the wall and handed it to Anthony.

My brother had already packed a supply of shot. "I'll take my horse instead of the wagon, Papa," he said. "Mary can ride with me as far as the Halsey house. From there I must ride with Wyandance and the Halsey boys. I'll not be home 'til the Pequots are captured."

Anthony mounted his horse and Papa boosted me up behind him. "God go with you, my children," he said.

I put my arms around my brother's waist with my face against his back.

Anthony must have felt my tears, for soon he spoke to me. "Mary, dost thou need to talk?"

"Why did this have to happen, Anthony? I just don't understand." My words came forth in gasping sobs. "What can I say to comfort my friend? Why did her mother have to die?" I wiped my eyes across the back of Anthony's shirt. "She was sweet and kind, and never did anything bad. Why did it happen? If God is so good and perfect, why didn't he stop the savages before they attacked?"

Anthony paused so long, I thought he would not answer. "Mary, dost thou remember the hatred between the royalists and the roundheads on our ship? How harsh Joshua Prentice's Puritan father was toward the Kingsley and Royall families because he had been branded and tortured? And how bitter those wounded soldiers were because they had suffered at the hands of the Puritans?"

"Yes, I remember. But it turned out they were all doing their duty as they saw fit. Quin Kingsley was as loving as Joshua."

Anthony took a deep breath. "Perhaps the warring Pequots believe it is their obligation to drive intruders from their land."

"But Anthony! Everyone says the Indians are heathens. Savages!"

"Hast thou not heard the story of the English attack on the Pequot fort, nigh onto 10 years ago? Hundreds of Pequots were burned alive when the fort was set on fire—men, women and children. The war that followed nearly wiped out the Pequots. If that happened to our people, wouldst thou forget so soon?"

I tried to put myself in their place. "'Twould be painful hard, but I cannot help the vengeful feelings in my heart. Mistress Halsey befriended us. Surely thou are not siding with the Pequots?"

Anthony patted the holster that carried his flintlock. "Within me there is often a struggle between forgiveness and revenge. Today I do what I must do. Pray for me, little sister."

When Mistress Halsey was buried on Saturday, with tearing eyes I stood by Elizabeth's side.

> Yea though in valley of death's shade
> I walk, none ill I'll fear:
> because thou art with me, thy rod
> and staff my comfort are.[48]

Instead of comfort, Uncle Robert's words roused only questions I could not answer. *Why? Why? Why?*

After the service, Aunt Alice, as the minister's wife, hosted a dinner for the Halsey family, in the parlor of the manse, with food brought in by the congregation. Mourners found a measure of consolation at the sound of

galloping horses and triumphant cries of their riders —
my brother Anthony, the Halsey brothers, the constable,
and other Southampton men.

"The murderers have been captured and taken to the
pillory!" Anthony shouted. "Lion Gardiner directed
Chief Wyandanch and his Montauk braves to join the
search,[49] and now we know that Chief is indeed the white
man's friend."

The constable continued the gladsome news. "Wyandanch keeps his word. He and his Montauk braves came
dragging the prisoners in, saying, 'We bring thee these
men. The arrow of the one called the Blue Sachem killed
one of your squaws. Deal with them according to the
white man's law. They are not of our tribe, but are Pequots from across the water.'"

John Halsey waved his musket over his head proudly.
"The murderer is locked in the pillory along with the
three who joined him in this heinous act, and they will be
conveyed to Hartford for trial.[50]

The mood of the mourners lightened and they began
shouting their gratitude and relief. "Huzzah! Huzzah!
These men will no longer extort tribute from our people
nor will they take our lives."[51] [52]

I stood beside Elizabeth, my arm around her trembling
shoulders. Her grief could not so easily take flight, but I
did feel a lessening of her tension and fear.

"Thank God," she whispered. "Our brothers have returned to us victorious."

After the mourners and other guests had left the Fordham home, Aunt Alice took me by the hand. "Mary, I
must speak to thee and thy Papa to ask a favor." Her
warm brown eyes took on a tentative look with one brow
raised as if asking my approval.

"Aye, but what wouldst thou have me do?"

"Come with me, Mary." Together we walked into the garden where Papa and Uncle Robert sat talking in low solemn tones.

"My husband, hast thou discussed our request with Will?"

Uncle Robert smiled and nodded.

Papa looked at me and took my hand. "Mary, wouldst thou be willing to live here with thy Fordham kin, taking on the responsibility of young Joshua's care?"

Uncle Robert continued. "Joshua is five years old now, but cannot see to read as other children even though he shows a real eagerness to learn. I sense a strong affinity between the two of you, and in thee, I see an inquisitive mind and a love of reading. Thine eyes could light his darkness."

My heart swelled with pleasure at the great confidence my uncle expressed. I turned to Papa, fearful of losing that moment of joy.

Papa was smiling. "My daughter, in giving my permission, I would be remiss if I were not sure of thine ability to assume the normal duties of a young woman when the time is ripe. But for a lack of maturity in the face of conflict with thy sister, thou hast proven thy talents worthy of any task." Papa's eyes were warm and approving. "Thou art indeed Thursday's child. I have always known thy calling may encompass a purpose beyond ordinary expectations."

Suddenly, in my exultation, a twinge of grief convulsed my heart, and my fingers twisted themselves in the folds of my homespun skirt. I could no longer hold in the hurt carried since the day Papa turned away from me as I sat on Boston wharf. "Papa, you wouldst have me leave thy house?"

His eyes took on a stricken look, and I plunged ahead, fearful of losing my courage to speak. "Canst thou never forgive me for the pain I caused my mama?"

"Forgive thee?"

"The day on the wharf when you turned from me—"

"Oh, my child, it is I who must ask forgiveness. When thy mother died, I was a beached whale, alone on an alien shore. When I saw thee sitting there on the wharf, the sun lighted thy fiery tresses like a halo, and in that emerald dress, thou wert the very image of thy mother on our wedding day. In that moment, I could not but turn away." Papa took a napkin from his pocket and wiped away my tears, then gathered me into his trembling arms. "Of course, you could not understand the insanity of my sorrow. Forgive me."

Finally home, I pressed my face against his warm chest. Simultaneously we heaved a great sigh as if we had both been holding our breath. Relief and contentment flowed through me. Together we inhaled the lovely, fragrant air of our new world.

21st Century
Memory Catchers' Office

By the time I finished editing the tape Grand-Mary had left me, the bayberry candle on my desk was burning low, and the clock read ten till twelve. Noon. Time enough left for a spell check of the ancient biblical translation Grand-Mary had quoted. When I entered a search: *e Bay Geneva Bible,* a view of a fully illustrated original appeared on the screen: *The Geneva English Bible 1610 with 1607 Book of Common Prayer; many engravings, maps. In its original handmade wooden case.* Views of various pages were still posted although the auction had ended. The winning bid: US $2,499.00. On the Psalm 23 page, I found the words just as Grand-Mary had remembered them.

An aroma from the kitchen—bay leaf in beef stew, awoke a different hunger. My crock-pot meal for two was ready and waiting. *Grand-Mary, are you coming back?* I snuffed out the candle and left the office.

After lunch, hunger satisfied, the doorbell's ring interrupted me. The USPS guy with a package. "Sign here, please." He climbed back into his truck. While heading for my office, I ripped open the box. Within a cushion of bubble wrap lay a lovely old wooden case and inside it, a Geneva Bible, just like the one pictured on e Bay. Stunned, I began crying, tears rolling down my cheeks.

"May I assume those are tears of happiness? Thou art pleased?" With a "cat-who-ate-the-canary" look, my longed-for guest settled into her chair.

"Gr-Grand-Mary! Wha'? Where?"

"What is it 21st Century Americans say? Don't ask, don't tell?" Her impish grin returned. "Oh, don't worry. It isn't stolen. I saw the Bible on e Bay, and recognized my mother's handwriting on the frontispiece. I dropped in on the buyer, and when I convinced him that I knew the original owner, he began trembling—turned pale as death. Thought I was a ghost. Imagine that. Do I look like a ghost? Forsooth, the man was quite ready to be relieved of the relic. Anyway, two thousand dollars ($2,499) was only pocket change to him. Jittery as he was, I'd say his fortune may be ill-gotten. He agreed to have the Bible and case mailed to thee, Overnight Express. It is thine. Now put it away and let's get back to work." Grand-Mary leaned back in her chair and changed the subject. "I can't wait to tell thee about Joshua."

Seven

~

By the time I'd moved my belongings to Uncle Robert's house to begin working with Joshua, my little cousin was already familiar with the house. He took me by the hand to show me around. "Here is the hall with the outside door." he said. "Feel its wide panels?" He surprised me by taking my hand and pressing it against the boards. "Door panels are not like the walls. I can feel and hear the difference, too. Can you?" Joshua put his ear against the door and listened. "Shh! I hear the owl hoo-hooting in the tree outside."

I closed my eyes. Yes, the oak panels were thinner than the walls of the house, and through the door I could hear the twitter of birds and the rustle of tree branches waving in the breeze.

He tugged at my bodice sleeve, ready to continue. "The stairway is next to the outside door. See? The stairs go up four steps—one, two, three, four—and then turn twice with four more steps before you reach the top. That's where I sleep and all of my cousins, too. In the room I share with Nathan, when I hear the floor squeaking, I know I'm right beside my bunk. See how easy it is?"

When I asked Joshua how he learned his way around so quickly, he said, "I *feel* what's in the room. And then I *listen*. Back in the kitchen, the fireplace tells me where I am. Come with me." He took my hand and led me down the hallway toward the back of the house and into the spacious kitchen where Aunt Alice kept the floor covered with clean, white sea sand, swept into patterns by a homemade broom.

"I like this room best of all. It always smells so good." He stopped and inhaled deeply. "Like Mama's kitchen. Bread in the oven and meat roasting on the spit."

Cousin Molly laughed. "Hungry again, Joshua?" She sliced a thick slab of bread and spread it with butter, offering it to him.

"M-m-m!" He licked his lips to catch the last crumb, then tilted his head.

"Dost thou hear the crackle of the embers, Mary? Hear the water bubbling in the pot? Feel the warm." He took my hand and held it toward the fire, then led me around the room. "Here on the wall next to the fire is the table. I can smell the beeswax Aunt Alice uses to polish it." He patted his way down the smooth planks—and then a bench, against the wall. Sometimes it is not where I expect, and I crack my shins on it. See," he said. Remembering the hurt, he rubbed his leg below the knee, at the hem of his new tan breeches, and placed my hand so I could feel the latest bump. He winced and scrunched his eyes, eyes fringed by long lashes, big blue eyes that could not see.

We continued our tour, back down the hallway to the middle of the house.

"Here's the big chimney. I like to put my hands on it. The right side is cool. Aunt Alice calls this side of the manse the "best" room. *Manse* just means the preacher's house, thou knowst. The best room is for weddings and funerals. I don't go in there.

"The other side divides in two. One for Uncle Robert's library where he reads." Joshua opened the door so I could peek in. "I can't see the books," he said, "but I think they're all around. And ink, dost thou smell ink? I think Uncle Robert writes his sermons here." Joshua motioned toward another door. "This other part is their bedroom. It has a great big mahogany chest of drawers and bed. Mahogany smells different from the other beds, and the whole room smells flowery like Aunt Alice. Sometimes baby Joe cries in the night, so there's a trundle that pulls out from under the big bed. That is were he sleeps, but I can not go in that room."

I laughed. "And how dost thou know so much about a room thou canst not go into?"

Joshua's innocent blue eyes were wide and solemn, then squinted as if to contain his laughter. "At first I did...'til Aunt Alice caught me jumping on the bed."

I could hardly have imagined the changes that small boy brought into my life. Taking charge of him was a full time job, leaving me little time for helping Aunt Alice with the housewifely chores I had so resented at home. Joshua was indeed—as Uncle Robert had said—bright and curious, with a most sturdy courage. Into everything. Eager to learn. Uncle Robert had a marvelous collection of books, and much of my time was spent in the library reading aloud to Joshua, reinforcing the studies taught him by Gideon—Bible verses, and numbers, with a peg board that helped him reckon the days and months and seasons. Part of his lessons were practical skills we all needed. He helped me pluck the down from geese and stuff the feathers into pillows. To the nearly constant music of the spinning wheel, he learned to card wool by feel, and after the wool was spun into yarn, to wind it into a ball and to knit it into scarves and mittens. He learned to weave flax and wool threads into cloth, his head cocked to one side as he listened to the clicking of the loom. With scraps left over from sewing, someone was always piecing another wool quilt, to be used on one of our beds or sometimes saved for guests or gifts, or displays at the fair. It was like painting, designing not with water and dyes but with colorful bits of cloth, one of my favorite tasks.

Much as I enjoyed reading after responsibilities were completed, Joshua more often wanted to spend time outdoors. In cold weather, I helped him into his waistcoat, hat, and gloves, then tied my bonnet strings tight under my chin. Grabbing my cloak from the hook by the door, we slipped out.

"What color is the sky today?" Joshua would ask. And I tried to explain in words he could *feel*. "Blue," I might say. "You remember blue, but the sun is making streaks of color across the blue sky." I held his mittened hand and moved it as if we were painting the horizon in broad strokes. "It's orange and red. Like fire."

"Hot like fire?" he asked.

"No, colored like fire. Dost thou remember?"

"Yes," he would say. "Hot colors."

We played a game we called "What Is Aunt Alice Doing?" so he could practice identifying sounds. I told him about everything I saw and heard when we were outside. We played "What Makes This Sound?" with his young

Fordham cousins. It seemed that Joshua could imitate anything, and no matter how difficult it was, he was usually first to recognize the sounds they heard.

In spite of knocks and bumps when he stumbled, he liked to hold hands with me and run. Down past the sand dunes and waving wild oats, we stripped off our shoes and knee-length wool stockings and walked barefoot along the seashore, feeling the texture and heat of the sand. We waded in the edge of the water where gentle waves splashed over our feet. Joshua bent to let his fingers glide through the water, and then touched them to his tongue.

"Taste it, Mary. It's salty like sweat." He took a deep breath and licked his lips. "Even the air tastes like the sea." He stooped to examine squishy green wisps of seaweed washed up by the waves, and sometimes he found a special object and thrust it into my hands. "See, Mary!" His fingers moved mine over his treasure, perhaps a small seashell.

Joshua giggled at the feel of a spider running up his arm or a slimy worm squirming through his fingers. He squealed when holding a crawly bug and insisted on sharing all of them with me—wiggly things that made shivers down my spine.

Uncle Robert's library also served as a schoolroom. Early in the morning, I spent much time with Joshua there, listening to Goodman Richard Mills,[53] the town teacher, as he read to school children from the Bible or helped them practice their ABCs on paddle-shaped horn books. Because Joshua was blind, Goodman Mills felt there was little the boy could learn and quite ignored him.

If Joshua heard rain on the roof, he began tugging at my sleeve. "Please, Mary, enough reading. Time to go out."

"Shush, young man!" Goodman Mills' voice was stern. "Thou art disturbing those who can learn." His remark offended me, but it may have been less offensive than the punishment Goodman Mills meted out to other students when their attention wandered: making them sit in the dunce corner or washing out their ears with a hot corn-cob.[54]

Once outside, Joshua whooped and hollered, enjoying the feel of rain on his face, splashing in puddles or stooping to draw numbers or whatever letters of the alphabet he could remember, squishing mud through his fingers. As the spring rain slowed to a sprinkle, we sat on a cedar stump and listened. I watched as the fog rose like a soft grey curtain and the sky changed from lavender to blue. Sorry was I that Joshua could not see it, yet mayhap he was more aware than I. "Listen, Mary," he would say, taking my face in his hands to be sure he had my attention. "The music of the frogs and crickets tell the sun it's time to come out and play."

One morning he caught a tiny creature in his hands. "Look, Mary. This little creature sounds like a cricket but it hath not the feel of one. He held it out to me "Touch his toes." They're so big for his body."

"Yes, it's a spring peeper, a wee frog. Those big toes help him hang on to plants when he climbs. And look at this, Joshua." I held his index finger and helped him trace the marking across the frog's back. "What letter is that, Joshua?"

"It is an X, is it not?" His smile widened. "Dost thou think froggies know their ABCs?"

I laughed and sang to him the song my Papa sang to me. "...Said this little froggie, I am lost you see; but I'll say my lessons over, A, B, and C."

Each day Joshua taught me the secrets of listening. When he placed his small hands on my cheeks, I could not but give him my full awareness, as if nothing in the world, for this moment, were of greater importance.

He loved to frolic in the meadow where Southampton families grazed their cattle, and he soon learned the way to the pasture without my leading. "Here's the white cedar fence," he would say, then reach out to touch the logs. "See this, Mary?" He grabbed my hand and placed it next to his. "Rough, smooth, rough, smooth." Past the fence, he began hugging trees, moving ever closer to the dark woods. "What's this tree called?" he would ask. Or, "Mary, what's this flower?"

In Uncle Robert's library I found a small book with answers to Joshua's questions, so I carried it in my pocket. At the edge of the woods we sat and he taught me to listen to the sound of leaves fluttering in the wind.

"Oak tree?" he asked.

"Yes, thou art right." I knew some of the names without looking in the book, and Joshua could often tell them apart by their aroma as well as by the sound of their rustling leaves. Pitch pines and oak, chestnut and hickory trees, low-bush blueberry and bayberry and swamp rose. He loved the sweet siren scent of the nectar of red-veined pitcher plants that nestled along the edge of a bog. "Look at this, Joshua. The flower is shaped like a pitcher, and a fly is caught inside, trapped by sticky hairs. It will drown in the tiny pool of rainwater at the bottom of the pitcher. The book says that's the way the flower gets its breakfast."

In the same way, we learned birds' names by finding them in the book after hearing their songs. The raspy, scraping, scream of red-tailed hawks high overhead: "Kree-eee-ar" The loud song of the tiny ovenbird: "Cher, cher, cher," ringing through the forest. The rich warbling of the orchard oriole.

To his delight, one day Joshua found a hairy worm. The book described it completely: Dark green body with head usually retracted into thorax and with rows of pale bars or spots....

"Oh, Joshua, this larva will turn into a beautiful blue-green butterfly like the one we found last summer. Remember how it fluttered its soft wings when thou held it in thy hand? The book says it feeds on the white cedar tree. Let's put it back."

His gentleness as he stretched to place it high on the rough trunk of a tree touched my heart.

Often we would follow the path to the north side of Southampton village, but when he begged to go exploring in the woods, I hung back, remembering my fall in the Matlock cave, Ben and Abby's Indian story, and Goody Halsey's murder.

"Come on, Mary, I'm not afraid!"

"Let me tell thee an old story, The Wolf and the Kid," I said. "A kid was perched up on the top of a house, and looking down he saw a wolf passing under him. Immediately he began to revile and attack his enemy. 'Murderer and thief,' he cried, 'what *dost* thou here near honest folks' houses? How dare thee make an appearance where thy vile deeds are known?'

'Curse away, my young friend,' said the wolf. 'It is easy to be brave from a safe distance.'"

"But being the kid is no fun," Joshua said, sticking out his lower lip. "I'm eight-and-a-half years old now." He straightened his shoulders and stood on his tip-toes — "And I'm almost as tall as thee. I'm not scared." He held my face in his hands to make sure I was paying attention. "There's a path where the Shinnecocks walk. The leaves there make a different crunching sound. I've heard them. We'll be safe if we stay near their path. And anyway, Uncle Robert says they are friendly Indians." Joshua grabbed my cloak and pulled me toward the path. "Come on! Let's play hide and seek. Close your eyes, Mary, count to twenty, then come find me." Off he darted.

I was twelve years old. Old enough, surely, to finally put my fears behind me, so I closed my eyes. I could hear him scampering away down the path.

"One, two, three…. At the count of twenty, I opened my eyes and entered the darkening passageway into the woods, listening as Joshua had taught me, peering behind any tree large enough to hide a small boy. I had not known him ever to commit the sin of lying, so I was sure he would keep his promise to stay within reach of the path.

Deeper I walked. No Joshua. My heart beat quickened, ker-thumpity-thump, and my legs ached — growing pains again.[55] Visions of Ben and Abby's near capture and Goody Halsey's death flashed through my brain. My throat tightened until only a high-pitched scream came forth. "Joshua! Where are you? Allee allee oxen free."

Finally, above my head, I heard him. "Here I am. Help me, Mary. I climbed a tree, and now it's got a hold of my hair and won't turn loose."

Peering upward, I espied his dilemma. On a bough that leaned downward nearly to the ground, he had shinnied up to the place where the branch of the oak was splitting away from the trunk. In the split, a golden lock of his hair was snagged. Even on tip-toes I could not reach him. I hitched up my skirt and then cautiously ascended the broken branch, skinning my already aching knees on the rough bark. I climbed onto a bough above Joshua's head, then reached down and loosened the lock of his hair. "There you are, Joshua." I took a big breath and then added, "I'm proud you stayed so calm. Now, can you ease on down the way that you came?"

He was on the ground in a flash, but the moment I attempted to follow, my skirt caught on a broken stub of a branch. As I turned to release it, a terrible muscle spasm seized my leg and I could not move. I heard a loud crack; the branch gave way and crashed to the ground. High overhead I heard the piercing scream of a red-tailed hawk. "Kree-eee-ar!" Then darkness swallowed me.

ANNO DOM 1650s
THE SHINNECOCK VILLAGE, LONG ISLAND

From the darkness, the hawk caught me up in his powerful talons and carried me into the sky, then finally deposited me in a huge nest of twigs and branches. There I snuggled into a bed of downy feathers. Strange, sharp odors woke me. Stinking hides. Fish and grease and smoke. In a room lit by firelight, I saw smoke curling up through a hole in roof. I made out dried plants and ears of corn hanging from poles overhead. My head ached and an anxious face blurred above me. Joshua!

"Mary, art thou all right?"

Other images floated in the space behind him. Frightening fuzzy images. Wild animal skins wrapped 'round painted bodies. Then I saw that I, too, was covered with an animal skin and lying on another.

Joshua touched my arm. "Thou art shaking, Mary. Do not be afraid."

"Where am I? How did I get here?"

"After you fell, I could not awaken thee, so I ran toward the Shinnecock village to get help."

My vision cleared and I could see a woman with shiny black hair stirring something in a pot over the open fire. A red circle was painted on each of her high cheekbones. Strands of colored beads—wampum—she wore in place of a bodice, and a deerskin skirt, embroidered with shells, scarcely covered her knees. I had seen Shinnecocks before, but never up close.

Another fuzzy image turned out to be a nearly naked boy clad in deerskin, deep reddish brown like his skin.

"This is Qolucksee," Joshua said. "I met him at the edge of the forest. The cry of the red-tailed hawk led us to find thee, and Qolucksee helped me carry thee here."

"The two of you carried me all this way?"

"We lifted thee onto his big sled, and his dog pulled thee to the village."

"My mother is preparing willow bark tea," the Indian boy said. "It will make thy head feel better."

The woman approached with a clay bowl of the steaming liquid. With great care, she helped me sit up and drink from the bowl. She began speaking in a strange tongue.

"My mother says the tea will drive away the evil spirit of pain." Qolucksee turned and touched the woman's arm. "They do not understand thee, Mother. Speak to them in their language."

Her broad face remained very solemn. "Do not be afraid, children. I am Nowedanah, Sunk Squaw and Shaman of the Shinnecock. My brother is the Great Wyandanch. We make thee our friends and show thee mercy as the Great Spirit has shown us mercy."

Blessed are the merciful. Strange how she echoed the very scripture Uncle Robert had used in last Sabbath's sermon. "Thank you," I said. "Thou art very kind."

Through the open passageway, I could see the sun lowering in the sky. Uncle Robert and Aunt Alice would worry if we weren't home before dark. "Joshua, we must be gone." I tried to rise, but the muscles of my legs were stiff and bruised from yesterday's spasms.

"You are in pain?" the Shaman Nowedanah asked.

"My head feels better, but my legs..."

"A devil lurks there. While you and Joshua eat, I will bathe and massage your legs with a special preparation, then replace your tattered skirt with pure white deerskins to chase away the evil spirit." She dipped corn meal mush out of a pot into wooden bowls, sweetened it with maple syrup, and brought it to Qolucksee, Joshua and me to eat. No spoons. Qolucksee dipped his fingers into his bowl and then licked them off, and his mother smiled at his enjoyment of the food. I'd have received a rap on the head for such manners, but hunger forgave my inhibitions. I supped as Qolucksee did. Joshua had already solved the problem by tipping the bowl to his lips.

Nowedanah smeared a warm salve over my legs and with gentle hands began massaging the ache away. It smelled like the roots of the herb Aunt Alice candied for special occasions. Angelica. Then Nowedanah wrapped and tied a skirt of soft white skin around my waist, removed my torn skirt, and laid it aside.

The sun silhouetted a tall, awesome man in an elaborate turkey-feather mantle approaching through the passageway. He entered the house and bowed to Qolucksee's mother. Adorned by wampum earrings and necklaces, his forehead was painted with yellow stripes. His head was bald and shiny except for a long tuft of hair on top, braided with scarlet-dyed animal hair, from which dangled several red-tailed hawk feathers tipped with copper.

Qolucksee bowed to him and said, "Father, these are my friends, Joshua and Mary. She was injured, and Mother gave her drink from the spirit bag of medicines."

The man turned to us and spoke in our language. "Welcome, children. I am Kockenoe, husband of Shaman Nowedanah of Shinnecock village."

I did not know if we should rise or kneel, but before I could move, he seated himself cross-legged before us, arms crossed over his chest. One glance at his formidable dark eyes made my breath quicken. Cold air brushed against my feet, and I drew my legs up under the borrowed skirt, surprised at how much the swelling had abated. I could not look at the man's face. Instead I focused on something almost as fearsome to me—the red feathers that hung from his braid.

Qolucksee joined the circle and said, "Father, 'twas your spirit guide, the red-tailed hawk, that led us to the spot where Mary had fallen."

Kockenoe nodded, and reached toward me with his long arm. I instinctively drew back.

"Do not be afraid, children." Gently, he clasped his hands over his heart. "You see the yellow markings on my face? They stand for peace." He turned and spoke directly to me. "Thou art a hawk person, my daughter. Thou hast been chosen by the Spirit. The visions and dreams it sends thee are not to be feared."

He raised a strong arm and gestured. "Thy gift allows thee to soar high above.

I remembered my father's long-ago promise to me: "Thou art Thursday's child, my little princess. That means you have countless visions to achieve. You will go far." I focused my attention back to Kockenoe's words.

"Just over the next hill is liberation and the freedom that keeps thee moving forward." His powerful voice reminded me of Uncle Robert's when he lectured from the Scriptures on Sabbath day. I sat spellbound, listening with full attention as I had been taught to do.

"Or if thy path is not appropriate," he told me, "the hawk points out a more favorable way. Sometimes the message you are given may not be what others want to hear." Kockenoe paused. "Take thy time. Soar above for a while and find the right words before speaking thy truth."

He touched his red-feathered totem as he spoke. "Stay hungry! If you sate your hunger, you will miss out on the joy!"[56]

Kockenoe placed his hand on my head, and I did not tremble. "Feel the words and the rhythms," he said to me. "The sounds, the sweat, the breathing in and out. Feel the laughter — and the fear."

He lowered his voice. "Walk slowly. Deeply. Listen to the music of the brook as it carves its way." His words were like a psalm. "Each step teaches life's mysteries," he said. "Enjoy each step."

Nowedanah came and stood beside her husband, and
Kockenoe's tone changed. He looked toward the passageway and then back at us. "Your family will worry if
you do not return soon. Can you walk?"

My head throbbed for a moment as I stood, and my
legs were stiff, but the pain had lessened. "Yes, I can
walk."

Feeling dizzy and a bit self-conscious about the length
of my borrowed skirt, I helped Joshua to his feet.

"Let me walk with thee," Qolucksee said. "I know the
paths through the forest. I'll help thee find the way."

Nowedanah nodded her permission, a proud look on
her face. She handed me the folded remnants of my torn
skirt. Her husband handed me a red feather like those in
the totem he wore.

"Thank you for thy kindness," I said. "We won't forget
you."

"Come again, children," Qolucksee said.

"Yes, come again. It is good for my son to learn about
unfamiliar customs," Nowedanah said. "Perhaps we are
more alike than different."

Anno Dom 1650s
Southampton, Long Island

As we arrived back home, the sun was setting. Thank
goodness, Aunt Alice had not yet begun to worry.

No one asked where we had been, and I, eager to tell
about our adventures, was sorely disappointed. But
Joshua, who often forgot that children did not speak until
spoken to, was bubbling over with information.

"Aunt Alice, I climbed a tree and Mary tried to rescue
me and she fell and hit her head and I ran through the
trees and —"

"Stop right there, young man." Aunt Alice paused and her eyes widened when she saw what I was wearing. Quickly she removed a skirt from the mending basket and wrapped it 'round my waist, covering my legs. "Well, it appears thou art all in one piece. Go wash your hands — the both of you. Supper is on the table. Whilst we eat, you may share your adventure with us."

We children stood at our usual places around the table, and Uncle Robert seated himself at the head and prayed. "Father we thank Thee for this food and especially for keeping watch over Mary and Joshua today. Amen."

My oldest cousin, Molly, practicing the housewifery arts that she might be ready for her approaching marriage, served the meal. When our trenchers were filled, Uncle Robert spoke. "Now, Joshua, you may begin thy account."

Occasionally I interrupted him to explain. "The Shaman Nowedanah's dwelling was dark and smelly, but they treated us kindly, not at all like savages might. She gave me willow bark tea to ease my pain, and after rubbing a sweet smelling salve on my legs, she exchanged my ragged skirt for a soft doeskin. I was surprised that they spoke proper English as well as their own tongue."

"Yes," Uncle Robert said. "I believe the man you met is Kockenoe. According to the story told me when we moved to Southampton, the Pequots captured him when he was but a young boy and then sold him to a man across the Sound. Kockenoe later met Rev. William Leverich, who attended Cambridge with me while we were studying for the ministry. Leverich preceded me to America and engaged in imparting religious truth to the Indians at Sandwich. He wrote and told me of his work, and said Kockenoe had helped him translate some of the scriptures into the Indian language. I heard later that Kockenoe made it back to his people on Long Island and began working with Wyandanch as a translator.[57]"

"The same Wyandanch who helped capture the Indian who killed Elizabeth Halsey's mother?"

"Indeed. Kockenoe married Nowedanah[58], the sister of the great Wyandanch, who appointed her chief of the Shinnecock—Shaman and Healer of the People."[59]

"Qolucksee and his parents invited us to visit them again, and I need to return the doeskin skirt."

Aunt Alice looked distressed at that thought, and she had further questions. "I can't imagine how the Indian boy and Joshua found their way back to thee after you had fallen, Mary."

Joshua was quick to answer. "We followed the cry of the red-tailed hawk."

"See what Kockenoe gave me?" I pulled the feather from my pocket. "He said I have been chosen by the Spirit of the Red-Tailed Hawk."

Aunt Alice shuddered. "I fear you are too accepting of the false notions of these heathens. I pray thee, put away that evil symbol!"

I turned to Uncle Robert, expecting to see the same fear in his eyes, but hoping, instead, to gain his permission to visit the Shinnecocks again.

A far away expression in his eyes vanished as he looked at me and smiled. "Mary, you remind me so much of your mother, my sister Clemence. She was always thoughtful and perceptive. She would be proud of you." From the mantle he picked up three small metal tools pointed on each end—muxes—to make the drilling of seashells into wampum beads easier and quicker.

"When you return the skirt, please offer these to the Shaman Nowedanah with my thanks for her family's kindness." He paused and then spoke softly. "I pray that my tolerance may never lead thee to suffer under our Puritan tenets."

ဢ

Our visit to the Shinnecock had to be postponed, for on Saturday a storm was brewing. Until evening, it consisted only of drizzle and some seldom and scarce perceivable thunder. By Sabbath morning on our way to meeting house, the wind was singing and whistling most unusually. Rattling thunder ran along the clouds and the sky turned black. We could scarce find our pew, so dark it was inside.

When the visiting preacher stood and began his sermon, his voice was drowned in the wind, and the wind in thunder. Rain and hail battered the meeting house. A dreadful storm ensued, swelling and roaring as if it were having fits. Amid the tempestuous noise of thunder and lightning, the preacher's voice rose as he read from the scriptures:

"In Job 37, the word of God speaks a warning: "Hear attentively the noise of His voice, and the sound that goeth out of His mouth. After it a voice roareth: He thundereth with the voice of His excellency; and He will not stay them when His voice is heard.

As if he were God himself, the Reverend's voice rose to a roar over terrible cracks of thunder, and he began pounding the pulpit as he preached. "Repent, ye sinners among us! It is God's vengeance you bring down. For He has set His face against all augurs and consulters with familiar spirits, against fornicators and coveters and gluttons, against all liars and those who swear by the name of the Lord our God, and against all who permit them to live within your city. They must be destroyed!

"Do not abide this wickedness to live among you." His fierce words beat against our ears as did the sound of the rising storm. Still he continued. "The black clouds of God's wrath now hang directly over your heads, clouds big with dreadful thunder ready to burst forth upon you! Hear ye not? Repent, ye sinners! Judgment against your evil works cometh from the heavens, greater than the strength of the stoutest, sturdiest devil in hell!"[60]

Immediately we were ear witnesses to an astonishing sound that struck the house and rent the door in pieces, opening it to the wind and rain.[61] The tithing man from his seat near the door began crying out. "Fire! Fire! God has caused thunder to rain fire upon the house. See how it blazes!"

The men rushed outside to discover the bolt had fallen upon the building next to the meeting house, causing lightning to set the house afire.

They rushed to bring buckets and vats of water, fighting the roaring inferno, burning in spite of the cold rain. Within minutes, another crack of thunder hit and struck Job Foulke dead. His seared body laid there in the rain with steam or smoke rising above it.

Seemed to me that was enough hell for any man, but even in the midst of the storm, the tittle-tattles were busy. Everyone had heard about the arrests and the trial not a fortnight before. Job Foulke and three others.

"Not a crime that extends to life and limb," the court decreed. For their sexual offence one boy was put in the pillory, one was scolded, and the two men were whipped.

"Oh, so that was what happened," one man said. "I passed by the town square that day on my way to the farm. Saw the boy in the stocks as I came riding through."

"'Twas good enough for the rascal!" someone muttered.

Once the fire was out, the rain turned into a light mist. Neighbors carried Job's body home, but the gossip around the meeting house continued.

"Can't say I feel sorry for Foulke," one said. Trembling as he spoke, he added, "'Tis the loud voice of God's retribution."

Others shook their heads, voicing their remembrance of Job's wife, grey faced and sitting like a statue of stone at the trial. Now her mortification had turned to mourning.

Uncle Robert's words were a compassionate reminder. "Thunderbolts knock all who stand in their way. May God have mercy on both the sinner and the sorrowing. May He have mercy on us all."

Twas blasphemy to question God's ways, but how could I stop the maze of questions running through my mind? I did not doubt His power—and yet I could not reconcile the contradictions in the scriptures, Old Testament and New.

Did God send forth the Spirit of love and life, or did He rain down retribution and death?

Wrath or righteousness?

Job's story or John's?

Had not Job Foulke's children suffered enough?

How could they bear the stench of their father's burned body?[62]

"For God so loveth the world...."

21st Century
Memory Catchers' Office

Head down and eyes closed, Grand-Mary sat quietly when I clicked off the recorder.

I reached for her hand. "What a terrifying experience! No wonder you remember it so clearly. But how did you recall the frightening words spoken by the visiting Reverend all those years ago?"

"My dear, time is relative. Three hundred years is but a moment once you have made the transition." Grand-Mary looked up and smiled. "In those days many people were illiterate or could barely write their names. The hearing of sounds and voices was of great importance. I was fortunate to have learned both reading and writing. But you recall also what I told you? We children were expected to listen with full attention that we might understand the discussion of the Sabbath sermon." She looked for my response and I nodded. "To help me remember, I took notes. Turn to the back of the Bible I gave you and perhaps you may see the words I scrawled in the darkening meeting house on that very day."

With a flick of her lavender shawl, Grand-Mary faded from my sight, and I was left to transcribe the words she had spoken.

I replayed the story she had just told me about the storm and as I listened, I typed the story, then reread it and then put it aside for her approval. Thinking of what an interesting Thanksgiving dinner guest Grand-Mary would be, I phoned a favorite buffet for reservations for my husband and me.

෩

Dinner time, Thanksgiving Day. On the way to dinner, my husband waited as I paused to straighten the colorful pheasant that perched on the grapevine wreath outside our door. Crafted by my mother with real pheasant feathers, the small bird, packed and unpacked for many autumn seasons, was a bit scraggly.

At the restaurant, I took pleasure in finding on the menu some foods Grand-Mary had mentioned—roast duck garnished with green grapes and berries.

Dinner over, we drove home, stuffed as holiday turkeys. Even before putting the key in the lock of our front door, I knew the afternoon nap I'd looked forward to would be postponed. The miniature pheasant perched on the grapevine wreath had sprouted a long red tail feather. Grand-Mary was back.

I hung up my jacket and held out my arms to greet her.

"Did you enjoy your duck? she said."

"How do you know what I ate?"

"I saw thee there. Thought I'd come and join you, but then decided the waiters might be uncomfortable serving dinner to a ghost." She laughed. "So I came here and read the new chapter. You did a good job." She fluffed up the cushions in her usual chair and sat down. "Shall we begin?"

I reached for the Sony and, like she had taught me, focused my attention on her as if, at this moment, her story was the only thing that mattered.

Recalling her return to the Indian village as if it had happened yesterday, she began.

"Grey skies continued for several days...."

I turned on the recorder to capture her soft words.

Anno Dom 1650s
Shinnecock Village, Long Island

Grey skies continued for several days and a constant drizzle kept Joshua and me inside. Finally, on Thursday the sun came out, and even though it was quite chilly, Uncle Robert gave his permission for us to return to the Shinnecock village. We donned woolen caps, mittens and capes and started north to the forest path. Although Joshua had made many changes since, as a six-year-old, he first came to live with the Fordhams, he still enjoyed the sound and feel of hopping in plashy pools left by the rain. I stayed my distance from him, trying to keep my shoes and skirt clean and dry.

As we approached the Indian village, Qolucksee's dog began barking, and both dog and master ran to welcome us. I had hardly taken notice of the structure of the Shinnecock lodges when we were there the previous week, but now I was amazed by the size of their dwellings — longhouses about 60 by 15 feet each. Oval in shape, they were made with hickory saplings, the tops bent and lashed together at the top forming a gallery. Throughout the length of these bent poles, narrow pieces of wood were woven. Bundles of blue vent grass were sewn fast to these, row after row, shingle fashion.[63]

When we entered Qolucksee's lodge, I could see that rushes covered the floor, and platforms swathed with furs ran along the sides of the house. A hole in the top of the dwelling was plastered with clay to let the smoke out without danger of fire. Below the smoke hole, several clay pots sat in the ashes of the fire, and old Indian women sat nearby thrashing beans out of their pods with a stick and adding them to a boiling pot of broth. In another corner of the lodge, women drilled pieces of shell into wampum. Others were weaving baskets and mats from reeds. Still others were braiding pieces of shell into belts, or earrings, or garments that looked like elaborate capes. They reminded me of the Southampton women at a quilting bee, but with less chatter. Later I learned that these women and girls all lived in this one longhouse, and that each longhouse provided shelter for fourteen or fifteen families together.

Qolucksee's mother, Nowedanah, came forward to greet us. "Welcome, children. Come sit by fire. Warm thyselves." She offered us bowls of steaming samp that tasted much like the corn meal mush we ate at home.

"I thank thee." Bowing to her, I handed her the doeskin skirt she had loaned me. I removed my cape and mittens, and then sat cross-legged by the fire, covering my stock-inged legs with my cape. Qolucksee sat between Joshua and me, sipping from his own bowl.

Men entered, all with only a central comb of hair, and wearing moccasins and occasional robes of fur over breech clouts. I tried not to stare or wrinkle my nose at their greasy, animal skin odors, and after a few curious glances at us, they were seated and the women served them thick samp from the steaming clay pot. [64]

A large shadow blocked the light from the doorway, and Kockenoe, after greeting Joshua, sat down beside me. This time he, too, wore a fur wrap instead of his turkey feather cape. Otherwise bare to his waist except for his amulet and strands of wampum around his neck, his dark skin glistened with a covering of grease and painted symbols.

"I see thou art wearing the red feather in thy hair. Did the hawk again guide thee to our village?" His voice was strong and intimidating. His face seemed void of emotion, as if unaffected by pleasure or pain, joy or grief, but his eyes were welcoming.

From my pocket, I withdrew his gift. "These muxes are from my uncle, the Reverend Robert Fordham, to thank thee for thy kindness to me when I fell from the tree. He said to wish thee pleasure as thy village uses these tools to create wampum from the beautiful purple shells."

A hint of a smile rent his stoic expression. "Tell thine uncle thank you."

Qolucksee and Joshua, having had quite enough of sitting still, slipped out the doorway.

Shaman Nowedanah spoke. "Would you like to see how our artists make use of the muxes?"

I nodded and she motioned one of the young women to come nearer, bringing the drilling sticks upon which muxes were fixed, and a basket of shell pieces, ground, polished and cut into small cylinders—white from the center column of the periwinkle or conch shell and purple from large clam shells.

I watched as she skillfully drilled each cylinder with the pointed end of the muxes, spinning the stick between her hands, a soft, whirring sound. Another girl came forward to string white beads together. The Shaman removed the red feather from my hair and handed it to the girl. She spoke to her in the Shinnecock language, and when the woman had finished her handiwork, Nowedanah took it from her—an amulet of white shell beads interwoven with the red tail feather of the hawk, hanging from a leather thong. She placed it around my neck. "Come again, my daughter, and Kockenoe will tell you more about the Spirit of the Red-Tailed Hawk." He nodded and rose, and motioning the other men to follow, he left the lodge. I gathered my cape and mittens and bowed to Nowedanah and the other women. Speaking in English, and then imitating the words they spoke, I bade them goodbye.

Joshua and Qolucksee communicated as if there were no differences between them, and we returned to visit the Shinnecocks many times while Joshua was in my care. While he and Qolucksee roamed the village and waded in the creek that ran through it, I was welcomed by the Shaman Nowedanah, who often shared with me her knowledge of herbs for healing wounds or coughs, chills or fevers: angelica roots, purslain, egrimony, violets, pennyroyal, elecampane, and sarsaparilla roots. Nowedanah believed that any disease common to the island could be cured with local herbs.[65]

Kockenoe was eager to teach me more about the ways of the Red-Tailed Hawk.

"The hawk soars above and the rabbit below, the rabbit weak and the hawk strong and powerful." With his hands Kockenoe gestured the movements of flight. "One spends most of its life flying in the air above, and the other below on the ground, running or hiding." He cleared his throat and asked, "Now which is evil and which is good?"

I searched my heart for the answer but could not decide. "Sometimes I have been frightened by the cry of the hawk, and in my dreams, sharp talons pierce my skin and carry me away to some fearsome place," I said. "But in other dreams, the prince who rescues me from danger comes in the shape of the Red-Tailed Hawk."

Nowedanah nodded. "Some would say that the hawk is evil, like darkness, but without darkness, how can we see the stars? I always wanted to be the hawk that flies above, but since last winters' long illness, I have learned from both. Without darkness we cannot appreciate the lights Cauhluntoowut gives us."[66]

"Cauhluntoowut?"

"Yes. Thy people call him Jehovah and you believe your souls meet him in the skies above." She turned to her husband and said, "Make clear our beliefs to her, Kockenoe, in the words she understands."

Kockenoe continued the account. "Our people believe that once their souls leave the body, they travel westward, where they are met with great rejoicing by others who have died."

Words struggled to get past the lump in my throat. "Do you think my mother will know me there?"

"Would that bring you joy?" Nowedanah laid her hand on mine. "We believe the Spirit of the Hawk can empower you to build bridges between thy ancestors and thy future descendants. You may not be honored and recognized for thy work here until long after you have crossed over."

Tears formed in my eyes, for I did not understand what work I had been given.

Kockenoe's solemn message continued, and I fixed it in my heart. "Never allow others to cause thee to lose sight of what is really important to thee! Trust in the messages the Spirit assigns to thy care and know that thy visions will bring blessings not only to thee, but also to many others!"

Eight
∾

ANNO DOM 1654
SOUTHAMPTON, LONG ISLAND, NEW YORK

Before my 15th birthday, Cousin Gideon returned from Harvard for a visit. The Fordham house was overjoyed to see him, but the pleasure was short-lasting for he and his father found a growing disparity within their discussions. I believe Uncle Robert had gradually moved toward the freedom to live a self-examined life and away from Puritan dogma. On the other hand, Gideon's strict Puritan beliefs had been supported and strengthened at Harvard College. When I openly joined in their argument during family discussion of the Sabbath sermon, Gideon acted as if I were heaping ashes upon his faith.

He turned to me, dark eyes flashing. "God's word says the good wife looketh well to the ways of her household. When will you learn your place? Do you never intend to become an honorable wife and mother? When will you bridle your tongue and learn to keep silence in subjection to those whom God has put at your head?"

Gideon turned and shook a clenched fist at his father. "How long, Sir, will you allow Mary to defy God by questioning the scriptures?"

Uncle Robert's mouth gaped opened. For a moment I thought he would strike Gideon, but then the deep wrinkle between his eyes relaxed, seeming to soften with tenderness. "Gideon, I must remind you that this is my house. It is not your place to—"

Gideon took a step backward, but his clenched fists did not loosen. "How long will you allow her to usurp the role of the male instead of surrendering to her God-given place as a woman?"

I wanted to cry out for the hurt I had caused between father and son. Gideon's face grew redder with each word. I could almost see the young minister of the future, pounding the pulpit and, with bitter lips, preaching hell and damnation to any who disagreed with his understanding of God's will.

Again Gideon raised his voice to his father. "How long, Father, will you permit this wayward girl to defile your house?"

I felt as if my heart were bleeding, wounded by the hateful arrows of my cousin's words. With tears streaming down my cheeks, I moved toward Gideon, wishing to ask his forgiveness, but he grabbed me by the arms and began shaking me. My amulet of red-tailed hawk feathers slipped out of its secret place beneath my bodice, and when he saw it, his face turned white as if a leech had sucked the blood out of his cheeks. "Thou art wearing a graven image? How long, Father, will ye shelter this daughter of Satan?"

A look of desolation and great sorrow shadowed Uncle Robert's face, a shadow that took my breath away. Puritans law based on Leviticus 20:9 from the Old Testament said, "A child who curses his or her parent shall be put to death." Surely he would not present Gideon, his beloved son, to the magistrate for trial! Fear stifled my breath.

Was it rage or love that made Uncle Robert's voice so soft I could barely hear him? "My son, forgive me if I have provoked you to wrath, but before you open your mouth again to seethe and shout and quote your accounting of the scriptures in my house, be sure you remember the fifth commandment: 'Honor your parents, so that you may live long in the land the Lord your God is giving you.'"

For a moment Gideon stood upright, shoulders back and fists clinched, face red as a blister. Finally, his posture changed, and anger seeped away like a spilled pitcher of water. "I am sorry, Father," he said, then turned away and entered his sleeping room. The door closed softly.[67]

The rest of the Fordham family sat speechless, their gaze moving from Gideon's door, to Uncle Robert's face, to me. I burned from the heat of their glances. But for the crackling of the fire, the great room where we sat was quiet as a grave.

Finally I could no longer bear the silence. "Uncle Robert, may I be excused to go to your study?" Once inside, I removed the amulet from my neck and tucked it away in the pocket of my apron. Perhaps Gideon was right to be upset with my wearing it. But to me it was not an object of worship but a memento of my friendship with our Shinnecock neighbors. "God," I prayed, "speak to me. Are they not also part of your creation? Did you not command us to love them as ourselves?"

In the stillness of the room, I heard only the voice of Kockenoe, the Shaman Nowedanah's husband. "Never allow others to cause you to lose sight of what is really important to you! Trust in the messages the Spirit assigns to your care...."

Taking a volume of John Calvin's *The Institutes* from the bookshelves, I dusted the aging leather cover but did not open it. In the last few years, I had searched through all 1200 pages, but the only mention of love I found was the love of righteousness and self-denial. If this great leader of the church omitted the second greatest commandment, I could not but question the Puritan way.

I took a seat in Uncle Robert's chair, thinking to read again that verse. On the desk his big Geneva Study Bible lay open to the book of Proverbs. A line he had marked caught my eye and provided a further answer to my questioning heart:

"Goe not foorth hastily to strife, lest thou know not what to doe in the ende thereof."[68]

The sun had gone from the sky, but before I had time to light a candle, I heard the clatter of advancing hooves, and then the call of the rider. "Are you home, Reverend Fordham? I fear there be sad news of John Carman, your dear friend and brother-in-law.[69]"

The family dissention was forgotten at the word that Uncle John, sailing home to Hempstead, had been stricken at sea and fallen overboard—lost and buried beneath the waves.[70] Uncle John Carman, who seemed always to be seeking greater religious liberty—or at least tolerance, had found peace at last. He was 48 years old. Surely he was too young to die. Too young to leave Aunt Florence and their six children—Abbie, Ben, John, Caleb, Thomas...and ten-year-old Joshua.

Uncle Robert dispatched Gideon to tell my father and siblings the sad news, and we gathered together at the meeting house to mourn the death of Uncle John Carman, Joshua's father.

In the quiet of this place of worship, Uncle Robert spoke in remembrance.

"Most of you did not know John Carman well, and none of you were here when he and my sister Florence arrived at the shores of this New World. John came first, in1631, as one of the investors in the Company of Husbandmen. He also came as a "familist" who followed the doctrine that religion lay in love, not in creeds, a dangerous theory and one liable to abuse. In 1632, John and Florence[71] became charter members of the church in Roxbury, and the next year he was admitted to the freeman's rights and took the freeman's oath.[72]

"I want to tell you of the man I knew:

"John Carman, as master of a ship of 180 tons, went from New Haven, Connecticut, laden with clapboards for the Canaries, being earnestly commended to the Lord's protection by the church there.

"On the way, he was set upon by a Turkish pirate ship of 300 tons and 26 pieces of ordnance and 200 men. He fought with her three hours, having but 20 men and but seven pieces of ordnance. His muskets were unserviceable with rust. The Turk lay across his hawse, so he was forced to shoot through his own hoodings, and even though these shots killed many Turks, their ship soon lay by his side and they boarded him with near 100 men.

"In the skirmish, the captain of the Turkish ship was killed. Fifty of his men were left on board. John and his men fought with those 50 hand to hand and slew so many of them that the rest leaped overboard.

"John had many wounds on his head and body, and divers of his men were wounded, yet but one slain; so with much difficulty he got to the island (being in view thereof), where he was very courteously entertained and supplied with whatsoever he wanted.

"Mr. Welde, John Carman's pastor at the church in Roxbury, was one of the most straitlaced of the Massachusetts Bay divines. Perhaps that added emphasis to John's constant search for tolerance and greater religious liberty.

"This honorable and brave man saw, as did I, the opportunity to establish a less restricted and more liberal community on Long Island. He sold his land in Roxbury, Lynn, and Sandwich, and induced a group of people to come with us to settle in Hempstead, in the middle west part of Long Island. We made a treaty with the Indians for this large tract of land, and in the winter of 1644, the Dutch confirmed our purchase by a patent that gave us full power to build temples of worship and exercise the reformed religion which we professed.

"God have mercy on the soul of this man who loved thee — our beloved father, brother, and uncle — John Carman. Amen."

Later in the week, when other relatives had gone home from the service remembering John Carman, Gideon packed for his return to school. After telling his family goodbye, he asked me that we might speak privately of his regret of the harsh words we had exchanged on the previous Sabbath.

"But, Mary, I must speak these words of warning." he said. "I hear thou hast brought jars of herbs from the savage Indians. Know ye not that ye could be arrested for owning these vessels judged by many to be instruments of witchcraft?" He placed his hand on my shoulder, and I saw the deep furrow that creased his brow as he continued his reproach. "I fear that thy mischief and creative tongue endanger both thy body and thy soul. If thou must speak, you should at least be telling the Shinnecock about the one true God." I heard no anger in his voice and saw none in his eyes. Only concern as he spoke. "Would thou not draw them from the dark night of heathenism to the bright light of the Puritan faith? In so doing, thou mayest raise these savages even to the heights we have attained."[73]

I could not bridle my tongue, and when I pointed out the similarities between the Puritan faith and the Shinnecock ideas of God and the devil, the drawn expression on Gideon's face and the stiff way he held his shoulders told me he was direly offended, yet his eyes held great sorrow.

"Mary," he said, "I am sore afraid that ye are not one of God's chosen."

"Then perhaps it matters not what I believe." Though my voice shook, I continued. "I reject the idea that the Shinnecocks are savages. And like Uncle John, I believe in love, not in creeds."

Gideon shook his head. "I cannot believe my father continues to defend thee." Without saying goodbye, he turned and left.

21st Century
Memory Catchers' Office

Suddenly, Grand-Mary, too, was gone, and I was left to transcribe her story of Gideon's visit. Hours later, I typed the last word, turned off the office light, and climbed the stair with only the monitor's ghostly glow illuminating my way.

Once in bed, I drifted to and fro from consciousness to a restless mosaic of sounds and colors—stormy waves and stark white burial sheets, the Shaman Nowedanah, shaking a long bony finger at me and saying, "Never allow others to cause you to lose sight of love. The bony finger morphed into a close-up of Gideon—red face and angry lips whispering as he pointed: "Thou art a witch!"

I roused enough to see my digital clock said 4:35. Filled with questions for Grand-Mary, I flipped on my night light and jotted them down.

Finally, I slept.

છ

The next morning, the aroma of bayberry told me that Grand-Mary was as eager as I to get back to work. After hurriedly dressing, I grabbed the notes I'd made in the middle of the night, dashed into the kitchen for a cup of coffee, and then down the hall to the office where Grand-Mary was waiting. She leaned over to retrieve the paper I had dropped.

"Phyllis, is this your writing? I can not read a word of it. No wonder you insist on taping my story instead of taking notes."

"Yes, it's hardly legible even to me. "

"So, what does this say?"

"Well, first of all, were Puritans in your day superstitious? Did they really believe in witchcraft?"

"Are not people in every age superstitious? Anything unknown gives rise to strange imaginings and beliefs, and I'll wager there are still some things unknown. When you think about it, it's only a short step from a negative faith in outlandish superstitions to a positive faith in God's word. 'The substance of things, which are hoped for, and the evidence of things which are not seen.'"

"That's from the Bible, isn't it?"

"Yes. Hebrews 11:1, I believe."

I turned on the recorder, and Grand-Mary continued.

Mid 1600s
Southampton, Long Island

Seventeenth century America was as superstitious as it was religious, and our Hamptons area was no exception: On the north side of Southampton Village were the Shinnecock Hills, a desolate wasteland. Even the most reckless wayfarer hesitated before crossing them. As the story goes, one dark and stormy night, a traveler defying all the spirits dared them to cross the hills. The next morning, he was found dead with nary a wound — except that of his missing tongue. Finally someone found it hanging on a prickly bush.[74]

Of course everyone in Southampton knew this was only a story. Otherwise the teller might have been tried for the offense of lying or drunkenness. In the town square where everyone could see, were the stocks. For lying, the penalty was five shillings or five hours in the stocks. For drunkenness, ten shillings for the first offense, twenty for the second, and thirty for the third offense.

I remember the summer when Thomas Veale's wife Sarah was held in court. For 'exorbitant words of imprecation,' she was sentenced to stand in the town square with her tongue pinched in a cleft stick.[75]

'Twas not the pain but the humiliation that rained down remorse and repentance, and oft it was the tongue that got a body into trouble. I could understand Gideon's warning to "bridle my tongue and keep silent, as becomes a woman." I truly was remorseful, for I had not only brought humiliation upon my own head, but also I had caused embarrassment to the whole Fordham family as they witnessed my disgraceful brazenness.

Most frightening to me was the trial brought forth by the tongue of poor little Lizzie Howell, though she was faultless. Not long since married, she gave birth to a baby girl, and one day, shortly after suckling the baby—perhaps it was the birthing fever that did it—she began carrying on and shrieking grievously.

"A witch! A witch! Now you are come to torture me because I spoke two or three words against you!"

According to her mother, poor Lizzie was totally out of her head, flailing her arms and crying. "Oh, mother, I am bewitched! There's a black thing at the foot of my bed, and Goody Garlick is at the corner."

That very evening Lizzie died.

The trial was soon the talk of the town. Goody Simons, who had been attending Lizzie, testified that the young mother "had once gotten terribly upset with Goody Garlick for being sharp-tongued with her."

According to Goody Simons, Lizzie had said to her, "Goody Garlick is a double-tongued woman! Did you not see her last night stand by the bed side ready to pull me in pieces? And she pricked me with pins."

Tongues wagged.

"My baby got sick after Goody Garlick fed her!"

"Did you hear of that child who died last week? And no one knows the cause."

"Our neighbor's fat sow and her piglets died during the birth last night."

"George's ox broke its leg Thursday last—right after he saw Goody Garlick pass by."

Everywhere I went, gossips were whispering about poor Lizzie—and about Goody Garlick. I heard one woman say that surely a witch was in their midst.[76] Looking around, I saw several others nod in agreement. And if one did not believe it, surely there were Puritan preachers to set them right.

John Calvin, himself, interpreting the first commandment,[77] wrote: "God will condemn to capital punishment all augurs, and magicians, and consulters with familiar spirits, and necromancers and followers of magic arts, as well as enchanters. And… God declares that He 'will set His face against all, that shall turn after such as have familiar spirits, and after wizards,' so as to cut them off from His people; and then commands that they should be destroyed by stoning."[78]

Lizzie's own father was heard to say that "Goody Davis starved her own child when she took an Indian child to suckle for lucre of a little wampum."

When local judges could not make a decision, the trial was moved to Hartford, Connecticut, where Goody Garlick escaped the death sentence. The jury found her not guilty.[79]

If my previous humiliation were not enough to quiet me, Goody Garlick's narrow escape was. Even Uncle Robert admitted that my behavior might be suspect in the eyes of some Southampton citizens. "You must watch your tongue, Mary, else you may be in danger of the same accusation."

Nine

~

ANNO DOM 1656
SOUTHAMPTON, LONG ISLAND, NEW YORK

In June, two months before my 17th birthday, my papa,
accompanied by my brother Luddie, came to say he had
found a suitable husband for me. The idea, to me, was
absurd, and I could barely hold back my laughter. I was
not looking for a husband. But the pleased-with-himself
look on Papa's face restrained me from expressing my
disdain although he may have guessed by the look he
saw in my eyes. At any rate, he began to press his case.
The Reverend Abram Hardwick, a Harvard-educated
minister visiting family in Southampton, was searching
for a suitable wife.

Luddie, too, seemed excited about the news. "He's
well-respected. Tall and handsome, too." Luddie's eyes
twinkled and he patted me on the head as if we were
children again, back in England playing Princess Mary
and Sir John Manners. He grinned and said, "Your prince
has come to carry you away on his white horse."

When the honorable Abram Hardwick came to call, he
was indeed, as Luddie had said, tall and handsome, with

a massive head sculpted as if it were overburdened with knowledge. Aunt Alice planned a dinner and invited several of the upstanding members of the community to come and meet him, and at their eagerness, it certainly seemed that the Reverend Hardwick was well-respected. After learning that Thom Scudder and the *Sea Hawk* were docked at Mecox Bay, Uncle Robert suggested that he also be included on the guest list. It had been nearly eight years since he had brought my family from Boston Harbor to Long Island, but I knew I would recognize him.

Taking a new role as an adult, after helping set the table with Aunt Alice's treasured pewter plates, I was to sit at the dinner table beside the Reverend Hardwick. Extremely respectful toward me, he held my chair as I took my place.

Goody Gabbler, dressed in a collar of lace that bespoke a station beyond her means, positioned herself across the table from me, her meek-mannered husband at her right. In her usual way, she set about learning everything she could concerning the honored guest. "Reverend Hardwick, are you married?"

He glanced my way, and I saw sadness in his eyes. "My dear wife died last year," he said.

Goody Gabbler continued her quest. "And have you children?"

"Yes," he said. "Four."

"Little ones? Babes?" Silently my thoughts echoed her question. Was I up to the task?

"Ah, yes. Reuben is but a year old, and the oldest is seven. "Perhaps you know, my good woman, that I have been invited to speak at meeting house on the Sabbath, but what brought me here was a different matter entirely." He smiled and looked at me. "I believe the good

Lord has led me here for a specific purpose. My poor children need a mother, and I would take a wife." Gently, he laid his hand over mine, and then released it to pick up his spoon and carry on with his meal.

Goody Gabbler gasped in surprise, and as she paused in her constant yammering, Thom Scudder took up the questioning. "Sir, have you the means to support a wife in goodly fashion?

For a moment I thought Reverend Hardwick might suggest it unseemly for a yeoman like Thom to treat the guest of honor so rudely, but he merely took another sip of ale and cleared his throat.

"My parsonage is near Salem, from whence I come. It is a lovely dwelling, a little larger than this one, with many rooms and real glass windows donated by the Conklin's, master glassmakers descended from the Concini family of Florence, Italy. Thou may have heard of them?"

Goody Gabbler's eyes were large. "Oh, my, such a job to care for a large home. And all those children to do for. Could a young, inexperienced woman fulfill the duties the Lord expects of her?" She looked at me and smirked, then turned again to the Reverend. "Of course thou may find someone like my lovely daughter who has been trained since a child to fulfill her womanly duties. With her generous dowry, she will make a fine match when the right man comes along."

When Reverend Hardwick replied, I heard a ring of re-proach in his voice. "I assure thee, my good woman, that I have property and wealth enough to provide a maid, as well as the nurse who now cares for my children. I am quite prepared to be the husband God decrees." Again he laid his hand over mine, but he continued looking di-rectly at Goody Gabbler. "Have you not read Ephesians

5:23? 'For the husband is the head of the wife, and he is her savior.' The good estate of the wife depends on the man, so that this submission is not only just, but also very profitable."

A savior? His different interpretation of the scripture was challenging, like a clarion call to splendid discussions we might have as we sat at our own dinner table.

He led the talk away from his personal affairs to the merits of the Puritan faith. Women, I knew well, were to keep silent on such matters, so I did my best. I did not wish to offend the suitor my father had chosen, though agreement was oft not within me. I suppose I spoke too freely.

As was his assumed right, the handsome Reverend Hardwick smiled at me as if I were a young woman in need of discipline, and then turned to his left to speak to Aunt Alice. As he continued his meal, with each bite he took, his right forearm brushed against mine. A warm blush flooded my being and my arm tingled where he touched me. A most pleasant feeling.

ဢ

On 10 June 1656, the night before Sabbath, I scarce could sleep. Finally, with a pure white angel pointing the way, a handsome man galloped into my dream,. With flourish of his purple and gold cape, he called out to me. "Princess Mary, I have come to save thee."

I awoke in a blur of reality and dream. Was it really a savior I longed for? The question faded as I recalled the tingling that flooded my senses at his touch. His smile reached an empty spot in my heart that until now, I had not known existed.

That morning, carrying my mother's Bible and a sharpened stick of lead for making notes, I took my place in the Ludlam family pew. When the rest of the family arrived and found their usual seats, my father, taking notice of my timely appearance, nodded his approval.

Never was I so attentive as when Rev. Abram Hardwick rose. He could have been a prince, regal in bearing, bringing good news to his subjects.

"From Song of Solomon 2:10-13, I read these Holy Words to you." He paused, giving the congregation time to turn to the scripture. In a voice sweet as honey, he began reading, and though he barely glanced my way, his words caressed my heart:

The voice of your beloved;
Behold he cometh leaping upon the mountains,
skipping among the trees.
Your welbeloved spake and said unto you,
Arise, my love, my faire one, and come thy way.
For beholde, winter is past:
the raine is changed, and is gone away.
The flowers appear in the earth:
The time of the singing of birdes is come,
and the voyce of the turtledove is heard in our land.
The fig tree hath brought foorth her yong figges:
and the vines with their small grapes have cast a savor:
Arise my love, my faire one, and come away.

Mr. Hardwick paused and then spoke with authority.

"The voice of my beloved—this is spoken of Christ who took on our nature. Behold he cometh leaping upon the mountains, skipping among the trees."

The minister's voice became stronger and more passionate.

"In this scripture, the wicked daughters of this world are as winter, producing only dried thorns in man's flesh. With great wisdom, Solomon looks to the future—the time when the winter is past."

Mr. Hardwick placed his hands, one on each side of the pulpit, and raised his voice.

"Oh, men of God, hasten the coming of springtime. Forbid the trifling pursuits of winter—the woman who wastes time in trifling visits with small departures from truth."

The sweetness had disappeared from his words and they touched my heart only as piercing arrows of disappointment.

"Oh, ye men of God, know ye not that ye are the vine that groweth in springtime? The woman is not your equal. God created her the weaker sex, and immediately she proved her sinful willfulness."

The Reverend Mr. Abram Hardwick certainly thought he had the answers. The only thing I knew for certain was that he didn't! My eyes smarted and blurred with underlying fury as I put away my writing utensils as his voice rose even higher.

"It is beyond the ken of my understanding to conceive, how a woman as ill-shapen as a shotten-shell-fish should have such little wit as to tempt men by transclouting herself with Salome's veils."

I had just read *The Simple Cobler of Aggawam* from Uncle Robert's new shipment of books, and knew that Reverend Hardwick's ill-shapen words were plagiarized from the *Cobler*. Then he switched similes in midstream.

"She is like a fox that cometh to you in the night to steal the seed of your grapes. Men, control the mouths of these vixens while they are young, when they begin to show their malice, before they destroy the vine of the Lord."

The preacher's face reddened, and he began pounding the pulpit, a different man than the honey-voiced prince I had first seen. For a moment, he fixed his eyes on Good-man Gabbler and his wife.

"Husband, control your wife as the Son of Man controls the church, for she is stubborn and opinionated. God's will is inscrutable, as is a husband's will, and disobedi-ence will lead contentious women to the depths of hell."

I glanced at my father, sitting in the pew across from me. His lips were pursed in a hard line. Surely he would understand my rejection of the mate he had chosen for me. Surely he recognized that I had no place in this man's life.

Following the afternoon service, the Reverend Adam Hardwick approached me and whispered in my ear. "Come take a ride with me, my dear. We have much to discuss."

The honey was back in his voice, and I wanted to be-lieve that his Sabbath tirade had been a temporary aber-ration. Wishing not to disturb the heedful congregation, with a mixture of trepidation and hope, I took his arm. In silence we walked to the grazing pen, and there we mounted our horses.

"Let us ride to the bay by thy father's mill," he sug-gested.

"Mecox Bay," I said. "Do you know the name 'Mecox,' is taken from the Shinnecock Indians for 'flat or plain country'? In 1640, when Edward Howell[80] announced he would build a mill for the grinding of grain into flour, the colonists expected him to construct a wind mill, but he had a different idea. He made his choice of land so that it included a lively stream which emptied into Mecox Bay. My father purchased the mill from him a few years ago. I'm sure this is the legacy he will leave my brothers and their sons to come."

"H-m-m. What a lot you know for one so young, and a female, too. Have you studied much?"

"I learned much from the fine books in Uncle Robert's library—" I flushed with modesty, not at all sure Mr. Hardwick approved of my answer, but I plunged ahead with the truth—"and from listening in on my cousins' classes. I can do numbers adequately, and I read and write, although only a little in Greek and Latin."

For the remainder of the three-mile ride, there was silence until we reached a secluded place where we could sit and converse privately, a leafy bower near the water's edge. Like a true gentleman, he helped me dismount and then secured our horses. The fury I had seen and heard earlier had faded from his eyes, and his smile was gentle when he spoke. "I can arrange my affairs to remain here for three weeks. We can get to know each other while waiting for our banns to be published."

Recalling the content of his sermon, I was not sure he would want to know me. Believing as he did, could he abide a wife who thought for herself, whose delight was to study and freely discuss the Word?

Above us, I heard the cry of a red-tailed hawk. As I looked up, it circled and then darted up into the sky and disappeared.

Screwing my courage to the sticking place, I spoke my mind. "Mr. Hardwick, why do you wish to marry me? You are a man of material worth and can hardly be interested in the dowry my father offered."

He hesitated and cleared his throat. "I hear good things about you, Mary. How you care for your blind cousin Joshua. How you have learned the art of housewifery. You have the skills of reading and writing. Under my direction, you can supervise my children in the lessons I assign them. It is proper that a woman learn to read the Good Book, and I would be proud to claim a wife who can sign her name…if ever there be need for it."

He offered no pretense of love.

Taking my face in his hands, he looked directly into my eyes, and I trembled, but it was not the tingling tremble of the previous night. His purple and gold cape had disappeared. His princely white steed had gone out to pasture. The fire was out. My disappointment was such that I could not hold back the tears.

Standing, he pulled me into his arms. His embrace became tighter, and he moved his body back and forth, brushing against my bosom. "Thou art my bride," he whispered. His breath ragged, he began panting like Qolucksee's dog did when he rushed to greet us.

"Let me go," I screamed, but when I tried to pull away, he threw me to the ground, fell upon me, and….

My disgrace was complete.

On weak and trembling legs, I rose to my feet and turned my head away as he shamelessly pulled up his breeches. When he attempted again to press me to him, I backed out of reach, and he swore at me.

"Depart from me, thou consort of Satan!" he shouted. "Thou art the daughter of Eve who has tempted me to enjoy your fruit, and I am drunk with the wine of your fornication." With a shove he cast me away, and I fell headfirst into Mecox Bay.

Gasping for air, I raised my head from the water, bitter with the waste from the mill. I could hear the receding clatter of horse's hooves on the dirt path, but the sound of lapping waves told me I was not alone.

Spluttering and spitting bits of sea lettuce from my mouth, I shook the water from my face, and opened my eyes to see the boat pulled in to shore — the *Sea Hawk*. Waving in the breeze was the banner I recalled from the time the Scudder boys carried my family and me to our new home on Long Island.

As I arose from the water, the disarray of my sopping hair mingled with seaweed and fell in tangled strands over my shoulders, hiding the wet fabric of my bodice as it clung to my body.

I heard laughter, and a masculine voice called, "If it isn't my Golden Aphrodite."

It had been years since Thom Scudder had rescued me from the waters of Boston Harbor, but he remembered. "I've oft imagined you rising again from the sea," he said, stepping into the brackish water, shoes and all, "and here you are, transformed from childlike nymph into a beautiful woman."

He retrieved my white bonnet from the water, and held out a hand to me, but his untimely laughter greatly annoyed me, and I jerked away.

"Prithee, do not think me a pathetic child," I said. "I do not need a man to save me." Embarrassed that I had spoken out so ungraciously, my resentment drained away, but a mixture of other emotions crowded in. I knew not whether to laugh or cry.

Thom Scudder grinned, and offering me his hand again, he led me out of the water. "Your face is as pink and pearly as a seashell!" he teased. Carefully he wrapped me in his cloak and held me, warming my shivering body, soaked to the skin. With a gentle hand he brushed the water from my brow, smoothing away the hot tears that ran in rivulets down my cheeks.

"What fool did this to you?" he said, avoiding my eyes. "The coward stole away when he saw me coming."

I could cast no stone. I could only shake my head. Once again my tears came unbidden.

"Don't you weep, Mary, sweeting. I'll get the blackguard for you and haul him into court!"

Fear and shame left me speechless, but the Goody Gossips would have plenty to say. How could I defend myself against a charge of lying, or worse, fornication?

Too much had happened all at once. I was chilled and trembling with anxiety and exhaustion, so Thom Scudder insisted on accompanying me back to the Fordham house, to make sure I arrived safely. He loosened my mare, and helped me on its back so I could ride behind him. There I leaned my head against Thom's broad shoulders. Before we reached Southampton Village, my shaking had stopped, but I was tired to the bone.

My father and siblings, who had spent the late afternoon with Uncle Robert's family, were just leaving as we arrived. "Where's the Reverend Hardwick?" my father asked, then noticed my bedraggled appearance.

Thom silenced further questions with his hand. "Mary's not injured. But she needs to rest now. Perhaps tomorrow…"

"Yes, prithee, tomorrow, Papa, I must speak to you."

With concern-filled eyes, he nodded in agreement "We'll go on home, but I'll be back early tomorrow. Thom, is the *Sea Hawk* docked at Mecox?"

He nodded. "Moon's bright tonight. Goods on board due in Hempstead on the morrow. Time to go."

"Then come, ride with us to the mill. Spare yourself the walk."

As soon as they had gone, Aunt Alice led me to my room. "Mary, do you need to talk?"

When I shook my head, she helped me remove my damp clothing and slip my night gown on over my head. Tucked into my soft feather bed, I immediately found asylum in an uneasy, sleep.

I awoke, grateful to the grey clouds shrouding the rays of the morning sun. So heavy was my burden that I felt I could not bear the light of day. I had barely dressed when Papa arrived, but before I had decided what I must say to him, there was a ruckus of barking dogs in the yard, and the sound of horses' hooves turning into the Fordham place. A loud knocking at the door came, and when Uncle Robert opened it, the men who entered identified themselves as authorities from Massachusetts.

"Where is the scoundrel?" shouted one of the men. "If the villain abideth here, bring the gallows bird out!"

Uncle Robert advanced toward them and held out his hand. "Whom do you seek? And who are you?"

The official who seemed to be in charge said, "We are constable's men from Salem, here to arrest the Reverend Abram Hardwick on a charge of rape and murder, brought by Judge Goodwin. Is Hardwick here?"

The most belligerent of the men began shouting. "I am the honorable Judge Jeremiah Goodwin of Salem, father of Annie whom the Reverend Hardwick employed as his children's nurse." Purplish veins stood out on the Judge's neck and forehead. "The Reverend must pay the price for his sins." Like a hunter searching for his quarry, the judge's wild gaze darted around the room. "My Annie heard him shouting, 'God will justify my vengeance!' Twas he that stifled the breath of his own wife when she spake out 'gainst his sinful enticement of my Annie."

"Where is the man?"

My oldest cousin answered. "I have searched his room, and although his baggage is here, I did not find him."

"Robert, where is the grey horse you gave him to ride yesterday?" Papa asked. "That horse was missing from the corral when I dismounted a few minutes ago."

"The blackguard has escaped!"

Bent on retribution, the men, convinced that their adversary had fled, jerked on the reins of their horses and sped away with Judge Goodwin in the lead. "The hangman's noose is too good for the likes of him!"

A flood of emotions filled my being—a strange combination of rage and relief. My face burned, but a frozen boulder of despair pressed down on my chest. Trembling, I grasped the edge of the table to steady my wobbly legs, then turned to avoid questioning eyes and quickly darted through the door to Uncle Robert's study where I took refuge. The conversation with Papa would have to wait for another day.

Four days later, when Thom Scudder returned from delivering goods to Hempstead, he stopped at Southampton to give Uncle Robert a missive from his sister, Florence:

6 June 1656
Dear Bro. Robert and my dear sister-in-law, Alice, The death of my beloved John Carman hath left me in good circumstance, but quite alone, for only Abby and wee Thomas are yet at home. I will this month wed John Hicks, a well-known settler

*in Hempstead, who is eager to manage my share of the estate.[81]
I am now able to care for my son Joshua.*
*Captain Thom Scudder assures me that he will happily bring
Joshua with him when he makes another trip to Merocke Bay in
Hempstead. I have great trust in the Scudder family for they
attended Salem's First Church when we lived at Roxbury. The
two towns are not far apart, and the Scudders were our
neighbors. Good people. I know Joshua hath grown in both
wisdom and stature in your care, and I offer my sincere thanks.
I ask the blessings of God on you and your family.*
Your sister, Florence Carman

Uncle Robert read the missive aloud and then turned to
Joshua. "Young man, it's time for thee to go home."

"Is Mama well now? Will she be there?" A slow sweet
smile spread across Joshua's countenance. "I hardly remember Mama's face, but I do remember the smell of her
bubbling halibut stew and the scent of pine logs burning
in the fireplace, and…

"I remember playing in a pond with my sister… and
almost getting lost on Hempstead Plains. The grass there
was taller than Abbie…higher than I could reach.…

"If I listen carefully, I can still hear my baby brother
crying.…" Joshua paused, as if deep in thought. "It's
been so long…Baby Philip will be in breeches already.
Five years old, and he won't even know me." Joshua began jumping up and down and then started giggling.
"Sure will be good to have a little brother."

Thom spoke directly to him. "According to your father's will, your brothers, Caleb and John are to care for
the property your father left you, and if you wish, you
can live with them."[82]

"Father's gone, isn't he?" Joshua's breath quickened as
reality dawned like never before. Pulling away, he es-

caped into the keeping room. I followed and found him sitting on his special stool by the hearth, resting his head against the brick facing of the fireplace. When he heard my footsteps, he raised his small chin and swiped away the tears with his sleeve. "I'll miss you, Mary —"

"Yes," I said, swallowing a lump in my throat. "We'll miss you, too, Joshua."

" — but it's time for me to go home to Mama." He held out his hand, and together we walked back into the great room.

"There you are, Joshua. Plans to make now." Thom spoke as if talking man to man, but he kept glancing at me. "You ready to go the first part of July? I have goods to pick up in Boston and several deliveries to make before I return to Hempstead," Thom said, and then turned to me. "About four weeks away, Mary. That long enough? No doubt Joshua will need you to help gather his belongings."

As we moved back to the great room, Joshua thought for a moment and then his lips spread in a grin. "So I can go to the Village Fair before I leave. Right, Captain Scudder?"

"The fair?"

"Yes," I explained. "We go every year. The whole family will be there. Papa and my brothers and sisters, too."

Cousin Nathan rubbed his stomach. "All Southampton brings their wares to sell or trade. You can sample the goods and buy whatever you want." Nathan was fourteen and always hungry.

Uncle Robert smiled. "Joshua loves the hullabaloo of the fair almost as much as he enjoys tasting and smelling the samples — Indian corn, summer wheat, oats, barley, and beans. Turnips, potatoes, and cauliflower and juicy strawberries are there to fill the senses. Maple syrup too, if anyone has it left by now."

"And maybe molasses taffy." Cousin Hannah licked her lips. "All you want to drink, too. Wine or cider, beer or ale."

"I'm glad you can stay a while yet, Joshua." Aunt Alice put her arms around him. "The Village Fair begins the first Tuesday of July each year," she said, looking Thom's way.

"And it lasts four whole days," Joshua added. "Maybe you can come, too, Captain Scudder."

Thom brushed the dark lock of hair from his forehead. The corners of his generous mouth twitched upward, and he glanced my way.

Remembering my mother's story of how she met Papa at the Scarborough Fair years ago, I felt a blush rising in my cheeks. I ducked my head, embarrassed by the far-fetched comparison I had pictured. Tarnished and un-worthy as I was, I could not hope for such a happy end-ing. Abruptly, I bolted to the door. "Time to feed the chickens," I said, excusing myself from the room.

I should not have chosen such a mindless chore. My fa-natical thoughts persisted louder than the cacophony of the hens' clucking and squawking. A rooster, reminding me that this was his clutch, strutted toward me. Brazen and fearless, he began scolding me, fluttering his wings and pecking at my shoes. I backed off.

"Shoo! Shoo away!" a familiar voice called behind me. "Only thing worse than being pecked by a jealous rooster is being attacked by an ornery old settin' hen." Thom's eyes twinkled with amusement. "Can't believe you're scared of a crowin' bird." His lopsided grin altered, and he spoke with solemnity. "Seems to me you're one of the most courageous women I ever met. 'Tis a rare woman who dares to live life by her own light as you seem to do."

"What do you know about my light, Thom Scudder? Some tittle-tattler been talking to you?"

He raised his brows at my question. "Remember the day your aunt invited me to join the family dinner given in honor of Reverend Hardwick? Think your Uncle Robert was taking my measure that day…" He paused and laughed, "but I was measuring you."

At first I was not sure if he was serious or teasing.

"Come sit beside me on the bench whilst we talk," he said. "By my measure, I think we can both fit here."

His comment annoyed me, but he ignored my flash of irritation.

"Speaking out at the dinner as you did was hardly the accepted way for the average Puritan woman. Showed you live by your own understanding, not that which was forced upon you. You may see things differently, but you have to trust in something—destiny, life, hard work, wealth or status, God, whatever. I admire the way you think for yourself."

My irritation was fast disappearing, but I could not resist a bit of mockery. "You, Thomas Scudder, appear to embody all the positive values held high in the community, but are you not a shameless heretic if you trust in anything but the God of all Puritans?

Again, that infectious laugh. "True that I strive for money or status. Good Puritans believe in ambition, hard work, and an intense striving for success. They tend to feel that earthly success is a sign of God's election. I know not whether I am "saved" and among the elect who will go to heaven, but worldly success assures me that I am furthering God's plans."

"Oh, ho, old man, 'tis a sermon you preach, and it's not even the Sabbath." Thom Scudder did not seem to mind my taunts, and in truth, he seemed still young for a man of forty years. "And is it not God's plan for you to re-plenish the earth? Where are your children, Mr. Scud-der?"

"I confess to you, Mary, I have waited long. There's more to life than achieving success in business."

Although I answered not, it seemed to me that he was well on his way to reaching whatever he desired and thereby furthering God's plan.

"Got to find what you love, Mary. That's as true for thy work as for thy mate. I want a relationship that gets bet-ter and better through the years. An exceptional woman with intelligence and a mind of her own. That's what I've waited for. The day I saw thee, bedraggled but beautiful, rising from the waters of Mecox Bay, I knew." He hesi-tated, and when he turned to me, I saw the yearning in his eyes.

Frightened, I looked away, then felt his hand on my shoulder. A gentle touch.

"Think I don't know what happened the day you fell into Mecox bay? I know. Didn't get there in time to save your innocence, but I was there when he shoved you. I saw him as he ran away. 'Twas not your fault, Mary."

His words let loose within my chest an overwhelming wave of relief. Suddenly I had the freedom to breathe. Tears ran down my cheeks, soothing as summer rain.

"Thou art a good man, Thom Scudder, but if you are asking me…. My answer is no. Though I was dipped in the water of the bay, I still came out tarnished."

"Not thy fault, Mary," he repeated.

I turned to him and saw him shaking his head, a look of perplexity in his eyes.

He leaned forward and kissed me ever so lightly. "Thou art an amazing, complex woman, Mary."

Noticing the angle of the sun in the sky, he rose from the wooden bench. "Work to do. Goods to deliver. Tell Joshua I'll be back for the first day of the fair." With that he spun away, headed in the direction of the bay where his ship was docked.

Ten

༯

ANNO DOM 1657
SOUTHAMPTON, LONG ISLAND, NEW YORK

The next few weeks were a paradox of anticipation and dread. I enjoyed Joshua's exhilaration as he looked forward to attending the fair and then returning home to Hempstead. I shared his sadness at saying goodbye to all the family and friends in Southampton, and his trepidation at meeting John Hicks, his mother's new husband. He looked forward to Captain Scudder's return—and so did I, but with considerable apprehension.

I feared Thom Scudder's attention. What if he talked to Papa; repeated the words of acceptance he had spoken to me?

What if he told Papa what happened the day I fell into the bay?

That knowing all my blots and blemishes, he still accepted me?

That he wanted a partner with intelligence and a mind of her own?

That, knowing all this, I still refused him?

How could I explain to Papa why I must refuse?

I entered Uncle Robert's study and took a piece of parchment, a quill, and my Bible from the shelf. I'd make a list of reasons why I must refuse.

Though hope against hope filled my mind, I dare not trust my quill to admit such far-fetched possibilities. Too many doubts prevented me, calling to mind the poem Anne Bradstreet sent to my mother when she found her own womanly talents lacking. Soon, my words turned into a poem, following Anne Bradstreet's pattern, but substituting my own doubts in certain lines:

Doubt and Fear
Does Janus live within him, frowns and smiles,
Yet values not such female wits and guiles?
My quest for question's answers, reprimand,
And say, a needle better fits my hand?
If what I doe proves oft not good, perchance,
Could any mate with surety advance?
O, does he yearn for common country mate,
Who rises 'fore the sun and slaves till late?
What if I cannot serve when stabbing pain
Comes fast within my weary legs again?
Could I become the wife to toil and spin,
Submitting to a husband's needs, no end?
Lay down my lovely Bible, book and quill,
For tedious deeds the nights and days fulfill?
Could I, through birthing pangs and pains prevail
And time and time again endure travail?
My mama bled and died, she gave her life;
Can I become self-sacrificing wife
Or hold a babe close to my milk-filled breast
With little time from dusk to dawn for rest?

I paused to dip my quill in the ink, considered my words closely, and then continued the poem.

But most of all could he forget the stain
That racked my soul with unforgiving pain?
Will rain of irksome tears forgiveness move,
Or water of my tedious tears quench love?
How could he 'cept my sinful rebel part,
Content to hold me near him, heart to heart?

Perhaps Papa would understand if I showed him the words of my poem. Perhaps Thom Scudder would understand why I must say no.

Late on the eve before the fair, as we were laying out the evening meal, Uncle Robert opened the door to the Captain's knock.

"Welcome back, Thom Scudder," he said as he held out his hand and then invited Thom to sit. "You're later than I expected. Was your trip successful?"

Thom's cheeks seemed to have fallen into deep grooves, and he appeared unusually tired and worn. "Terrible trip! Saw something yesterday I never want to see again.

"You ran into trouble?"

Thom took a deep breath, and slowly shook his head. "Stopped at Plymouth to take on a load of goods bound for Hempstead. Business took me to the center of town, where I heard the most terror-filled screams—" His voice broke, and it was a minute before he could go on.

"She was red haired. Young like Mary." A spasm crossed Thom's face as a stone convulses the still water of a pool. "Asked the blighter next to me what the poor girl had done and he just sneered. Without the slightest scruple, he told me that the vixen's name was Mary Everett. Said he saw her tried last month, a common whore, convicted of fornication.

"With what proof? says I. And he told me the dead babe was proof enough. Hideous and misshapen, it was.

"Then an oafish man with skin pocked like a walnut husk spoke up, eager to tell the vicious tale. He said the snivelin' girl had been sentenced to stand for an hour with a rope 'bout her neck, an' t'other end cast over the gallows in Town Square. The hateful man seemed to think that should have taught the girl a lesson. Oblivious to the girl's suffering, the man gnawed greedily on a chunk of bread and cheese, licking drool from his lips.

"Another of the bloodthirsty audience, an old hag, grinned as she told me the girl had got 30 lashes at the public post. I can still see her toothless leer and the delight in her shrill voice. 'Blood trickled down the little Jezebel all the way to the street,' says she."

Thom paused and wiped his brow. "A red-nosed man with watery eyes took up the story then. Said a crowd of them stripped her to the waist, followed her at the cart's tail, and whipped her through the town. 'Can ya' believe, the wicked chit was still rebellious, wouldna' tell who the father was,' says he. 'Jus' clenched her teeth and said she'd druther die! Then the impertinent little twit wiped her dirty snivlin' nose and asked what any of us knew of pain or torment, or aught else. Made Judge Percy so angry he ordered her to wear a badge two-inches big, cut out in cloth of a different color to her clothes, and sewed upon her upper garment on the outside of her arm, or on her back, in open view.'

"I turned away from the man, but he grabbed my arm, eager to finish the story. 'You'd think that'd be 'nough to make her confess, but no! Ya don't see 'er wearin' any letter now, do ye? So today, she's bein' burned on the face with a hot iron,' says he. 'That's what all the screamin's about.'"

Thom's hands fisted against his jacket as he continued the gruesome story. "I started to protest. 'Isn't that too —' but a red-haired man with a cold, shut look shoved his hand out to stop me, indignant that I would question the law. Told me to read my Bible where it says, 'If a daughter be taken in whoredom and dishonor the name of her father, she shall be burnt with fire." Thom, unsteady on his feet, shook his head forcefully as if to clear the scene from his memory.

Uncle Robert put his arm around Thom's shoulder. "Alice, get out the ale. Looks like we need it tonight."

Mugs were brought out, and the lines in Thom's face relaxed a bit in spite of the shadow in his eyes.

Suddenly a small boy bounded in the door. "Captain Scudder! You're back! Now we can go to the fair!"

Thom took another sip of ale and smiled. "Told you I'd be here, Joshua. Are you ready to go?"

Joshua nodded, his wide grin changing to a pout when he heard Aunt Alice calling.

"Young man, if you're planning on going to the fair in early morning, you'd best get to bed."

"But I'm not —"

The man he idolized interrupted. "See you in the morning, Joshua."

As the rest of us went to our sleeping rooms, Uncle Robert led Thom Scudder into his office to talk. Not until later did I recall that I had left my poem lying open on the desk.

෫ා

Before the first streaks of dawn lit up the sky, Joshua was up and dressed and rousing the family from their beds. "It's Tuesday. Time to go to the fair!"

My young Fordham cousins were as excited as he, and I was little more capable of containing my own eagerness. Still, over an hour passed at the fair before Thom managed to separate himself from his small admirer. I watched him as he eased his way down the rows of wares to the spot where I was choosing cloth and thread and an emerald ribbon to trim the dress I would sew from the mint-sprigged cloth I had found.

"You think I may be Janus, eh?" Thom wrinkled his brow, scowling as he spoke. In the flicker of a moment his face broke into a teasing grin, and I could only blush.

He fingered the cloth I was choosing and looked at me with mischievous eyes. "So, a needle does fit your hand?" I ducked my head.

"I like your words, Mary. Did you think I'd not stand for poetizing? It's not a quiddling occupation, but the very expression of your soul."

To my surprise, his speech was no longer clipped, quite at odds with his usual banter.

"I would ask no more of you than what I could give, both wit and smiles," he said softly. "Put your doubts behind you, Mary. Together we could grow and reap a fine harvest, me thinks."

He took my hand, and under the watchful eyes of the Southampton village, he strolled with me through the market displays, greeting with a friendly wave the many smiling citizens he'd met beforehand at Papa's mill.

"I took no time to break fast this morning, and it's near noon. Are you hungry?"

I laughed, for I was filled with happiness, and my thoughts were not of food.

"Going through town this morning, down at the end of the street I saw men tending a pit filled with roast pig," he told me. "Let's try that out."

As we walked along the cobblestone way, never before had I known such contentment.

Thom stopped at a booth with metal wares. "Look at these pewter plates, Mary, and cups to match, 'graved with scripture. *'Many waters cannot quench love. S of S 8:7.* My mother would love something like this." He looked at me, one dark eyebrow raised. "She's a lot like you, Mary. Her strong opinions oft exasperate my father, but they have a love that abides in spite of troubled waters."

A loving son, I thought. I smiled at him and nodded. "She'll treasure them."

After an agreement on the barter, the artisan wrapped the gift and handed it to Thom.

When he turned back to me, his merry brown eyes seemed barely able to hold back his pleasure. "For you, Mary, sweeting," he said. "These will serve us for years to come. Someday we'll have a mantel where they will stand as a reminder of this special day."

In the hurly burly of the crowded fair, a clear voice sounded in my ears, as if God himself were speaking. I held my breath, and Thom cocked his head as if he, too, were listening:

"Didn't I promise you I would do a new thing? Now it shall spring forth; shall ye not know it? I make a way in your wilderness, and create fresh rivers in your desert.[83]"

A pristine hope leapt up within me.

With a lift of his shoulders and tilt of his chin, Thom took my arm and led me toward our destination.

Suddenly my legs began trembling, not with the gripping pain so long accustomed, but as if my bones had turned to water.

"Wouldst thou sit a while, Mary? Come, here is a bench beside Fordham manor. Rest a while."

I sat, and trying to overcome the quavering I felt within, I took a deep breath. A sorry decision, for immediately the smell of roasting pig, fat and greasy, overwhelmed me, and my skimpy breakfast of samp came roiling forth, spewing onto my skirt and shoes. Again I retched, and darkness overtook me.

When I awoke, Thom was hovering while Aunt Alice, wet linen towel in hand, gently wiped my face. Her eyes were wide, questioning. Behind her, I saw an instant of shocked revelation flicker like summer lightning over Thom's face. His color paled. His green and gold flecked eyes were glassy with tears. I did not understand.

Courteously, Thom spoke. "Goodwife Fordham, perhaps Mary would like to rest. May I accompany her into your home? We have things to discuss."

Not until I was comfortably seated on the cot in the study did Thom speak again, and then it was bit by bit, as if he'd rather swallow his awesome words than give voice to them.

"Mary, you were young yet when your mother died, and too young when your Aunt Alice—" He stopped, and then started again. "You have never met my beloved sister Elizabeth, and I have not had chance to tell you the news so full my mind was of other things." Thom paused, swallowed hard. "On the way down to Southampton, I passed by New Haven where she and Samuel live. I have oft been there, and seen her suffer the expectancy of their nine children. Each time, at the beginning, she was direly ill at the smell of roasted pig, so ill she could seldom prepare the meal without help. Roast pig, Mary."

For a moment there was silence as I struggled for understanding; then a staggering sense of violation assailed me—loss and grief and isolation. My fingers clawed and twisted in the folds of my apron as my dreams spiraled out of control like a pelican with a broken wing.

"Never fear, sweeting," he says. "Nothing is lost, only changed."

Misery welled up from my tight chest. Suddenly I had a strange feeling. I'd known this would happen. I could not hold back my cries. "Oh, now, is my name to be Mary Everett? Shall I be burned for my transgression?"

Gently he answered. "Remember that heat may burn, but it can also warm a household, or draw family together. You are my family, from this day forth, you and your babe."

"How is it possible that you still want me?"

"I won't argue about whether or not this is possible. I know it is, because this feeling within me, this caring for you, is so big I can hardly hold it inside."

Thom wrapped a soft quilt round my shoulders. "Lay down your head and rest, Mary," he said as if he would brook no argument. "Tomorrow things will be different."

The next morning Thom left very early, and I knew not where he had gone. By the time morning chores were finished, he was back again.

"Mary, I must talk to you." he said. "I went to the mill to visit your father this morning, thinking I must have his blessing if I were to ask you to be my wife. He always treats me with the utmost respect, so his demeanor as well as his answer surprised me." Thom reached out to me. "Mary, talk to him. He's retreated, shriveled inside of himself."

I shook my head. "I have not seen Papa since that awful day last month."

Thom looked at me with pleading eyes. "He needs your forgiveness, Mary. He's full of recriminations for thinking he could decide whom you should wed. 'The Devil lured me with new guises,' he said to me, 'and I saw an opportunity for my sweet Mary to receive wealth and honor and respect as the wife of such a revered man.' Have you seen him, Mary? Your father can hardly speak, so desolate is he. Says he's ashamed to look you in the face. He's chastising himself for such a flawed judgment in your regard. So, you'll not give your blessing? says I. And all he would say is that you are stubborn like your mother was, but you know, better than he, what is right for you. You always have, he says.

"Talk to him, Mary. He's aged, in just this short of time. Told me to trust *thee*, not *him* for knowing what's best for you."

Alas, I had focused so on my own desires and disasters that I had not considered my own family's distress. First of all, Papa, but also the dear Fordham family. What disappointment and dishonor Uncle Robert and Aunt Alice would feel if townsfolk were given reason to focus their gossiping tongues on me. Tears smarted my eyes. "I'll see Papa tomorrow."

Again he said to me, "Remember, Mary. Nothing is lost, only changed. As soon as our banns can be published thrice, we can be wed. Early August. I'll speak to your uncle before I leave."

"Are you sure, Thom?"

With eyes as honest and clear as brook water, he nodded and caught me hard against him, kissing me softly on the mouth.

"Tomorrow, I'll return to my new land in Babylon. Seven hours away, Mary. No one will guess." His words spilled out in a rush of ideas. "A rough cabin sits there. Small it be, with only sand for floors. Closest neighbor is five miles away, but I'll be with you. And next spring I'll find a midwife to help you through the birth. Together we'll build a better home."

I could see the list of plans as Thom added to them, one by one.

"A fireplace and mantle, a cot and a cradle. Our first home, Mary."

With single-minded urgency, he plunged on. "I'll pack my boat with needed goods, and the first week of August when I return from Babylon to pick up Joshua, we'll be wed. Thursday, August 3, after the last banns. Sound like a good day? I'm partial to Thursdays." Thom inhaled deeply, a satisfied sound.

On the morrow, although waves of doubt still tossed me to and fro, Thom was steady as a rock. He accompanied me to Mecox Bay, so I could talk to Papa. Then, with everything settled to his satisfaction, he boarded ship and sailed west to Babylon.

Although Joshua was disappointed that Captain Scudder had left without him, he wanted to say goodbye to Qolucksee before going home to his mother, and I prayed for some sort of confirmation that the path I was choosing would find favor not only with my family, but also within the wisdom of Shaman Nowedanah and her husband, Kockenoe. Out of respect for their beliefs, I once more placed around my neck the amulet they had given me, and then, on a gentle horse from the Fordham pasture, we rode to the Shinnecock village, Joshua mounted behind me. Grateful was I for the warm day and relieved that we would have no need to sit inside the lodge where smells were overwhelming.

The bustle of the Shinnecock village seemed unusually subdued, except for a group of young boys who immediately joined Qolucksee and Joshua and headed toward the river.

Beneath a bower of leafy saplings, the Shaman Nowedanah sat cross-legged on a mat woven of reeds. "Welcome, my friend." She held out her hand in greeting. "Come sit and meditate with us. Today we ask the Spirit's blessing on the new lodge we are building. Kockenoe will join us here as we listen to the Spirit voices."

Quietly, I took my place within the canopy, a place as peaceful as the domed cathedral of St. Giles — the place in England where my family worshiped when Mama was yet alive. The sun shone through the open spaces above, lighting Nowedanah's face with a golden glow. Here, with little sound but the cry of birds, the wind itself seemed to whisper: *Be still and know.* The words came clear to me, and I knew that was exactly what I needed. Quiet. Calm. Time to ponder.

High in the still, blue sky, I could see a pair of Red-tailed Hawks soaring in wide circles. "Look," Kockenoe said in a low voice. "The male dives down in a steep drop, then shoots up again at nearly as steep an angle. He repeats this maneuver several times, then approaches the female from above.

"They are courting," Nowedanah whispered. "Look how he extends his legs and touches her briefly. Sometimes the pair may grab onto one other and spiral toward the ground."

Kockenoe nodded his agreement. "Hawks mate for life. Perhaps they bring thee a message, my friend. I see you still wear the amulet. What Hawk persons needs is someone who can accept and honor their gifts and talents, giving them the space they need to soar high above."[84]

Nowedanah touched my hand as she spoke. "Your mate will allow you to bring your visions and ideas to fruition before soaring off to the heights again.[85] Have you found that person at last?"

With a sigh, a tremendous burden escaped my rib-bound prison, and for the Shinnecocks I breathed a prayer. "Thank you, my friends. I'll never forget you."

Once more, they sat in silence, listening for the Spirit's song. I rose and silently slipped away. Leading my horse to the river, I picked up Joshua, and we waved goodbye to Qolucksee.

On the following Sabbath, the whole town was still buzzing with the arrest of the Reverend Abram Hardwick.

When Uncle Robert rose and read the very scripture Abram Hardwick had chosen the month before:

"Winter and summer, springtime and harvest, sunshine and rain; through change and similitude, God loves us. He has not given us a spirit of fear, but of love. We have been restored to a right relationship with God, not by our own merit, but by God's love."

The whole congregation seemed to lean forward, waiting for his next words. Surely he would not continue where the Reverend Hardwick had left off!

Uncle Robert paused and slowly turned to look directly at each member of the gathering, speaking straightforwardly to each.

"God's people are neither a select group of the self-righteous, nor an exclusive group with rigid determinations regarding who is chosen. No! We are a cast of people, male and female, who are not only equally privileged but are also unentitled beggars at the door of God's mercy!"

The congregation sat straight in their pews, more attentive, even, than usual.

"Life is a bundle of paradoxes. We believe and we doubt, we hope and we get discouraged. We love and we hate. We feel guilty about not feeling guilty."

The people nodded in concurrence. Who had not experienced these riddles?

When the minister raised his voice again, no one slept. The young had no need of the tithing man's rod nor did the old have need of his tickling feather to awaken them.

"Husbands, love your wives as Christ loved the church. Never believe any union will be smooth and easy, or that anyone who embarks on the voyage can measure the tides and hurricanes he will encounter."

At these words, in the pew to the right, I saw Goodman Gabbler smile at his wife and nod at Uncle Robert's words.

"What I tell you is this: love your enemies and pray for your persecutors. It is only human to strike back when we have been hurt or abused or insulted. But God requires forgiveness; else we may simmer in bitterness."[86]

A rush of forgiveness flooded my soul. Warm as summer rain, it melted the icy condemnation from my heart.

In spite of this happy release, this holy day in which we could neither laugh nor play, nor work nor travel, seemed long. Lonely.

Observing the Sabbath, I put off writing until the next morning when the words in my heart came clear to me. In the quiet dawning, I went to Uncle Robert's study and lit a candle. There I took out my quill and turned to a blank page at the back of Mama's Bible.

21ST CENTURY
MEMORY CATCHERS' OFFICE

Grand-Mary's voice faded as the Sony beeped its warning. The sound card was full. Pressing the off button, I reached for the Bible Grand-Mary had given me and carefully turned to the back. There, just as she remembered, were the words she had written on that long-ago day.

Certainty and Faith
by Mary Ludlam
O strange! Now he hath eastward sailed away
I weary grow, so long the dreary day
And if to me he westward bound shall turn,
Then shall the brightness of my day return.
Whilst he's away my spirit mourns in black,
Though summer's here, my soul's late zodiac.
Yet whilst with him, no fearful frost I felt,

My lurking doubts his tenderness doth melt.
He listens, tells me that he loves my mind,
Requests I walk beside him, not behind.
Forgiving, gentle, kind, but far from weak.
Shares thoughts with me,
Yet thinks 'fore he doth speak,
And he be witty, learned, comely, strong.
If ever I do wed, could this be wrong?
He's waited long for love and faithful friend,
Who'll always be committed to the end.
Oh, may your absence quite confirm my test
That with you I wouldst be forever blest
If two be one, it's surely thou and I;
Return, sweet Thom to cusp of Gemini. [87]

AUGUST ANNO DOM 1656
SOUTHAMPTON, LONG ISLAND

Aunt Alice, certain that a wedding was in the offing, had stocked up on foodstuffs from the wares displayed the last day of the fair. Each course at the dinner, she told me, would include a soup, followed by a wide range of baked, roasted, and boiled dishes. "Of course, the whole community will be invited to the feast," she said, looking at me for approval. She was in her glee, scurrying about with first one preparation and then another, adding to the repertoire of delights she had prepared for previous family celebrations. Her recipe for wedding cake came straight from Gervase Markham's *English Huswife* [1615], the same cake she made for her own daughter, my cousin Hannah's wedding.[88] Of course, Aunt Alice thought everything had to be cleaned and polished. Linens were put out to air. "And, Robert, dear, don't you think we should have the bricks of the fireplace and the hearth cleaned?"

Uncle Robert looked at her with raised eyebrows. "Do you suppose you might be overdoing things, my love? We would not wish to offend God by being too fussy and decadent."

She looked quite startled at that suggestion. "Robert Fordham, except for fasts and Holy Days, this feast is one of the few celebrations Puritans permit," she said. "Mary is a dear motherless child, and I'm only doing what her mother would have wanted. Put ye not a damper on my pleasure."

Aunt Alice continued with much ado, fussing over details. From the cookbook, to separate main courses one from another she planned entertaining sotelties — sculptures made from edible ingredients, mostly sugar and pastry dough — perhaps a pie with exotic spices, and an elaborate model of my old St Giles church made with pastry, using colored marzipan for windows.

When the wedding plans seemed to Uncle Robert to be growing out of hand, he called me into the library. "Mary, is all this fuss to your liking?" He took a book from the shelves. "Have you read, 'Canterbury's Doom'? he said. "The satire is probably somewhat exaggerated, but if you read it, you may comprehend why I became a Puritan, giving up the outrageous, empty ceremonies of the church, and you will appreciate the unease I feel at overmuch celebration."

He handed the book to me, saying, "It's Prynne's account of Bishop Laud's consecration of the Church of St. Catherine Cree twenty-six years ago in London. Read the concluding paragraphs.

Opening the book to the last page, I read:

"The Bishop approached the communion-table, bowing with his nose very near the ground six or seven times.

Then with his two fat chaplains upon their knees by him in their surplices, hoods and tippets, he himself came near the bread, and gently lifted up one corner of the napkin, like a boy that peeked into a bird's nest in a bush, and presently clapped it down again and flew back a step or two."

If I were somewhat nervous about all the wedding preparations, this was the relief I sought, and I burst out laughing.

"Oh, go on. Read the rest," he said. I could see the laughter in his eyes.

"Then Laud laid his hand upon the gilt cup of wine. So soon as he had pulled the cup a little nearer to him, he lifted up the cover of the cup, peeped into it, then flew nimbly back and bowed as before. After these, and many other apish, antic gestures, he himself receded and then gave the sacrament to some principal men devoutly kneeling near the table."

"Uncle Robert, I can just picture you in a red hood and tippet, peeking into the cup, then jumping back like a puppet on a string. How could people keep a straight face in the meeting house with you carrying on so? They'd be rolling in the aisles."

Uncle Robert wiped away tears of laughter, and then his expression sobered. "Oh, my little Mary, what joy you give me. If only you had been born my son. Have you any idea how many people take every word literally, not understanding the wit behind such satire? Promise me—"

Holding back welling tears, I grinned, raised my hand and assumed a teasing tone. "I solemnly swear to expect no bowing and scraping when you and the magistrate read our vows to us. And I promise that Aunt Alice will bake no pies filled with more than four and twenty blackbirds to fly out and astonish the guests."

Aunt Alice borrowed chairs, tables, dishes, and utensils from willing neighbors, all eager to join the festivities. Within the week, my cousin Molly, now married to Lizzie Howell's brother-in-law, Edward, Jr., came home to practice her well-learned hostess skills. Even Cousin Hannah came. Married to Samuel Clark and moved off to Stamford in Connecticut Colony, she was still suckling their fourth son and expecting a fifth—another boy, no doubt.

At Richard Mill's tavern, the sleeping rooms over-flowed with guests from Southold and parts further, mostly Thom's friends and family. And of course Thom had a room there.

"Your eyes are shining as if someone had lighted a candle behind your face," he said when he saw me. Words I tucked away in my heart.

On Thursday, the day of the wedding, the parsonage filled with cousins and my siblings—Luddie and Eliza-beth, married earlier this year, and all the rest, from Me-cox.

Best of all, Papa was there, solid and physical and smelling slightly of sweat and milled flour. Feigning a tetchy look, he greeted me. "What kind of business can I run when there's no work being done? Might as well close the mill for the day and come to the wedding!" He held his arms out to me, and although I suspected the glow of pride on his face was bolstered by an extra flagon of beer, warmth and gladness overwhelmed me.

Outside the front door stood a gigantic punch bowl, hollowed out from a boulder, filled with spiced cider combined with sugar, lemons, and limes from the West

Indies. Tankards were filled and drained. Aunt Alice opened the big parlor, and from the kitchen the women folk brought out the main courses—fish and clam chowder, stewed oysters, duck, potatoes, and baked rye bread. Surprisingly, my Shinnecock friends appeared— Nowedanah and Kockenoe and Qolucksee—bodies shiny with oils, arms laden with cornbread and pumpkin pudding sweetened with honey. I placed their gifts of goodies between the wedding cake and an exotic dessert of Indian pudding studded with dried plums and served with a sauce made from West Indian molasses, butter, and vinegar, and beside trays of fresh fruits and vegetables, nutmeats and broken blocks of candy made from maple sugar, butter, and hickory nuts. Next to that was a table laden with gifts from the townspeople to help Thom and me begin our lives together.

Some guests, even my dear friend Elisabeth Halsey whose mother had been killed by marauding Indians, tried to exhibit hospitality to my Shinnecock friends, but to my chagrin, some of the guests wore expressions of repugnance, recognizing only the outside appearance rather than the tender, loving hearts within.

Barely audible, a gruff voice whispered, "Such gall *they* have. Intruding where they were not invited!"

"Well," another laughed and sneered, "better keep them away from the ale."

Noticing Goody Gabbler wrinkle her nose as the Shinnecocks walked passed, I quickly led them through the crowd to the place Thom was standing.

I introduced Thom to them, and gracious as I expected, he bowed, and then held out his hand in welcome. "Qolucksee, Mary has told me how you rescued her when she fell from a tree a few years ago," he said. He turned to Nowedanah and Kockenoe. "And I believe it is because of you and the red-tailed hawk that she finally gave me the answer I wanted." With great solemnity, he said to them, "Long have I waited for a woman with such gifts and talents. Thank you for giving us your blessing."

We sat with my Indian friends and shared some of the delicacies they brought as well as some of Aunt Alice's goodies. Obviously noticing some discomfort at their presence, they left early, but not until I let them know they were welcome and how happy I was that they had come.

Since my family had migrated to Southampton seven years ago, the town had grown from twenty-nine families to nearly sixty. Because Thom had often sailed his sloop across the Peconic Bay bringing supplies, they knew him and liked him and respected his fair prices; the same people who traded with Papa at the mill; people in Uncle Robert's congregation; a close knit community who was sure God had given them the land where once the Indians roamed free. I felt blessed by the people who had helped build this town, but saddened that they had so soon forgotten the help the Shinnecocks had given them in the days of the first settlement.

After the sumptuous meal, guests drank healths to us and offered prayers, and we thanked them for their presence and the many gifts they had given us. One, in particular, brought tears to Thom's eyes— the cordwainer had cobbled two pairs of fine shoes from leather prepared by a skilled furrier—Thom's oldest brother, Liam, who had died in Salem not six months before.

Soon my brothers, Anthony, Luddie, Hal and ten-year-old Joseph, came to Thom with the typical man's gestures, boxing and punching shoulders, offering their help.

"Your Southold kin have gone to finish loading the *Sea Hawk* for you. We've packed the wedding gifts in our wagon." Teasing as always, but also being helpful, Anthony said, "May we carry them to the sloop while you are distracted by the wedding vows?"

I could see that Thom was pleased with their acceptance as well as with their offer to help.

"Do not forget my bag," I called as they started to leave.

"Ho, Mary," Luddie said, laughing. "This is your wedding night. There'll be no need for clothing."

I could feel the blood rise to my cheeks, but my brothers slapped each other's backs, roaring with laughter as if this were the best joke yet. "Our Mary's a feisty one," Anthony called. "Good luck, Thom."

In Uncle Robert's library, Magistrate Edward Howell waited patiently, ready to preside at the wedding. With only Papa, Aunt Alice, and Uncle Robert attending, Thom and I softly repeated words of betrothal in the Magistrate's presence, taking each other for husband and wife—a private civil service according to the Puritan way.

Cautious that gold adornment might bring offense to strict Puritans, Thom placed his grandmother's plain gold band in my hand and closed my fingers over it. When a sudden shyness overtook me, he lifted my chin with the back of his hand and searched my upturned face. "Mary, beloved, the inscription within the band is my vow to you. *Amorem Nostrum In Aeterno*: Our love for eternity."

Fervently then, and devoutly, Uncle Robert asked God's blessing on our hearth and home.

My gaze slipped around the room and came to rest on Papa. I caught his eye, and we smiled at each other as he moved toward me.

"Fare ye well, lass," he said. "May you be a loving, dutiful wife to this fine man. I could wish ye no greater happiness."

Breathing deeply of the perfumed air of that warm and beautiful afternoon, I stood in the doorway with Thom, wedding garland on my head. Realizing the ceremony was over, friends came forth from the parlor to bid us farewell.

From the corral, Luddie, back from the sloop, led Thom's white horse on which he had placed a crimson cushion for a saddle. "You must ride like a princess, not plod along through the dust and heat of the afternoon all the way to the *Sea Hawk*."

Thom grinned his approval, for I had shared with him my childhood fairy tale. Cupping his hands for my foot so I could mount without trouble, he boosted me up onto the cushion; then putting his foot in the stirrup, he bounded into the saddle behind me.

A sudden wariness niggled at my heart, and my breath quickened, then blossomed into spicules of cold panic. "Wait, my husband! I beseech thee! Forsooth, we are forgetting something."

Thom's face was blank, then red with embarrassment. "God in heaven, we've forgotten Joshua."

Luddie laughed and nudged Anthony with his elbow. "Methinks the bride and groom have else on their minds. But don't worry, Mary. Cousin Joshua's already stowed his bags on board the sloop, and he's waiting there for you. Hal's staying there with him 'til you're ready to cast off."

"Hal or Henry?" Thom said, raising one eyebrow to match a sardonic grin. "My brother or yours?"

"Both, I believe. Two of a kind." Luddie chortled and slapped one knee. "And between the pair of them, they've probably eaten all the foodstuffs in the galley by now. Best you hurry along or that young imp Joshua will sail home to Hempstead without you."

21ST CENTURY
MEMORY CATCHERS' OFFICE

The tape came to an end and I typed Grand-Mary's last sentence. Her descriptions of the wedding and celebration were silken threads of a lovely tapestry, weaving the colors of her life. But the image was far from finished. Where was she? I could not weave the story without her soft-as-silk words.

As if she heard my words, suddenly she was seated beside me in her favorite chair, eager to continue the story.

Eleven

᷾

Anno Dom 1656
Babylon, Long Island, New York

Once on board the *Sea Hawk,* we found an impatient but well-fed Joshua, and after bidding our Henry and Hal goodbye, we set sail.

From the moment we were out to sea, Joshua was constantly in motion, exploring the sloop, from top to bottom, scurrying down the steps, into the galley, back up the steps, stern to bow and back again, then stopping to ask questions, barely waiting for Thom's answers.

"How soon will we be home? How fast are we going? Is this boat as fast as my Papa's was? Can I be your skipper?"

Some of Thom's crew might have looked at a small blind boy as a nuisance, but as usual, Thom showed both kindness and enthusiasm toward Joshua's interest.

"Here, young man. Put your hands on the wheel, and you can help me steer," Thom said, smoothing back the lock of hair that was wont to fall over his forehead. "Breeze's good today. We'll dock at Merockes[89] in about five hours—before dark, I'm sure. That's on the water's edge of South Hempstead, you know. Just a short walk to your mother's house."

Joshua nodded. "We walked to the shore to meet Papa when his ship came in. I think I remember the sound of the waves there, but I do not remember how big his ship was."

"That's because your Papa's ship was too big to dock in the bay. He'd have used a small boat to sail from the barrier island on to Merocke."

Seeing how attentive Joshua was, Thom continued his explanation. "With a favorable wind, the *Sea Hawk* can travel about 11 knots, and with her shallow draft she can sail in the channels and inlets where larger vessels would run aground."

"Like pirate ships? Uncle Robert said my papa won a battle with a pirate ship."

The corners of Thom's mouth tilted upward. "That he did! Those vessels were much larger than the *Sea Hawk*, although pirates often favor a single-masted sloop like this one. The bowsprit—the spar on the front of the ship—is almost as long as the hull, so she can mount an enormous amount of sail in relation to her size. That makes her very fast and agile, so she can outmaneuver larger vessels."

Warmed and relaxed by the sun and rhythm of the ship, I found a place to sit and watch my two seamen. After the hustle and bustle of the day's events, I was happy to sit listening to the sounds of the sea and gulls that swooped and swirled above the sloop. As we neared Merocke, the blue of the sky was not yet darkening, and rosy-hued clouds covered the sun in the west.

Joshua trembled with eagerness as we docked at Merocke Bay. With feet at last on shore, he began calling, "Mama! Mama, it's Joshua. I'm home."

Thom rushed to grab Joshua's hand. "Here," he said, "I'll walk with you. It's not far."

'Twas a joyful reunion although Goodman Hicks, Aunt Florence's new husband, was gruff and standoffish. The only child left at home was young Philip, the little brother Joshua was so eager to see, so the house seemed quieter than he remembered it. His big brother John and wife, Hannah Seaman, expecting their first child, were living on the land left to him by his father. Ben, now 22, and Caleb, 17, were working for John; Abbie, 21, was working for the Coe family and living with them.

"You'll have a meal with us," Aunt Florence said, "and I've prepared a bed for you two in Abbie's old room."

We thanked Aunt Florence for her kindness, but declined her invitation to spend the night. "Want to set sail at first light," Thom said. Lots of work to be done at our place at Babylon. Moving day, you understand."

Joshua and Aunt Florence hugged us goodbye, she with a knowing smile on her face, and we slipped away to spend the night on the boat.

The night was lovely and warm, and the rising moon reflected in the waters of the bay, silhouetting the black fringe of trees on the far horizon. Thom dismissed the crew and they went to their cabins, leaving us alone. We rolled feather-stuffed bolsters out on the deck of the *Sea Hawk* for sleeping, Waves lapped against the hull and the hum of summer insects accompanied the sounds of gulls, gliding over the darkening waters with peaceful lowing cries. In the lovely darkness, I stood trembling, hugging myself. Trepidation and nervousness flapped beneath my ribs like a panicked flock of chickens.

Noticing my apprehension, Thom spoke quietly, so quietly I could hardly hear him. "We've no netting to protect us from mosquitoes on deck. Shall we rub this oil on our skin? It hath not a pleasant smell, but it's better than insect bites."

Wrapping determination around me like a cloak, I took the jug of oil from him and began slathering the smelly substance over Thom's arms and face, then proceeded to his back and chest.

He took the oil and began a delicate game of gentle movements, slowly applying the odiferous repellant to my skin, often pausing as if uncertain whether or not to proceed. I let out my breath, not realizing I had been holding it, and leaned my head against his chest, feeling his warmth and the strength of his arms around me. Soon forgotten was the unpleasant odor of the oil. Finally I grasped Thom's hands, pulling him closer to me. Turning so his lips were just below my ear, he whispered gentle, loving words to me. Balancing his yearning with my uncertainty, he let me set the rhythm of our movement. Several times I felt him pull back, as if resisting. Finally he relaxed, and we came together, melting as one in a strange, warm mingling of identities.

After a time, he sighed and snuggled against my back, cupping my roundness in the nest of his thighs. "I love thy satisfied sounds," he whispered.

Surely the blush of my cheeks lighted up the sky, yet I could not refrain from asking, "Why did I sense your hesitation? Have you doubts about me?"

He did not answer immediately, and I felt my breath catch in my throat.

"Forgive me, Aphrodite. 'Twas my upbringing. I was suddenly fearful of the loss of myself, but more than that, of the passion that swept over me. Puritans, you know, believe they must be careful not to love anyone more than God. But the Bible did say, 'Thou shalt be one flesh.'"

"And remember Solomon's Song," I said. "*Both wisdom and love are gifts of God, to be received with gratitude and celebration.*"

The joyous sound of Thom's laughter bubbled forth as he said, "I can't think of a better way to celebrate." After a long pause he said, "Are you as restless for the morrow as I? It's too late in the year for planting our land, but there's much work to be done before spring." He paused again, and then said, "Have you read Hesiod? Nearly a thousand years ago, he wrote,

> And if longing seizes you for sailing the stormy seas,
> when the Pleiades flee mighty Orion
> and plunge into the misty deep
> and all the gusty winds are raging,
> then do not keep your ship on the wine-dark sea
> but, as I bid you, remember to work the land.

"Yes, I remember. Uncle Robert had those very lines marked in Hesiod's poem. He said it could have been the Puritan's Song of Songs. Do you remember the title? 'Carpe Noctem,' it was called. Seize the Night!"

I went to sleep in Thom's arms and awaked hours later with the wind singing in my ears. The glory of the Milky Way still stretched overhead from north to south with not yet a glimmer of dawn in the east. A thin sliver of moon silhouetted Thom's figure, standing at the helm. Lo and behold, I realized that my fear of bedding with a man had gone, but in its place, an ultimate gift—the intimacy we had shared. It was as if my dreams had blended with his, wrapping our union in a lovely coverlet firmly stitched with faith, hope, and understanding.

"There's a good west wind," Thom called. "Better get up. Your new husband's hungry." His broad grin warmed my heart.

Breathless, eager to reach our new home, I flung back the coverlet, smoothed my hair, and made my way to him. The quizzical expression on Thom's face told me he was expecting my many questions.

"Will you know where to dock?" I asked. "How far is our house from the shore?"

"Don't worry, sweet. I'll recognize our cove when I see it," he said. "The house is inward about two miles at the edge of a small, green patchwork of pines, oaks, and aspens. A pool with a spring and smooth grass. A pretty place."

"Tell me about our house again."

Thom took one hand from the wheel, put his arm around me and drew me close. "One large, drafty room, with a walled loft above and a small lean-to at the back for storage. It's only a start, I'm afraid." He raised an eyebrow, as if seeking my approval.

I smiled and nodded. "Go on, prithee."

"Goodman Michaels, a neighbor who came from Netherlands, told me the man who started building the house died in an accident before he could finish the job. He had cleared some of the land, and from the logs, Michaels had helped him saw the clapboards—thin boards they used to frame the walls. A wattle and daub cottage, but one of the walls still needs the 'daub.' We can finish that to-gether. By winter, we'll have a warm room."

"With windows?" I said as I dug through the crates of our belongings, searching for the basket of cheese and breads Aunt Alice had packed for us.

"Yes, my sweet. Openings have been cut in the front and side walls, but not on the rear. Warmer that way. For now, we'll cover them with oiled paper to let in light, but anon we'll make a trip to Boston, and I'll buy you some real glass."

"A place for a garden?"

"Oh, yes. The man had riven pales and driven them into the ground, the beginning of a palisade."

Thom wolfed down the cheese and bread I had found, and followed that with a cup of beer.

"Is the palisade to protect us or the garden?" I asked.

Thom grinned. "*I'll* protect *you*. The fence is for the garden. Without it, animals will eat the crops as soon as the leaves poke through the ground. Deer, especially, and rabbits."

I looked around at all the crates of goods and wedding gifts to be unloaded. "How will we carry all of this the two miles to our house?"

In his eager and organized fashion, Thom laid out his plans. "Jan Michaels, the neighbor I spoke of, offered to meet us at the cove with his ox and wagon this morning. He'll be there an hour after sunrise. And I'm going to put the crew to work."

"And where will the crew live?"

"On the sloop, of course. When they're in port, they'll have some time for hunting, fishing, and gathering food for daily survival and for times when they're at sea, as well as for replenishing fresh water supplies. In wintertime, they'll likely haul the boat up onto the beach for sail and rigging repairs. I hope to keep them busy most of the time carrying oil and hay to other towns. If we need protection from Indians or pirates, they can help build some kind of encampment, a fort."

So much to do and so many skills to learn! Skills in felling and sawing logs, building fences, constructing and maintaining buildings and carts, shaping shingles for our own use, and maybe some left over for market. Then there would be butchering, smoking, salting and packing away meat, rendering lard, candle making and soap making. Before winter we would be making fodder of meadow and salt marsh grasses. Someday soon, Thom would teach me the skills I knew not. Here in our own Garden of Eden, I would be his help meet.

My reverie was interrupted by Thom's words. "This is Saturday and we can easily get everything loaded into Goodman Michaels' wagon and carried to our place before Sabbath begins at sundown. And then, in the new week, and for the next month or so, the crew can help me with the heavy labor while you set up house. Only one or two of crew needs stay with the boat."

While you set up house, he had said. I tasted those delicious words and rolled them around on my tongue, savoring the thought. *A pretty place. A house of my own.*

AUGUST, ANNO DOM 1656
CABIN AT BABYLON, LONG ISLAND

As Thom had told me, the interior walls of the house were a woven network of thin branches and saplings called wattle. The network of three of the walls had been finished, filled with daub—a mixture of clay, sand, and straw. The intertwined branches of the fourth wall, the one by the bed, still bare, let in air between the gaps.

Crowded it was once the men had finished carrying our goods from ship to cabin. Kegs of beer; barrels of flour and grain; and chests, boxes, and crates of goods littered the room. But by laying a board ceiling, accessed by a ladder, over the main chamber, the crew helped Thom create a loft for storing dried foods as well as some of the chests, boxes and baskets of personal items.

I found that the previous owner of our cabin had left furnishings that came with the purchase. Against one wall stood a solid ark of oak—a chest-like box for storing peas or grains with a lid I could turn over to use as a kneading table. Next to that was the fireplace, and on the other side, a table and a long bench. In another corner was a bedstead with a wooden frame laced with rope.

I began unpacking our wedding gifts. On the bed frame I spread our featherbeds, pillows, and the lovely linen sheets Grace had spun. Over the top of them I spread the patchwork quilt my Fordham cousins and I had stitched last winter. Each piece of the quilt brought forth a lovely memory. Each woolen wisp of cloth we had spun and dyed and sewn into garments—scraps from my Sabbath dress, the first breeches my baby brother Joseph had worn, richly colored with chestnut brown, Abbie's yellow bonnet—usually unsuccessful at restraining her lovely blonde curls, Papa's bright blue cloak, and most of all, the rich fellowship we shared while stitching the varied pieces together. Memories that warmed my heart. As I smoothed the quilt and began unwrapping each gift, I said a prayer of thanks for such dear friends and family members.

Above the fireplace, Thom hung his musket and two fowling pieces, and on pegs by the door, we hung our cloaks. Already, it was beginning to look like home.

To please me, Thom built special shelves for our treasured books, adding his collection to mine—the newly revised *Bay Psalm Book; The Odyssey, Aeneid, Canterbury Tales*, and other books Uncle Robert had given us as a wedding gift. With all the work there was to do, when would we ever find time to read them? I took pleasure in arranging them—brown leather bindings, gilt titles and edges—on the shelves Thom had hung on the wall above the table.

On each end of the top shelf I placed the green bayberry candles and candlesticks from my dearest friend, Elizabeth. "When you are lonely or afraid," she had said as she hugged me, "just light one of these candles and remember our friendship."

Above the door, I hung the wedding garland my little sister Abbie had woven for me with rosemary and roses from her Mecox garden.

On one shelf of the cupboard that stood against the wall, I put our linens. On another, cooking pots, bowls and mixing spoons. Our carpenter friend John White had carved the spoons from wood scraps and initialed them with a delicate "S" for Scudder, my new name. Another shelf held the copper kettle and a warming pan with a copper bowl and a long wooden handle, fashioned by the Veale brothers, Southampton's blacksmiths. On top of the cupboard, I arranged the pewter plates and cups Thom had bought for me at the fair. My fingers traced their engraved scripture—*Many waters cannot quench love.*

The finished array made me feel like "Ye Compleat Decorator."

On the second afternoon after the Sabbath, Thom and I paused from our labors to sit in the shade of the canopy created by the limbs of a giant tulip tree. "Did you ever make mud pies when you were a child?" he said.

"Mud pies?" I grinned. "If you're hungry for pie, I think I can do better than that. Blueberries, perhaps? The meadow is bursting with them."

Thom laughed. "Blue's nice I suppose, but brown mud will work better. Tomorrow let's finish the bare wall by our bed. Daub will make the house cooler for sleeping in this heat. And warmer in—Oh, look, someone's coming."

It was Jan Michaels again, but this time he was not alone. Without wasting words, he got straight to the point. "Goodman Scudder, I could use some extra help with my fall harvest, and since you have just kom hier and have no harvest of your own, I offer a trade. My help during the winter on any building projects you might have, for your aid with harvest."

Thom offered his hand in agreement, and then with a welcoming smile, he gestured toward the woman sitting beside a young man in the wagon. "Goodman Michaels, this must be your wife?"

"Indeed it is. Thirty good years we've had together." He stepped down from the wagon and turned to offer her a hand. "Lisbet, this is Goodman Scudder and his wife Mary, our new neighbors. With a look of pride he added, "And this rascal is my grandson, Dirk, come to help out on the farm."

Once on the ground, the goodwife's round face, barely wrinkled in spite of her years, broke into a broad grin. "Welcome to Babylon. Is good to have someone this close to visit. Sometimes is quite lonely here, away from hustle and bustle of New Amsterdam where first we lived." She turned back to the wagon. "Dirk, hand me the basket, please."

Thom cleared his throat. "Mary, perhaps we could offer our guests some beer? Five miles in this heat would make anyone thirsty."

Inside the cabin, I invited the Michaels family to sit while I poured drafts from the jug, delighted that in such a short time, I had been able to make our home orderly and hospitable. Aunt Alice would have been pleased.

After draining their mugs, the three men excused themselves to look over possibilities for the land, leaving Goody Michaels and me alone in the cabin. Alone, but certainly not lonely. "Call me Lisbet, please," she immediately said, then continued to talk non-stop as if a dike of solitude had suddenly been released. Years ago, her husband had been a soldier in Leyden, Netherlands, she told me. In exchange for his service as a soldier, they had gained passage to New Amsterdam to follow his trade as farmer and carpenter. She paused to tuck a strand of straight grey hair behind her ear. "I was an English girl who moved from Sussex to Leyden with my parents in 1618, expecting to soon sail to the colonies." She shook her head, and a shadow of sadness flitted across her face. "When the ship that was to have sailed with the May-flower had problems and could not sail, there was not room for everyone, and my parents and I were left behind."

"Is your husband from England, too?" I said.

"Oh, no, no. He was a Leyden boy. But the first time I saw him, I was sure we would speak the same language, so handsome was he. Now, my tongue is more Dutch than his. Over half my life we have been wed." She smiled, and smoothed her neat white apron. "Three sons, all grown and married and living in New Netherlands Territory, but my darling Jan's dream is to farm, far away from the crowds of the city. With Governor Stuyvesant's blessing, we moved from the salt meadows of Vlissingen near the river, east across Hempstead plain, and on to Babylon. I'm hoping our boys and their families will follow us. With such plentiful land, we can soon have our own little village."

Hesitant to interrupt, I lifted the jug. Raising an eyebrow, I motioned toward her empty mug.

She shook her head, pausing only long enough to take a breath, and then continued. "You and your Goodman Scudder, you came from England, *ja*?"

"Yes, but Thom was here long before I was. He and his parents sailed to Massachusetts Bay Colony a dozen or more years before my family immigrated. The Scudders came from Kent and settled in Salem in 1635. My own father, William Ludlam, left Matlock in Derbyshire after my mother died in childbirth. Their eighth child. I was only eight then. My siblings and I followed him to this new land on the ship called the *Triall*. That was 1648."

"The *Triall*, was it? I believe we may have mutual friends then. Did not John Bowne come from Matlock on that same ship?"

"John Bowne? I haven't seen him since we landed in Boston. You know him?"

"Indeed I do! When first he came to New Amsterdam, he built a place in Vlissingen,[90] not four houses down from us. I danced at his wedding last May. Did you know? His wife is little Hannah Feake, great-niece of Governor Winthrop of Massachusetts Bay. A delightful young couple, but she speaks out so fearlessly, far beyond the place of women. Even though Netherlands tolerates religions of all kinds, oft I've heard her complain there is no liberty of conscience in New Amsterdam. It's true. The law of New Amsterdam says we can worship only in Reformed Dutch Church. I fear the poor dear will soon be in trouble."

Lisbet sighed and shrugged her shoulders. "Perhaps it's good that her cousin Tobias is the sheriff of Vlissingen, although I'm not sure how much good that will do. Hannah says she's joining a new religious group lately come across from England. The Religious Society of Friends."

"Sounds harmless."

A vertical crease between Lisbet's iron-grey brows deepened as she puckered her lips in a round shape of dismay. "Oh, but the Society of Friends meets in secret—someplace in the woods to avoid persecution, and so strong is young Hannah her belief that she tries to convince John to attend their meetings." Lisbet rolled her eyes and then paused, a sudden blush of embarrassment splotching her apple cheeks. "*Oh, hemel!*" She reached for the basket she had brought. "So busy I have been with the talk, I forgot." She set the basket on the table and folded back its white linen covering. "Here, my dear neighbor Mary, I have brought fresh-baked breads for you, and today's butter. Find a cool spot for it before it melts away, *ja*?"

I thanked her and then placed the bread in a basket on the table, and the butter in its wooden mold on a lower shelf of the cupboard. Without a pause in her newsy chatter, Lisbet once more reached into the basket. "Have also brought sage plants for your garden."

"It's not too late?"

"Oh, no, no," she said. "These summer seedlings will grow even in autumn. It's not too late to plant a mixed herb bed. Perhaps your husband will plant it for you.

I think it was the appreciation on my face that encouraged her to continue her advice, for she looked around the room and gently shook her head. Laying her hand on my arm, she leaned toward me and whispered, "My dear, may I suggest...." she paused only a moment and then went on. "Placing a bed facing north and south brings misfortune." Quickly Lisbet jumped to her feet, saying, "*Kom hier*, Mary. I'll help you move it to a more pleasing spot."

New as I was to the business of housewifery, I protested not, and by the time the men came in, wiping the sweat from their brows, our living quarters were neatly rearranged. Thom's face showed surprise, but nothing like the start Lisbet gave him when he removed his hat and tossed it on the bed. "Oh, Goodman Scudder," she gasped, "'tis bad luck to put hat on bed. Must at all times hang it on a peg by door."

Thom, always cordial, quickly covered his astonishment. "Well, we certainly don't need that," he said as he moved his hat to the peg. With a twinkle in his eyes, he smiled at me. "Goodman Michaels tells me his wife is an experienced midwife. 'Twill be good to have one close by."

"Oh, ja," Lisbet said, again flashing her broad grin. "One of my great pleasures is helping bring little ones into the world."

I smiled, lowered my eyes, and smoothed flat the gathers of my apron. Surely she could not yet tell my condition.

After enjoying another cup of beer, the three of them bade us *adieu*, with a promise to come back soon. Thom and I watched their wagon until it disappeared in the trees, and then he pulled me to him, brushing back locks of hair on each side of my head to kiss the lobes of my ears.

"What are you doing, you crazy man?" I asked.

"Just checking to see if she talked your ears off," he said with a grin.

"She's a veritable mother hen, isn't she? — always clucking as if to gather stray chicks under her wings with her advice. Perhaps my own mother would have done the same." For an instant, a sense of loss I hadn't felt for ages filled my heart, but it was quickly replaced by a warm feeling toward Lisbet. "Leastwise," I said, "'twas good to hear another woman's voice. And if she has her way, we'll have several more families nearby. She's hoping her sons will all bring their families here to live."

Thom nodded. "Good land," he said. "They could hardly find better."

After lunching on some of Lisbet's fresh bread slathered with butter and topped with chunks of cheese, we pushed a small tip-cart down to Skookwams Creek. There we filled the cart with damp clay dug from the banks. Next we gathered hay from the prairie, laid the straw across a large concave stone and with a rock — much like the Indians made their corn meal — we pounded it into workable bits. Adding the bits of straw and sand from the nearby beach to the clay in the tip-cart, we worked the mixture with our hands to create a smooth daub for our cabin wall. "Need more water," Thom said, pointing to the bucket.

Obediently, I dipped a bucketful of water from Skook-wams Creek and carried it back to our makeshift mixing trencher. Suddenly, a sharp spasm seized my hand, and the whole bucket of water spilled into the clay and sand. The resulting splash of muddy water caught Thom squarely in the face, and I could not stop laughing. His expression of shocked astonishment changed quickly to that of a mischievous young boy as he grabbed a handful of slimy daub and took aim. Although my right hand was cramping, my left was not. And so began the battle. Giggles, chuckles, and hoots attended our volley of mud balls, until we were both weak with laughter.

Thom sat back, grinning, hands on his knees. "Haven't had so much fun since my boyhood in Salem," he said. For a moment he seemed lost in reverie. Then, in a sudden leap of thought, "How would you like to meet my parents?"

Raising my chin, I feigned a look of solemn dignity. "Do ye suppose we should clean up first?"

Laughing, with little probability of watching eyes, we waded into the creek and stripped off our clothes, rinsing the mud from them in the clear, flowing water. After wringing out our garments and spreading them on bushes, we took turns washing each other. Finally we found a grassy spot on the bank and sat there in the sunshine waiting for our clothes to dry.

"I'm glad you do not suffer from the sin of false modesty," Thom said, a teasing sparkle in his eyes.

"I have other flaws," I said, returning his smile

"Is that so?" He gently stroked my back. "Tell me more."

In sudden gravity, my mood changed as I realized there was indeed something I had not told Thom. Something that could greatly hinder me from performing all the expected duties of a Puritan wife. Hesitantly, I placed my hand on his arm. "I poured not the bucket of water into the clay intentionally. It was…a terrible accident."

"Hush," he said, laying a finger across my lips. "Nothing you do could make me love you less."

"Listen," I said. "I have not told you about my deficiency. At times, I cannot grip even small objects without getting painful cramps in my hands and arms. Even as a small child, sometimes I could not walk without my legs screaming out in pain." In a rush, my fears gushed forth. "I know the Bible admonishes me to follow the path of Solomon's wife, the good Bathsheba, but now and then I cannot do the work a woman should do. If a cramp doth grip my limbs, I cannot spin, or hoe in the garden, or carry firewood." I held my breath, waiting for Thom's response.

He reached down, plucked a blade of grass and placed it between his teeth. Still silent, he shied a stone at the water, watching it skip across the creek.

"Not as able as Bathsheba?" he said softly. "Neither am I as wise as Solomon. Tit for tat, I would say." His eyes met mine and then moved slowly downward, all the way to the tips of my bare toes. With an impish grin he said, "I think I'm getting the best of the bargain."

He pulled me into his arms, and I snuggled there, sheltered from the cool breeze that had arisen from the bay.

"You're shivering, my Aphrodite. Shall we dress and return to the job at hand?"

ജ

Within the next week, when our bare wall was thoroughly daubed and dry and the house put in order, I began packing for Salem. Even though we had few garments to choose from, fearful that I had made the wrong choices, I repeatedly removed them from our bags, then put them back again.

Thom noticed my trepidation and reassured me. "'Tis only natural, my sweeting. Every young bride feels this way when meeting her in-laws for the first time. They'll love you." Thom paused and patted my still-flat belly. "Can't wait to see you blush at their pleasure when we tell them we're 'fruitful and multiplying.' "

"You're going to tell them?"

"Of course. Spring, I will say. Nothing would please them more than another little Scudder grandchild."

Tilting my head to one side, I stole a look at him.

"We'll stop by Southampton on the way back and tell your family, too," he said. "Springtime."

With a business-like movement he turned toward the door, finalizing plans in his rapid-paced manner. "Going over to talk to Jan Michaels—see if he'll allow his grandson to keep an eye on our place while we're gone. Only a week or so. Maybe Lisbet can help you pack while I'm out putting plans in motion. My crew has a good supply of cured fish ready to sell. Tomorrow they can sail over to Whalehouse Point with me to see if Isaac Stratford has any whale oil ready to trade.

"We'll go to Salem to see my parents and you can stay there while my crew and I take our products to trade in Boston. Cornelius Conklin, the glassmaker, still lives in Salem. Only glassmaking house in Massachusetts Bay Colony. [91] Before we sail home, I'll get those windows for you."

I smiled, pleased that he remembered. "Hurry home, my sweet. I have bread ready to bake for supper. And when you're at the Michaels, tell Lisbet she's always welcome," I said with a quick wave goodbye, "but do not worry, I'll be ready."

When Lisbet arrived that afternoon, she was horrified to find that I had planted the sage seedlings myself. "Don't you know," she said, "is bad luck to plant your own sage, and even worse, to plant it in a bed alone. *Kom*, Mary, my child!" Removing a container from her wagon, she said, "For you. Yesterday, we go into woods, my grandson and I, and cut stems from wild herbs to mingle with the sage. Coriander for muscle cramps, and chamomile for colic and watery flux, and lemon balm good for salads or whatever ails you. Already rooted, ready to plant. 'Twill make the sage right with the world."

Lisbet was a veritable lexicon of herbs and their uses, combined heavily with superstitions, both English and Dutch. Which, I wondered, should be taken with a grain of salt?

While helping me plant the cuttings she had brought of dill, parsley, and thyme, Lisbet continued a constant barrage, as if finding pleasure in reciting all she knew. "The hedgerows are thick with berries," she said. "Currants, blackberries, elderberries—they're everywhere. Wild strawberries, too. And raspberries are plentiful in this area," she said, tamping the damp earth around the last chamomile root. "There's no end to the usefulness of raspberry leaves for decoctions—bedwetting, sore throats, sore eyes. And if one of these days you be bothered by morning sickness, sip tea brewed from the leaves to stop the vomiting. Later on, makes easier the child-birth, too."

I was so young when my mother died, and after that, I had never been around a birthing. Little did I discern about either birthing or tending a new baby. Knowing that Lisbet was experienced and willing to help greatly relieved my anxiety. Still, some of her ideas seemed a bit far-fetched. Perhaps I could find a good book in a Salem shop, teaching me which of her "facts" I should take as the gospel truth and which were merely old wives' tales.

"A newborn child should not be first laid to the left side," my neighbor assured me, "or it will grow up to be ungainly. Happened to a neighbor's poor infant, back in New Amsterdam. She just would not listen to my advice, but with three boys of my own, and now a dozen darling *kleinkinderen*—" Lisbet shook her head, clucking over the clumsy little fellow's ill fortune. "Suffered so when he cut his first teeth, too." She looked up at me, her round face solemn. "That woman didn't know, until I told her, that when you see a child's first tooth, immediately slap his face, and he will teethe easier."

"Lisbet, you are a good-hearted soul," I said, turning away lest she see my amused expression. Thanking her for the herb cuttings, I invited her to come in out of the heat and have a glass of beer.

After only one glass, she suddenly glanced out the west window. "*Oh, hemel,*'tis growing late!" she said, taking notice of the position of the sun. "I have yet to *bakken* bread for Jan and Dirk's supper. Such appetite the boy has!" She smiled, a look of grandmotherly pride on her face.

"Thom, too," I said, "but I'm used to helping Aunt Alice prepare meals for a large family, and I made too many scones for breakfast this morning. Please, won't you take some home with you?" Not listening to her polite protests, I grabbed her empty basket and filled it with scones in a clean linen cloth. "There now! Your bread baking can wait until the morrow.

Lines of pleasure crinkled around the good woman's eyes. "Thank you, Mary dear."

Carrying the basket of scones, I walked with her out to her wagon, where the grey ox waited, swishing an occasional fly from his back with a bristly stub of a tail. I placed the basket in the wagon while she yoked the animal to the cart and climbed aboard.

"Dirk promised your man to keep an eye on the place while you're away in Salem town. I'll remind him to keep the herb garden watered. He's a good boy. He'll do well for you." She tucked a strand of graying hair under her white bonnet and smiled. "Have a pleasant visit," she said. Then reaching over to pat my arm, she added, "And don't worry. Your in-laws will love you."

21st Century
Memory Catchers' Office

Grand-Mary let out a big breath, as if the uncertainty she felt at the prospect of meeting Thom's parents was fresh as yesterday. I stopped the tape to let her pause for a moment.

"So," I asked, "you were anxious about meeting the Scudders?"

"Indeed! It had not occurred to me that Thom might have found talking to Papa difficult before we married. Papa and Thom had known and respected each other for years. But now that the boot was on the other foot..."

I laughed. "Yes, and the meeting hasn't gotten any easier through the years. My own father tried to withhold
judgment when meeting my future husband for the first
time, but I must admit that he nearly dropped his hymn
book when my young man walked into church wearing a
scrawny, Vandyke beard."

Grand-Mary covered a giggle with her hand. "Like the
painter? Oh, the poor boy!"

"My father-in-law, Hap, was even worse than my own
father at torturing suitors," I said. "Hap took delight in
scaring poor young fellows away, usually quite successfully. Still, he was not totally devoid of sympathy. Once, I
remember, when waiting for his daughter to make her
entrance, Hap noticed the pale face and trembling legs of
the boy who'd come courting, and in a booming voice, he
ordered, "Sit down, Son, before you beat yourself to
death!"

Smiling again, Grand-Mary took another deep breath
and relaxed into her chair. "Some things never seem to
change."

"Oh, Grand-Mary, forgive me. I didn't mean to take
you traveling into the 21st century. It's not my story we're
writing. Let's get back to 17th century Babylon."

I flipped on my recorder, and, with a forgiving nod,
Grand-Mary began where she'd left off, readying for a
trip to meet her Salem, Massachusetts in-laws.

Twelve

ᴥ

No sooner had my good neighbor Lisbet left than my husband returned home with plans nearly finalized for the trip to Salem. Thom took a seat at the table, sharpened the point on his quill, and dipped it into the inkhorn to begin his list—everything we needed to pick up in Boston. "Sit down," he said. "You can help me think of things we need. Wheat meal and oats we can purchase at your papa's mill till our first planting."

I nodded. "We can pick that up on the way home."

"Salt pork to last till I can slaughter a wild boar. Jan Michaels will help me butcher. Can you salt and cure the meat?"

"I can learn."

"This winter I'll have time to make my own flail and fork handles," he said, "but I need tools essential for spring planting— shovels for moving dung, mattock and spade for digging in the ground and such, and hoes to weed the crops."

Thom closed his eyes for a moment. "Until the land is cleared and crops are established, God will provide fish and oysters and scallops as well as wild game."

I looked over Thom's shoulder and read from his list: Writing paper...,"

"Writing paper?"

"I notice you are about out."

"Thank you, Thom, although I think there may be little time for writing anything but lists." I continued reading his list:

"...Flintlock rifle, ammunition pouch, supply of black powder, bars of pig lead, a bullet mold."

Thom added replacement flints to the page. Then, in response to my questioning nudge, he laid down the quill and turned to me, sliding an arm around my waist. "You know the old Fordham plantation is not many miles away. Isn't that where the Carnarsie Indians tried to capture your young cousins? We must not become complacent," he said. "Not everyone is as peace-loving as your Shinnecock friends at Southampton."

His arm tightened around me, and I sensed the determined set of his shoulders. "As long as there is an Indian threat, settlers must stand guard as soldiers."

My husband's foresight and consideration warmed my heart, and I smiled as I brushed back the dark hank of hair that fell over one side of his forehead.

The list finished to his satisfaction, Thom wiped the tip of his quill, sealed the inkpot, and was up and headed for the door again. "Isaac Stratford is waiting for me at the Point. Have to load the oil on the ship now so we can get an early start in the morning."

"Oh, do tarry for a moment, Thom. Are you not hungry?" I reached for the basket of scones. "Here, take some of these. A trifle stale, but with butter, they'll make do." I grabbed a kitchen knife, sliced one of the biscuits in half, sandwiching it with a thick layer of Lisbet's butter.

He took a big bite, folded the rest within a linen napkin, and tucked them into his pocket. "I'll be back soon."

Although the day was warm, a chill wind suddenly whipped at my heart. "I beseech thee, my husband, be careful." But he was already out the door and down the trail.

When the packing was finished, I hung up my apron and helped myself to a scone and a big chunk of cheese — more than I needed, but, after all, I was eating for two. The image of a tiny form within me, nibbling on the biscuit, gave me pleasure. A little life within me.

I spread the remainder of the scones with butter and placed them in a basket to take with us for the morrow's breakfast. I wiped the knife clean and brushed the crumbs from the table, then paced around the room, smoothing the quilt on our bed, straightening the books on the shelf, checking the fireplace for hot coals. All set and in order, yet a nameless feeling of unease distressed me. Was I leaving something undone? Perhaps I was only tired — drowsy from the heat of the day. I took a seat on the bench outside our door and shaded my eyes from the late afternoon glare, gazing in the direction of Whalehouse Point. The sun sank lower in the sky, and I heard the lone call of a red-tailed hawk.

"Kree-eee-ar!"

Leaning back against the wall of the cabin, I dozed.

Yellow eyes blazed through a dismal grey sky, and a marauding savage with a wolf-like head appeared, whooping and howling. The creature's wide brow and toothy leer reminded me of nothing more than that awful Rev. Hardwick.

I jerked awake at the clip-clop of hooves galloping down the hard-worn trail toward our cabin and realized the whooping sound in my dream was a high-pitched "Halloo, there! Thom, are you home?"

I jumped up, and with a shaky hand straightened my apron and tucked a straggling strand of hair under my cap. In the dusk I could see the dark silhouette of a man on horseback. The rider dismounted quickly and secured the reins around a branch of the tree in the yard. Seeing me in the doorway, he called out, his voice high and raspy. "Mary, where is Thom? Where is he?"

Swiping at the sweat on his brow, Thom's brother, Henry, paused for a moment as if fighting to control his face before he spoke. "Father Scudder is gravely ill—" fearsome words he'd held inside from his home in Southold to ours in Babylon. Henry took a deep breath. "We must hasten to Salem before it is too late."

Still shaking from my dream, the breathless alarm I heard in his voice was contagious. "Thom is at Whalehouse Point loading the ship," I said. "We're on our way to Salem."

I jotted a note telling Dirk we were leaving while Henry loaded our baggage, tying it behind the saddle. Closing the door behind me, I tucked up my skirts and set my foot in the hand Henry offered. With a thwump I swung up onto the padded pillion Henry had placed behind the saddle and he mounted in front of me. The mare grunted at the extra weight, laid back her ears and took off at a gallop.

"Move it, Frost, you pokey old mare!" Keeping a tight rein, Henry shouted and spurred the sweating animal. "Hie, hie, hie!"

Upon reaching the bay, we saw the *Sea Hawk* approaching from the Point, already loaded with casks of oil. Having passed the news of their father's illness on to Thom, Henry jerked on Frost's reins and coaxed her onto the sloop, and with the crew already aboard, we set sail, not waiting till the morrow. A full moon would light the way through the break in the barrier reef and on around the island to the east and then north to Salem town.

Thom brought mugs and a jug of ale from the galley, and we sat on the deck in the moonlight with the rhythm of the waves acting as a calming tonic. Soon, Henry and Thom were reminiscing and telling me about their father.

"I was twenty when we landed at Salem," Thom said to me. "Henry was only nine, so we recall our immigration from wholly different perspectives. But one thing we always agree upon. No one in the family became seasick...except Father."

Henry nodded and chuckled. "I remember hearing him gasp after a terrible bout of vomiting, saying, 'Check the basin, Son. I think I lost my toes with everything else.' Sick as a hound he was, but never lost his sense of humor."

"Oh, yes, I remember that." Thom laughed and shook his head. "Mother kept giving him ginger-root tea to settle his stomach, but with every gust and gale, the rocking ship triumphed. Up came the ginger tonic. I think that's why I've never cared for gingerbread. Can't get it out of my head—Father's groans and gagging, and the sharp odor of ginger-root tea. Phewie!"

"Oh, your poor father!"

"Yep! Pitiful." Henry took another sip of ale. "The minute we landed, Father swore he'd never set foot on another boat. For nigh on twenty-one years, he's stayed right there in Salem."

Elbows on knees, Thom leaned forward to prop his chin in his palms. "I'd guess that's one reason he's been careful to keep his own counsel. Didn't want to be chased out of town like his hero, Sam Gorton!"

My ears perked up at the mention of this man. "Gorton? The minister who got kicked out of Boston for his outspoken beliefs?"

"One and the same. The Puritan government of Boston was so vexed with Rev. Gorton that they threw him in prison because his maid smiled at meeting house."

Thom raised his head and tilted one eyebrow as he turned to his brother. "Henry, do you remember what Father said to us almost every Sabbath morning?" Henry nodded and Thom turned to me.

"Father would keep his face straight and with great pretense of seriousness, he'd look around at the eight of us and say—"

Henry cleared his throat and lowered his voice in his best imitation of his father. "Now, children, be careful not to smile in meeting house today! I don't want to be spending time in a stone cold jail."

"And Mother would scold him." Thom grinned at the memory and raised his pitch to mimic her voice. "Hush, Thomas. The neighbors might hear you."

The brothers slapped their thighs, laughing.

Henry wiped his eyes and said, "Mother resolved to present the perfect image of the proper Puritan wife. She cared deeply how things looked to others. Still does, I suppose."

The wind was rising, and I wrapped my cloak more tightly around my shoulders. "Tell me more. Your parents were good church members, of course?"

"Well, after they settled in Salem, Mother joined First Church right away. But even though he sat in the meeting house every Sabbath, proper as any pious citizen, Father never became a member. I never knew why."

"Nor did I," Henry said. "Father's a courteous and friendly man, and very open-minded, but he usually keeps his opinions to himself.

"Believes we should have the right to make our own choices — without interference."

"So," I said, "when he moved his family to the colonies, he was looking for religious freedom?"

"Oh, no, that wasn't it at all. In spite of the fact that he was the oldest son of his father, he never thought it fair that he should inherit the wealth and the others do without. Thought it was a mockery to leave beloved daughters only a cow or two. He wanted us all to have the opportunity to work and grow and prosper. Said he couldn't change the whole of society, but he could improve the lot of his own family."

I hugged my knees and leaned closer. "I'm surprised he isn't at odds with the church government officials."

"Oh, Father is no raving zealot. But the old codger gets by with gentle comments that some magistrates might interpret as blasphemy."

Thom refilled his cup and turned to face me. "Perhaps this will surprise you. Father says women deserve the right to speak their minds. Says they should be listened to. Townspeople think he's only jesting. Everyone knows such a proposal 'twould be a sin against God's plan. They admire Father as a fine example of the Puritan work ethic. If they need a hand, Old Goodman Scudder's always there for them."

" 'Old Goodman Scudder goes the extra mile, just like Jesus,' one will say." Thom stretched, and then grinned, remembering his Father's droll reply. " 'Well, I may have been born of a virgin, but the similarity stops there.'"

Henry nodded. "Yep, I've heard him say just that. Then, in a spirit of camaraderie, they'll have a good laugh—unless it's Sabbath, of course."

"Salem town is blessed to have had liberal thinkers in the pulpit since we came in '35. Perhaps they take the focus off Father's peculiarities." Thom said. "Salem suits him."

I could no longer hold my eyes open. Thom helped me roll out a feather bolster, and the last I heard, Thom and Henry were still reminiscing about their father.

∽

From the ocean, we entered a Salem cove and sailed into the narrower Cow House River where we dropped anchor. Tension returned, tight as a sailor's knot. Wasting no time, we embarked and hurried along the water's edge toward the Scudder property. The path was so thick with damson trees and grapevines that the house was unobserved. Soon Thom spied a familiar landmark—Governor Endicott's sugar pear tree, laden with fruit. "We're almost there," he said. "God willing, we're not too late."

Within minutes, Thom's middle brother, John, came running down the trail to meet us, arms open wide. Nearly out of breath, he shouted as he came.

"Good news, brothers. Father's better. His fever's down, and he's dressed and sitting up today. I swear Mother's chicken broth and willow-bark tea will cure anything."

"Father may fall down six times but he'll get up seven. Hallelujah!"

Arms wrapped around their brothers' shoulders, they pounded each other on the back. Their laughter startled a cloud of twittering tree swallows out of the bayberry bushes, scattering wisps of down in their wake.

Father Scudder was sitting in the garden when we arrived. I'd have known him anywhere. Sun-weathered skin, crinkled around the eyes. Broad, high cheekbones, a long, straight nose, and dark eyes. Falling over his brow was a hank of dark hair. A single streak of grey matched the feathery tufts sprouting from his ears.

His eyes twinkled when Thom introduced me, and he smoothed back his hair with one hand—hair that brushed his shoulders, an anti Cromwellian statement if I ever saw one. Then he steepled his fingers, peering over them at me, as if taking my measure. With a quick upward curve of thin dry lips, he cocked his head to one side.

"So you are Mary."

Suddenly he engulfed my hands in his own, and his smile widened. "Thought Thom was never going to find you." His voice wavered only slightly. "Elizabeth, come out here."

Thom's mother immediately came forth, bearing a wooden goblet. "Here, my husband. A drop of broth with ale in it to strengthen you." Suddenly aware that he was not alone, she looked up and nearly dropped the ale cup.

"Thom! Henry! John, why did you not tell me your brothers were here?"

I stepped back while the Scudder boys enfolded this lovely woman in their arms. Like a typical Puritan wife, she wore a neat white apron and cap. Silvery-pewter tendrils had slipped from under her cap to frame petal-pink cheeks and smiling blue eyes. She was slim and wiry and moved with a youthful energy.

"Mother..." Thom turned to me. "I want you to meet my wife, Mary." The warmth of his expression echoed the pride in his voice. Her lips curved in a lovely, welcoming smile as she took my hand.

With his arm around me, Thom said, "I hear Henry and Catherine will add to your list of grandchildren in January."

"Yes," Mother Scudder said. "Isn't it wonderful? Baby Jonathan's going to have a new little sister or brother. That will make nineteen grandchildren."

Mother Scudder nudged her daughter. "Lizzie, are you going to share your news with your brothers?"

Lizzie blushed. "The Bartholomews are so fruitful, it is hardly a surprise. Another baby in May. That makes nine little Bartholomews. We'll have to build a bigger house over at Bartholomew Pond[92] and add another table before our next family gathering. That makes twenty Scudder grand-children."

"Twenty-one." Thom's eyes twinkled with news he could contain no longer. "In spring, Mary and I will make it twenty-one."

Again the Scudder brothers began laughing and clapping each other on the back. "It's about time, Thom, old man. Thought we were going to have to give you lessons." Henry elbowed Thom and then doubled over laughing.

Father Scudder beamed at his eldest son. "Elizabeth, I believe that's the medicine I've needed." He inhaled deeply. "Is that venison stew I smell? Someone help me in to the table. My knees are stiff as hasty pudding."

What a joyous reunion we had that day! Liam's widow and son, and Thom's sister Lizzie and her eight children joined us for dinner along with her husband Harold Bartholomew. He was a commissioner seated in the General Court with Captain William Hawthorne, and I half expected Lizzie to be a bit...well, niminy-piminy, married to such a prominent man, but she was not overly prim at all.

I found myself drawn smoothly into the flow of Scudder family life, and though Thom had moved to Southold several years ago, it was as if he had never left home. Mother Scudder and Lizzie, too, hovered over me like anxious broody hens, and I quite enjoyed the attention. I took this as a God-given opportunity to glean all the birthing and child care information I could, tucking it away in my memory to be retrieved in the spring.

Thom left me there in Salem while he and his brothers sailed on down to Boston to unload the whale oil and purchase a midwife's birthing book, the glass window panes he had promised me, and the tools and supplies on his list.

Thom's father liked to talk, and since I hadn't heard his stories before, whilst his sons sailed down to Boston, he took pleasure in telling me the tales that the rest of the family had heard over and over.

"You've heard of the great storm of August 1635? A ship called *The Angel Gabriel*," he said, "sailed as a consort to *The James,* the vessel that carried our Scudder family. The two ships were caught when a terrible thunder storm slammed into the area and blew them off course. The *James* first anchored near the Isles of Shoals, and The *Angel Gabriel* off Pemaquid on the coast of Maine. That ship sank, taking several lives down with it. The *James,* sails in rags, limped into Boston Harbor where it finally rent in sunder and split in pieces." No one perished, but oh, such seasickness we suffered." To Father Scudder, the trip was not the great adventure Thom and Henry remembered.

"I swore by all that's holy never to set foot on another sailing vessel. Besides..." Father Scudder paused and smiled. "Why should I go to sea? Salem has been good to me. I have been able to help my children find success in their endeavors. I'm richly blessed with grandchildren. I have a good woman who far surpasses David's Bathsheba in wisdom and beauty and industry."

His list reminded me of Thom's bent for detailed plans.

Father Scudder paused and scratched his head. "I may never understand the ways of the Lord, but the scripture says, "He maketh his sun to rise on the evil and on the good, and sendeth rain on the just and on the unjust." Perhaps I am not one of the chosen, but I *am* refreshed by the rain. I am blessed." He crossed his hands over his stomach and remained motionless for a long moment, eyes closed. Then he opened one eye and looked at me. "You still here?" He smiled and nodded, answering his own question. "You are a good listener, Mary. You remind me of my Elizabeth. Thom was right to wait for you."

Wafting in from the kitchen was the most delicious aroma. "Father Scudder," I said, what is it I smell?"

He smiled and said, "That is Mother's hot cross buns. Would you like to try one? If I remember right, they were favorites of Thom when he was a growing boy. Has he not asked you to make them?"

"Oh, yes, he has. They were my favorites too when my mother was alive. But I could never remember the special ingredient that made such a lovely aroma."

"It's cardamom," Mother Scudder said as she came in and passed around a plate of the buns for us to sample.

Such delight! A scene of my own mother kneading dough and shaping the buns flooded my memory—sweet on my lips and tongue—the taste and aroma of love. Even the sugary glaze on Mother Scudder's delicacy tasted just like Mama's.

"I believe I have the recipe you remember," Mother Scudder said. "Your Aunt Florence gave it to me when she was first in Salem. I'll send some cardamom pods home with you if you wish. Just grind them fine and add them with the other spices."

"My papa told me that Mama believed every day we live should be celebrated, so we enjoyed the buns time and again."

Mother Scudder nodded and smiled. "I quite agree. I hope you'll serve them often."

Autumn Anno Dom 1656
Salem, Massachusetts Colony

I enjoyed being with Thom's family and took pleasure in the hustle and bustle of Salem Village—the public market every Wednesday from 9 to 4, the friendly people—housewives and children, carpenters and planters, coopers and shipwrights, blacksmiths and merchants—each to his calling. No idlers.

Each investor in Salem had received private ownership of a half an acre of ground for each fifty pounds adventured in stock—a site for a house, ground to be fenced in and prepared for crops, and pastures for his cattle.[93] The Scudders owned rich bottom land on the south side of Cow House River, not far from Governor Endicott's acreage.

On the Sabbath, we joined Thom's family at First Church, and listened to the Rev. Edward Norris.[94] I sat in the women's pew with Thom's mother. Across the aisle, Thom caught my eye and smiled as he joined in the affirmation he'd made each Sabbath day for twenty years:

> We covenant with the Lord
> and one with another,
> and do bind ourselves
> in the presence of God,
> to walk together in all His ways,
> according as He is pleased
> to reveal Himself unto us
> in His blessed word of truth.

I brushed away an unexpected tear, suddenly homesick for... for a place that existed only in my dreams. Our own community of believers. A meeting house that would one day become First Church of Babylon, with pews for Goodman Thom Scudder and his wife and children.

Before we left Salem, Father Scudder presented us with a book from his library.

"My Uncle Henry wrote it," he said, "so I treasure it. I don't always agree with what he says, but it does give me something to ponder. Perhaps it will do the same for you."

Smiling, Thom reached to receive the gift, then drew back his hand. "Father, are you sure? This book is dear to you."

"Yes, I'm sure. Anyway, I've memorized the good parts. Time I passed it on to you. My farewell gift."

Dear Father Scudder, God willing, not farewell.

I couldn't see Thom's face clearly, couldn't see if his eyes, too, were filled with tears.

Thom handed the book to me, and I carefully opened it to the title page.

THE CHRISTIAN'S DAILY WALKE
in Holy
SECURITIE AND PEACE

by the Reverend Henry Scudder
a Presbyterian clergyman

summoned by King Charles to serve at
Collingbourne, Wiltshire, England

Printed in London, 1628
First Edition[95]

The crew of the *Sea Hawk* raised the sails and the anchor as soon as Thom and I and his brothers boarded. In a box on deck, I found goods Thom had bartered for—a cheese press and a churn, and a goodly supply of the salt I craved. Below deck, the crew had stowed the rest of Thom's purchases—a noisy crate of six hens and a rooster; an ox he immediately named Blue, and a milk cow he called Bossy.

"'Twill be good to have our own milk and butter,' he said. "Have you ever milked a cow?"

I laughed. "Somehow I can't picture the biblical Bath-sheba with a milk stool and bucket, but if that is part of the requirements of a yeoman's wife, I can learn."

We landed first at Southold on the northeast end of our island where Henry and John lived with their families. While they unloaded their baggage, Thom slipped the halter on Frost to lead her off the ship.

"Wait, Thom." Henry blocked his brother's way. "Since Mary suffers with muscle cramps if she walks very far, why don't you keep Frost for a while?"

"Won't the mare be having her catch-colt soon?"

"Near the end of the year," Henry said.

Catch-colt?

As if he could read my mind, Thom turned to me. "That's what the Indians call the foal of a mare that was bred ... accidentally."[96]

"Who knows what the foal will look like." Henry cleared his throat. "Anyway, the colt is yours, Mary, if you want it. In a year or so, when it's grown big enough to ride, you can return the mare."

My joyful shout startled the brothers and they started laughing. "Guess that means you accept?"

Once that was settled, Thom took the helm and steered the ship east and south around the tail of the island, west toward my family at Mecox, and then home. But for the call of gulls and the lapping of waves against the vessel, all was quiet. Though I stood by his side, Thom seemed lost in thought, totally oblivious to everything around him.

With a gentle nudge I brought him back. "Hatching an-other list, are you?"

Thom took a deep breath. "Hm-m-m. Well, a list of a different sort, perhaps. Now that we're to be parents, should we not set the spiritual tone in our household by keeping the Sabbath Day holy? What do you think? Cease our labors at mid-afternoon on Saturday as they do in Salem? Southampton, too, I'm sure. Rest of the day we can spend preparing for the Sabbath—isolated though we be. Someday we will have a community of folks around us and we will build a meeting house—"

"—with a bell that will call everyone to worship. Yes, I'd like that. I still miss the sound of the bells at St. Giles, back in Matlock."

Thom took my hand in his. "Until then, each morning and evening we can read to each other—from my Great Uncle Henry's book of devotions and your mother's Geneva Bible—"

"And we'll talk?" A hundred questions ran through my head. Who was the elect of God? Did he not love all his children? How could I accept what I could not understand? Dare I admit my many doubts? "You may find some of my ideas strange," I said.

"Even blasphemous?" Thom laughed. "Your questioning can hardly astound me. Remember, my father and I were both named for the Doubter. Thomas didn't believe, though he saw Jesus with his own eyes—until he touched the nail prints. So, 'forgive us our doubts.'"

"I think it be 'debts' but I'm sure He forgives mistranslations, too."

My teasing banter suddenly changed into fully-bloomed joy as I looked toward the afternoon glow of the sun shining across the waters. "Is that not Mecox Bay just ahead? A few more miles and we'll be with family again."

"Homesick, are you?"

"We've been so busy there's little time to think of that."
I turned my face toward Thom. "I do miss sleeping in our
own bed, but for a day or two it will be good to see Papa
and the rest of my kin." With both hands I smoothed and
patted the front of my gathered skirt. "Do you think
they'll guess?"

"Not unless there's a soothsayer among them. You're
still flat as a plank." Thom's eyes twinkled as he placed
his hands over mine. "Can you imagine your papa's
wide grin when we tell him he'll be a grandpa come
spring?"

By the time we dropped anchor at Mecox, it was of an
hour to cease Saturday's labors and prepare for the coming Sabbath. At eventide, after hearing that I would give
birth to a child come spring, the Ludlam and Fordham
families gathered for prayer and thanksgiving..

Across the table from Papa, Uncle Robert feigned a
stern warning. "Brother Ludlam, if the tithing man is
alert tomorrow, that broad smile of yours will surely earn
you a rap on the head."

"I'm going to be a grandfather! However can such good
news be contained in a solemn face?" Papa's sun-crinkled
eyes crinkled a bit more. "I only pray that my joy may
not turn into laughter."

Grinning, Uncle Robert offered him no relief. "Just be
thankful thou art not the one in the pulpit."

I knew they were jesting, but if, according to the scriptures, Jesus wept, did He not also laugh? I looked at my
husband, and by the mischievous look in his eyes, I
guessed he might well be tempted to ask the same question.

છ

Monday morning, we said goodbye to family members, set the course, and sailed home with the tide. The sun slowly vanquished the grey curtain of fog, and we could see the horizon. The morning air was brisk. Lapping waves of the flowing tide mirrored a flawless dome of sky going from gray to blue. Soon, I heard Thom's cry. "Look, Mary!" He pointed northwestward, across the thin strand of the barrier reef that guarded our stretch of land from the open sea. "There's our tulip tree." The eagerness of his voice echoed my own thoughts.

Almost home.

Dirk saw the sail of the sloop and came down to the shore to welcome us. "Isn't this a beautiful day!"

Indeed it was.

Dirk helped Thom and the ship's crewmen carry a load of purchases to the cabin. I lagged behind, admiring the changing season. A light coating of frost had become a nightly affair. The last goldenrods had died and the asters faded. Bristly black caterpillars seemed to be everywhere. When I picked one up and held it in my hand, it curled into a tight ball. Thom and the men were already headed back to the ship for another load of provisions.

Look, Thom," I said. "Look how narrow the orange band is around the wooly bear's middle. Not wide like last winter."

"I noticed," he said. "Thin bands like that mean we're in for a bad winter." That was all the reminder Thom needed of the work that must be done.

"No time for fishing today," he said to the men. "We need a barn for our animals."

"Goodman Scudder," Dirk said, "with your permission, I'll ride on home. My *oma* is eager to come tell your goodwife our good news, and *Opa* Michaels will help with the barn raising."

While I hurried on to the cabin, Dirk headed down the trail, and Thom's crew returned to the sloop for broad axes, a bow saw, and a froe—cutting tools for hewing trees and for riving the logs for the fence pales and shingles. When they came back to the cabin, one of the men handed me a left-over parcel of the cured fish like we had enjoyed on our trip to Salem. "'Twould be good for our midday meal, perhaps."

I thanked the crewman and then watched as the men began clearing oaks from a field where crops would grow next spring.

"We'll rough-hew the logs into planks," Thom told them. "I have the measurements ready." Thom's rapid-patter directions seemed to encourage the pace of their work.

"Big enough for a cow, an ox, and a mare," he said. "Divide the inside into three sleeping stalls. We'll open them into a fenced-in barnyard where our animals can run free, protected from wolves and wildcats."

He brushed the lock of hair from his forehead as if clearing his vision into the future.

"Might as well section off a private corner for the mare," he said. "Come winter, she'll need it for birthing. For bedding, we'll layer the floor with fresh-cut meadow hay." I saw a muscle twitch near the corner of Thom's wide mouth.

"What's so amusing?" I said.

"Well, if we layer the floor with hay, Frost can have her bed and eat it too."

So hot and tired we were from the long morning's work, our laughter turned into childish giggles.

"Have her bed and eat it too! That's a good one, Captain Scudder."

"Lucky horse," another said. "If she gets hungry long towards midnight, she can just take a bite of her blanket."

Laughter eased our weariness. Refreshed, the crew returned to their labors.

I turned away and carried the package of salted cod into the cabin. I had yet to find places to put all our purchases for the house, but I knew the men would soon be hungry. I stirred the fire, then turned to the cupboard for flour and other ingredients for bread and fish stew. Up to my elbows in flour, I didn't notice Dirk's return with his grandparents until Lisbet popped in the door.

"Couldn't wait to tell you." she said. "The wife of my youngest son is soon needing a midwife. Their second child." She found a spoon to sample the large kettle of stew hanging over the fire. "Needs more thickening," she said. Grabbing a handful of flour and a sprinkle of basil leaves from the cupboard, she stirred them into the pot as she chattered.

"Next month, Dirk will accompany me back to Vlissingen. 'Twill be good to see my sons and their families again." She took a clean napkin from her apron pocket and wiped a stream of perspiration from her forehead.

I added a final pat to a batch of bread dough, dusted it with flour, and plopped it into a long-handled skillet before offering my congratulations. "That's wonderful news, my friend!" With one hand I shielded my face from the fire, and with the other, shoved the pan into the back of the fireplace to bake.

I turned to Lisbet who was finding places to put the rest of the supplies. "It is my turn to lend a neighborly hand while you're gone. We have brought home Henry's mare—Frost's her name— so I can ride now. While you're away, I will watch over whatever still needs care after the harvest."

Lisbet gave a nod and brushed at a strand of hair that adhered to her cheek. "And when I see the Bowne family, I'll give them your greetings."

∞

After we finished putting the cabin in order following the midday meal, Lisbet and I went out to see the progress on the barn. The men had added a manger where the animals would feed, and near the door, they mounted hooks where tools, buckets, and Frost's bridle and saddle would hang. By nightfall, all but the roof was in place.

Thom was indeed pleased. "Haven't seen better work since the barn raisings in Southold. Come back in the morning and we'll add the roof."

The Michaels family bade us goodbye until the morrow, and the crew returned to the ship.

Thom poured cups of grain and bunches of hay into the manger, and then led the animals into their proper stalls. "Come watch, Mary. It's milking time." He grabbed a bucket and a T-shaped stool fashioned from scraps of wood.

The way he balanced on the stool beside the cow and clenched the bucket between his knees looked effortless. He leaned his head in toward her flank, and grasped two swollen teats. "Easy there, Bossy." Over his shoulder, he looked up at me. "See," he said. "You squeeze first one teat and then t'other, top to bottom." I watched the level of foamy milk rise in the bucket.

Thom stood up and handed the stool to me. "I left the front teats for you." He grinned with only a slight hint of skepticism. "No other way to learn," he said.

At Bossy's side I squatted over the stool and then carefully planted my bottom on the rough seat. The stool wobbled and I drew in a quick breath. Thom raised an eyebrow, then handed me the half-full bucket of milk.

"Clasp it between your knees," he said.

With feet planted wide for balance, I brought my knees inward to hold the bucket.

"Now grasp the front teats."

I followed Thom's directions and with sweaty hands, I squeezed. Nothing happened.

"Try it again. Squeeze harder and pull down a bit.

Suddenly the cow objected and a kick sent the bucket a-spin. Milk splattered my stockings, and the pail bounded across the floor. The stool tipped and I fell backwards, landing with one hand splat in the middle of a fresh cow pile. E-e-u-ew!

Thom doubled up with laughter. "Soft landing, eh?"

If anger were arrows, I'd have aimed a full quiver at his backside. Better yet, I'd have grabbed a handful of the warm, greenish manure and thrown it at him.

Reason prevailed and I wiped my hand on the hay. If Thom could milk a cow, so could I.

I retrieved the bucket and seated myself on the stool. Speaking softly, I rubbed one hand over a hairy brown flank to gentle the cow. "Whoa, Bossy. We'll both feel better when this is over." She turned her head and peered at me with soulful brown eyes as if giving me permission to try once more. Seizing a teat in each hand, I squeezed. Splish……splish….splash, splish…splash..splish. Rich milk squirted into the pail.

Finished with the chore, I handed Thom the half-full-again bucket. I arose and stretched, then stepped to the end of the barn and hung the stool on its hook.

"Old man, do you know how to work butter after it's churned?" I looked at him and raised an eyebrow. "Know how to use the cheese press?"

Thom shook his head.

I made no effort to hold back a smug smile. "Then I expect we'll see who laughs last."

ഏ

Father Scudder had warned that idleness gave occasion for excess and mischief, but in the ensuing weeks we had little chance of that. While the *Sea Hawk* was at anchor, if Thom needed not their help, the crew assumed a dawn-to-dusk ritual: fishing, cleaning, salt-curing the catch, and spreading them in the sun to dry. With an adequate store for our own use, there'd be enough left for a goodly trade in the city.

I recall little of those months, only a dreadful tiredness that seeped into my very bones.

Come the dawn, upon my first waking moment, I started a cooking fire, stoking the flame with logs we had carried in the previous evening. An iron kettle hung over the fire continuously, like a peas-porridge pot, and the wood fire smoldered throughout the day.

By lantern light, Thom saw to the morning milking and tended the animals. In the early light, I took the short walk to the spring, filled two kettles with water, and carried them home on a yoke that sat across my shoulders. I first poured part of one container into a basin, then hung the other over the blazing fire. Into boiling water, I stirred a measure of ground grain for breakfast porridge, then moved the pot farther from the center of the fire so it could simmer. Sometimes after adding a handful of currants to the porridge for sweetening, I cracked eggs into a skillet heating on a trivet in the fireplace, or heated salt pork or cod. Thick slices of yesterday's loaves spread with butter completed the meal.

When Thom finished his barnyard chores, he carried in the bucket of warm milk and set it aside for cream to rise.

While I filled our bowls or trenchers with the meal I had prepared, Thom dipped his hands into the basin of water, splashed it over his face, brushed back his hair, and took his seat at the table. Eager to get on with the meal, his grace was short.

After eating, I rushed to put the room in order while Thom reached for the Bible and his uncle's book. We seldom missed devotions. We read to each other for a few minutes, free to question the verses we did not understand. Finally, Thom took out his work list, and we went over it together. After asking God to guide us, we arose and directed our energy towards each project, first to last. When one was completed, we drew a bold charcoal line through it. A mark of satisfaction.

I usually came back to the cabin ahead of Thom to prepare the midday meal. While bread baked and stew simmered in the pot, if the cream had risen to the top of the milk by then, I skimmed it off, saving some to pour over the berries Thom enjoyed. The rest I churned into butter, worked it, salted it, and packed it away in wooden molds for storage or trade.

We stopped only briefly to sup at midday and then returned to our tasks, toiling until well past lantern light.

After evening chores were finished, we shared a meal of bread and cheese and perhaps leftover stew. Then Thom would lay down his spoon and read to me for a few minutes from his uncle's book of devotions:

DIRECTIONS HOW TO END THE DAY WITH GOD

Look back and take a strict view of your whole carriage that day past. Reform what you find amiss; and rejoice as you find you have done well. Fall asleep with some heavenly meditation, Then will your sleep be more sweet and secure, your dreams fewer, or more comfortable; your head will be fuller of good thoughts, and your heart will be in a better frame when you awake. (See Prov. 3:21-25 and 6:20-23.)[97]

From Mama's Geneva Bible, I read the scripture Uncle Henry's book suggested: My sonne, keepe thy father's commandement, and forsake not thy mother's instruction.

Thom's eyes met mine, full on. "I'm only beginning to realize how blest I am to have such godly parents."

I nodded. "Yes, and I know thou wilt be as good a parent as Father Scudder."

I hesitated. "I'm not so sure about me. I'm scared and unprepared. But the time draws near, ready or not...."

I felt some reassurance when Thom took my hand in his, waiting for me to continue the verse. "What does it say next?"

"Verses 23 and 24 say...the commandement is a lanterne, and instruction a light: and corrections for instruction are the way of life. Then shalt thou walke safely by thy way: and thy foote shall not stumble. And when thou sleepest, thy sleepe shal be sweete.

With that thought, we said goodnight and crawled into bed.

℘

I remember a day Thom's list was longer than usual, so I took over his morning chores. By then I had developed the knack of milking, but this day, the task made my hands and arms knot with painful cramps. Back in the cabin, I rested at the table for a moment, laying one hand across my stomach. Could the baby within me feel the throbbing pain? I moved my hand. My head ached, and worry overtook me. Where would we get clothing for this child? With cramps like these, I could not hold a sewing needle to stitch a baby dress.

A blue jay began pecking out a rat-a-tat-tat, as if someone were knocking at the door. In the recesses of my mind I heard a deep voice. Perhaps it was God himself.

"Your heavenly Father feedeth the birds and clothed the lilies," the words reminded me. "Are ye not much better than they?"

The cramps in my hands let up. I took the quill, inkhorn, and a scrap of paper from the shelf and began making a list—Thom would want a list—of items the baby would need:

Swaddling clothes, extra linens, woolen blanket, cradle.

I did not notice the sun until it was high in the sky. I jumped up, grabbed a basket and hurried to the herb garden to gather sorrel and leaves of lemon balm. I'd add it to hot butter dip for the lobster. On the way back, I stopped in the barn for a moment to feed Frost a handful of the leafy greens.

Thom came in at his expected mealtime, worn-out and more than a little tetchy. The cabin was empty, the table strewn with paper and writing utensils, and worse, nothing in the pot but boiling water.

As I hurried from the barn, I saw him standing at the open door, fists clenched.

"Can you not stop your dilly-dallying long enough to ply the pipkin for your husband?"

I swallowed hard and squared my shoulders. "There are oatcakes in the oven, and fresh-churned butter to go with them, and 'twill take only a minute to heat yesterday's leftover lobster."

"Lobster again? Can you cook nothing else?" His voice was bitter as the sorrel I'd gathered.

I could hardly abide such criticism. "Wherefore doth you protest, Thom Scudder? Has it not been seven days since you last brought fresh meat to the board?"

The dismissive toss of his head made me even angrier, and I did not hold back my wicked thoughts.

"Day after day I labor with you...and for you. Undertake this, do that, whate'er's to be done, and all the while carrying a child. Can you not grant me one moment's respite?"

"My mother carried six babes, and I never heard her complain."

"I hope you value your mother's worth."

"She said it was God's will that she endure the pain of childbirth."

"And I say, her God has a strange sense of fairness. Why should women pay for Eve's sin?"

Thom gasped. "It is good that we live *not* in Salem. There the hangman's *knot* would surely silence your tongue."

With my head held high, I picked up the container of leftover lobster and pitched it into the yard. Suddenly, I burst out crying.

By the time I had dried my tears, I was alone in the cabin. Though I remember it not, I suppose Thom found something to eat before he went back to work. I only recall thinking that this life was just too, too trying.

After work, we spent the evening in dour silence, and I was not sure it was only coincidence that called Thom away the next day.

"The weather in Southampton has been unusually dry, and their cattle need hay," Thom said. His crew and the Michaels men helped him load some of Babylon's surplus hay harvest, and then he sailed away to Southampton. I missed him even before he was out of sight.

Thirteen

؏

FALL, ANNO DOM 1656
BY THE RIVERS OF BABYLON ON LONG ISLAND

In the barn, I lifted the saddle from its hook and carried it to the mare. "Hello, Frost." Her whinnied greeting made me feel less alone. I patted her nose and rubbed my hands down her back and over her belly. It seemed to me that Frost's middle had expanded to an alarming size in the last month. According to Thom, it took almost a year from conception to birth of a colt, so she had a month or more to wait. I slipped the bridle over her head and threw the saddle over her back. "Easy there, Frost." The mare nudged me with her nose, and whinnied again as I tightened the girth. "I know the waiting is difficult, girl." I led her over to the grain box and used it for a step up so I could more easily reach the stirrup.

"No need to hurry, girl." We moved at a gentle pace until we reached the clear mineral spring at the head of Skookwams Creek. Frost lowered her head to drink.

Heavy, silvery-gray clouds deepened my feeling of isolation and loneliness. I missed Thom, though his harsh words loitered like a skulking wound. My eyes prickled as I sat on Frost's back, resting there under the trees.

We rode on toward the shore. About a mile in from South Bay there was only sand and salt and sedge meadows as far as I could see on either side, then a fringe of oak trees that I knew to be a mile or two deep. From there northward five to ten miles was a barren pitch-pine and scrub oak plain—a bed of sand, with occasional thin strips of sandy loam. Babylon was inhabited by very few colonists, and then only near the heads of creeks. I was alone. Neighbors were at least five miles away. A sudden chill in the air made me shiver.

I missed the sound of human companions, of family. I missed the sounds of Southampton—the neighborly sounds of women batting their laundry and sharing gossip as they spread the garments to dry on sweet-smelling lavender bushes. I missed the music of Salem's church bells, the call of the town crier, the clatter of horses' hooves on cobblestone streets.

I missed Thom.

The rasping cry of cicadas had been silenced by the cold leaving only the slumberous fiddle sound of a few late crickets. Only the autumn sounds of the wilderness remained: A rising wind. The drawn-out howl of a wolf. The muted babble of water falling over rocks and on down to the soft, ceaseless sighing of the sea.

I turned Frost toward the cabin. It was still hours before feeding time, but I gave her a handful of grain and slipped off her saddle and bridle. Later, after finishing barnyard chores, the usually short autumn evening stretched on interminably. From the top of previous days' milk, I spooned cream into the wooden churn, then finally relaxed to the soothing rhythm of the paddle while chanting a long-remembered rhyme: "Come butter come, come butter come. Papa is here, a-waitin' for some." After a time, clots of butter swirled in a thin, milky liquid. I poured the buttermilk into a mug, and the butter onto a platter, then worked the thickened spread with a paddle until the last drop of liquid was removed. After packing the butter into a mold and setting it aside, I pulled Uncle Henry Scudder's devotional book from the shelf. With one finger, I skimmed his table of contents.

CONCERNING BEING ALONE

When you are alone, be sure that you are well and fully exercised about something that is good, either in the works God has appointed you, or in reading, or in holy meditation or prayer.

I removed Mama's Bible from shelf and let God guide the place it should fall open.

Psalm 137:1 By the rivers of Babylon, there we sat down, yea, we wept, when we remembered Zion.

Clutching the Bible to my heart, I closed my eyes. Was there something I should remember about Zion? Listening with all my senses, I could not find solace, could hear neither God's voice nor Thom's. Alone by the waters of Babylon, I wept.

The next morning stretched out before me as wide as the horizon of muddy-grey clouds. At the barn, I fed the animals, Blue the ox; Frost and Bossy, and then did the milking. On the way back to the house, I scattered grain for the chickens that scurried across the yard, squabbling and bickering over who would get first peck.

I was not hungry. I could not eat alone. I might have ridden to Lisbet's house, but I had been there the day before Thom left.

No. Lisbet couldest think only of preparations for her trip back to Vlissingen. I could not abide another hour of her cheerful chatter and her fastidious fall cleaning frenzy.

Returning to the barn, I saddled Frost and rode eastward. When I came to the banks of a stream, I followed it inland. Beyond a distant knoll, an ascending ribbon of smoke appeared. Indians? Fear o'ertook me, but in spite of potential danger, I could not check my curiosity when I heard the whinny of a horse. Perhaps Frost was as lonely as I, for at the sound, she broke into a joyous gallop. At the top of the rise, I pulled back on the reins and Frost halteth. Not too many yards away were a small, newly-built cabin and a grey horse in a pine log corral. The newcomers heard Frost's answering whinny and ran out to meet us.

"Good morning, neighbors," I said. "I'm Thom Scudder's wife, Mary. We live about a half-hour's ride southwest toward the sea."

The young man introduced himself and his consort—Rev. Ransom True and his new bride, Rachel.

"Wilst thou come in, Goody Scudder and share our breakfast?" the comely woman said.

Rev. True's brows drew together, but his gentle voice implied a forgiving spirit. "Whatever art thou doing out riding this holy morn? Keepst thou not the Sabbath?" He held out his hand to help me alight.

I'm sure my face turned red. I had not marked the long hours. Surely the Sabbath had come and gone. "Prithee, forgive me, Sir. My husband is away, and I have lost track of the days."

He nodded his head, and I was much relieved when his expression softened.

Joyous I felt at finding settlers less than an hour's ride north from our cabin—souls who received me with Christian affection.

After sharing their breakfast from the day-old kettle of porridge, Rev. True rose from the table and invited me to stay for the sermon he had prepared—"in case God sends someone to listen."

Surely God had done just that, for Rev. True's scripture was the verse from Psalm 137 that had but a few days ago set me to pondering.

By the rivers of Babylon, there we sat down, yea, we wept, when we remembered Zion.

The preacher cleared his throat and continued. "Zion, as it is referred to here," he said, "is a symbol for Jerusalem, the city of the Jewish people. Captives, they were lonely for home. Why would they not weep? Here, they had no freedom."

Rev. True looked around the room, as if seeing filled pews in a new meeting house. "Many colonists travel to the colony to find a home where they can worship as they see fit. Yet, the rigid rules of the hierarchy suck their hopes dry.

The Rev. True lowered his eyes and folded his hands. "Here on this island may we conduct ourselves according to the commandments Christ himself gave to us: First: Thou shalt love the Lord thy God with all thy heart, and with all thy soul, and with all thy mind. Second: Thou shalt love thy neighbor as thyself. On these two commandments dependeth the whole law and the prophets."

His words of benediction brought me hope and warmed my heart.

Ransom and Rachel True promised to visit us soon, and I bade them goodbye and swung myself onto Frost's back. As we traveled down True's creek toward home, a presentiment of the future filled my eyes. Homesteads and lodges of peace-loving people—Indians, and white men of differing faiths: Congregationalists and Dutch Reformed and Quakers as well as free thinkers. Yeomen and craftsmen, housewives and children—settlers adding their names to the myriad creeks like Skookwams and Sampawams, streams that flowed south to the sea:

Shotbolt and Rowe, Longstreet and Ludlam;
Jones, Seaman, Kelly, and Carman too,
Heath and Howell, Halsey, and Fordham,
McDonald and Murch, Wright and True.

As I rode toward the shore, the vision joined a rich babble of voices in a cantata of joy.

ဆာ

In the kitchen Monday morn, I mixed a handful of sweet currants into the bread dough, believing that Thom must surely be on his way home. Still, at the sound of quickening footsteps outside, I could but remember the heartless words he had said to me. I gripped the edge of the mixing table. Had I not the right to my anger?

When he reached for me, I pulled back, stiff as Lot's wife.

Thom's eyes darkened. "Were you worried, Mary?" His words came forth in breathy gasps for he had run the distance from the ship. "I was at your Papa's mill Saturday morn, ready to sail home, but a traveler stopped me." Thom paused to catch his breath. 'Twas my brother

Henry. He'd ridden down from Peconic Bay, and he brought a package for you from the Scudder family. Here 'tis." He handed me the gift, but without waiting for me to open it, he continued. "Henry and John have sold their Southold land at a goodly profit, and have purchased new land up at Huntington. A grand opportunity lies before them, and they are eager to move. Wanted us to join them there, but I said no." Thom stood still for a moment, then leaned forward and kissed me gently on the forehead.

"By that time," he said, "the sun was far in the sky. Time to stop labors and prepare for the Sabbath with your Papa."

Tears welled in my eyes. I reached up and covered his lips with my hand. "It's all right, my husband." I leaned my head against his shoulder, soaking up strength and the warmth of his arms around me.

"I swear by all that's holy," he said, "harsh words will never again separate us for even one night." With the tip of his tongue he flicked away a salty tear that had tracked its way down one of my cheeks and across my lips.

Distracted, I pulled away. The stirring in my belly, like bubbles bursting, was much stronger now than before. Oblivious to my husband, I looked down and placed my hands over my stomach. "Oh, my tiny catch-colt. Is that you I feel?"

"Mary, what is it? The baby?" Thom put one hand lightly over mine. "You must not call our baby a catch-colt." His smile broadened as he felt the gentle kicks. "Have you thought of a name?"

His question suddenly awakened me to fearsome reality. In five months or so, I would face the pangs of birth.

"Aphrodite, I will be with you. Don't you know? You are my family, you and our babe. The child is not fatherless. He is heart of my heart for I have loved you both from the day I led you out of the water."

I smiled then, remembering his concern. "Surely you would not call our babe 'Moses?' I was considering 'Sarah' "

"Oh, it's a boy," he said. "See how hard he kicks." Thom threw back his head and let out a great peal of laughter. "I think I know how Abraham felt when God told him he would be the father of many nations. Abraham's laughter, like mine, came forth in sudden joy." Thom paused for a moment, still holding his hands over the baby's nesting place. "Let's name him Isaac."

Butterfly wings fluttered again inside me.

"See, he already knows his name," Thom said. "Isaac Scudder." He smiled at me, then knelt and pressed his lips lightly against the beating wings.

"Hello, little Isaac."

ဆ

During October and November, Thom helped Jan Michaels gather in the harvest, cutting, curing and carting most of the hay from the marshes to northside homes. Then they fit up his dwellings against winter. The Michaels' garden, sheds, and barn, as well as their cabin, were surrounded by a high fence—a palisade to keep out intruders, animals and savages alike. Jan planned to enlarge the enclosure, giving his animals more room within.

I often rode to the Michaels' with Thom so I could help Lisbet prepare meals for the men, using fresh produce from her garden—cabbages, parsnips, turnips, garlic and leeks, too. All ready to be gathered in.

"After harvest, we'll go hunting," Jan said to Thom. There be great herds of deer and flocks of wild turkeys in the woods. All sorts of eggs, and an abundance of water fowl. And, then, Thom, you can help me butcher the pig. You had no time to plant crops this year, so we will share our bounty with you.

Not to be outdone by his neighbor's generosity, Thom offered what he could. "My crew will help you with your harvest, and we will share the goodly supply of cod and shellfish they have already salted, with more coming— plenty for trading after our families have stored all we need. Trout that the crew have caught will taste good, too. Skookwams Creek is choked with trout."

Jan patted his round belly and smiled. "Nothing I like better than trout dipped in ground corn and fried in a skillet."

By the time harvest was finished, the weather had turned cold. Butchering weather, the men decided. Lisbet had raised an orphaned piglet after their sow burrowed under the palisade one night and led her litter off into the woods. There a wildcat had killed the sow and all of the litter but one. So attached Lisbet had become to the tiny piglet now grown into a fat hog, she could not bear to witness the slaughter.

Some of the fresh pork we boiled with dry beans in the kettle over the fireplace, an ever-ready meal for the whole workweek. The rest of the pig we preserved, rubbing the back legs down with a salt-based cure flavored with sugar—Lisbet's closely guarded family recipe. Salt pork seemed to be the one ingredient that no recipe lacked.

I'd helped Aunt Alice the previous year when Uncle Robert's congregation had come together to butcher a pig for them, but I was nervous lest I embarrass my husband with my ignorance. I should not have worried. Nothing was more pleasing to Lisbet than to demonstrate her huswifery skills.

Some of the pork we cut into small pieces, then ground the meat, seasoned it with hot sausage spices from Lisbet's neat cupboards, and stuffed the mixture into entrails cleaned outside in a wooden tub. I was of little help there. I—or perhaps it was baby Isaac—could not abide the smell.

After wrapping the salt-cured meats in linen sacks, we hung them from the eaves of the low roof that jutted out from the kitchen—a small brewing room they had built on the coolest side of their cabin.

The scraps of fat we rendered into lard, some for cooking, and some for making lye soap. A smelly process that burned my nose and made my stomach roil.

The peas in Lisbet's garden were not worth gathering, she told me. "I fear they were too late sown. They came up well and blossomed, but the sun parched the blooms before the pods had set on."

The tangled squash vines were laden with yellow crook-necks. Fat pumpkins peaked through the autumn-orange leaves. In the woods, brown nuts were falling, grapes were purpling, and all sorts of berries—blackberries, blueberries, raspberries—were ripe for picking.

We'd have enough dried beans and berries and pumpkin, as well as salt pork and fermented cider, to last well into next May.

When the fruits of the harvest had been gathered and stored, the crew of the *Sea Hawk* invited us to a clambake celebration. By the shore, they had dug a deep pit, built a fire in it and then let the fire burn down to coals. On top of these coals, they placed layers of seaweed, dripping with ocean water. Between layers, they put clams and lobsters, then after a while added ears of corn and chunks of squash. Steamed by moisture in the kelp, the aroma created was better than that from any iron kettle.

Thom and I rode over to invite the Rev. Ransom True and Rachel, his wife. Jan Michaels surprised us when he asked if he might invite the Indian families who had helped them so much with their first planting. Of course we agreed. "'Twill be almost like having our Shinnecock friends eat with us."

Dirk rode westward to their small village to invite them to share with us, and soon came leading them back with him. "They don't speak English too well, but then I can't speak their language either," Dirk said, laughing.

The Secoutagh Indians were from the same Iroquois family as the Shinnecocks, so before long we were pointing and speaking in broken sentences, and calling each other by name. I was drawn to the serene comportment of the woman Lisbet introduced to me.

"Tania is gifted in the healing arts," she said. "She helped me when I burned with fever last winter. And if ever again I have need of a midwife, I'll call on her."

She turned to the woman. "I'm going back to Vlissingen next week to assist my daughter-in-law's midwife. Another Michaels' grandchild," Lisbet told her.

Tania smiled and nodded as if she understood.

It taketh not a common language to enjoy food together. Before the Secoutaghs went back to their lodge, our faces were not only covered with juices from the clam bake, but were also wreathed in friendly smiles.

∞

That first autumn of our marriage, Thom and I shared much of the work and responsibility — the closest we ever came to real equality. Later in November, Thom and I hitched up the ox and cleared land that had not yet been cleared by the Indians. It was good that Blue and Frost had been trained to plough and halter. We moved rocks and felled trees for fields to be planted to wheat, rye, oats, or barley when the weather warmed. After the planting, there would be harrowing, hoeing, and weeding, and then harvest again — threshing, winnowing, carting, cleaning, milling, and storage of grain.

I spent most of my mornings preparing food for the day ahead. A big morning meal to break the fast now that Thom was toiling and moiling such long hours — porridge, turkey eggs I had found in hidden nests in the woods, wild berries with thick cream, and salted cod.

Our midday meal combined the pungent taste of freshly picked sorrel or watercress with a modest lobster or cod fish stew or trout caught from our waters.

When Thom took time off to go hunting, we had stewed squirrel, goose, turkey, pheasant, or one time, venison — from a deer Thom caught marauding our garden. Some of the meat we shared with the crew and our neighbors, and some we salted and cured.

In the evening, we washed down cheese and bread with the beer Lisbet taught me to brew. It took only a walk in the woods to find hops growing wild, which we combined with barley harvested from Jan and Lisbet's fields.

One cold and dismal morn, a violent gale with heavy rain turned into blowing snow, the first of the season. The wind came in gusts, and we could barely see across the yard. The previous day, Frost had started acting out of sorts, getting up and down, rolling and showing signs of discomfort. I tried to soothe her. Perhaps she was colicky. According to the lay of shadows, it must be early December, too soon for the foal's arrival.

The next morning, Frost began wandering in and out of the shed and around the yard, frequently lying down, then rolling and getting up again as if looking for a calm, comfortable nesting place.

"She will probably give birth in the middle of night," Thom said. "It's important to keep her away from the other animals but close to our cabin in case she needs help.

By evening the snow was still falling. Gusts and gales had piled huge drifts everywhere. Thom and I bundled up in warm woolen cloaks and mittens, and with a lighted lantern in hand, we tramped through the snow to check on the mare. In the barn we found Frost lying in a large pile of hay, wet with sweat in spite of the cold. I knelt beside her and ran my hands down her neck to comfort her. I could feel the thump-thump-thump of her pulse and hear her labored breathing. She got up, and then lay down again in a position that suited her better. Slight contractions soon increased in intensity, coming closer together. The mare continued her actions, lying down, then standing, pacing about, then lying down again, making nests in the hay.

Suddenly, I heard the rush of her water. My breathing quickened as the mare's contractions grew stronger. Her legs strained. With each push she grunted. "Uh-h, uh-h."

The foal's front feet emerged, one more forward than the other. The nose appeared, black and shiny. The shoulders slanted through the birth canal. To my surprise, every part of the foal I could see was enclosed in a nearly transparent, shimmery gray sack. When it tore open, I heard Thom gasp. His eyes were bleak, his expression a mask.

I tried to read his face, and then said, "My birthing book says some babies are born with a caul. Is that what I'm seeing? That's supposed to mean they are born to good fortune."[98]

Thom took a deep, unsteady breath and with a dark look, turned to me.

"You are a gullible child, Mary. This is a horse, not a human."

I had never heard that scoffing tone in my husband's voice before. It rankled. With trembling hands, Thom brushed a lock of hair from his eyes and with single-minded urgency, turned back to the mare.

Tearing off his mittens, he got in position to help. Sweat poured down his face. I stepped forward, kerchief in hand to wipe his forehead.

"Thom, let me—"

"Get back, Mary," he said, holding up an unyielding hand to hush me. "I've done this a hundred times before. Just stay out of the way."

With another push from the mare and a pull from Thom, the foal was half way out. They rested for a second, then one more push and the foal was born.

Frost's once distended belly and flanks now appeared hollow. She rested from the effort, then sat up and turned her head to see her baby. A healthy colt. Before his back legs were even out of the sack, he was trying to get up. Unsuccessful, he tried again but fell to the ground, exhausted.

Frost turned her head and rubbed the nose of her foal, nickering. The umbilical cord broke naturally as the new colt succeeded in rising and then took a step or two. Wet but beautiful, he lay down beside his mother and she began licking him dry. Finally, she stood and nudged him to rise. On wobbly legs, he made it to his feet and began poking at his mother's swollen teats with his nose. The effort was tiring, and he lay down again next to her in the nest of straw. Folding his long legs under him, he curled up in a ball.

Silently, Thom and I made our way toward our cabin. The snow continued. The wind whipped my hair and skirts, and I shivered and pulled my woolen cloak tighter around me.

The fire had died down, but it would take more than another log to provide the warmth I craved. I could not rest with this cold tension between us.

"Thom, we must talk."

He jerked away, turning toward the ice-covered window. His voice was low. "Mary..." He paused, as if searching for words. "What we witnessed tonight with the foal was a miracle. It took my breath away. When I saw the sack tearing too early, I was afraid the baby colt would die without ever seeing the day."

Thom's shoulders sagged. When he turned to me, his eyes held a hint of the shadows I had seen when Henry told him his father might be dying.

"I have hurt you," he said. "Forgive me for speaking so harshly…for pushing you away." Thom rubbed the back of his hand across his eyes. "It is not your fault I was afraid. With the birth, so many emotions rose up in my throat, I could scarcely swallow. It made me appreciate even more the gift of the life you are carrying within you."

I smiled, and reached out to him. "I forgive you."

For a moment, we stood locked together, but even within the warmth of his arms, the cabin was frigid.

Together we scooted our bed closer to the fire, and while Thom added a slow-burning log to the grate, I hung our outer wear on pegs by the door. We slipped into long, wool-flannel nightshirts, and then, beneath several quilts and coverlets, we nestled together like two spoons. Thom laid an arm around me, and with his hand, caressed the small round swell of my belly.

I tried to hide my tears by burying my face in the feather pillow, but Thom heard me sniffling. He pulled me closer.

"I beseech thee, sweeting, don't cry." So soft was his whisper, I could scarcely hear him. "Have I further disheartened thee?"

"Another quarrel."

He hesitated. "Yes."

"Know thou not that we can share the bad times as well as the good? You can trust me. Let us not have *this* quarrel again. Keep in mind, though, if we remain true to our own selves, there will be others."

Thom laughed. "Here I thought I loved thee because of thy buxom bosom and soft plump bottom. And now I find it's also a wise woman I've married. Oh, Aphrodite! I am fortunate indeed."

With my back to him, he could not see me smile. "There is something else we need to settle before we go to sleep."

"Yes?"

"Henry told me how the mare got her name."

"Yes, I remember. 'Jack's Frost.' 'Jack' because that was her sire's name, and 'Frost' because of the storm the day she was born."

"So what shall we name her foal? 'Snowball'?"

With a gentle laugh Thom relaxed and again caressed the small roundness of my belly. "We'll call the foal 'Blizzard.' 'Blizzie' for short."

§ෆ

The snow had stopped by the time we awoke the next morning. Thom cleared a narrow path from our cabin to the corral so we could attend to the animals. At the horse yard, I was pleased to see Blizzie had gotten the knack of nursing. Twisting low, he tilted his nose upward where he could grasp hold of his big mother's teats. Watching, I felt a brief tingling and tried to imagine what it would be like to have a tiny child nuzzling my breast, finally learning to grasp hold and suck. Surely one of God's miracles.

Except for similar white stockings on their forefeet, Blizzie was dark where Frost was white. When dry, the colt's long face, ears and forehead had lightened from black to chestnut. Two white spots on his forehead looked like fuzzy caterpillars. Their upward tilt reminded me of Father Scudder's expression when I answered one of his questions with uncertainty.

A chestnut saddle shape lay across the foal's back, and the same rich reddish brown color splashed in outrageous patterns across flanks and chest. All the rest was snowy white—from socks and knobby knees to his neck, and back to a wavy-haired tail. Catch-colt he might be, but what did it matter? He had claimed my heart.

∽

South winds blowing across the bay brought a return of warm weather the following week. After devotions Monday eve, Thom laid aside his quill and read through his list. When he looked up at me, I sensed his disquiet. "The mare and her colt are doing well. Do you think you could manage the chores here for a couple of days? I have yet to deliver goods sent from Southampton and intended for Merocke. Jan Michaels has asked me to take his horse along so I can ride on up to Vlissingen to pick up his wife and grandson. The new grandbaby has surely arrived and been christened by now. If I leave in the morning, I can be back by Wednesday." Thom hesitated and raised his eyebrows as if he were soliciting my agreement.

I nodded. "Of course. Everything's going well here. I'll never miss you now that I have Blizzie."

Amusement flickered in his eyes. He enjoyed our gentle sparring as much as I did. Suddenly I remembered the package Henry had sent home with Thom months ago. I pulled it from the cupboard. Within was an etui filled with needles and pins, a spool of thread, scissors, a generous length of lace trimming, and a piece of fine white cloth.

Thom laughed. "Henry thinks you are a seamstress?"

I bit my lip to hold back an impertinent reply. "When you get back Wednesday, you'll see. If Bathsheba's hands could hold a needle, so can mine."

Never have I regretted a vow so deeply. As I began cutting out the baby's gown, my right hand curved tight into a useless claw. When I tried to force my cramping fingers open, extreme pain shot all the way up my arm. It was as impossible as prying open a clam shell one-handed. Some days I could wait it out, but today, time was short.

Outside the cabin, last week's snow lay in slowly-melting drifts. I gathered some in the wash basin, brought it into the house, and thrust my hand into the icy slush. *Oh-h-h!* My tingling fingers turned numb. My arm ached. With small scissored cuts in the fabric, the cramp eased enough that I was able to continue. Slowly I snip…snip…snipped the cloth into a long, ragged-edged T-shape. By the time I got to the neck opening, the claw was back.

At one time I'd learned to write a crooked line of letters left-handed. If I wanted to finish the dress before Thom's return, I could not wait for a better solution. Between my teeth, I clenched a big-eyed needle. Looking downward, eyes nearly crossed, I picked up the thread left-handed and, after several tries, slipped a strand through the needle's eye.

With the cloth held steady between right thumb and cramping fingers, I used my good hand to push the needle through one side of the garment's seam, then out the other. Over and over again. Slow, uneven stitches, each one a promise fulfilled. To Thom. To baby Isaac.

The candle burned low, and my eyes drooped, but I could not stop. It was dawn before I began sewing the last bit of lace around the tiny gathered neckline.

Suddenly I heard a fearsome ruckus in the barnyard. A pathetic whinny crescendoing into a piercing cry. A terrified snorting. A ghastly cracking as if a madman were attacking the fence with the broad side of an axe.

Like trees engorge with sap, so my limbs had swelled with tension, pain-ridden and stiff as stumps. I dragged myself to the fireplace and with my left hand grabbed one of Thom's fowling pieces. Could I load the gun? No, the effort would be too slow. Futile! I dropped the weapon and scuttled out the door. The side of the barn lay in splinters—a mother's fierce attack against a marauding wolf. Powerless to stop the raid, I could only scream. Thom was suddenly beside me; I heard the click of his weapon as he loaded it. A shot rang out.

Oh, my husband, we are too late, too late!

Crimson tracks in the snow marked the wolf's escape. Inside the barn, in a mound of bloody hay, the colt lay still.

Fourteen

ے

In the coming days, so great was my sorrow and rage, I found it difficult to pray. How could a loving God allow such calamities? How dare He allow such innocence to suffer?

Difficult it was to erase the memories. The red-stained tracks across the snow. Blizzie lying on blood-soaked hay.

Often I ran to the barn expecting to see the colt nuzzling her mother's teats or lying on a clean nest of straw. He cannot be gone!

The remembrance brought a torrent of tears that I could not seem to quench.

"If only I'd been more watchful," I said as I wiped my eyes. "If only I had been able to load the—"

"'Twasn't your fault, sweetings. I should have been here." Thom's eyes and voice seemed filled with remorse. "I should have let someone else make the *Sea Hawk's* delivery."

Finally I took up the quill and poured out my grief on paper.

Mourning

Quick beats my icy heart, I know and yet
God let this be not true; let me forget
The scarlet tracks across a snow-white stream,
The blood a wolf tracks 'cross my fearful dream.
Oh, God, who gave the catch-colt life and breath,
Why paid the blameless babe with cold, dark death?
I know all things are possible for Thee,
So let me understand, if lov'st Thou me,
When there shall be no sorrow, no more pain,
Will innocent loss be then repaid with gain?
Oh, will I meet him 'gain past this farewell
In 'blivion's bliss, in heav'n, or graven hell?

For several days, Frost milled around the corral, rejecting the handful of offered grain, poking her nose into corners, raising her head in a loud whinnying call. She grew thin and skittish.

Lisbet came calling and found me slumped at the table, my fingers grasping a tangled strand of grey yarn and a pair of knitting needles. "Whatever is the matter?" she said.

After hearing about the colt, she reached out and touched my shoulder. "'Tis hard," she said.

It must have been obvious that I was not ready to give up my grief, for Lisbet changed the subject. "You know I have a new grandson?"

Her chirping reminded me of a grasshopper, leaping from one bit of information to another.

Lisbet folded her arms in front of her, and her brows creased in a scowl. "Can you imagine? Though I have helped women deliver thirty-nine babes since my own children were grown, my daughter-in-law would not let me near her childbed. 'Twas not my fault that the last two—" Suddenly Lisbet stopped in mid sentence and brought a hand up to her mouth.

The last two? I wondered at her words, but instead of explaining, Lisbet leapt again to the latest birthing.

"Ah, well, I know when I'm not wanted. The hired midwife did well enough without my assistance. The birthing was easy, so it mattered not that I was there as a maid—fetching and carrying this and that. Poor little babe, though. I fear he will never know the pleasure of nursing at his mother's breast, so cross she is!" Lisbet lowered her voice to a whisper. "I suppose you know that if a mother is overcome by sleep, a faery creature may steal her babe and replace it with a changeling. To thwart the theft, one must lay a pair of men's breeches over the cradle." Lisbet's mouth tightened. "Well, in this case, someone should have thrown the breeches over my daughter-in-law's marriage bed. She is the changeling. Not at all the sweet bride of a few short years ago."

Lisbet's eyes held a look of sorrow as she continued. "She screams vile names at her husband—my son Wilhelm! And she calls their first child 'little worm' or 'dummy.' A child will not grow properly if you call him demeaning names." Teary eyed, she shook her head. "One should not chastise a child with the same whip used to punish an animal." She slipped a han'kerchief from her apron pocket and blew her nose.

I lay down my knitting and rose to comfort her. 'Twas then she noticed my rounded belly, and a smile blossomed on her face.

"You are with child! Oh, hallelujah!" With barely a pause, her joyful words turned to reproof. "Mary, dear, it is better not to knit while you are with child. Knitting can cause the babe confusion." She caught a quick breath. "Have you a midwife? May I be of service? There's nothing better than helping a baby into the world."

"Thank you, Lisbet. I'd like that."

As if staking a claim, she reached out and patted my belly, judging the child's progress. "When will you deliver?"

I smiled. "In the spring."

"Oh, then I must plant your kitchen garden for you. If a woman walks over a garden bed within six weeks of giving birth, nothing will grow on it. I can tend your garden and the baby at the same time. I'll get Dirk started on my own planting and hoeing early each morning, and Thom can stay with you and the baby until I get here. I'm sure you know that women should not be left alone for six weeks following the birthing."

"Why is that?"

"Oh, my dear, for those weeks, the devil has more power over you."

Sometimes Lisbet's chatter made me weary. The devil? Perhaps she was right, although I'd never heard that before. If idle hands were the devil's workshop, as I'd heard, certainly mine had never given him invitation, nor had the busy hands of my mother.

Back in England, Grandma had told me it was God's will that Mama died when little Joseph was born, but I could not understand such a God. Was Lisbet right about the power of the devil? Many women died in childbirth. I shuddered. Though it had been ten years, I could still hear my mother's awful screams. I could still see the midwife's hands stained with blood when she came out of Mama's birthing room.

What would Thom do in this wilderness with a tiny baby if I was not there to care for it? I closed my eyes. *Please, God....*

With a start, I realized Lisbet was speaking to me.

"...pulled them by the roots. Valerian is good medicine. Here, dear. I've steeped some roots in warm water for you. There's enough in the pot for several nights. 'Twill calm you and help you rest. I'll come back another day." She handed me the cup and then slipped out the door.

Even with Lisbet's potion, restless dreams disturbed my sleep. A wolf with bloody fangs. A baby whose crying reminded me of Blizzie's scream the day he was killed, and an awful burden of unreasonable guilt. Sometimes in the winter nights when I could not sleep, I heard Thom cry out, and I wondered what he was dreaming.

I had told Thom about the strange scripture I read in Revelation when he was gone, so one morning after barnyard chores, we opened the Bible to that last book.

Thom began reading:

And I stood upon the sand of the sea, and saw a beast rise up out of the sea, having seven heads and ten horns, and upon his horns ten crowns, and upon his heads the name of blasphemy....

Thom paused, brow furrowed. "That reminds me of something I heard at the Globe Theater when I was a boy." He scratched his head. "I remember. 'Twas in one of Shakespeare's plays. *O judgment! thou are fled to brutish beasts, and men have lost their reason. My heart is in the coffin there with Caesar.*" Thom looked up from his reading. "Do you suppose the Bard of Avon had been reading John's Revelation when he wrote those lines?"

"And the beast was John's symbol for Caesar?" I said.

Thom cleared his throat and continued reading.

And upon a woman's forehead a name was written, Whore of Babylon, the mother of harlots and abominations of the earth....

And an angel cried mightily with a strong voice, saying, Babylon is fallen, is fallen, and is become the habitation of devils, and the hold of every foul spirit, and a cage of every unclean and hateful bird.

"What are we supposed to learn from this?" Thom shook his head and slammed the Bible shut. He reached for his Uncle Henry's devotions. "What does Uncle have to say about John's Revelation?"

"I've already searched for his comments," I said. "There's not a word about Revelation in the whole book. However, I am glad he encouraged us to carefully consider the truth of each line of scripture. At least our questioning has his blessing."

"Strange imagery it is," Thom said. "Strange as my dreams: An animal eating bloody flesh. A mother's despairing cry." Thom shivered, and his face seemed drawn. "I know you haven't been sleeping well, nor have I. Oft I awake feeling an odd burden of guilt," he said, "yet I do the best I know how." Thom shrugged, straightened his shoulders, and put both books back on the shelf.

Taking the last bite of his breakfast bread, he asked me for the list I'd made—things the baby would need. "Pleasant and not too cool today," he said. "Fine time to ride up to Southold to return the mare. Trade for another horse there. Feel like riding with me? From Southold we could catch a ship to Salem, purchase an extra blanket or two. Warm woolens from England. Baby clothes on your list."

I adjusted my sitting position. "I think I'll stay home if you don't mind."

My forehead seemed overly warm, and my feet were beginning to swell. Though Lisbet told me 'tis oft thus for a woman with child, I didn't feel like sitting a horse for all those miles. I shifted my position again. "Perhaps I'll yoke the ox to the cart and ride up to visit with Rachel True while you're gone," I said.

I walked to the corral with Thom, and as he saddled Frost and slipped the bridle over her ears, I gave the mare a farewell hug and then kissed her nose. "I'll miss you, girl."

Thom grinned. "Much as you'll miss me?"

"Well, it is different with the mare. She won't be back." I put my arms around my husband and kissed him goodbye.

He held his cheek against mine for a moment. "You feel a little warm, sweeting. Are you sure you're all right?

"Of course I am. Hurry back, Thom."

Hot and aching with weariness, as soon as Thom rode away, I returned to the cabin and without finishing my breakfast, I threw back the glass window to cool the room, crawled back into bed, an unspeakable action for a goodwife.

I was thirsty, but not hungry. Nothing would taste good. I tipped the jug of ale, refilled my cup and drank, yet the draught cooled not my tongue. In bed, I could find no comfortable position. A fire raged within me. I had no need to reheat the brick that lay at my feet.

I threw off the coverlet and rubbed my burning eyes. My sight blurred, and through a swirling haze, an apparition arose at the foot of my bed. Horned angels. The shrill chorus of their voices faded, then swelled as they read from a great book:

"Come with us to the fiery pit, O great whore of Babylon, for thou art damned."

Their long, thin arms reached out for me. I struggled against their power, kicking and screaming.

Their damning voices convicted me without a trial. "Thou, O whore of Babylon, hast committed blasphemy and fornication."

I reached for the cold brick hiding beneath the bedding. With all my might, I threw it into the midst of the fearsome beings. A great shattering sounded. Ricocheting pieces of glass splattered over the room. Something wet and warm trickled into my eyes. Through a crimson curtain I saw the demons heads broadened, and their horns became fangs, dripping with blood.[99]

In the struggle, my hair loosened and its tangled thickets fell across my shoulders. I brushed a thick strand out of my eyes.

Flaming words, like swords, shot from the demons' gaping jaws. "Shameless woman, in torment thou shalt burn."

Oh, what penance was there for me?

Reflected in the dwindling light of a lone candle, an object on the mantle caught my attention. In near darkness, sharp stones pierced my feet as I staggered, stumbled, and nearly fell. Finally I grasped the handle of the glittering blades. Screams echoed in my ears—

Blizzie's? Frost's? My own? Darkness enveloped me.

I awoke to the sound of knocking and Lisbet's voice calling my name, but I was too weak to go to the door.

"Mary, are you there?"

She pushed open the door and came on in. As she glanced around the room, her eyes widened and her mouth gaped in a disbelieving "O."

As I followed the path of her glance, blood rushed to my cheeks. I saw the disgraceful array of my clothing, rumpled and wrinkled. The bed sheets scrunched up, almost in knots. The inside of the cabin was even more ruined than I.

Mama's precious Bible, one page torn, sprawled open on the floor; my beautiful window lay scattered — broken shards of glass. Cold sweat poured down my face, burning my eyes.

Lisbet frowned and I heard the censure of her clicking tongue.

"Oh, Mary, what happened? What have you done?" Her words echoed my thoughts exactly. I blinked and rubbed my eyes, hoping to clear the scene from view.

"Lisbet, are you …. Are you real? I've had a horrible dream about...."

I could not bring the dream into focus, did not want to remember.

With lips pressed tight, Lisbet grabbed the broom and began sweeping up glass mixed with what looked like yarn, bright as a copper coin, thick as wood shavings in a carpenter's shop. Within the heap of refuse, she discovered the scissors. Gasping, she looked straight at me, her eyes taking in my sinful desecration.

Not until I raised my hands to my head did I comprehend that the bright strands lying on the cabin floor were...my hair.

"I could shake you, Mary! Don't you know a haircut during these months can shorten the lifespan of your unborn child? Don't you also know that raising your arms will cause the baby's cord to wrap around its neck and choke it?"

Her warning was like a hard blow to my midsection, knocking the wind from me. Instinctively, I doubled over, hands across my belly until finally my breath returned.

Lisbet stooped to pick up a copper-colored curl, and when she lifted her head, I saw her eyes, wet with unshed tears. "My poor Mary," she said softly. "You knew not what you were doing." She put aside the broom and removed my cap from its hook. With gentle fingers she combed through the damp stubble of my hair, and then slipped the cap over it. "Oh, my child, I had thought 'twas shame that dyed your cheeks scarlet, but you are feverish," she said as she tied the strings under my chin. "My dear, I'll brew a concoction to cure what ails thee. And you must stay in bed till the fever is completely gone!"

I fell back against the pillow. I could but obey her command, for my eyes were heavy and my limbs limp as water. I barely knew when she spooned the bitter herb between my lips.

ℝ

Low voices woke me. Lisbet's familiar chatter. Thom's solemn response. For a moment I lay quietly, enjoying the familiar rasping noise made when Thom rubbed a hand over the stubble on his chin.

"Are you hungry, Goodman Scudder?" Lisbet said. "There's meat and broth in the kettle."

Suddenly I was starved! "Prithee, save a bowl for me."

Thom whirled around, and his lips spread into a beaming smile as he held out his hands in greeting. "Guess who's awake."

I put my legs over the side of the bed and sat up. "I'm not the only one who's awake. I think Isaac knows your voice. See how he kicks."

With great gentleness, Thom laid his head on the round of my belly. "Hello, little one," he said. Isaac kicked again.

"Strong one, isn't he? Seems as if he's grown in the short time I've been away."

While Thom crossed the room to pull a package from his bag, Lisbet brought me a bowl of broth, and then slipped out, closing the door behind her.

Thom's hands trembled as he ripped the wrapping from the parcel. "Look what I brought our baby. Every item on your list but one."

"You forgot the cradle?"

"Thought I'd like to make it myself. Something to keep away the idleness of winter days. Think he'd enjoy a rocking cradle?" The look in his eyes was tender and warm. "Oak. Four hands wide at the bottom. Nine hands long — room to grow."

I took a deep breath. "Did Lisbet tell you what happened —" My voice cracked, and for a moment I could not go on. I tried again. "Did she tell you what happened to…to the window?"

He nodded. "It's only a piece of glass, sweeting. There are others to be had. Until then, we'll hang a rug over the opening to shut out the cold." He paused. Waited for me to continue.

"'Twas…. 'Twas Lisbet who put the cabin back in order. But she could not mend…"

Perhaps he saw the anguish in my eyes, for he did not make me finish. I felt the warmth of his fingers as he gently laid his hand over my cap. Slowly he untied the strings, and with a carefully blank expression, he slipped the covering from my head.

"Aphrodite," he said, leaning to kiss the back of my neck, "you've never been more beautiful." His voice was hoarse with emotion.

"No more bad dreams, my sweeting. I swear I will not leave again until after our baby is born."

I covered his lips with my hand. "You are as much sailor as farmer. Will you not miss—"

"Not nearly as much as I miss you when I'm away. You are my heart."

March, Anno Dom 1657
Babylon, Long Island

The weather that winter, as forecast by the narrow orange band around the wooly bears, was bitter and freezing. Without a word of reproof, Thom fastened a heavy rug, tightly woven of bright blue woolen strips over the window I had broken. It darkened the cabin but kept out the icy blasts. With scraps of fabric, I stuffed a long tail-like pillow of yarn and tucked it against the doorsill to block out the frigid air that sought entrance through even the tiniest crack.

The candles my Southampton friend, Elizabeth, had given us were nearly gone, so I was thankful that Lisbet had helped me set in extras, even enough to sell at market, from the fragrant bayberries we had gathered in the fall. They brightened the room as well as my mood.

Our fields lay ready to be planted in the spring, so Thom took care of the animal chores both morning and evening, chopped, stacked, and carried in firewood when needed, and made an occasional trip to the *Sea Hawk* to see if his crew had need of anything.

On days when the weather was not too cold, he saddled Banbury, our new white mare, and I rode with him. The beauty of the shore changed with the seasons. In February, we watched harbor seals frolic in the bay. Winter birds — gyrfalcons and rough-legged hawks — patrolled the treeless area of the barrier beach, swooping and diving to snatch their prey. Nearer our cabin, yellow-rumped warblers hunted for berries in brush and thicket, and crossbills searched for pinecones in evergreens.

One day in early February, after morning chores, breakfast, and devotions, Thom began fulfilling his promise to craft the oak cradle for baby Isaac. He pulled the table over in front of the fireplace and placed the wood and tools on it. Then, to my surprise, he pulled from the loft a marvelous gift from the crew.

"Under the bosun's direction," Thom said, "my men replaced the jib — the foremost sail of the ship — with new canvas. Then, following the measurements I had shown them for the cradle, they took the old sail — worn soft by wind and weather — and fashioned a sack for the cradle bed, thick enough to keep a babe warm. They stuffed the sack with soft down from deserted nests of eider ducks. Took them a while to find enough," Thom said, smiling. "See how soft it is!"

I plopped my back-side onto a bench. Holding the long, fluffy pillow, I rested my head on it. Here beside the fire, I could admire Thom's artistry as he worked.

First, from thick oaken planks, he cut panels for the ends, bottom, and sides of the cradle. He smoothed each piece with a tool he called a carpenter's bench plane, and on the next day, he fastened the parts together with pegs. One morning, he whittled two curved rockers from short lengths of a branch, and rubbed them with handfuls of dense, dark sand until they were smooth. "I'll attach these to the bottom of the cradle when it is finished," he said. Another day, Thom carved the Scudder crest on each side panel, and stained it red. [100] Across the top of the crest he fashioned three of the five-fingered leaves of the cinquefoil.[101] As he carved them, I heard him chanting what sounded like a blessing.

Suddenly, the baby kicked, and I placed my arms over my burgeoning belly. "What is that you are singing, my husband?"

"It's a toast to our son." he told me. "In the days of the knights, cinquefoil was an ingredient in a magic potion for celebrants who gathered round the table and lifted their glasses high: 'May your net be filled with fishes and your heart be filled with love.'"

He ducked his head and returned to his work. Below the leaves, Thom placed a horizontal band displaying three black gun stones. Again I heard his murmur: "I will always protect you, my little one."

Around the bottom half of the crest, he curved a streamer and inscribed it with the family motto in Latin: *nunquam non paratus.* "I am ready for you, my son," Thom said as he laid aside the carving knife and attached the rockers. We stood together, admiring his handiwork.

"Those Latin words mean *Never Unprepared*, do they not? How can you be so sure of yourself, Thom? In another week, my time will be here, and I am still uncertain about my own readiness." I reached for Thom's steady hand and looked up at him. As he drew me into his arms, the fire threw deep shadows on his face—a face fixed with determination and confidence, yet gentled by the curve of his smile. I had never loved him more.

"By my calculation, this is the seventh day of March. Saturday. Nearly time to stop work and prepare for the Sabbath," he said, releasing me from his warm embrace. "Would it give you comfort for the Michaels' family and Ransom and Rachel True to spend the morrow with us? I'm sure the Rev. True has a sermon ready. What is it he always says?"

"...in case the Lord supplies a congregation?"

"That's it."

The joyous anticipation of guests on the morrow made me forget the painful cramps in my back. "Oh, and the crew, Thom. Would they like to come? I want to thank them for the baby's gift."

"I'll ask them," he said. "Drifting ice beyond the barrier island has brought sailing to a standstill. The *Sea Hawk* won't be going anywhere."

"Oh, do invite them. By the time you get back, I'll have bread enough in the oven, and a big kettle of beans and ham hanging over the fire. 'Twill take no work at all on the Sabbath."

As Thom rode off, I stood with a thumb on each side of my waist, fingers in back, rubbing the nagging pain. My feet were swollen. Fat, puffy sausages replaced my ankles. I sat for a moment, but could contrive no comfortable position.

Enough whining. I refused to let such bodily discomforts detract from a wonderful Sabbath. Fifteen guests in our small cabin. Oh, happy day! But with only two benches, where would they all sit? Perhaps Thom and the men could rig extra seats with logs and leftover planks.

No time to waste. I pushed myself up, and waddled across the floor to sprinkle flour on the kneading table and began to shape loaves of bread, readying them for the oven. To the kettle of water hanging over the fire, I added beans and chunks of salt-cured ham to serve fifteen.

∓

On March 8, 1657, I didn't feel right when I awoke on Sabbath morn. My head ached. My hands were red, my ankles puffy, and I had terrible muscle spasms in my back although I could not think of anything I had done to bring them on. As soon as the Michaels family arrived, Lisbet hung her wrap on the hook, smoothed her apron, and took over in her usual way. "Now you just sit here by the fire and prop your feet up," she said, handing me a mug filled to the brim with beer.

I watched as she chose a linen cloth and a large bowl from the cupboard, poured in a generous cup of vinegar, withdrew a small bottle of liquid from her pocket. After splashing a dollop into the bowl, she scurried over to the fireplace where she added hot water and then stirred it all together. Surely she did not plan for me to drink this decoction!

"Now you just lie back and keep your feet up. I'll bathe them with this vinegar and rose water. And don't you worry," she said as other people began arriving. "I'll see that everyone finds a place to sit."

I felt like a guest in my own house, allowing others to wait on my every need. There was nothing for me to do but sit and listen. I know not whether I was, for once, in complete agreement with the message of the sermon, or if I was merely too weary to contemplate Rev. True's words. At the benediction, a blast of icy rain rattled on the glass of the west window. The weather was worsening, but we were warmed by the sharing of our meal together. The crew left after eating, but soon we heard the deep voice of the second mate, Garrett Jones. "Ahoy, there, Captain Scudder!" He came rushing into the cabin. "At the shore we hear voices — cries that seem to be coming from the barrier island. I believe there is a ship stranded, just across the bay. The *Sea Hawk* is too iced in to sail, but with your permission, Sir, we can lower the yawl boats and row out to help them. Surely they are in a desperate plight in this terrible ice storm."[102]

Thom nodded. "Garrett, you and the crew go on ahead. Take the first boat and row out to find the wreck. I'll bring the three men here along to manage the second boat. God speed!"

Thom and our guests, Jan and Dirk Michaels and Ransom True, began throwing on their weather-proof cloaks, preparing to aid with the rescue.

Thom looked at Rev. True and raised a questioning eyebrow. "You don't object to working on the Sabbath?"

"I'll follow the Lord's command," Rev. True said. "What man shall there be among you, that shall have one sheep, and if it fall into a pit on the Sabbath day, will he not lay hold on it, and lift it out?[103] Surely these lives are of greater value than a sheep."

Thom nodded as he grabbed his sealskin boots and slipped them on. "Pray, Reverend, that there be no injured or dead for you to attend." He looked around. "With all of us, there'll be enough men to manage the second boat." Abruptly, Thom stopped. "Oh, I cannot leave now! Mary is nearing her time of travail. I must not leave her!"

"Hush, Thom." I said, biting my lip to keep from crying out. "Lives may be in danger. You must go!"

Lisbet looked at me and then turned to Thom. "A first child takes longer than others to be born. Your wife will have plenty of warning, and you surely will not be gone long."

"I'll be all right." I said. "Lisbet and Rachel are here to help me. You must go, Thom!"

It was decided. Thom turned to the men. "Dirk, ride to the Secotaugh's lodge and ask for their help. They'll have canoes that can reach the shipwreck. We must rescue the sailors first, of course. We'll need blankets. They may be freezing. Then, if their ship is breaking up, we may still be able to save some of their goods."

Lisbet and Rachel, insisting that I remain seated with my feet up, hustled about gathering blankets and quilts. Then, with a quick goodbye, the men left.

As we waited, my pain went from bad to worse, until at last I could no longer keep my mind on Thom and the other rescuers.

My vision blurred. My head ached. The spasms in my back were overridden by pain across my belly. I began vomiting, and Lisbet's cure-all did little to abate the problem. I could feel the rapid beating of my baby's heart. The pains grew stronger. Exhausted from the hard work, I lay panting at the end of each contraction.

No wonder it was called travail!

The sun was dying in the west as Lisbet stirred the fire, then held a small stick to the flames and with it lit the candles on the table. I heard alarm in Rachel's voice as she called out to Lisbet. "Look," she said, "Mary's face fades from red to white."

I clamped my lips through the next contraction, holding in a shriek. Lisbet took my hands in hers. "Here, lovey, grab hold and squeeze."

The next contraction came. "Let me wipe the sweat from your face, Mary." Lisbet laid a cool cloth on my forehead and crooned to me as if I were her child, half lullaby, half lament.

The sky was dark. Not a glimmer of sunlight came in through the west window and still Thom had not returned. The baby had not kicked since long before candle lighting time. Suddenly, within my body I felt an agonized ripping as if the child were trying to push his way out, yet could not.

I barely recognized my own voice, ragged, pleading. "God, can't you do something to help me? Why are you hiding your face from me?"

"Sh-h-h, Mary," Rachel said softly. "Ransom says childbirth is the curse God has visited upon all the daughters of Eve. But through it we gain the hope of redemption for our sins."

Another wrenching pain, and with it, as clear as midday, I heard my mother's dying scream. In anguish, I cried out. "If I die, tell Thom…"

Amidst the growing fog of semi-consciousness, I felt a rending pressure that nearly cleaved me in two. Lisbet lifted the cover from my limbs, reached to knead my belly with the next contraction. Were her hands stained with blood when she withdrew them? I could not see them clearly.

The door swung open with a bang, admitting a blast of cold air. Through the pain, I heard familiar footsteps, hastening toward me.

Lisbet attempted to prevent him. "No, Goodman Scudder. 'Tis not fitting for a man to be in the room when his wife is in travail."

I knew that would not stop my husband. At that moment, I felt the gush of warm liquid. "Oh, Thom, I am bleeding! The quilt under me is soaked."

"'Tis as it should be," Lisbet said calmly. "The water breaks before the baby comes."

In my exhaustion and confusion Thom held me, smoothing the hair back from my face. He grasped my hands when another pain came. "Here, sweeting. Squeeze my hands. No one will hear you. Cry out, my love."

With one more push, the baby shot into the world.

Not until Lisbet started crying did I know something was wrong. I, who had been afraid of dying like my mother, had never imagined it would be little Isaac instead. By the dawning of first light, March 11, 1657, I glimpsed his wee body. Wide blue face. Unseeing eyes.

The fog thickened around me.

❧

From the agony of a nightmare I awoke, drenched with sweat, and knew it was not just a dream. There was no cradle beside my bed. Baby Isaac was gone. My heart was as icy as the storm that continued its rage.

Lisbet spooned a decoction into my mouth. Kelp from the sea; coriander and seeds; basil, dried and ground; nuts, legumes, and grains, she told me. "'Twill stop the seizures. Here, you must take another bite. I told your dear Thom that turkey would be good for you, so he went hunting and shot one, and it's roasting in the fireplace with dried tomatoes and shallots. You must eat. You cannot stand another spasm." Her voice sounded a long way off.

I remember frigid blasts of the wind, beating against our cabin and the mournful sound of the doves that perched under the eaves. I have little memory else of the happenings of those days. My heart felt like a solid block of ice; I shivered and shook like a sapling weakened by the wintry blast. To warm me, Thom gathered my body close to his under a pile of quilts and cloaks. When at last the ice thawed, in its place, a hellish fever raged.

Brief images of Thom's grieving face floated before me. Large, gentle hands held me, cooling my face, my body, with damp cloths. Blurry images of someone spooning sips of an herbal tea between my burning lips. Sage and parsley, and something bitter as gall.

Sometimes it was not Thom's face I saw above me, but... "Nowedanah?"

"No, sweeting," Thom's voice drifted through the haze. "This is Tania. The Indians say she is gifted in the healing arts. Look what she found down by Skookwams Creek where we gathered mud for the walls."

Into my hand Tania tucked a familiar small bundle of white shell beads interwoven with the red tail feather of the hawk. My amulet.

Again, I slept. In my dreams, I heard Rev. Hardwick screaming, "Thou wicked daughter of Eve, you have tempted me to enjoy your fruit, and I am drunk with the wine of your fornication." Then one of the seven angels said to me, "Come. This is your punishment." Endlessly, I carried stone tablets of painful guilt pressed heavy against my breast. Over and over, one by one, I tried to roll them away, and when I finally escaped their weight, they stood mocking me like tombstones each graved with a name: Mama. Blizzie. Isaac. Judgments of guilt.

The fever cooled, and I awoke with a clearer mind. I blinked against the light that shone through the window. Thom was there, leaning over me, his face gray and worn. "Mary?"

"Thom, tell me. Did I see our baby? I can't remember."

Thom blenched, and then covered the movement with an immobile face masked with sorrow. With a mixture of both despair and awe in his voice, he answered. "Yes, you saw him. I watched while you held him, marveling at the length of his fingers. You slipped one of your own within his closed fist, as if imagining what it would be to have him grasp your finger and hold on tightly."

His voice faltered, but he went on. "Small, he was. I held him in the palm of my hand. He had tiny light eyelashes, nearly hidden by eyelids, puffy as if he had slept overlong. We wrapped him in that soft linen christening gown you had stitched, and I tucked him within the folds of the tiny blanket in the cradle..." Tears streamed down Thom's cheeks as he gave me back the memories of our lost child.

A faint smile crossed his face, and I smiled too, but Thom's voice had faded in my ears. It seemed as if I were listening to some far off sound. Something only I could hear. Baby Isaac?

An old memory came clear. With legs too short to reach the floor, I sat in Mama's big chair rocking my baby brother and listening to his babbling—ma-ma-ma.

"...guests were still here, of course," Thom was saying. "Bound in by the storm. Rev. True baptized baby Isaac, and as soon as the wind abated, they helped me bury him."

"Where doth he lie, Thom?"

"Safe within the palisade." His voice trembled. "Under the red-bud tree where the land is high and dry."

"How long have I been...asleep?"

"Today is Friday. Good Friday, March 27, 1657."

"How long, Thom?"

"Over a fortnight." His voice shook. "Since the day I left to rescue strangers and left you alone."

I saw a tear trickling down his face, but I was numb, empty, devoid of anything but sorrow. I could not reach out to him.

"What can I do Mary? How can I —"

"How can you bring me comfort? Can you raise the dead? Give me back my child?"

"No, I cannot."

I gathered myself tighter and whispered through my teeth. "Let me be awhile. Give me o'er."

21st Century
Memory Catchers' Office

A few days later, when I came in to my office, Grand-Mary was back. There she sat in her usual chair reading my transcription of her last interview, her lips tight as if she were yet holding in this long remembered grief. Finally, her expression softened, and a small, wavering smile appeared. She reached out and gathered me into her arms for a moment. "You know what it means to lose a child, don't you? I saw your daughter's Memorial DVD on your computer screen. I'm so sorry."

I nodded, and tears welled in my eyes. I brushed them away and cleared my throat. "How ever did you gain the strength to go on after little Isaac's death?"

"Oh, Phyllis, my dear, one never forgets. There was a time when I believed there would never be a single day I thought not of Isaac. Still, even in the depths of sadness, I clung to my faith in the victory of life over death. That faith is everything."

Discomfited by her strength in the face of my weakness, I lowered my eyes. "Grand-Mary, do you think it's strange that I don't go visit her grave?

"Strange? No. I never visited Isaac's grave. He wasn't there, you know. 'Twas only his natural body we buried. I think that is what the scripture means when it says: *That which thou sowest, is not quickened, except it die. O grave, where is thy victory?* That is why I love springtime. It reminds me of the resurrection, the new life we inherit."

I looked up and was utterly encompassed by Grand-Mary's aura of peace and compassion, as real as the sweet aroma of Easter lilies. I took a deep breath. "No more sorrow. No more pain. That gives me comfort."

Grand-Mary nodded, and then continued. "Puritans, you know, did not celebrate Easter. But I will never forget the Lord's Day that followed the first full moon of spring that year. April 4, it was, 1657. I had a weird and wonderful dream. In it, my legs were stiff and scarred, and so wracked with pain I could not stand, but in a moment of healing, I escaped the bonds of earth and soared like a red-tailed hawk across the sky. I looked down and saw myriads of children. Ordinary men and women. Great leaders. Loyal followers. People of great dreams."

"Did you recognize them? Who were they?"

Although Grand-Mary looked toward me as she spoke, her sparkling eyes seemed focused on a faraway place.

"My descendants, of course. My reason for being. More-over, my dear Phyllis, I heard a voice as clear as could be:

Mary, thou canst not let the scars of death and devasta-tion deprive thee of thy purpose.

"An unutterable sense of peace crowded out my fear and grief, and I felt a great longing. Still my limbs trem-bled so that I knew I could not stand alone." Grand-Mary paused and cleared her throat. "Again I heard the voice:

Concerning the resurrection of the dead, have ye not read the Word? I am your God and the God of Isaac. I am not the God of the dead, but of the living.[104] *I cannot guide thy footsteps if thou art not willing to put thy feet on solid ground. Come now, Mary. My peace, my love, will empower you.*

Grand-Mary paused with her head bowed, and my of-fice seemed infused with...peace. When she looked up at me, she was smiling.

"A dream?" I said.

"Perhaps. But sometimes dreams are stronger than real-ity. When I opened my eyes, not only the cabin but my heart also was filled with the glow of the rising sun." Suddenly conscious of the present time, Grand-Mary smiled at me. "Shall I continue my story now?"

I nodded, and turned on the Sony.

Fifteen

☙

Spring, Anno Dom 1657
Leaving Babylon, Long Island

In spite of my dream, the gloom of loneliness insinuated its way into a hollow spot in my heart. To lighten his own dark shadows of guilt, Thom created busyness, but he, too, suffered. I tried to comfort him. "You only did what was right," I told him. "You could not have stopped the angel of death that carried away our little Isaac."

Often Thom searched the scriptures, and at our morning devotions, he read the verses that brought him comfort, or, on the other hand, chapters that called him to question the ways of God.

"Why, Mary? Why does it seem that God blessed us with plenty in our new Babylon home, yet turned away his face — punished us by taking away our child? Verily, I am confused. And is confusion not brought about by godlessness?"

From the recesses of my mind, I heard the slam of the rod against the desk, and my Cousin Gideon's stern voice. "Pay attention, little brothers. The Greek word for Babylon is 'Babel,' a symbol of confusion."

Oh, such a tumult. I pressed my hands to my aching temples and then shook my head back and forth as if to rid it of my bafflement. "Even my dreams are babble in my ears. Enlighten me, Thom. What do they mean?"

Thom took my hand in his. "Tell me about them, sweeting."

So I told him of my dream, and the voice that called out to me.

Thom reached for the Bible. "Does that not sound like God's promise to Abraham?" Quickly, he ran his finger over the pages of Genesis. "Here it is! Genesis 12. When Abraham left Haran—see, that's north Babylon on the map—" My husband began reading:

Now the LORD had said unto Abram, Get thee out of thy country, and from thy kindred, and from thy father's house, unto a land that I will shew thee. And I will make of thee a great nation, and I will bless thee, and make thy name great; and thou shalt be a blessing under God's promise that he would become the father of a great nation.

"See here, Mary, the study notes say, 'In appointing him no certain place, Abram proves so much more his faith and obedience.' "[105]

"Well," I said, we know Canaan was Abram's Promised Land, but how shall we prove *our* faith and obedience if we know not where to go?"

From the barnyard, Bossy gave a loud, demanding moo as if in response to my question. Thom and I both laughed. "That moo sounds like Greek for "How long must I wait? Such an educated animal we have! I think she's calling you, Thom."

He grinned as he took his leather jerkin from its peg and slipped it on. "I hardly think that's the voice of God, but it is time to go."

I handed Thom the milk bucket and then moved to stir the pot of porridge simmering over the fire. "In another month, we'll be eating strawberries covered with sugar and Bossy's rich cream, but this morning you'll have to settle for samp." I turned to stir the pot as Thom headed for the barnyard. Bossy was waiting.

I'd hardly spread the board when I heard men's voices and hearty laughter outside. The door swung open and Thom burst in with his brother Henry close behind. Both were grinning. "Mary, I've found our promised land. Get packed! We're moving north across the island, to Huntington Village." Then, for a moment, he hesitated. "Would that please you, sweeting?" Without pausing for an answer, he resumed a rapid pace that reminded me of the funny medicine-wagon man who hawked his wares as he traveled through Southampton. I knew not whether to laugh or cry. In spite of my mixed emotions, Thom hurried on, pitching his proposal.

"Henry, the fortunate fellow, already has a house. Or rather his little Jeffery does. Remember when Catherine's father, Jeffrey Este, died earlier this year? Well, he left his house and lot in Huntington to his grandson. Just think, the babe's barely learned to walk, and already he is a property owner. The will makes Henry the guardian of the property until Jonathan is of age."

"And where are we to live?"

"We'll build. We Scudder boys did it in Southold. Now we'll do it again. Brother John and his Mara will need a house big enough for their five young'ins. And Henry says there's a lot and land where we can build our house right by the waterside of Huntington Bay.[106] We'll have neighbors, and a church, and kinfolk nearby."

Forsooth, Thom's eagerness was contagious. "How soon are we leaving?" I said. "I'll start packing."

The next day, Jan Michael signed an agreement with Thom for one of the Michael sons to live on our Babylon land, letting our house to him as his own.

It was mid April, 1657, and Henry, though impatient to get back to Huntington to oversee moving into the Este house, stayed to help Thom and the crew load our household belongings and hurry the animals onto the *Sea Hawk*. Then they heaped Thom's stock of carpenter tools, buckets and barrels into our two-wheeled cart. With Henry's horse hitched to the cart, the bumpy, twenty-mile trail from our Babylon property north to Huntington Village could be covered in a day. Thom and I were taking the long way around. As soon as the tide was right, we sailed toward Southampton and Mecox to see my family. From there we would travel on around to Southold and west to Huntington Village.

ℴℝ

When family and friends at Southampton learned of baby Isaac's death, they enfolded me in their love and concern. Caught up in the flurry of a large household and village, I had little time for solitary mourning, and that, too, was good.

"Twill be an exciting prospect to live in Huntington," Uncle Robert assured Thom. "I almost wish I could go with you. Build again from the start."

Thom nodded. "Great opportunity. Huntington has a fine harbor. Shipping is sure to be good. Plenty to keep the *Sea Hawk* crew busy. Vessels travel up and down the Sound. Maybe even as far away as the West Indies. And an abundance of cleared land—we have the peaceful Matinecock to thank for that. Now, after only four years growth, the settlement has hired a schoolmaster, built a mill, and soon, I am sure, a meeting house. Already twenty-four settlers and more coming every day."

My friend Elizabeth took great delight in telling me her news. "Mary, just see how our wee Eliza has grown. Already she is trying to walk, and now our second child is on the way."

Pain lanced through me, but I was determined to be happy for her. Suddenly aware of my grief, she gasped and covered her mouth, eyes wide. "O-oh, I'm so sorry, Mary."

"God has richly blessed you and your good husband, Elizabeth. Don't you fret; someday I will have my turn."

Good it was to worship at meeting house once again, sitting with my sisters while the men took their places on the other side of the house. I could hardly hold back the tears when dear Uncle Robert took his place at the pulpit and began reading the text from his Geneva Bible.

To all things there is an appointed time, and a time to every purpose under the heaven. A time to be born, and a time to die: a time to plant, and a time to pluck up that which is planted. A time to slay, and a time to heal: a time to break down, and a time to build. A time to weep, and a time to laugh: a time to mourn, and a time to dance.

Then, a time for farewells. Godspeed.

Luddie, newly wed, surprised me with his suggestion. "My own dear Elizabeth has Smith family relatives near

Huntington whom she sorely misses. Perhaps the town needs another miller?"

"Oh, Luddie," I said, "twould be a delight to have you near."

At the idea of Luddie leaving, Papa hesitated, then with a shrug, turned back to me. "Now don't you worry, my little Mary. We'll see each other soon." He put an arm around my shoulders and hugged me close. "Your brother Hal's doing well at the mill, so I can surely get away to visit you in your new home."

Papa walked us to the *Sea Hawk* for one last goodbye, then after lending me a hand as I boarded the sloop, he turned to Thom. "Times are fast changing," he said. Won't be long, I reckon, until we have a road instead of an Indian path straight through from here to Huntington Village. Twenty-some miles—not a far piece at all." Papa's voice wavered, and he cleared his throat. "I swear by my hope of heaven," he said, "I will see you again soon."

Thom gave the orders, and the crew of the *Sea Hawk* raised anchor and set sail toward the east end of Paumanok, the Indian name for our big fish-shaped Long Island.

After the lively commotion and chatter of family and friends and the strain of adieus, I was tired to the bone and grateful for the quiet lap-lap-lap of the sea as the ship moved through the water. Laughing gulls, dipping and swirling through a bright blue sky, startled me as they let out a burst of ha-ha-ha's. On the deck of the *Sea Hawk*, Thom rolled out bolsters for us and pulled me down to him. With gentle hands, he removed the pins from my hair and ran his fingers through the twisted strands. Warmed by the nearness of his body and lulled by the rhythm of the waves, I could stay awake no longer.

Perhaps it was the laughter of the gulls that woke me, or perhaps it was the wail of my own lament. I reached for Thom, shook him awake. "Oh, my husband, can you not hear the crying? The baby.... Listen." Grief shook my body, and I could not stop the flow of tears. Thom reached for me and took me in his arms, calming me as if I were a small child. In the light of a cloud-shrouded sun, I saw his own grief tightly reined that he might comfort me.

Willing myself to be calm, I took a deep breath and wiped my eyes. As if God approved of my determination, the sun broke through the clouds, gilding the waves. I heard Thom catch his breath at the sight.

"Your hair shimmers with gold, my Aphrodite." With a mischievous grin, from the bolster he rose on one elbow. "As I recollect," he said, "this is the first day of May. Years ago, the English celebrated this date. That is 'til the Puritans reacted to the rites with pious horror. Since then, the celebration has been forbidden." With a tender touch, Thom smoothed my hair back, but the expression on his face held a veiled hint of merriment. "You were too young to remember the day, my sweet, but I fairly enjoyed the festivities," he said. "A young man's sinful delight." Thom's face held not a trace of guilt. In fact, the gleam in his eyes gave evidence of quite the opposite. "May Day," he said, "celebrated human fertility and renewal." Thom snuggled closer to me and went on with his story. "Young men and women made merry by staying out together to greet the May sunrise," he said with a chuckle. "But I remember an angry old Puritan who apparently had forgotten the giddy days of his youth.

'Whatever is this world coming to?' he said, then went right on complaining: 'Why, I heard of ten maidens which went to see the May sunrise, and nine of them came home with child.'"

Hearing the evocative gaiety in Thom's voice, I felt a twinge of envy. Oh, to bring back the halcyon days before such strictness ruled. Was it not the very God of the Puritans who created this time of fertility and renewal? With measured deliberation, I took Thom's hand in my own, gathered my courage and lifted my eyes to his. "Remember when I asked you if you could give me back my child? You said you could not, but now I think I have a better answer. God willing, you might give me another."

ॐ

My heart rejoiced at the sight of dawn's glory—pink and purple brushed across a gray-blue horizon. Something Uncle Robert had said echoed in my mind. A time to build...a time to dance. Slowly the sun peeked over the horizon, and the sky turned blue. I could think of no greater testimony to God's power than the promise of a new day.

Thom was stirring, and I laid my hand on his arm. "Look, my beloved, God is in his heaven, ready to fulfill his promise to us." I handed him my Geneva bible. "Read it again, Thom."

He rubbed his eyes, sat up, and took the book, but he opened it not. "I remember it by heart," he said.

Get thee out of thy country, and from thy kindred, and from thy father's house, unto a land that I will shew thee. And I will give to thee chil-

dren and make of them a great nation, and I will bless thee, and make thy
name great; and thou shalt be a blessing under God's promise.

"How much farther is it to our promised land, Thom?"
How soon will we be there?" I could hardly contain my
joy.

Well," he said, "it took the Israelites forty years, but
what is time in the eyes of the Lord? His word is true.
He'll keep his promise."

Sixteen

~

ANNO DOM 1657
ON LONG ISLAND—FROM BABYLON TO HUNTINGTON

We dropped anchor at Southold and soon Thom's brother John, his wife, Mara, and their nest of five chirping children, ages 8 to 14, boarded the sloop. With the help of the ship's crew, the family's belongings were quickly loaded, and again we set sail. Never have I seen greater excitement!

"Uncle Thom, can I help thee steer the ship?"

"Where are our bunks, Uncle Thom?"

"Daddy, Daddy, how far away is Huntington? When will we be there?"

As parents, John and Mara had evidently removed themselves from the strict orthodoxy of Massachusetts where children were to be seen and not heard, and I rejoiced in the sounds of the happy voices.

Except for the clatter of children's feet as they explored the ship and their insistent pleading as they coaxed the galley cook to supply treats before mealtime, the rest of the trip to Huntington passed without incident.

"Where are we going to live while our dwelling-house is being raised, Papa?" twelve-year-old Aaron asked John.

Samuel punched Aaron's shoulder. "Hush, little brother with the big ears. I think you know the answer for you have been eavesdropping, have you not?"

John interrupted the squabble before it got out of hand. "Enough of that, boys. Uncle Henry and Aunt Catherine have asked us to live with them. Their new dwelling house was built for children, and they have more than enough room. Your Cousin Jonathan's cradle taketh up but little space."

Beth pulled at her father's sleeve, demanding her share of attention. "I've missed Baby Jonathan so much since they moved from Southold," she said. "Do you suppose he can walk yet? Do you think he will remember me?"

John laughed and shook his head. "Your Uncle Henry says your little cousin goes to sleep every night hugging the pillow you stitched for him. I'm sure he will remember you, my pet."

By mid afternoon, outlined by the light of the sun, the tree-covered hills of Huntington came into view. But even before we sailed into the bay, the militant beat of drums I heard sent shivers down my spine. Thom and John busied themselves anchoring the Sea Hawk and paid no mind to the sound or to the rag-tag band of militia, diversely outfitted but orderly with muskets propped over their shoulders, guarding the harbor.

"Soldiers!" Mara said. She seemed angry, not frightened as I, and her forehead knotted in a deep frown. "Is there no place where men do not wage war? Look!" The sun glinted off the visor and shield of a tall soldier stationed at the top of a lookout point, ready to sound warning.

I stepped toward the prow where my husband stood. "Thom..." I took a deep breath to stop the quavering in my voice. "Are we in danger here? Is that why those men are standing guard?"

"Here we are in our promised land, and already you are afraid?" Thom scowled and his voice was sharp. "Have you forgotten the militia at Southampton?" Suddenly his voice softened and he moved to me and put an arm around my waist. "Remember how the men took their turn standing guard in case of Indian attack?" He smiled and gestured toward the lookout point. "We'll be well protected here. From his coign of vantage the soldier can see approaching danger, whether it be the Dutch or Indians, but neither have caused any conflict for several years."

How could I lose faith so easily? With some relief, I spied a fort the early settlers had erected. I took a deep breath and squared my shoulders.

"May I carry your baggage?" Thom asked as he hoisted our bags and slung them over his shoulder. "The household goods and chattels we'll leave on the sloop for now." He turned and took my arm to steady me as I eased my way from ship to pier and then stepped foot on the rocky soil, our promised land. Surely, the dark days were now behind us.

My thoughts were interrupted by the sad voice of an Englishman, accompanied by the strumming of lute strings.

"O be drunk again, Quaker.
share thy bottle and shake her[107]

For thou, Peter Wright,
Thou art wrong.
Know ye not where you're heading?
With the devil yer bedding.
Friend, why must you be so headstrong?

Be on thy guard, son
If Rebecca ye've won.
She's a Wright,
And you must not choose wrong.
Propose not the wedding—
Ye'd be worse for the bedding.
That woman will pitch you headlong.[108]

The singer somewhat absentmindedly disembarked a few feet from the place where we stood. I watched him as he moved toward us. Plain dress, the simple style of a fervent Puritan. Thick, shoulder-length hair and dark beard, silver with age. Tall and thin, with a somewhat rounded belly and slightly stooped shoulders, yet his mien was striking, that of no common man. Long, graceful fingers stroked the smooth wood of the lute for a moment before slinging its carrying strap around his shoulder. Long face, sad as the song he sang. As he drew nearer, I could not help but notice his eyes—grey, expressive, and deep as pools.

As if suddenly aroused from unfathomable thought, the man looked up at the militiaman nearest the shore and spoke to him. "Good work, Ezekiel. God be with thee." I felt my cheeks redden when he turned and caught our group gaping at him.

"Good folk, I humbly beg your pardon if my caterwauling hath disturbed thee. I have just returned from Oyster

Bay and am all amort[109] by my dearest friend's confession. Alas, he, Peter Wright, hath become a Quaker."

The Englishman gave a deep sigh and blinked as if he could not quite comprehend such a turn of events. "But that's not the whole of it," he said. "I have learned of my youngest son's declaration of love for Peter's fair niece, Rebecca. I am fully baffled." The poor man swallowed hard and tilted his head in our direction. "Forgive me," he said. "I have no right to inflict my pain on thee. Let me introduce myself. I am the town miller. William Leverich, by name." [110]

"Leverich, eh?" Thom and John reached for our greeter's extended hand and shook it.

"Welcome to our village," Goodman Leverich said. "It's a fine ship ye have there. From the appearance of thy load, may I assume ye seek refuge in our bustling township?"

"Quite so," John said. "Tell me, is the militia on call because of some current danger?"

"Ah, no. Over west at Oyster Bay where I first settled, we English had trouble with the Dutch, but the Treaty of Hartford resolved that conflict seven years ago. Indians are plentiful here, although pestilence hath swept many away. Thirty or so families left. Never since we purchased the land from the Sachem Mohannes hath there been a conspiracy here of Indians against the White Man.[111] Distracted from his former anguish, the Englishman spoke in a vigorous and spirited voice. "Still," he said, "it is good to be vigilant."

Thom nudged me and I leaned toward him to hear what he was saying.

"Mary, do you hear the quality of this miller's voice?"

"Yes, I noticed. The man hath no trace of a low country accent," I whispered. "He sounds quite like my Uncle Robert, a Cambridge man."

Goodman Leverich looked our way and lifted an eyebrow. Perhaps deciding we were yet in doubt of our safety, he said, "Worry ye not about Quakers though they become thick as locusts settling in the fields." His eyebrows furrowed. Then his lip twitched as if on the verge of laughter. "Knowst thou what these shakers call themselves? He paused and cleared his throat with a grand harrumph before answering his own question. "Children of the Light," he said. "These folk claim the Holy Spirit dwells within *all* people; therefore they totally discount scriptural predestination. Quakers do not attend meeting house nor do they pay their tithes as Puritans do." He clicked his tongue. "'Tis disrespectful of them!" Then, perhaps feeling the need to reassure us further, he said, "Fear not. Thou hast no mortal reason to worry. Quakers believe violence is unjustified, no matter the cost."

I saw the dark flush on Mara's face and heard her low muttering. "Can my family never escape persecution by these self-righteous Puritans?"

"Sh-sh, my wife!" John placed his hand on her shoulder. "Do not be so quick to judge."

Mara shrugged away her husband's hand. "The man speaks well, but such a rude fellow is he! If only the wrathful Puritans would silence their yammering and then listen as we Quakers do, they might hear God's voice and know the truth."

We stood on the shore for a moment, hoping Henry would soon come and lead the way to his dwelling.

"Well, stranger," Goodman Leverich said as he tilted his head Thom's way, "where are you headed?"

"Do you know the Esty place?"

"Old Jeffrey Esty? Poor soul. Had his mind set on marrying the widow Burns. He had just completed a fine dwelling house big enough to hold all her children when he fell ill and died.[112] Guess he left everything to his wee grandson, Jonathan. Now the old man's daughter and her husband are moving in. Scudder's their name."

"So, you've met them?" Thom said, grinning.

"Verily, I have. Their dwelling house is less than a furlong from mine. A fine young couple they be." He turned and peered down the path toward the village green. "My ox and cart will be here shortly. Wait a bit and I shall give thee a ride. Hast thou baggage to carry?"

"Only our personal belongings. Until we have raised our own dwelling, we will leave the rest of our goods on board the *Sea Hawk*. It will be safe, I am sure, with the militia guarding the bay. Thank you for your offer, Goodman...ah...Leverich?"

"Yes, William Leverich. And you?"

Laughing at their cautelous joke on the man, John and Thom said together, "We're the other two Scudder brothers."

Goodman Leverich's eyes crinkled and he joined their laughter. "So I guess you two have known Henry Scudder longer than I have. Is he as good a brother as he is neigh—Ho, here is the love-besotted Eleazer, my youngest son, with the ox and cart."

The young man nodded in greeting, and together the men loaded our baggage into the cart. Young Eleazer Leverich flicked the whip, and the ox began moving down the trail.

As we walked the narrow trail with him, the elder Leverich held the wooden bed of the cart with one hand, freeing the other for impressive gesturing. Without missing a step, he told us his story.

"When I first came to Oyster Bay, the move was not without its misadventures." Leverich shook his head, smiling widely as he retraced his journey. "At the time," he said, "the Dutch and the English were at war, but the conflict ended quickly." Leverich's eyes gleamed and his voice sounded like that of a royal bard, clear and strong. We could not but listen.

"In the spring of 1653," Leverich said, "with two friends, I organized an expedition to Oyster Bay to expand our trading territory. The place offered great benefit—a deep sheltered harbor that owed duties to neither the Dutch nor the English."

Leverich went on with his discourse. "For a large portion of land at Oyster Bay and Huntington, we—Sam Mayo, Peter Wright and I—paid the Indians a mere pittance—coats and stockings, kettles and bottles, hatchets, awl-blades, and shovels, and a meager trifle of wampum, £4 silver.[113] Then I engaged Sam Mayo to send his Captain Dickenson to sail back to Sandwich on Cape Cod for our chattels and personal goods."[114]

When young Eleazer looked back to check the load, I saw something that quite amused me. Thom noticed it too, for he came up beside me, grinned, and nodded toward the boy. "Mary," he said in a low voice. "Look at Eleazer's face. I'll wager he's heard this story many times before."

"Yes. The son mouths every word his father says."

At the same moment Goodman Leverich gestured toward the east, Eleazer turned his gaze to the path, and with a wide flourish of the whip, urged the ox on its way.

On the trail ahead, a red fox looked up startled, and then scampered off into the forest.

The story continued. "That first year, some of the purchasers stayed at Hempstead with families that had settled there earlier. Others set about constructing dwelling-houses at the site of the present hamlet of Oyster Bay."

Leverich paused and looked around at his listeners. He raised his voice. "Because Captain Dickenson ran the Dutch blockade above Hell Gate, the *Desire* was considered a suitable Prize of War, and as such, any black-hearted pirate might claim her."

Eager for more of the story, we listened.

"That's right," he said, "A prize of war. Therefore, when a brigand by the name of Thomas Baxter sighted her that morning, by force of arms he boarded the vessel loaded with our household goods. The scoundrel claimed the sloop as his own and sailed his prize of war over to Fairfield harbor."

Goodman Leverich's clenched fist slammed into his opposite hand with a loud smack. "That was his undoing! After putting up a considerable fight, he was arrested there. At the trial, the judge ordered Baxter to return the *Desire* to Goodman Mayo, and we got our possessions back."[115]

"That was three years ago. Life was simple then." Leverich took a deep breath. "Simple but often difficult. Having few possessions, the early arrivals created their own household furniture and basic tools. With the tools, they cleared the ground and seeded their fields. Peas and beans, grain and corn. The settlers scratched along that year, building up their stock of animals and fowl to supply their needs — meat and milk; wool, hides, and leather; and feathers for bedding — bolsters and pillows."[116]

Ahead we saw the rail fence and hickory tree Henry had described as the marker for the northwest corner of his acreage. Through the trees, Henry's deep voice called out, interrupting the storyteller. Down a narrow path leading off from the trail, we saw him coming toward us.

"Hail, miller! I see you've gotten acquainted with my brothers, John and Thom and their families."

"Verily, I have, Henry, and passing fair they be. It's good to see the town grow. More business for the mill," Leverich said. A hint of mirth became a sudden burst of laughter. "Perhaps I'll see thee at the mill soon, although when my work is caught up, I need visit the Indian village. The poor souls are in darkness and under the shadow of death. I must try to bring them to Jesus Christ."[117]

"Ah, yes," Henry said. "But that can wait for the morrow. Come with me, all of you." Henry motioned down the path and then led the way toward his dwelling.

At the door of the Scudder dwelling, two women appeared, one carrying a squirming child on her hip. "Look, Jonathan. Da-da hath brought your favorite cousins."

I recognized Catherine, of course, but the other woman was a stranger to me.

Goodman Leverich stepped forward. "Ellen, my dear, I thought I might find thee here. These are our new neighbors, the Scudder families, come to stay at their brother's dwelling until they can raise houses of their own." He turned back to us, gesturing as he spoke. "Thou mayest have perceived this woman who visits

Goodwife Scudder is none other than my own fair consort, Ellen, mother of our sons Caleb and Eleazer."

By that time, Eleazer had unloaded our belongings and piled them at the door. Leverich turned again to his wife: "Come, dear Ellen, you've men to feed. Wouldest thou ride? There is plenty of room." Giving her a courtly hand, he helped her onto the seat beside Eleazer who had again taken the reins.

"Wait a minute, Eleazer." Goody Leverich put her hand on her son's sleeve, and then turned to Catherine. "Remember Bible study at my house on the morrow. Mid-morning while we are still unblemished by mundane household duties—and bring your sisters with you. A good time for becoming acquainted." She smiled, and after Goodman Leverich had bidden us farewell, they went on down the trail toward their own abode.

"Wave bye-bye, Jonathan," said his mother.

Instead, little Jonathan held out his chubby arms, squealed and laughed, showing two front teeth. "Da-da!"

Henry took his son from Catherine and hugged the babe to his chest. He motioned to us. "Come on in, now. If I know Catherine, she hath dinner simmering in the pot, enough for all."

Catherine nodded and smiled. "If you will each pick up a pack of your belongings, we'll find a place for it inside." Crossing the threshold, she led us into a spacious room blooming with the aroma of beef stew and fresh bread.

"Who is that Goodman Leverich who speaks so eloquently?" I asked when we had all found places at the board and scooped our trenchers full.

"From what I'm told," Henry said, "he's a preacher—the Reverend William Leverich, educated in Cambridge,

England. Too bad Huntington Village hired him as miller rather than minister. If the Reverend's Sabbath sermons are as good as his stories, I could more easily listen to him for three hours than the layman who speaks now."

"Reverend Leverich, is he? Methinks I've heard of this man before," Mara said slowly. "A woman I know told me about a Puritan preacher named Leverich who was on Cape Cod a few years ago. His wife was the talk of the town. Seems he was offered the presidency of a new university being established at Yale, but his shrewish woman, violently averse to his moving to New Haven, made him turn the offer down."

Catherine gasped. "Oh, my! I would never think of doing that to Henry. It is difficult to imagine Ellen Leverich speaking out like that! She is such a kindly soul."

The expression on John's face was sardonic, to say the least. "Oh, my yes," he said. He cast his glance Mara's way, and quirked his eyebrows humorously. "It is indeed hard to imagine a woman speaking out like that."

Mara ignored his remark. "Leverich supposedly told the town folk at New Haven that he turned the offer down because he had overmuch invested in learning the language of the Cape Cod Indians." She laughed, making a derisive sound in her throat. "Actually, his own flock complained that he was so conservative he made the Quaker way look conventional." Mara's voice rose and her words rushed. "An arrogant man. He—"

I felt my hands clenching at my sides. "Arrogant? He seemed genuinely humble. Did he not introduce himself only as the town miller? Never did he flaunt his standing as an ordained minister."

Mara frowned and the line between her eyebrows creased more deeply. "But you were not present at Cape

Cod," she said, "nor could you have been. None might be admitted to town rights there without his consent. The law was emphatically enforced."

Henry grunted concurrence. "Yes, dear sister-in-law, we all know the law. That duty is given to ministers and the town council. It keeps out the riff-raff."

Mara rolled her eyes at Henry's remark. "Believe me, enforcing this law did not gain Leverich any converts. According to what I was told, many at Sandwich were offended, and in their animosity, they invented charges against him. Accused him of novelties in religion; of using the services of the Anglicans in Baptism and Holy Communion, following the rituals of the Mother Church of England."

I sighed. "And that brought about his dismissal?"

"Well, local gossips say so," Mara said with a furtive smile. "They laughed at the reasons given for his banishment. In truth, they could no longer abide him; hence, his removal."[118]

With Mara's contentious talk, a realization came to me. I was not as tolerant of variance with society's rules as I had thought. Mara's tetchy manner seemed to me to be intolerable in the sight of God and also in the eyes of her husband. Was that the Quaker way? Perhaps she stepped beyond the bounds of what women were allowed. Or perhaps I was seeing in Mara a reflection of my own flaws.

I cast a cautious look at Thom. Would he wish me to keep silent, to still my questioning of God's ways? Must I try to become a more submissive wife?

Time enough for that conversation later. Now there was work to be done.

ANNO DOM 1657
SETTLING IN AT HUNTINGTON, LONG ISLAND

That night, snuggled under soft quilts in the great room at Henry and Catherine's waterside home, sleep eluded me. Where would we build our own house? How soon could it be finished? Could it be waterside? How I would love watching the daily ebb and flow of tides. Finally, Thom pulled me close to him and I drifted off, dreams awash with voices—Miller Leverich's song, his wife's friendly invitation to her Bible study, and Mara's cross words.

I awoke early at the sound of baby Jonathan calling for his Da Da. Catherine and Mara were preparing the morning meal, so I dressed and slipped away to the sloop with Thom and his brothers.

"The Town Commons is open to the public," Henry said. "We can take your cattle there to pasture."

With Henry showing the way, we herded our animals off the boat and down the path to the east. Like the proud discoverer of a great treasure, he chattered rapidly each step of the way.

"You'll find we're self-governing here, and the first of the free men to settle in Huntington have been very busy. They have already organized a Town Meeting to distribute town-held land and regulate the pasturing of cattle, and to resolve disputes and any other matters that concern the town as a whole."[119]

"In the February Town Meeting," Henry said, "we made education a priority."

"That's excellent news," Thom said. "Mary and I have prayed for such a place."

Henry smiled. "Yes, isn't it. When we offered Jonas Houldsworth the job as the first schoolmaster, straightaway he agreed. 'I'm sure God would wish all villagers to be able to read. How else can we study the Bible?'"

Then, according to Henry's report, the man made certain stipulations. "If you would hire me to teach, first, supply me with a dwelling house and a cleared lot next to it. I know cash money is hard to come by, so I will accept butter, wheat, Indian corn, and cattle as part of my salary. The rest you can make up in wampum—enough for goods and clothing that I might need each year."

By that time, we had reached the Town Commons, and I stood with my mouth agape at the loveliness of the place. Indians and early settlers had cut the forest away, leaving thickets and wild bushes. The cattle could amble toward the edge of the forest to chew their cud in the shade of hickory trees when the weather warmed, but today they hurried toward a miry pond to drink.

Henry pointed. "See how the land slopes down to the bay on the west?[120] The Indians call it 'Opcathontyche.' They tell me the word means 'wading place creek,'[121] but we call it Big Cow Harbor. Altogether, it is a fifty- or sixty-acre plot."[122]

High above the trees a red-tailed hawk circled. Bright splashes of yellow and violet—early-blooming wild flowers sprinkled the grassy hills and vales, announcing the arrival of spring. For an instant, a scene from my childhood skipped through my memory. I was with my beloved brother Luddie, tending cattle in fields of England...the day I fell down the mineshaft...the day my mother died.

The sunshine of my memory disappeared behind grey clouds but with a quick shake of my head, the childhood scene faded. In

Huntington Village on Long Island, the morning sun was rising and the air smelled fresh and new as the first day of creation.

21st Century
Memory Catchers' Office

Abruptly Mary ended her story. "My dear, look how dark the clouds are!"

A loud rumble of thunder shook my office and for a brief instant, the lights flickered, went out, and then came back on. Yet not even a shadow remained in Grand-Mary's chair.

A great sorrow descended upon me, like a death in the family, and I could hardly hold back the tears.

I set the recording back to the beginning of Grand-Mary's interview and transcribed the latest chapter. The sound of her voice lifted my sadness.

Spring, Anno Dom 1657
Huntington Village, Long Island

In Huntington Village, the Town Fathers met and assigned lots to John, Thom, and other new settlers. Our lot was, as I had hoped, by the waterside.

So much to do! Before carts, barns, and fences, we must build our dwelling ere we wear out our welcome at Henry and Catherine's home.

At night, when all else was still and I was lying in Thom's arms, we whispered ideas in each other's ears. Two chimneys on west end, one on the east, with the house facing south. We'd build a kitchen with a huge fireplace, a hall and a parlor, and another room to hold all the cooking utensils, buckets, and earthenware. Two stories in front with chambers above for our future offspring's sleeping rooms, and storage on the north under the eaves for foodstuffs and out-of-season tools.

But first, for the men folk there were trees to fell, timber to saw, and shingles to shape.

While our Henry, Thom, and John and his sons prepared for the house raising, they also took charge of the oxen and horses, and readied the land for the planting of fields and orchards.

In the meantime, my sisters-in-law Mara and Catherine and I, and Mara's three dutiful daughters, Hannah, Martha, and Betsey, shared the labors of ordinary housewifery. We prepared meals and attempted to keep the house in order, rooms filled with twelve souls and their baggage. Together we cared for the family's clothing and bedding—washing, drying, knitting, sewing, mending—the labor seemed unending.

Our days began at first light. The men donned heavy work clothes and set about their daily labors. The first of the women to arise coaxed flame from the bank of hot coals in the fireplace and hung pots of water to boil. Then Hannah, my eldest niece, with Mara, Catherine, and me headed for the barn to tend the chickens, sheep, and hogs and to care for and milk cows that had recently calved. The younger girls, Martha and Betsey stayed in the house tending baby Jonathan and preparing breakfast—cheese, bread toasted over ever-burning coals in the fireplace, and the remainder of yesterday's dinner—often boiled meat and turnips.[123] When the meal was ready, the three families gathered around the board, asked God to bless our day's endeavors, and then filled our trenchers with the food the girls had prepared. Then back to work.

I enjoyed this time of getting acquainted with my husband's side of the family. Together, we women cared for the animals and planted gardens — potatoes, parsnips, carrots, watermelons to supplement our daily needs. What a sight we were. Catherine, great with child; Mara, relentlessly fanning her flushed face with her apron; and I, limping along with cramps in my legs. I soon understood that Mara's crossness had reason. She suffered from hot flushes and sleepless nights like Aunt Alice had experienced when I lived with her in Southampton. Mara was young to be going through the change, but she never shirked her duty.

"My mother taught me that to see what must be done and not to do it, is a sin," she said. "After all, it is not as bad as the curse." She paused in her work to wipe the sweat from her face with the tail of her apron. "At least I won't be having a dozen babes like most women do. Five are quite enough, and my John is happy with our two sons as heirs."

Some afternoons when the sand was damp from rain, we strolled along the shore, filling our eyes and ears with the joy of nature all around us. Groves of dogwood in bloom. Apple trees showing their first sign of buds. White oaks hinting at new leaves.

Geese, filling the skies with their harsh honking, veed their way back from the south. Small, sand-colored piping plovers darted along the shores, lining their nearly invisible nests with colored pebbles and shell fragments. Huge ospreys and an occasional swan or pelican took wing. My heart sang with the "kon-ka-ree" of the red-winged blackbirds, the discordant gobbling of wild turkeys, and the sight of a red-tailed hawk looping and diving in a cloudless heaven. Predators might lurk in the darkness of the forest, but we saw only frisky squirrels and rabbits skittering through the new grass.

We rested on the grass under the fragrant canopy of a peach tree in full bloom, but in spite of the joys all around us, Mara began sobbing. I put my arm around her shoulders. "Mara, dear, are you feeling ill today?"

She wiped her eyes with her apron. "Did you hear of poor Humphrey Norton over in Southold? When he lately criticized Rev. Youngs in church, he was arrested and sent to New Haven. There they fined him twenty pounds and whipped him till his back was bleeding." Mara sniffed and blotted the tears from her eyes again. "But even that cruelty was not enough," she said. "With a hot branding iron they seared the letter H on his hand and banished him from Southold."[124]

"I didn't know you and John were close friends with Goodman Norton," Catherine said.

Mara shook her head. "I do not know him well, but I know Norton is a rebel like my father. Filled with the love of God. He would harm no one. I cannot think of him for imagining the brand of a heretic being burned into my father's hand."

"Is your father not William King? Are you saying he is a Quaker like Goodman Norton?" I asked.

"In all truth, he claims that faith in Christ frees him from the laws of the Old Testament. Fear not, he does not disregard the moral law. But he believes that Christians are saved by faith rather than works, as antinomians believe."[125][126]

Catherine gasped. "Oh, Mara, are you not afraid for him? That is the belief of Anne Hutchinson, and you know what happened to her."

"I know. She was cruelly banished and driven out of the Colony with her husband and children."

"And after her husband died, by faith she moved away to start a new life where she would no longer be persecuted. 'Twas there that warring Indians killed them all."

"Yes," I said. "I remember Uncle Robert telling Anne's story back when my family first arrived in Long Island. She became my example of what a woman could do."

"Your example?" Catherine raised her eyebrows as she spoke. "Why ever would you say that?"

"Because she stood up for her beliefs and was not easily intimidated. Is not the ability to think and question a gift? If a loving God bestows on us this gift, why must our freedom forever be limited by men?"

"Oh, I pray that you are never brought into court for your beliefs, my dear sister-in-law," Mara said. "You could be hung for such heresy."

"Yet your father is not afraid?"

"No. As he oft says that perfect love casts out fear." Mara shook her head and got to her feet as if to put her worries behind her. "Come," she said. "We dare not shilly-shally longer."

Before returning home, we scooped up shellfish from an inlet on the bay—clams, oysters, muscles and scallops—for our late meal. At evening devotions, Thom obliged me by reading from my favorite book in the New Testament—I John 4:18. A verse I had long ago written on my heart and from it, gained peace and quietness. *There is no fear in love; but perfect love casteth out fear: because fear hath torment.*

May, Anno Dom 1657
Huntington, Long Island

Settlers came from every guild and trade—teacher, tanner, shoemaker, weaver, whaler. One might have the calloused hands of a blacksmith or a brick maker, a carpenter or a cabinetmaker. He might wear a magistrate's wig or a minister's robe. But first, if he and his family were to survive, he must care for the land.

છ

As soon as Thom and his brothers had prepared the materials for building, neighbors welcomed us with a house-raising, a social gathering that rivaled community celebrations I recalled at Southampton. Bringing their saws and hammers, planes and levels, hatchets, axes and nails, men hurried to the lot Thom and I had drawn for our dwelling place—by the waterside of Huntington Bay.[127] From there, a cart path lead southward toward the Town Spot—the village green.

I heard the welcome sound of my husband and his brothers entering into the boisterous conversations and booming laughter. House-raising was a time for celebration, a coming together. It was a breathing space, a respite from isolated labors. And in Huntington Village, helping thy neighbor was the Christian thing to do.

So many friendly faces, so many names to remember— Jonas Wood, Edward Higbee, Thomas Skidmore. Robert Seeley, John Ketcham, Jonas Houldsworth. Isaac Platt, Thomas Jones, Thomas Weeks. How *ever* could they afford to cease their own labors and tend to a new neighbor's needs? Everyone labored from dawn to dusk.

Think ye not that women had a lesser load. I could fill a whole book with the list, yet we, too, found time to join in the house-raising. Come midday, in a cacophony of chattering and gaiety, goodwives and their daughters descended on our lot by Huntington Bay. Some carried babies on their hips; some hobbled, bent with painful lumbagos; several were large with child; yet all came laden with pots of food and baskets filled with rum and sugar cakes to share with their worker-husbands and sons. On boards laid across trestles, we spread the meal. Early that morning, the men had dug a pit and thereby roasted a young pig. By noontime, it was giving off a delicious aroma. Hungry laborers filled their trenchers with hunks of roast pork and with stews rich with broth, and then mopped them clean with chunks and crusts of hot breads and topped it off with rum and sugar cakes.

When the men returned to work, it was the women's turn to eat, but I could not join them. The odor of the roast pig permeated the air, and my stomach roiled. I counted the days on my fingers, and it was then that I knew. By next February, Thom would surely have constructed another cradle. Never before had I experienced such a premonitory emotion. I was sore afraid.

Anno Dom 1657-1658
Huntington Village, Long Island

Our house was soon completed, [128] and the very first night in our own room and bed, I told Thom the news. So happy was he that he jigged around the room as excited and energetic as a young lad.

Laughing, he grabbed me and swung me around as if we were charter members of the forbidden English Folk Dance Society. "Now that we are happily settled on our own property in a growing community," he said, "my dream is coming true." Around and around we skipped until I was so dizzy I collapsed in his arms and we both fell to the floor in a Ring-around-the-Rosy heap. The lump of anxiety in my chest relaxed as we lay there giggling like children.

With his forefinger, Thom caressed my cheek and then laid his palm gently over my belly. "Oh, Aphrodite, thou art so precious to me. Long have I dreamed of the sons that would one day inherit the fruits of my labors. Now I know it will come to pass."

I could not dampen his happiness. I could not admit my terror of the days to come. No, I could not.

εϽ

It was late in the season for planting crops. Some of our land had already been cleared by the Indians, and neighbors pitched in to help with the rest. Then came the digging and manuring, the plowing and sowing the fields with flax, oats, corn, wheat, rye, barley, turnips, and potatoes. The planting of fruit trees.

Thom had been toiling dawn to dusk, but now the energy and time he put into his work seemed to double. I hid my fears from him, and in truth, so occupied was he with his own labors, he scarce had time to notice. At night, he came in, supped, and then fell exhausted into bed and was immediately snoring. I sorely missed the nights when we lay in each other's embrace. I missed the way he used to pull me to him and curve his body around mine until we both fell asleep.

The Scudder brothers eagerly joined in community interests, helping to lay the town's foundation of government, education, and morals, as well as establishing their own occupations and enterprises. Thom saw heaven's work before him, improving barely touched land, recreating England with its fields of wheat and barley and its barnyards of cattle, sheep, hogs, and geese.

Although government and religion were as one in my day, Huntington was not really a theocracy. Because we were far from the seat of Royal Government, we were, in effect, self-governing and verdicts of Huntington Town Meetings were law, without any appeal to a higher court.[129]

At an early Town Meeting, the townsmen decided to build a tavern, a public house or ordinary it was called, near the Village green and appointed Goodman Swallow as its keeper. Though designed as a lodging house for travelers, the tavern served a variety of purposes. Town Meetings convened there, and after adjournment, the men lingered for a time of social amusement and conversation. Selectmen held court there, acting as both judge and jury, meting out punishment to wrongdoers. To add insult and humiliation to the sentence, they constructed public stocks where the entire village, like the audience at an entertainment, could taunt the condemned.

Goodman Powell, the town clerk, who struggled with words of more than one syllable, sipped his ale as he sat at a table in the tavern,[130] recording sales and transfers, marriages, deaths, estrays, and earmarks. Perhaps that explains the splotches of ale and the lingering odor I noticed when Thom asked me to go look up the description of his newly purchased pastureland.

Henry Whitney, the village lay preacher, as well as visiting ministers, were oft seen entering the tavern of an evening, perhaps to be sure he knew which idler or tippler most needed his prayers.

The militia also met at the tavern. Each freeman from 16 to 60 was responsible for possessing his own gun and ammunition for militia service and for watching out for foxes, wolves, and wildcats that competed with farm animals for existence.

Thom, after occasionally hearing his name called in the drawing to determine whose turn it was to serve, would load his bag of powder and shot, put his musket over his shoulder, and head to the tavern where the militia or trainband captains planned for the town's protection. When, at the nine o'clock curfew, Thom came home smelling of smoke, sweat, and ale, I imagined the dimly lighted room where he and other men of the town took their accustomed places at the bar, gossiping and telling stories between gulps of ale and beer. I was not without envy.

Living in our new dwelling was a blessing, but sometimes I missed the bustle of the household when we were all staying at Henry and Catherine's home, and I missed the respite of the daily companionship of my sisters-in-law.

One lonely day when I walked to the Leverich house for Bible study, I arrived before the rest of the women. Ellen welcomed me, asked me to sit, and then poured me a mug of ale.

"Mmm," I said, after taking a sip. "Never have I tasted better ale. Did you make it yourself?"

Ellen Leverich nodded and tucked a loose strand of iron-grey hair under her cap. Her wide smile expressed pleasure at my compliment. "'Tis certain more agreeable than the putrid substance we sipped once we arrived at Sandwich twenty years ago." Ellen wrinkled her nose. "I had a terrible time drinking that stuff, so while my husband was off preaching to the Indians on Sandwich, I learned the art of the brewer."

"I've heard that your husband is a minister."

"You can't tell it by looking at him, but yes, he certainly is. Reverend William Leverich. Huntington Village paid Henry Whitney a goodly amount of produce to build a mill at the head of Huntington Harbor and they asked my husband to run it.[131] Ye can not have much of a village without a miller, thou knowest. They made him an offer he couldn't refuse, but he still hath time for his calling. He hath learned the language of the Matinecock who live between here and Oyster Bay so he can bring them to Christ. Back in England, he was an ordained clergy. A priest of the Anglican Church. I met him when he was preaching in Suffolk, east of Cambridgeshire, and there we wed. Then, when he fell afoul of the church authorities because of his non-conformist beliefs, he decided to sail to the New World — to Duxbury in Plymouth Colony. They already had a minister there, so he moved on to Sandwich on Cape Cod. That's where I joined him, and both of our sons were born there."

"Cape Cod? My aunt and uncle, John and Florence Carman lived at Sandwich a few years ago. Did you happen to know them?"

"The Carmans? Oh, my, yes. Dear, dear friends. Both of our families had sons named Caleb. The same age, too. If I remember, they left Sandwich just before we did. Goodman Carman and the Rev. Fordham had determined to purchase a large tract of land from Tackapoushe, the One-Eyed Sachem in Dutch territory." Ellen reached for the jug of ale and refilled my cup. "How are the Carmans? I have often thought of them. I believe your Aunt Florence was expecting another child at the time they moved."

"Yes. She delivered soon after they first moved to Hempstead," I said. "Aunt Florence and the babe caught the measles, and she wasn't well for some time after, but worse yet, the baby lost his sight. Joshua, they named him. He was only a little tiddler,[132] but he was a wonder child."

"And how is your uncle, Goodman Carman?"

I shook my head. "Uncle John's dead now. Sailing home to Hempstead, he was stricken and fell over-board — lost and buried beneath the waves.

"Oh, God have mercy. And Goody Carman, your aunt Florence? How doth she fare?"

"Married again — to a Goodman Hicks. He's farming Uncle John's land now, along with my Carman cousins." I carried my empty mug to the cupboard, and then re-turned to our conversation. "When did you and your husband leave Sandwich?"

"Well, like your Uncle John, my husband was always searching for more land, added opportunities for growth, and greater freedom, but in truth, we were banished. The Quakers there gave the authorities no end of annoyance, but many other settlers were also independent in their thinking and no longer supported the strict Puritan the-ology espoused by William and other ministers like him. Attendance at Sabbath meetings was compulsory, you know, but without the presence of a constable, the rule was often not respected." Ellen paused and nodded to-ward her husband's office study. "Perhaps it was Wil-liam's work with the Indians at Cape Cod that drew the settlers' resentment most of all. I was never sure what they meant when they said he was 'too conscientiously humane' for the times." Ellen raised her brows, as if still puzzled by the outcome at Sandwich. She sighed and then continued. "With a group of other dissatisfied Puri-tans, he soon formed a company to purchase land at Oyster Bay. Sam Mayo was chief negotiator, but my William handled the dialogue with the Indians. They purchased a broad expanse of land here along the north shore of Long Island. Now he works with the Matinecocks living between Huntington and Oyster Bay. Some ministers and governors claim God's plan is to clear the land of the Indians, making way for us, his chosen people. But my conscientious William shall never agree with that. Often he goes among the stricken Indians, teaching in the wigwams amid the terrors of death, and giving them bread or a cup of cold water in the Name of the Master."

A knock at the door interrupted our conversation, and before Ellen rose to admit the women's Bible study group, she said to me, "I'm sure my husband will invite the Scudder men to share his pew on the Sabbath. Mary, would you and your Scudder sisters like to share mine?"

Anno Dom 1657-1658
The Sabbath Meeting

Everyone owned a dog or two in our village. Because the woods harbored wolves and other wild beasts that preyed upon the flocks of sheep pasturing therein, the town treasury paid up to five shillings as bounties for wild animals the settler's dogs destroyed.

Not only were they a necessary part of the community, they were also regular attendees at the Sabbath meeting house. There was a good deal of empathy between them and the wretched boys, for both received retribution when they disturbed worship. As was his duty, the tithing man rapped the heads of the miscreant boys and beat out the dogs."[133]

His duty, also, was to control those who could not refrain from smiling when the monotony of a three-hour sermon was broken by an occasional dogfight with boys shouting loud cheers of approval to their favorite. If a man dozed off during the sermon, the tithing man gave him a tap on his head, or if the snorer were a woman protected by a bonnet, he woke her by brushing her face with a fox's tail. Later in the week, howls of laughter at the tavern encouraged imitators of the snorers.[134]

The Town fathers had soon discovered Henry Whitney, the carpenter, to be a cantankerous man when crossed, but when he volunteered as a lay preacher, they accepted his offer for they had found no other pastor. The first Sabbath our Scudder families attended meeting house, Goodman Whitney described the fall of Adam and Eve: "The Bible tells us," he said, "that the first woman, Eve, was seduced by the serpent and then made Adam eat of the apple, so God chastised them both." Whitney raised his voice as though he were God himself, condemning Eve for her disobedience: "I will multiply your pains in childbirth. You shall give birth to your children in pain. You will long for your husband, but he will lord it over you. Justly so, for it is because of the sin of Eve that man must forever till the soil by the sweat of his brow.[135] [136]

"Women's subjection to men, and the pain they bear in childbed, is God's inescapable curse." Whitney shook his fist at the women's side of the meeting house.

I heard faint sighs of weariness from the benches behind us. How disheartened these women seemed, how dependent on their husbands for everything. Even their thoughts must be censored.

I tried to stay awake during the long sermon, though oft my head nodded and mine eyes drooped. Even the dogs were restless. A welcome distraction. *Oh, God, forgive my sinful thought.*

Finally, the discourse ended. We stood for the final Psalm, and from the men's bench beside us, the bass growl of someone's stomach accompanied the words. The noon repast was overdue.

On Monday, the workweek began, and I looked forward to the respite and companionship as well as the discussion of the sermon when we women gathered at the Leverich abode.

Ellen opened the door to my knock. "Welcome, dear Mary. Are your sisters not coming today?"

"No," I said, "Catherine asked that she be remembered in prayer. Her birthing time draws near, and she is not feeling well. Mara, too, asks to be excused for she wishes not to cause dissention with her Quaker leanings. Her parents, William and Dorothy King, live at King's Cove, Salem, near Royall's Neck. In Salem, they are oft in conflict with the Puritans, for as Quakers, you know, they believe that once a person hath accepted the Lord, the Holy Spirit dwells within them."

Ellen nodded her understanding, led me to an empty spot at the end of a bench, and introduced me to the woman on the bench that adjoined mine. "Mary Scudder, meet Dora Cummings."

I smiled as Dora ducked her head and pulled her spinning wheel close to begin working the treadle. "Forgive me that I work. I have so many children to clothe."

The low chatter of the women, the sighing of the fire, and the humming of the wheel were pleasant to my ears. "Dora, are you oft in attendance here for discussion?"

"Oh, yes," she said, "though words come hard to me."

A woman beside me interrupted Dora to introduce herself as Deriah Catswaller. "Thou wilt soon make the acquaintance of all the women here," she said. "They attend church without fail and sit rapt while the minister expounds on the week's text. Most of the women here have enough education to read the Bible, and we read and meditate on the scriptures each week."

Tilting her head upward enough to look down her nose at me, she said, "Art thou trained in the art of reading, dear Goody Scudder? Without the ability, thou mayst find it difficult to join in our activities. We make our way through the Old and New Testaments at least once each year," she said. "And we pray and fast and repent our sins as zealously as the most devout men."

I bit my tongue and turned from her, avoiding the sharp reply that first tickled my tongue. No need to search for a soft answer to the Catswaller woman's remarks, for the others had already begun to discuss Whitney's sermon of the previous Sabbath.

Deriah Catswaller. Her name, I was sure, would be an easy one to remember. I turned my attention to their discussion.

"Why must God punish us all for Eve's disobedience?" a bold one asked.

The question revived in my heart the punishing pain of Isaac's delivery and death barely three full moons ago to the day.

Two of the women across the room, very young and with child, sat uncomfortably on their hard bench. "My time is near," one said softly, "and I am sore afraid. My first child nearly died when he was but three months old."

Ellen nodded. "My little Hannah was born before we came to the Colonies. She was but a year old when I found her stone cold in her crib. Though we sailed here to the Puritan Utopia that very year, I suffered five years of grieving ere I could tolerate giving birth to another."

My heart had found kindred souls.

Silently I began weeping, and when Ellen observed my tears, she held out her hand, a gesture of comfort and understanding.

"Why," I asked, "must children die in their infancy? Why must we suffer such loss, such pain?"

"There are herbs to prevent conception," a woman said quietly. "Is that a sin against God?"

Ellen raised her hand. "My husband is an ordained minister and a great scholar of the Old Testament. He says procreation is the key to the economic survival of the colonies. We must not frustrate the ordinance of marriage nor hinder the generation of mankind. It puts the future of the colonies in jeopardy. God's decree makes my husband the head of our house," Ellen said, "so I bow in obedience to him."

The women began talking all at one, like a brood of hens released from the confines of their nests for a brief reprieve. Some shook their heads, but most spoke out in agreement with Ellen. Their increasingly loud cackling quieted to a gentle clucking when the Goodman Leverich stepped into the room from his book-lined study to scatter a few grains of wisdom our way.

"Read your Old Testament, goodwives," he said. "Ye should be discussing last Sabbath's discourse, rather than debating religious and ethical ideas that are beyond your discernment."

Goodman Leverich apparently felt it his duty to listen in on the women's discussions to keep them from going astray. Being good Puritan wives, they accepted his counsel with nary a frown.

"Women," he said sharply, "you are to be domestic, separated from the linked affairs of church and state." He turned to go back to his studies, then paused and turned to us for a few last words. "Women would best derive their ideas of God from the contemplations of their husbands."

After Goodman Leverich's comments, I better understood my friend Ellen Leverich's meek manner. I also felt a mite sorry for her, and perhaps others did also, for at once, the women began to rise, straighten their bonnets, and put on their wraps.

As they were leaving, Ellen took my arm and asked that I stay and chat. She bade me to sit so she might tell me more about the loss of her little Hannah before inquiring about my loss. "Perhaps, my dear, it would help if you might share your grief with my husband," she suggested. "He could give thee good counsel. Ask your husband if he would permit."

My heart was so full I could answer only in mumbled words. I waved goodbye, then thanked Ellen for her hospitality.

On the day of our second Sabbath meeting, the sermon was again on the sins of women. Pastor Whitney used the Jezebel Anne Hutchinson as an example. It had been less than 20 years since Anne's banishment. "Her greatest sin," he reminded us, "was that she invited women to her house for discussion of the sermon, and then stepped out of her place to challenge ministers and disagree with them. Though men also began joining the women who met at her home, she was yet considered the ringleader. At her trial, the judges focused on her failure to adhere to her proper female role." Whitney's voice took on the sound of reprimand. "Women should not teach at meetings, especially men, for that disrupteth hierarchies in Puritan settlements." His brow creased in a stern frown and he shook a long finger at the women's row of benches. "When ye follow her example and step out of thy proper place, ye, like Anne Hutchinson, have rather been a Husband than a Wife, a Preacher than a Hearer, a Magistrate than a Subject."

His sermon again relied on the Biblical story of Eve in the Garden of Eden. As he looked to the men's side of the meeting house on the right, he spoke boldly while gesturing to the left. "Be ye men warned of the danger. Eve is their foremother; the female is innately inclined toward evil. Women are more susceptible to temptation and easily become emissaries of Satan. Women are more likely to give in to passions, more likely to become witches. Lack of social and economic power makes women angry and leads them to avenge themselves through the Devil."[137] The pastor glared toward the pews on his left, then turned to the men again. "How to counter this threat?" He pounded the pulpit. "Make women totally subordinate. Keep them in line. Deliver them from the paths of temptation and sin. Insist that they must submit in marriage as Christian believers submit to Christ." Pastor Henry Whitney paused and looked directly at Ellen Leverich. "Heed ye this clear lesson," he said. "Mrs. Hutchinson would not cease her preaching and teaching, but obstinately continued in her gross errors. For that, she was justly tried, excommunicated, and exiled from the colony." Again, he turned to the right. "Men, we must not allow our wives and daughters to weave their evil ideas into the fabric of our Puritan society."

That week when the women's study group met to discuss the admonitions of the sermon, a few women, lead by the suggestions of Deriah Catswaller, proposed that we contain our opinions of the Anne Hutchinson case ere we do serious wrong—we should meet together only to pray, read the Bible, and edify one another according to the warning words of the pastor. Otherwise, our discussions would surely become disorderly and without rule.

Jedidah Higbee, with a babe at her breast and another apparently due soon, looked first for approval either from the Catswaller woman or from her neighbor, Pastor Whitney's wife, Sarah, before nodding her agreement.

"Summer is fast approaching, and we have read only through Leviticus," one woman said. "We shan't even get through the Old Testament at this rate."

Though I suspected the preacher's wife as a spy in the group, I dared to suggest that if we fell behind in the reading, we might skip to the New Testament. "Do you not take comfort in the two commandments Jesus gave us in his simplification of the Old Testament law? The good news of the New Testament does not abolish the precepts of the law, but rather it confirms them," I said.

This drew glaring glances from Deriah Catswaller and her obsequious fawners, the haughty Jedidah and others. Still I could not restrain from admitting my doubts of the irrevocable power of the male hierarchy, even questioning the harsh, judgmental Puritan God of the Old Testament. I could hear the rapid scratching of Sarah Whitney's pen. No doubt, her husband would be pointing me out as the embodiment of the wayward wife during next Sabbath's sermon.

Anno Dom 1658
Huntington, Long Island

I found much to take my mind off disagreements at Ellen Leverich's Bible study. A woman's work was never done.

Stoic settlers rose early and went straight to barnyard chores that demanded their attention. Then, returning to the house, they drank the usual mug of cider or beer and gulped down a bowl of porridge or cornmeal mush that wives had set to cook all night over the embers. They washed the meal down with more cider or beer.

In many kitchens, meals were a quickly-prepared monotony of choice—chiefly salt beef, pork and fish and more often rye than wheat bread, all prepared over the fireplace.

Thankfully, the book Aunt Alice had given me— Gervase Markham's *English Huswife*—inspired variety.

For breakfast, a Johnnycake with fried pork. Dinner was the larger meal, served in the early afternoon. A typical farmer's dinner when goods and money were scarce was a chunk of salt pork and a boiled pot—Indian pudding boiled with potatoes in an iron kettle.

The one rule that served me in almost any situation was Mara's maxim: "To see what must be done and not to do it, is a sin." Urged on by this saying, when my cramping legs prevented me from ordinary housewifery and community service, I volunteered for simpler tasks. Sewing, mending, scrubbing clothes, and ironing them were never-ending responsibilities.

When a severe cramping spasm hit, my stomach rejected food and my whole body clenched as if I were being caught in the refiner's fire and squeezed in the smithy's vise. With my body swollen and bruised, words oft came to me from the scriptures I had learned as a child, sometimes harsh words from the Old Testament:

But who may abide the day of his coming? and who shall stand when he appeareth? for he is like a refiner's fire, and like fullers' soap[138]*: And he shall sit as a refiner and purifier of silver: and he shall purify the sons of Levi, and purge them as gold and silver, that they may offer unto the Lord an offering in righteousness.*[139]

On the other hand, phrases from the New Testament oft brought me control, courage, and comfort:

Though I have the gift to understand all knowledge; and have not love, I am nothing. Though I bestow all my goods to feed the poor, and give my body to be burned, and have not love, it profiteth me nothing. Love defers wrath, and is kind; love envieth not; love is not puffed up, does not behave itself unseemly, seeketh not <u>her</u> own, is not easily provoked, thinketh no evil.[140]

I pondered the word "her" in describing the gift of love. How far I was from that perfection! I could no longer ignore duty without feeling guilty. It was "a still, small voice," to be sure, but sharpened by my own discernment.

To avoid cramping, I learned to start work slowly, move slowly, and then rest and wait for restored energy or strength. A sweet treat at breakfast seemed to help. Once I had learned to avoid squatting, kneeling, or sitting cramped for long hours, spring gardening became a joy.

The kitchen and household demanded gathering of eggs, wild roots and herbs for seasoning and preparation of medicines. Books I had read from Uncle Robert's library, and the lessons in herbal remedies from my Indian friend, Nowedanah, and from our Babylon neighbor, Goody Michaels, helped me with duties of nursing the ill.

When the men finished shearing sheep, women's labors increased. Wool washing, carding, spinning, and weaving of fabrics for linens, skirts, capes, and breeches; knitting of woolen caps, mittens, and stockings. We lessened the burden by hauling materials, supplies, spinning wheels and weaving looms to one another's homes. Companionship made light work, and I was able to trade labors with those more competent while I served in the kitchen, preparing meals for the next day, dishes the women could take home to hungry families.

Until fresh meat was more plentiful, preparation required desalting of brined foods and the grinding of corn from storage barrels for bread, baking and yeast. I could not yet abide the kneading of bread, but many were the kitchen tasks I could do, first at home, beginning with dawn's light. And then perhaps to my neighbors' kitchens where they were pleased for the respite from cooking chores.

With summer came crops to harvest, vegetables and fruits from the garden, wild berries and seasonal greens picked from the field. Once again, I applied the recently discovered means for dealing with the painful cramps I had long endured—start slowly, move slowly, and then wait for renewed strength.

Garden and field crops were plentiful, and in an attempt to become a good huswife—pleasing to my husband—my stews often included pork, sweet corn and cabbage, or other varieties of vegetables and roots. Of course, I prepared our Sabbath meals on the previous day to avoid breaking the law.

Eels, clams, and fish were plentiful. Wild game abounded, and these fresh meats and fish relieved the monotony of salted food.[141] Often, for a late meal after Sabbath meetings, we invited John and Mara and their five children as well as Henry and Catherine, their growing little Jonathon, and the two new arrivals, Rebecca and Moses, to share with us. Sometimes William and Ellen Leverich or shy Dora Cummings and her husband and seven timid children came to dinner—a perfect time to include the children in a discussion of lessons learned from the sermon that day. Sometimes, particularly if both John's family and the Leveriches with sons Eleazer and Caleb were there, the discussion turned quickly to disagreement, with Eleazer, much to his father's vexation, often siding with John and Mara. Disagreements were especially rife on the rare occasion when my dear old friend from Matlock, Quaker John Bowne stopped by as he and his wife were passing through Huntington. He had married Hannah, one of the Feake girls, grandniece of Governor John Winthrop. Our guests were more varied than the combination of ingredients in Gervase Markham's epicurean recipes.

Had New Haven's blue laws, so-called for the color of paper they were written on, been in force in Huntington Village at that time, the Bowne family would have been excluded, for the first law stated that no food or lodging should be offered to a heretic. The Blue laws also decreed that "2) No one shall cross a river on the Sabbath but authorized clergymen. 3) No one shall travel, cook victuals, make beds, sweep houses, cut hair, or shave on the Sabbath Day. 4) No one shall kiss his or her children on the Sabbath or feasting days."

Even Goodman Leverich's lute was outlawed: Another of the Blue laws said, "On the Sabbath, no one shall eat mince pies, dance, play cards, or play any instrument of music except the drum, trumpet, or jew's-harp."

In the fall, we preserved food for winter, pickling, preserving, and drying. We processed milk into cheese, made sausage, and salt-cured hams and bacon.

Once we were well settled, I oft prepared a soup to precede the first course—meats plus meat pudding or deep meat pies containing fruits and spices, pancakes or fritters, and the ever-present condiments—sauces, pickles and catsup. For the second course, I might prepare an assortment of fresh, cooked, or dried fruits, custards, tarts or sweetmeats, and I found recipes for cakes of many varieties: pound, gingerbread, spice, cheese. At dinner, Thom was a good trencherman, a big eater, but often, after a late supper of a simple bread, samp, hominy, or pudding with milk, he would nearly fall asleep in his chair at the head of the table, so wearied to the bone was he.

Winter arrived early in Huntington in 1658, but winds were mostly from the south and southwest, and by Thom's best guess, temperatures rarely dipped below zero.

The child growing inside me became heavy and burdensome. Though in good health as far as my condition was concerned, I soon needed respite from the entertainment of guests and the increasing seasonal toil. The baby was due in February, less than a year after little Isaac's death, and the closer drew the date, the more fearful I became. I oft repeated the scripture, "Perfect love casteth out fear," but forsooth, I felt neither love nor joyous expectancy for this coming child.

When I admitted my shameful fears to Ellen Leverich, she tried her best to comfort me. "I well remember," she said, "how the ache of my daughter's loss stayed with me, but the memory of my birthing pains soon faded."

She paused, and with a look of sudden inspiration said to me, "I have an idea for you to consider, Mary. You are going to need a woman in the house as your birthing time nears. There is a dear woman from the Matinecock tribe where William hath been ministering. Her half-breed husband recently drowned in the bay, and though her orphaned babe is sickly, she would be a good servant for you, and she does so need to find a place where she can lay her head. Her name is Anna Wing."

"Tell me more," I said. "Is she dependable and honest?"

"Oh, my dear, yes. And a hard worker. Anna Wing is a Christian, although she mixes her belief quite thoroughly with her Indian ways. Besides that, she speaks English as well as her native tongue."

Anna Wing sounded like an answer to my prayers, and when I told Thom about her, he was happy to employ her in our home. Within the week, she and her babe had moved in. She chose to bunk by the fireplace where her ailing babe would stay warm. She agreed to keep the fires stoked, rise early to prepare breakfast, feed the farm animals and chickens, and milk the cow.

How good it seemed to sleep past the rooster's crowing, even though it felt strange to give my wifely duties to a stranger.

Ellen also brought other wonderful news. Her husband's worldly occupations — miller and general mer-

chant selling cloth and other articles — occupied quite a
large part of his time. So that he could give more hours to
his mission work and his studies, he had sold the mill to
my brother, Luddie Ludlam, who would soon move from
Mecox Bay to Huntington with his wife, Lizzie, and Little
John, their first child. I could look forward to the company of another dear sister-in-law.

With Reverend Leverich freed from running the mill,
the town hired him as minister, replacing Henry Whitney, somewhat to this lay preacher's annoyance. The
schoolhouse the town fathers had built for Jonas
Houldsman, served as the meeting house, and it seemed
to me that in the makeshift pulpit, Reverend Leverich
rose to a commanding height, straight as an arrow, eyes
burning, voice ringing. I could not but listen.

From that time, when I attended women's prayer meetings hosted by Ellen, at the Leverich dwelling house, I
could see Rev. Leverich through the open door to his
study.

"He's working on an index to subjects within the
course of his study of the Old Testament," Ellen said.
Later, I learned that he had about 100 pages of hand written notes in Latin, a running commentary on the first
fourteen books of the Old Testament, but in part copied
from the commentary of the learned Aramaic scholar, Jo-
hannes Piscator.[142] [143]

"Goody Leverich," I said, "my Uncle Robert Fordham
told me that he changed his faith to become a Puritan
and then when he and Aunt Florence left England, the
Church took away his license to preach. Did that happen
to Reverend Leverich?"

Ellen's mouth flew open. "Your uncle is the Reverend
Robert Fordham? Why, I believe he and Reverend Lev-

erich were in school together at Cambridge. But we left England several years earlier than he did and went right to preaching. It wasn't until later that the Church of England began withholding the license of ministers who had left for the colonies."

"Yes, you are right. Nevertheless, I think Uncle Robert enjoyed the life of an adventurer when he could not preach. He had a plantation in Hempstead for several years and returneth not to the ministry until they moved to Southampton about twelve years ago. When our family arrived from England, I stayed with my Fordham kin. And when I asked Uncle Robert why he had left England, he told me that the Church of England had grown to prefer ceremonies rather than a spiritual religion, and that many of those who wanted to make changes were punished and even put to death. But Reverend Leverich preached here from the time you first arrived, is that so? Did he leave England because of persecution?"

Ellen nodded and cleared her throat. "Here," she explained, "we were to construct a completely pure society, uncorrupted by the conflicts of Europe. My William says that the Separatist pilgrims erred when they established a group *outside* the Church. William and other like-minded ministers wanted to clean the *inside* of the cup. Get rid of offensive practices and rituals. Purify, not break away— and for that, they were persecuted as sowers of sedition. Some were branded with hot irons, or had their ears cut off.

"William and the other New England Puritans will tell you that God hath led his elected people to the Promised Land to establish a New Jerusalem governed by the laws of the Old Testament. A City on the Hill shining its light to the entire world.

"Under Governor Winthrop, they have established a government according to the Laws of Moses, a theocracy founded on literal Biblical prototypes from the Old Testament — rules for all the Colony's institutions and activities — an earthly expression of the will of God. And to keep this covenant with God, they must strictly control any who incite rebellion or discontent."

"So they are free to believe as they choose, but cannot allow the same freedom to others?"

Ellen's face creased in an uncharacteristic scowl. "You may be thankful, Mary, that you settled not in the strict confines of Massachusetts Colony. With all your questioning of the Puritan belief, you could well have been dragged into court like Anne Hutchinson."

Ellen wiped her brow and continued. "By the time the Puritan converts — men who wished to purify the Church of England — decided to leave England, King Charles I and Henrietta Maria of France, his Catholic wife, were in power."

"Yes, I remember," I said. "As a child in England, my friends and I played war, one group taking the side of King Charles' Cavaliers, and the other taking the side of Cromwell's Roundheads. Later, when my family sailed here on the ship *Triall*, I met travelers from both sides, escaping to a better life in the Colonies."

Ellen moved toward me and patted my hand, "You were fortunate to move to Long Island. Town meetings here are the New World's first example of government by the people. They are remarkably advanced in some realms, more liberal than the English legislation in promoting individual rights."[144]

Until then, I had seen the Leveriches as contrapuntal. William talked. Ellen listened. Whether writing in his study, teaching, or preaching in the pulpit, William Leverich was a fountain of language, issuing forth streams of words. Now his wife was doing the talking.

"Ellen, thou dost surprise me," I said. "Thou art not the silent partner I had thought."

"No, but I have learnt silence is oft more prudent. When we lived at Sandwich, my dear William was invited to become the first president of the newly-planned Yale University. This meant he must leave his pastoral duties and his employment with the Society for the Propagation of the Gospel." Ellen shook her head. "After all the hours he spent learning the language of the Indians of Cape Cod and Plymouth Colony, I could not bear the thought. Are we not to bring the Gospel to heathens? These savages needeth Jesus Christ. I believed that with all my heart, and I defied my husband in a fierce burst of temper. My violent averseness to him going to New Haven caused him to miss what might have been the opportunity of his lifetime.[145] Yet daily, I hear my husband praying that someone at Sandwich may water those poor souls as are in darkness.[146] And mine own prayer is for forgiveness that I stepped out of a woman's place."

I raised my eyebrows at the blush of shame on her cheeks.

She lowered her eyes. "'Tis not easy, but I have learnt to hold my tongue in submission to my husband as well as to God. Remember, dear Mary, that although my William can be sensitive and accommodating, he is an Old Testament man with a Puritan regard for woman's place. Take heed, Mary. Women here should be silent and modest, and live in the private rather than the public sphere."

Seventeen

∿

The next two years for Thom and me were times of troubles and sorrows.

In February 1658, Anna Wing, our Indian servant, became ill and went home to the Matinecock longhouse with her ailing child to recuperate. Days grew short, giving Thom long evenings to carve again a cradle for our child. Pleased with the results, he set it rocking beside our bed.

My sister-in-law Mara was nearly over the curse of the change, and while the Scudder men went about their work, and I neared my delivery time, she oft came with her youngest daughter, nine-year-old Betsy, to help me with my housewifely duties. I enjoyed watching the two of them work together. Even when Betsy erred, as every child is wont to do, Mara shunned the rod and the Puritans' stern way of breaking the child's will.

"I believe God plants a spark of divinity in every child," Mara said. "It is a mother's obligation as much as the father's to nurture the light within each child, though oft it is hard to set a holy example. Sometimes I forget myself and scream in frustration at the Puritans' insistence that only their way is of God. Sometimes I rail in anger. How can a loving God permit his people to suffer so?"

I stirred the pot of stew hanging over the fire, and then eased myself onto a bench, propped up my swollen feet, and picked up my knitting. "You and I are not so far apart in many ways, Mara. I, too, search for the answer to that question. How can we not rail at injustice?"

A tear began trickling down Mara's cheek, and sweet Betsy put her arms around her mother. "Don't cry, Mama. Don't worry. Look how beautiful the day is. God is in his heaven."

Mara smiled and smoothed Betsy's hair with her hands. "How lovely is the light of your faith, my daughter." Mara looked at me and said, "It's hard to make our home a haven from the world when my own father is being threatened with banishment." Mara's hand trembled as she wiped the tears from her eyes.[147]

ℒ⃝

One winter afternoon, Betsy brought in more wood for the fireplace, and after dumping it in its place, she stood by the fire, shivering and rubbing her hands together. "Looks like a storm coming, Mama," she said. "Just listen to the wind."

Mara peered out the window, then took her wrap from the peg and motioned to Betsy. "Your father will be in soon." She turned to me. "Will you be all right now? Is there anything else we can do?"

"No, thank you. I'll be fine. You two hurry on home." I stood to see them off, and then, "Oh!" suddenly sat and clutched my middle when a stabbing pain hit.

"Mary, what is it?" Mara said. "Is it time?"

"No, no, it's only the turnips," I said, letting out my breath. "Our mid-day stew always gives me indigestion when there are turnips in it. Go on home. Thom will be here soon."

Mara and Betsy bade me goodbye, and I closed the door behind them. Within minutes, darkness filled the corners of the room, and the flames of the fireplace cast eerie shadows. A cold wind roared around the house like a mythical lion, howling its way in through every little crack. Shivering, I eased my way across the room to our bed and wrapped myself in a woolen quilt. Where was Thom? Alone in the house, I heard every creak of the rafters, every shriek of the storm raging outside. My pain grew sharper, intense, as if some great-clawed creature grabbed my belly and squeezed. Was this the pain of labor? So ill I had been last year when Isaac was born, that I knew not what to expect.

By the time Thom burst through the door, my own shrieks were echoing the noise of the storm, and there was little doubt in my mind. There was no time for him to go for help.

"I can do this, sweetheart. Fear not." Thom stationed himself at the end of the bed, and without more ado, the infant almost flew into Thom's hands.

"It's a girl!" he shouted, holding her out for me to see.

Relief flooded through me. "Thank God for deliverance!" I whispered.

The baby's hands waved weakly in the cold air and she uttered a thin cry. Then her breathing stopped, and I knew God was only a child's fairy tale. He could not answer prayer. Oh, blasphemy! In one breath, one instant, I called forth both blessing and curse.

When Thom pressed his mouth against the baby's, I turned my face away. I could not bear to watch, but the stillness of the room was even worse.[148]

Moments passed, and all I could hear were breathy little puffs coming from Thom. Suddenly, the baby let out a tiny gasp, then a lusty cry.

"She lives!" Thom's voice exuded relief and joy pressed into one. He withdrew his knife from his scabbard and cut the cord.

My whole body felt limp and battered as if I had been tossed into a butter churn and tumbled about.

Life, kerthump. Death, kerthump. Hope, kerthump.

Thom wrapped the baby in swaddling bands and placed her in the cradle, then turned to me. Exhausted, I lay trembling, numb.

"Aphrodite, thou are extremely pale. Stay awake for a moment. Let me give you something to help stop the bleeding." Again, he took his knife, and I saw blood on his fingers as he tucked a small chunk of something warm and wet into my cheek.

"Suck on this, sweeting" he said. "Like you would if you cut your finger and sucked the blood from the wound."

Tired as I was, I yet attempted to spit out the morsel he gave me.

"Trust me, Mary. I have heard my mother talk oft enough when she was a midwife. 'Tis but a bit of the afterburden[149] I have given you."

He went to the cabinet and returned with the jar of arnica ointment I often used to rub into my cramping legs. "Let me knead this into your belly," he said.

Weary, I submitted to his ministering. Sleep lapped at me like the unalterable waves of the tide, comforting and inescapable.

 හ

The next day the storm was past and the sun shown brightly. News traveled quickly, and when Thom answered a knock on the door, he found Reverend Leverich with our Matinecock servant, Anna Wing, gray-faced, but stoic. "Anna is well, but her wee babe hath passed on," he said, "She insisted on coming to you. Says hard work will help her sadness heal."

Blessed Anna. Grieving, yet willing to fulfill her God-given station.

හ

For baptism the next Lord's Day, Thom swaddled the baby in fresh, white linen bands and wrapped her in a warm woolen blanket and an embroidered quilt. "Do you think she will be warm enough, Mary?"

I braced myself, and set my jaw. I could not care.

The meeting house was not far, well within walking distance, so I wrapped my woolen shawl around my shoulders, and moved to the fireplace, where I withdrew a warming pan. The meeting house would be frigid, but the warming pan would keep my feet warm. I insulated it with a pad of linen, and then carried it out the door.

Thus, as Thom carried our baby to be baptized, I walked beside him, with Anna Wing following behind in her proper place.

From the pulpit, the clear voice of Rev. Leverich rang. "The benefits of God are to be kept in fresh memory and propagated to posterity.[150] The sacrament of baptism throws the divine seed into the human heart, and as God wills it to grow, it cannot fail to do so.[151]And so, following the Covenant God hath made with us, we come here today to baptize the infant of Thom and Mary Scudder."

To my ears, the minister's voice took on an ethereal and strangely tentative sound as he moved to the font.

"O Lord, from whom we have received this babe, we consecrate this little one according to Thy bidding. By right, she is more Thine than ours. Thy grace alone canst make her happy for we have handed her into a miserable world; and have conveyed to her a corrupt nature. Yet we present her to Thee for Thy blessing. If it shall please Thee to remove her out of this sinful and troublesome world before she shall become capable of transacting with Thee personally, take her to Thyself.

"If Thou shalt please to spare her life, we solemnly promise to do all that lies in our power; by wholesome instructions, and serious admonitions, parental counsels, seasonable reproofs, and suitable corrections, as we can discern occasion." [152] The Reverend Leverich paused and looked toward Thom. "What name hast thou chosen?"

"Elizabeth," we said together.

The minister received our baby into the crook of his left arm and dipped his right hand into the font. "I baptize thee Elizabeth Scudder, in the name of the Father, and of the Son, and of the Holy Spirit."

As the icy water splashed over her wee head, Elizabeth squalled and kicked in protest, but when the minister looked up, he and Thom exchanged satisfied smiles. Thom reached for Elizabeth and tucked the warm quilt around her. "Sh-sh-sh, little darling," I heard him whisper. "Save your tears. God will warm thee with His blessings."

As we turned to take our seats, I glanced toward my friend Ellen Leverich. Tears were streaming down her face, yet strangely, I felt nothing but the February chill of the meeting house.

It seemed as if my motherly instinct had died with Isaac. Poor little Elizabeth. I could not abide holding her for more than a few minutes at a time. I was worn out, body and soul. It was up to our servant girl, Anna Wing, to wet-nurse and otherwise care for the child.

At bedtime, Thom rocked and cuddled Elizabeth and then laid her in my arms. "See how she rests her little head on your shoulder and clutches your neck with her hand?"

For a moment, there was delight and innocence in my life again, but weariness soon overtook me, and I called Thom to take her from me.

"How can you resist such sweetness?" he said before putting her down to sleep. "Do you not love your own child?"

Burdened with guilt and worthlessness, for weeks I suffered. Elizabeth's infant wailing overwhelmed me — although it may be that I cried more than she. She fought sleep. I longed for it. I took no interest in Tuesday's Bible study and made excuses to miss the women's Wednesday marketing excursions. Though my heart seemed to be either racing or skipping beats, I felt lifeless. God, if

He even recognized my existence, resided so far away I could not talk to Him. I was a lost sheep so unworthy that the Shepherd searcheth not for me.

By the end of her first month, Elizabeth smiled when her father placed her in my arms. Instead of joy, I felt only embarrassment and shame at my sinful lack of caring. "Please, Thom, take her. I know not how to hold so small a child. I fear I will drop her."

In an effort to lessen the anguish of my spirit, Ellen Leverich came and talked to me about the slough of despair she suffered when her baby Hannah died. For once, words were slow coming to me, but finally I said, "Dost thou believe God is punishing me for my sins? First, my baby Isaac died, and now I can feel no love for my little Elizabeth. Yet I have obeyed the command and submitted to my husband as Christian believers submit to Christ." A deep sigh welled up from the pit of my chest. "Why would God allow me to walk through nine months of futile preparation? Why would he multiply my pains in childbirth and yet not give me a mother's love for my own babe? Am I being punished for the conception of Isaac? Or for his death? I would confess my guilt, but I know not what evil I have done."

"Mary, dear, I am not suggesting the popish ritual of a confessional, but if you would talk to Reverend Leverich, I have faith that he might help you cast off your burden of guilt. My beloved husband is now in his study, but on the morrow, he will be working amid the Indians. Wouldst thou meet with him today while he is able?"

The Rev. Leverich, undeniably had been blessed with skill of listening with his full attentions, and I did indeed find relief in telling him of my guilt and grief. Trembling with shame, I could not lift my eyes to his as I put the fearful question to him. "Am I being punished for the fornication that gave me Isaac?"

"Do not charge God foolishly," he counseled. "If in your heart thou art muttering against Him, remember then the days of creation, how He created the darkness and the light. Even in these dark days of winter, you can find blessings if you will look and listen."

I am sure the look on my face only proved to him what a doubter I was. But he was not ready to give up on me.

"Do you recall St Thomas Aquinas's writing I spoke of from the pulpit last month regarding the conditions necessary for the commission of sin?"

"Yes. I wrote it down that day. The first condition is that it be wrong, and secondly, that one give full consent to it," I said.

"According to St Thomas, when the intelligent creature, knowing God and His law, deliberately refuses to obey, that is sin.[153] You, Mary, did not refuse to obey God. Your participation was against your will."

The room was exceeding still, and Oh! Then I heard a sweet voice saying, "There is One, even Christ Jesus that can speak to thy condition." And when I heard it, my heart did leap for joy. I felt as if a light beamed from within me, and with great eagerness, I told Reverend Leverich what had just happened, expecting him to rejoice with me.

Instead, he turned pale and in his eyes, I saw a hard light, a sinister glare. In a voice of doom he shouted, "Damn George Fox[154] and his cursed sect. He hath spread his evil beliefs even on my island."

Quickly he regained control and a note of contrition sounded in his voice.

"My advice, if you suffer from the late winter despondency, is to get outside. Look. Listen."

"Now you sound like a Quaker."

Reverend Leverich grimaced and said, "I pray thee, what have I said that ye might consider me thus?"

"They believe they hear the voice of the Lord when they sit and listen, do they not?"

"But how do they discern whose voice it is that they hear? Doth it come from God, or from the evil one?" With his fist, he thumped the Bible that lay before him. "No, my dear child, if you seek the voice of God, you will find it within these pages."

Hard as I might try, I found nothing in the good Book that spoke to my condition, and I wept. I found more comfort, and sometimes an ease of heart and gratitude for my child when I sat at the banks of the stream. There I listened for the voice of God, and though no words reached my ears, I did find a measure of peace and an inner delight in the quietness I found there.

Sorrow visited us again when we received word from Salem that Thom's father had died. I knew not how to console my husband, but he seemed to find comfort in holding and rocking two-month-old Elizabeth. As he rocked, he crooned silly old ditties with made up words wailed mournfully off-key.

As I look'd over the castle wall
To see what I could see,
O what should I spy but my own father's ship
Come a sailing along the sea,
Come sailing along the sea.
"Is it thy brother Henry?" you said,
"Or is it thy Johnnie fair?
Or is it my Grandfather Scudder

Come home to meet his heir?"
"Then where are his red and rosy cheeks
That even in winter bloom?
And where is the long and dark brown hair
O Grandfather, lost too soon?"
 "The ground have rotted it off, my dear,
For the worms are quick and free,
And when you're so long lying in your grave,
The same will happen thee."[155]

When finally he laid Elizabeth in her cradle, he turned to me. "Mary, my father hath left me his schooner. I must ride to Salem, see that my mother is comfortable, and then bring the ship home with me. This may be the last night I spend in a bed for sometime. Come lie with me."

I snuggled obediently to his chest. The musky smell of his body infused the air around us, and the room glowed in the light from the fire. Shadows of purple hid my secret places, but with gentle hands, Thom found them. Surely, this was a promise of better days to come.

While Thom was away, I scrubbed the floors, cleaned the cabinets, and brought fragrant dried herbs from the loft to spread around our rooms. I took pains to create a new boiled stew recipe with Thom's favorite spices and meats, and roasted walnuts dipped in sugar, sweet comfits for his pleasure. Only when all this was in readiness did I retreat to my spring garden, the favorite of my housewifery duties. By the time Thom returned, there would be fresh lettuce and peas to pick.

At night, after Anna had nursed the baby and put her to bed, I bathed and brushed my hair until it shone like gold, read from Uncle Henry Scudder's book of devotions, and then took out my ink and quill. When I was finished writing, I spread a new counterpane on our bed. Aneath the quilt, I placed on Thom's fresh linen-covered pillow a sweet comfit and my poem of love and gratitude for all the blessings of our marriage. He would find it there before he took me to him again.

The sound of a barking dog alerted me to Thom's arrival. I ran to greet him just as both he and the dog crossed the threshold to our home. "Here you are, Shep," Thom said in a voice filled with pride. This is your new home."

The unruly animal bounded around the room, wagging his tail, leaping upon the table with his muddy paws, into and out of Thom's chair, with ruin following in his wake. With one leap on the bed, he nosed out the comfit, and sent my poem flying to the floor. The sweet treat disappeared with one gulp. Satisfied, he settled himself on a rug by the fireplace. Thom had taken no notice of the dog's rambunctious exploring. Full of his own adventures, neither did he heed my mundane achievements, and instead of gathering me into his arms, he went first to Elizabeth's cradle. With a defiant look at Thom, the dog, and the ruination of the room, I turned away, grabbed the milk bucket, and rushed out to join Anna Wing in the barn. I dare not speak. In the barn, I planted the milking stool next to Bossy, leaned my head into her soft, hairy side, and burst into tears. Anna, stoic as always, rose from the cow she had milked, and nudged me aside. "Let me finish," she said. "You have mending to do inside."

I rose and wiped my tears. A hot flush of shame encompassed me. Anna had lost both husband and child. What reason had I to weep? Contrite, I mumbled thank you and ran to the house.

Thom was sitting on the bed, holding Elizabeth to his chest with one hand and the besmirched poem he had retrieved from its landing place in the other. His shoulders shook, tears rolled down his cheeks, and the look of grief on his face pierced my heart like the blade of a butcher. Except when the news arrived that his father died, I had ne'er seen Thom in such distress.

Slowly he raised his eyes to me. "Aphrodite, thou art like the yellow orchid I saw in the middle of the woods, and I am but a prickly cactus. How do you survive here?"

I kissed his cheeks, damp and salty. "Hush, my love. Where else would I be? This is our promised land."

Elizabeth was sleeping and he laid her in the cradle, and then quietly enfolded me in his arms. Finally he spoke. "What do you think, Mary? The Bible says He is the God of all comfort. But what if God is wroth and will not send comfort?"

"I do not believe He is ever wroth with those who love enough."

"Everywhere I turn, I see my father. Although he would never step foot on board ship, I hear him planning the business of the crew. He stands on the pier, watching as we sail the schooner into port. Sometimes I talk to him though he is gone. Does that mean I'm daft?"

A sudden wave of remembrance washed over me, grief both recent and long past.

Slowly, I shook my head and in a hushed voice said, "I do the same. When I was sick after baby Isaac, I imagined my mother there with me. I think it is God's consolation that brings her to me."

With my fingertips, I smoothed the wrinkles from Thom's brow. "Tell me now about your trip. There must be something besides that unruly mutt that you can share with me."

Thom grinned. "He'll make a good sheep dog." Suddenly, it was if a dam opened, and his excitement poured forth. "Mary, I'm going to build a tannery, right here on the bay. And with the Scudder schooner and my sloop, we can increase our shipping business. My father's crew came with me and is ready to work. I am more eager than ever to greet the dawn. So much to do!"

Before I drifted off to sleep that night, by the light of the fire I saw that Shep had made a place for himself next to Anna's sleeping pallet. Eyes closed, she reached to pet him, a peaceful smile of contentment on her face.

&

Before the year was out, we learned that Oliver Cromwell, Protectorate of the British government, had died. Stability and civilian rule in England had ended. Soon the monarchy was back with King Charles II on the British throne and his half brother James waiting in the wings.

Those two years in the colonies, 1658 and 1659, were filled with droughts and storms and crop blights and winter cold beyond anything we had known before. There were epidemics of smallpox, typhus, measles, and respiratory illness. According to a dispatch Thom brought home from one of his trips to Salem, Boston officials had ordered the town drummer to drown out the gallows speeches of Quakers Mary Dyer, William Robinson, and Marmaduke Stephenson. After a short trial, the two men were hanged, but Dyer's husband, a friend of Governor John Winthrop, secured a last-minute reprieve — against her wishes, for she had refused to repent and disavow her Quaker faith.

ଛ

God's blessings were on our town, for in Huntington we suffered not from epidemics and drought. Basically self-governing, we were little affected by the Boston trials. What went on in Salem, though, seemed much closer to home: Mara's father, William King, Jr., because of his Quaker belief, was judged guilty by the Court for his disrespect toward the established Church. On October 8, 1659, he was sentenced to be whipped and banished from the colony.[156]

Thom's brother John, dispirited by his father-in-law's persecution, moved Mara and their family from Huntington to Newtown where a Quaker colony was growing.

Thom, too, was disheartened. While at Salem, standing near the tavern on the green, he had been an ear and eyewitness to William King's punishment. He saw this peace-loving man stripped and bound to a post in the center of town. Thom told me that when he turned his eyes away, he could still hear the awful sounds of the three-corded rope come down across King's back. Thirty-three lashes. When he looked again, ribbons of blood ran down the man's back and legs, soaking the legs of his britches and dripping onto the cold cobblestones. William King was not to be pardoned or allowed to return to his home until he agreed to withdraw from the Quakers.

ଛ

Oft I read discontent on Thom's face. Although he participated in Town Meetings, he could not hold office in the local government for only church members qualified. Because he had experienced no Damascus Road, he felt he could not give testimony of conversion,[157] nor could he become a full-fledged member.

"What is it you want so much?" I asked.

His lip jutted out in the stubborn way I had come to dread. "My father taught me there was no need to be Puritan to build new and free in a new land," he said, scowling. "As long as I pay the price, they do not stop me when I want to buy land. But all the acres I have added and my tannery by the bay does not satisfy. Where are the sons to receive my inheritance? Where is God, that He hath not called me to His church though I sit there each Lord's Day?

"Unlike my father, I cannot be 'Old Goodman Scudder.' And I cannot squat like a pheasant in the autumn sedge, making myself invisible to the falcon's claws. I cannot. There must be a better way."[158]

To ease his troubled heart, Thom doted on little Elizabeth, and from the days of her first steps, she liked nothing better than to please him.

Elizabeth and I were not close. Perhaps I resented her. As she grew, she could do all the things that I could not. Though Thom and I both read to her and taught her to read, she had little interest in book learning. Instead, she followed Anna Wing around, begging to help her with the cooking or mending, or cleaning.

Of course, we continued to attend meeting house each seventh day, sitting with due attention to Reverend Leverich's sermons from the Old Testament, followed by my weekday women's study of the scriptures and contemplation of the message we had heard on the Sabbath.

Reverend Leverich's eavesdropping on our discussions made me uneasy, and Goody Whitney's inauspicious note-taking bode not well with me. I determined to keep my beliefs to myself, to be satisfied with writing them in my journal or in sharing them with Thom during our daily devotions. The minister could hardly object to that although I was sure some of my questions could be considered heretical if Leverich wanted to intrude. There were times, though, when words burst from my mouth before I could stop them.

Like the time at the Bible study after I had shared my sadness at Thom's report of William King's grievous punishment. I had also told the women how much I missed my dear sister-in-law Mara now that they had moved away. How her caring way of guiding her children, to my way of thinking, seemed more likely to please a loving God than the harsh rod of the Puritan. On the next Lord's Day, Reverend Leverich preached on the holiness of the Mosaic Law, taking his text from Deuteronomy 13. It seemed that the vindictive light of his eyes aimed directly at me as he read.

If thy friend, which is as thine own soul, entice thee secretly, saying, Let us go and serve other gods, ...namely the gods of the people which are round about you thine hand shall be first upon him to put him to death, And thou shalt stone him with stones, that he die.[159]

"Ye chosen of God," he said, looking toward the men's side of the meeting house, "the law of Moses contains over six hundred commands. Here in the New World, we have established a society, a government, a religion that will not, must not, change one tittle from the law that descended from God's own mouth. The law guides every move we make."

I wanted to stand and protest. How could anyone possibly carry out all six hundred Old Testament laws? Does not the New Testament fulfill them all with the two great commandments? I fear I shall never attain the peace God promised, for I possess both blessing and curse—a doubting, questioning mind.

Anno Dom 1659-1660
Huntington, Long Island

When my brother Luddie bought the mill from Reverend Leverich, he moved his wife Lizzie and baby John north from Southampton to Huntington with him, leaving our brother Hal in Mecox Bay to help Papa run the mill there.

"Makes no sense for both of us to stay at the mill," Luddie said. "Only one can inherit it from Papa, and Hal always got along with Papa better than I did. Besides, Hal's sweet on pretty little Jane Shaw from over at East Hampton, so he's not inclined to move." Luddie's dark eyes twinkled. "Wait till I tell you..." he grinned, and then sobering he said, "I'm thirty-three soon. Time I found my own fortune. The Huntington mill is a God-given opportunity for me, and Leverich tells me there is plenty of room for me to pasture cattle here. Nothing more like Eden than a meadow in spring."

I was pleased when Thom not only sold Luddie two heifer calves so he could start his own herd, but he also loaned Luddie some tools until he could fashion his own for plowing and planting.

It did not seem possible that Luddie was almost as old as Papa was when I was born, and had only one babe to his credit—Little John, on whom he doted. Tall and lean as ever, Luddie still sounded like the dreamer he was as a young man. Having him nearby brought forth happy memories of our childhood.

Often that month, one of our town whale watchers spotted a baleen whale coming close to the shore, and the call went out. Luddie and Thom, as well as other townsmen, dropped their axes and plows and raced to the boats. They speared the huge creatures for their blubber and oil, an important source of revenue. Nothing was wasted. Even the flexible bones sold in London for umbrella spokes, bustles, bodices, collars, ruffs, and hoop skirts. Whale hunting brought an exciting change from the usual men's work.

Except for birthing times when women gathered at a home to help, housewives found little in their work that was other than routine. Still, the mundane jobs allotted me pleasurable time to ponder the ways of God and the inequities between His way and that of the Puritan faith. I tried to hold my tongue at our women's Bible studies, for to mention these differences aloud was sure to bring harassment or worse.

One day, not long after Luddie and his family arrived, I invited Lizzie, his wife, to our women's Bible study at the Leverich dwelling. That day, as was often the case, Reverend Leverich was directly in my view as he worked in his study. The poor man must have had a ferocious headache, for oft I saw him drop his quill and grasp his head between his palms, with his face contorting in a pain-filled grimace.

I directed my attention back to the women's group. Across from me sat sad-faced Jedidah Higbee, her apron stretched tight by the burgeoning child soon to be born.

We had wept with Jedidah and her five fatherless children when the court declared Edward lost at sea a few months before. On this day, I watched in surprise as quiet little Dora, ignoring past insults Jedidah had heaped upon her at previous meetings, took a seat beside the suffering widow and reached for her hand. "I've been praying for your husband's return. Have you any word?" Dora asked softly.

Jedidah half-closed her eyes and gave a breathy grunt. "Hmph! What good does it do to pray for the lost," she said, "since God hath already locked outsiders out of heaven?"

Lizzie, not being acquainted with the poor woman's grief, said with a smile, "Perhaps God could declare a general pardon of the non-elected?"

Forgetting the eavesdropping minister, I could not contain myself. "That's a very beautiful idea of yours, Lizzie. A hell emptied of sinners. I like it."

With a long, bony finger, the new magistrate's wife, Deriah Catswaller, pointed at me and gave forth with a strident and most unseemly laugh. I cannot imagine why she found that idea of hell so amusing, but out of the corner of my eye, I saw Reverend Leverich as he scraped back his chair, rose and threw down his notes. As if on the borderline of violence, he burst into the midst of the women.

"You may be a blessing to men when you are doing housework, tending children, or on your knees before God," he shouted. "But when you pit your brain against God and man, making light of the seriousness of the scriptures, you only create misery."

The women sat wide-eyed, gasping at his hostility.

With a flourish, he spun on his heel, and then before entering his office, he turned and shouted, "It might be better if you spent your time gossiping."

The study door slammed behind him, and poor Ellen rose to apologize.

"I fear a husband's will is as inscrutable as God's, and obedience to it is dreary hard at times." Pink faced, she caught her under lip with her teeth. "In recent weeks, my dear William hath suffered terrible headaches. Some days he is gentle as a lamb, but in an instant, he changes to a bilious, roaring lion. A most awful melancholia." She shook her head. "Neither feverfew compress nor willow bark tea gives him relief."

The women were sympathetic toward Ellen, at least in appearance, but I noticed Jedidah and her close friend Sarah Whitney whispering behind their hands, with derogatory glances at our hostess. They tucked their notes into their Bibles, slipped their quills and ink bottles into their pockets, and turned to leave. The uppity Deriah Catswaller, backed by Sarah Whitney's notes, would be the first to carry tales to her husband.

ℴℴ

Lizzie and I became great friends, and oft we shared our work, going to one house or the other. Sturdy little John and our Elizabeth were the same age, but he preferred riding his stick horse to Elizabeth's clamorous banging of pots and pans. They entertained each other mightily while Shep howled in accompaniment. Dear Anna Wing held her hands over her ears, laughing at their noise. "Children will surely bring on a rainstorm with music like that," she said. Indeed, we did endure a spell of bad weather, shutting us inside more often than not.

Perhaps that is what brought on a long season of bickering and lawsuits. Although the workload of 1659 was no lighter than usual, neighbors seemed to have more than enough time for hauling one another into court over the most trivial matters.

In January that year, Henry Whitney began by suing Rev. Leverich in town court, claiming that his pay had been unjustly withheld for building the corn mill that Luddie had just purchased, and a few days after, followed it up with a suit for slander. The town knew Reverend Leverich as a frank, outspoken man, and when a charge was true, he would acknowledge it without waiting for proof from his opponent. However, many of the town folk had recently witnessed or had at least heard of Leverich's increasingly violent temper and provoking tongue. Leverich claimed Whitney's charges were not true, and in his defense, he claimed that Whitney had not finished the mill in season, or in any way that the contract required.

Back and forth they went, like wrangling children. Reverend Leverich retaliated with four suits of his own against Goodman Whitney. One for slander, one for breach of contract, one for defamation, and another for debt. To settle the lawsuits, the court required both parties to make a public acknowledgement that they had done wrong, or submit to a fine of five pounds.[160]

Their feud considerably disturbed the peace of the community and especially the church, and the collection of taxes allotted to pay the salary of the minister fell short as squabbling parishioners aligned against him. The sweltering days of summer seemed to encourage continued bickering. Who knew what man would next bring his neighbor into court.

One fall morning after family devotions, Thom said to me, "We have a load of whale oil and stacks of whale-bone ready for market, and the crew are eager to be on their way. With nearly a thousand residents in Boston now, there is a ready market, and what local shopkeepers do not buy, London traders will be eager to purchase. As soon as the *Sea Hawk* is readied, would it please you to go to Boston with me?"

I'm sure Thom could read the eagerness on my face, for he waited not for my reply.

"We could invite Luddie and Lizzie to go along," he said. "In fact, I already asked Henry and Catherine if they'd tend Little John and Elizabeth while we are away."

"Oh, but does Catherine not have her hands full? Four babes in five years." I shook my head and laughed. "My goodness, but your little brother seems in a hurry to populate the earth with little Scudders."

"Yes, very few quiet moments at their house." Thom grinned. "I could not help but laugh yesterday when Luddie and I were there. Jonathan's always into mischief, and what he does not think of, Becky suggests, with Moses toddling right along after them. It's good that baby Miriam is still in swaddling bands." Thom cocked his head and looked at me with quizzical eyes, then added, "Catherine suggested she would appreciate Anna Wing's help while we're gone."

I suppose God knew what he was doing when He left child care to the women. Men would never understand how complicated it all could be. At any rate, the trip was in the offing. Henry, with the help of Lizzie's brother,

John Smith, agreed to complete the fall farm work, and William Leverich, feeling somewhat better at the time, offered to take care of the mill so Thom and Luddie might sail the town's produce to market.

A few days after arriving and unloading the ship at Boston Harbor, we stopped at a tavern for a meal before traveling on to Salem to visit Thom's widowed mother and his sister's family, the Bartholomews. The tavern was agog with gossip. I heard one gruff voice above the crowd. "Murderin' bastard. Thought he could scape the eagle eye of our judge, did 'e."

The news spread quickly. "At least his poor children didn't live to see it," one woman whispered.

"No?"

"No," came the answer. "Did you not hear? They are all dead. Their loyal maid and all four children died of the diphtheria that raged through Boston last winter."

In every tavern, every place where people gathered, we heard the news. Even sitting in the Scudder pew with Thom's mother and sister at Lord's Day meeting in Salem, I heard the whispering.

"Who was it that was hung from the gallows?" Thom finally asked.

"Abram Hardwick," came the answer.

"Wasn't that the man Papa chose—" Luddie stopped abruptly, catching his breath. He laid a gentle hand on my shoulder, and on the other side, Thom put his arm around me.

My hands unconsciously twisted together, and then relaxed as somewhere in the depth of my heart a hard lump of bitterness melted. As if I had been holding it in for a very long time, I let out a long breath.

Strange, the comfort that death can give. Not only Hardwick's, but also that of the poor children. May they rest in peace.

ॐ

Pleasant it was on the last day of our trip to visit with Thom's sister Elizabeth and her husband and ten children, now nearly grown. And dear Mother Scudder. Silvery-pewter hair framed her lovely features—clear blue eyes and serene smile. I could see in her many of the traits I loved in Thom. Her kind, down-to-earth manner invited confidence and made me again feel like a part of the family. How I appreciated her. She also welcomed Luddie and Lizzie and instantly made them feel at home. It had been two years since Thom's father died, yet nearing 70 years of age, she looked well, walked to First Church of Salem when Lord's Day weather was good, and otherwise drove her own horse and cart as she went about quietly helping the poor and needy. An amazing woman.

All too soon, the days passed. As we climbed into the Scudder wagon to head for Boston Harbor, Mother Scudder handed Lizzie a basket of fall fruits from her garden. She surprised Thom with a second basket. "These books were your father's," she said. "I know how you loved to read them when you were a boy."

Taking the basket on one arm, with the other he gave his mother a tight squeeze and softly kissed her cheek. His eyes were wet when he turned away and stepped into the wagon.

⁊ꙅ

At the pier in Boston where the *Sea Hawk* was anchored, whom should we meet but Mary Wright, one of Peter Wright's young daughters traveling alone back to Oyster Bay. She seemed quite bedraggled and worn. A piteous sight. She recognized us as friends of the Leverich family, and when Thom invited her to come aboard for the return home, she gratefully accepted. We invited her to eat with us, and while Lizzie prepared a meal of cheese and bread and fruit from the basket, I showed Mary Wright to my cabin, offered her water and a towel, and loaned her a clean bodice and skirt to wear. She appeared much rested after eating, and eager to talk. And what a story she had to tell!

"I'm sure you've heard about the latest hanging from the tree on Boston Commons," she said. "All Boston is awash with the news. Did you perchance see the hanging?" Breathless, she spoke, agitated, though weary. "One of the Puritan's own ministers. Shows you that men in power are not always as sinless as they claim."

"You came to Boston alone?" Lizzie's eyes were wide. "To see the man hanged?"

"No, no. 'Twas quite by accident. I came to protest the murder of Ann Dyer who was hanged from the same tree a few short months ago. Can you imagine a crowd standing round to jeer at a poor woman's lifeless body? What had she done but to share God's light as it was revealed to her?" Mary Wright raised her eyes, as if looking for a kindred soul who would stand with her. Then she shook her head and continued her story. "'Tis said some self-righteous Puritan jested, 'She hangs there as a flag for others to take example.' When I heard that, how could I not come rally to that flag? What better example could I take than to testify to my own faith as did Mary Dyer?"

How I admired this young girl, surely not yet eighteen and powerless as any woman, but brave enough to protest publicly the authority of ministers and magistrates. My own dissent, my own questions, were cautiously guarded, and for the most part, kept to myself, shared openly only with my husband. "Did anyone listen to your protestations?" I asked.

"Listen? Listen?" Bitterness and irony overflowed in her laughter. "Oh, they heard me, all right. I was immediately jailed. The next day I was set in the stocks, exposed to public derision, all because I answered the call to speak out against evil. Then at eventide, I was loosed and driven out of town. I hid near the docks until this morning. Thank God I recognized the sails of the *Sea Hawk* and found you loading your ship."

Luddie rolled a bunk out on the deck where the Wright girl could rest, and we set sail. Perhaps life back in Huntington would seem dull, but I was ready for that.

While Mary Wright slept, Thom and Luddie rolled out other bunks and the four of us relaxed in the sunshine and the rhythm of the waves.

"Let's see the books your mother gave you," I said.

Thom began removing them from the basket. "Look at these treasures," he said with glowing face. "Here's Shakespeare's *Hamlet*. My father took us to see that play in London before we sailed to America. Here, Luddie," he said. "We'll put on a play for the women. You be Hamlet and I'll be Horatio."

Thom opened the book. "Here it is, Act V. I remember this scene because it sounds so much like the Bible that I thought Shakespeare must have copied it."

Luddie scooted closer to Thom, and they read:

HORATIO

You will lose this wager, my lord.

HAMLET

I do not think so: since he went into France, I have been in continual practise: I shall win at the odds. But thou wouldst not think how ill all's here about my heart: but it is no matter.

HORATIO

Nay, good my lord,--

HAMLET

It is but foolery; but it is such a kind of gain-giving, as would perhaps trouble a woman.

HORATIO

If your mind dislike any thing, obey it: I will forestall their repair hither, and say you are not fit.

HAMLET

Not a whit, we defy augury: there's a special providence in the fall of a sparrow. If it be now, 'tis not to come; if it be not to come, it will be now; if it be not now, yet it will come: the readiness is all: since no man hath aught of what he leaves, what is't to leave betimes?[161]

ༀ

Our husbands bowed deeply, and Lizzie and I clapped so loudly that Mary Wright stirred in her sleep.

Lizzie laughed. "Now I know why you two characters never judged acting to be your God-given talent." She helped Thom stack the books back in the basket, and then took her husband's hand. "Now, Luddie, this is the perfect time for you and Mary to tell us about your years as children in England."

And so he told them the stories I had loved to hear as a child—about Haddon Hall and our distant cousin Benedicta Ludlow and Sir Richard; Sir George Vernon, the fine-looking King of the Peak, and his two beautiful daughters—Margaret the elder and Dorothy the younger; and about Dorothy's elopement with her handsome suitor, John Manners, after she had signaled him from the tower. Even grown-ups enjoy fairy tales.

When Luddie finished, Thom and Lizzie clapped and begged for more.

Luddie shook his head and laughed. "Enough! Enough!"

"But Luddie," I said. "You haven't told them the best story of all. If it weren't for you, I'd be in a cold stone grave."

Luddie grinned. "You exaggerate, little sister."

"Oh, no. When I fell down the mine shaft, if it hadn't been for you, no one would have ever found me."

Thom and Lizzie looked at me with questioning eyes. "You tell it, Mary," Lizzie said. The wind caught a lock of Luddie's hair and with a smile, she reached to smooth it down. "Luddie is too modest for such a story."

And so I told them of my seventh birthday, the day I stumbled and fell into the dark cavern, and how when Luddie found me, he brought Papa who tied a rope around Luddie's waist and lowered him with a lantern, into the hole. How Luddie begged Papa not to be angry with me, saying it was all his fault.

"You saved my life, Luddie." I smiled as a tear trickled down my face, and I leaned to kiss him on the cheek, a rare caress.

"I see why the two of you have such a special attachment." Thom began to laugh softly as he nodded. "Mayhaps I should kiss thee also, Luddie. If it weren't for you, I'd never have found my sweet Aphrodite."

Chuckling, Luddie backed away. "Enough of that, old man. I've been well enough thanked."

A gentle wind blew strands of hair across my face. The air felt chilly, and beautiful grey fog began to creep across the water, nearly blocking our vision of home.

"The water seems unusually still," Thom said. "Perhaps it may rain later on. Does anyone want to go below deck?"

Lulled by the waves gently lapping against the boat, no one answered. We snuggled into our wool comforters and slept until daybreak.

When the *Sea Hawk* finally docked in our own harbor, the stillness was alarming. Something was wrong. Where were all the workers we usually found at the dock? Why was the group of militia who guarded the bay so small? Only a few men stood guard, and some of them looked ashen and wan.

Once we disembarked, we learned that many townsfolk were recuperating from a bad case of chills and fever — ague. At the mill, Luddie found his grinding wheel damaged and two signs posted on the open door:

> *Mill closed because of illness.*
> *Signed, William Leverich*

Door locked, miller gone.
Forced my way in. Ground my corne.
Here's payment, my rightful share.

Signed, Henry Whitney.

The way of the town was that whenever there was bad feeling between persons and either of them was imprudent enough to condemn the other liberally, he was immediately taken into court—but I never imagined the plaintiff in the next court case, October 5, 1660, would be my brother Luddie. The town clerk wrote the charge as it was read: "William Ludlam plaintiff against Henry Whitney Defendant ... of trespass for breking the mill and grinding several times without leve to his greate damages ... the Defendant deny the breking of the mill but confesed he opened the dore and grounde his corne....[Plaintiff claims] damage of an hundred pounds sterling ..."[162]

Eighteen
の

ANNO DOM 1660
HUNTINGTON, LONG ISLAND

Unfortunately for Luddie, the court, led by Jacob Cat-swaller, aligned itself on the defendant's side. Whitney was only acting in his family's best interest, they said. His family was sick and hungry at the time and that he had left payment for its use. Perhaps someone else had done the damage.

Other events at Huntington that fall were also most unexpected.

As the sermon ended the next Lord's Day and people poured out of the dark and stuffy meeting house, who should come riding up but Edward Higbee, back from the dead! Seeing his wife, he called, "Jedidah, me darlin'. I went lookin' for thee at home, and not seein' thee there, I borrowed the neighbor's horse and rode out to find thee."

Jedidah, trailed by their brood of five young ones, rushed to meet him.

"Papa!" shouted the children.

"Edward, my dear, thou art alive?"

With a flourish, he dismounted, embraced Jedidah, and kissed her, to the shock and amazement of the whole town in Sabbath attendance.

Twas the Lord's Day! Such blatant conduct could not be dismissed.

"Edward Higbee, in the name of the law, I do arrest thee," the constable said as he placed the man in shackles.[163] "Thou knowest as well as anyone, that for a husband to kiss his wife on the Sabbath is against the law." With that, he dragged Higbee to the pillory post next to the meeting house greens.

Some of the watchers nodded their agreement. Others seemed more forgiving, yet the law must not be broken. Higbee would spend the night in jail and then appear in court on the morrow.

We women returned not to the afternoon sermon, for Jedidah Higbee's pangs of childbirth began the moment her husband was arrested. We carried her home and took over our duties as midwives. Several of the older girls took charge of the Higbee children, feeding them the noon meal prepared the previous day, rejoicing with them at their father's return, and comforting them through their mother's travail.

Goody Leverich, as the eldest of the group, took charge, and within minutes, the baby made its entrance into this sinful world and began crying lustily. "It's a healthy girl." Ellen announced. "Praise God."

Lizzie, standing at Ellen's side, handed her a piece of yarn and a kitchen knife. Quickly Ellen tied and cut the cord and then disposed of the afterburden in a waste bucket next to the kitchen fire where it would be burned after everyone had gone to bed, as custom decreed.

Handing the baby to Lizzie, Ellen said, "Find towels and swaddling bands. Keep her warm."

"Look, mistress," Dora said softly. "The mother's face groweth white as milk."

Ellen Leverich reached under the birthing sheet and then sadly shook her head as she withdrew her hands. "More towels, please. Overmuch blood." With a shudder, she wiped her hands on her apron and suddenly sagged to a chair as if her bones had turned to water.

For a moment, it was again my seventh birthday, and the blood on the apron was that of my mother. I felt myself ridiculously close to tears, but courage told me to push myself forward. "Help me keep her awake, Dora," I said. I put my hand on the woman's shoulder and shook her. "Stay awake, Jedidah. You must choose to live. Command your bleeding to stop. Your children need you. This new little girl needs you."

Jedidah's eyes fluttered. "Yes, I know," she whispered.

"Then cling to that thought while I get something to help stop the bleeding."

When I grabbed the knife from the table where Ellen had laid it, though my right forearm cramped, I was able to go to the waste bucket at the fireplace and cut off a piece of the afterburden as Thom had done when Elizabeth was born. Quickly, I turned to the birthing bed. "Suck on this, Jedidah," I said as I tucked the piece into her mouth with my left hand. "Suck on it like you would if you cut your finger and sucked the blood from the wound."

I saw Deriah Catswaller's eyes widen and heard Sarah Whitney whisper, "What? Is this healer in league with Satan? Is she a witch?"

A chill skittered down my spine, but I looked Sarah in the eye. "Without this, she will surely die." From my pocket, I withdrew the jar of arnica I carried with me and handed it to Deriah Catswaller. "Knead this into her belly," I said.

With a determined set to her jaw, Ellen Leverich rose from her seat. "Do as she says, Deriah. And Sarah, put the baby to the mother's breast. Twill help stop the bleeding."

"Well done, my good and faithful servant," a voice whispered in my ear, but no one else seemed to notice.

Around me flowed a kind of love I had not felt before, and the emptiness in my heart suddenly lifted. I could hardly wait to get home to hold my own little Elizabeth.

When I opened our door, I spied my baby toddling around after our Indian maid. Overflowing at last with a mother's love, I reached for her, but she pushed away my hands.

"No, Mama," she said in the sweet voice of a three-year-old. "I help Anna now."

℅

The townspeople rejoiced at the news of the new baby at the Higbee house and the return of Edward Higbee. However, good or bad, words that soak into the ears are whispered... not shouted, and nothing can outpace the speed of gossip. Before nightfall, Luddie, Henry and Catherine, and even Reverend Leverich came to warn us of the whispers saying that I must be in league with the devil, and that I had falsely foretold that Jedidah would surely die. [164]

ANNO DOM 1660
HUNTINGTON, LONG ISLAND

No scripture could have seemed more fitting than that with which Edward Higbee opened his plea in court: "The Sabbath was made for man, not man for the Sabbath," he began reading from his Bible.

The tavern, used as a courtroom, was packed and if anyone had missed hearing the Lord's Day sermon, Higbee's oration would have served the purpose, so eloquent and sincere he seemed.

"Seven months ago on the way home from London, my ship was boarded by French pirates who killed the crew and held me for ransom. Evil men," he said. "But God hath brought me out of the land of iniquity, for I did escape from their snares with naught but this precious book. Yea, verily, and on the seventh day of the seventh month God brought me back to my wife and family. Yes, on the Lord's Day. Yet here am I in bonds."

So piteous was his voice that some in the audience brought out their handkerchiefs, and their tears further watered the fervor of the preacher.

Higbee's soliloquy went on. "Where is the wine of celebration?"

"Yes, where?" echoed a few voices in the audience.

At that, Higbee waved the leather bound book in the air as his voice took on the pitch of a pleading preacher, with a Shakespearean tone of grave acquiescence to divine destiny.

"Are not two sparrows sold for a farthing? Yet we are of more value than many sparrows. Is it not fitting that ye should rejoice when God brings the lost sparrow home to find his wife and children at meeting house,

waiting for his return? Should he not kiss her in rever-
ence to the One who hath saved him from evil?"

Encouraged by his captive audience, he opened the book,
and as if he were truly in the pulpit, he began to read:
"There's a divinity that shapes our ends; rough-hew
them how we will. There's a special providence in the fall
of a sparrow. Whatever is, hath already been, and what
will be, hath been before, and God will call the past to account."

Across the room, I saw Luddie whisper something to
Thom that made them both double up with silent laugh-
ter. Lizzie nudged me and raised an eyebrow. "Is that the
Geneva Bible he's reading?"

"I think it's Higbee's Hamlet," I said. "What a performance."

Nevertheless, Higbee's silver tongue was convincing,
and ere it was time for our midday meal, the court had
voted to set him free without punishment.

The trial spectators, suddenly athirst, moved to the bar
to celebrate Higbee's release.

"Drinks all around," he called.

Luddie moved forward to order pottage, ale, and
cheese for the four of us, and then carried the trencher
back to the bench where we sat.

Not a quarter hour later, Higbee was encouraged to tell
his tale again, reinforced by his second or third round of
the innkeeper's latest shipment of Barbados rum.

"Like I tol' you afore, those black hearted pirates
boarded my ship, killed all the crew, beat me within an
inch of my life, and then tied me in the hold. Couldn't
understand a word those thievin' Frenchies spoke, but I
suppose they planned to ask for ransom. I'm a friend of
Young John Winthrop, you know." Higbee raised his cup

and emptied it with a gulp, then wiped his mouth with his sleeve. "They pulled my boat into a hidden cove somewhere between here and Southold, and while anight they cavorted and celebrated their fortunes with the enticements of dark-skinned beauties and Jamaican Rum, I managed to escape, and with a bag of their booty, too."

From his belt, he withdrew a bag of gold. "Drinks for everyone," he bellowed, more garrulous and rowdy than before. "Drinks a'round." He motioned to the bartender to fill his cup again. "Here's to my new youngin', Patience Higbee," he said.[165] "Named 'er Patience 'cause she waited for her old man to get home."

"Huzzah," shouted his listeners as they egged him on.

"Thank the Lord for Patience," cheered one companion as he sipped his fourth cup. "Took her nine months to get here and her father only seven. You'd a looked bad, Higbee, if it had been tother way round." His bawdy remark was greeted by a bedlam of guffaws and backslapping and another toast: "Huzzah, huzzah, here's to the courage of Captain Edward Higbee!"

"Dutch courage, I'd say," Luddie muttered.

"You're looking pretty good for having undergone all the pirates could dish out, Higbee," Thom said with a grin as Higbee came nearer, circling the inn to include a larger audience. "Guess your wounds have all had time enough to heal, eh?"

"Whadya mean by that, Scudder?"

Another man took up the jibe. "Sounds like you may have had overmuch of the pirates' potion, Higbee. First thing you know, I suspect some of those dark skinned beauties will have their bellies full of little Higbees, just like your wife."

Another man laughed and said with a sneer, "What is this, your sixth one, Higbee?

"Yeah, six or eight," Higbee said. "One ever' other year. Rachel's always ready with a warm bed for me when I get home."

"Rachel? Thought yer wife's name was Jedidah," said the quarrelsome Joachim Ferret, an aptly named man. "How many wives do you have, Higbee? One in every port?"

With feet spraddled and hands on hips, Higbee locked eyes with Ferret. Suddenly Higbee swung at his maligner, bellowing vile threats.

Immediately, Thom grabbed Higbee in a neck hold and held him back while Luddie stepped between Higbee and his rat-faced opponent.

Oh, Thom, I thought as I dug my fisted hands deep into the pockets of my shawl. A fine specimen to make an enemy of. I willed my face to remain expressionless

"Lemme go, Scudder, you bastard," Higbee yelled, "or I'll burn down your house, you and that snivelin' wife and brat of yourn."

A few of the town's militia unshouldered their muskets, and the fight was over, but the look on Higbee's face told me he would not soon forget his threat.

∞

To ward off future conflict, toward the end of October, Thom brought suit against the defendant Edward Higbee.

Nineteen

21ST CENTURY
MEMORY CATCHERS' OFFICE

The recorder stopped, and Grand-Mary was gone from her accustomed chair.

Curious, about Thom's lawsuit, I did an Internet search and found the court records of Huntington in the year of 1660. As I transcribed Grand-Mary's recollections, I added the court records verbatim. She'd like that, I was sure:

> *Thomas Skodar plaintive against Eadward higbe, in action of defamcion to the damage of £100. The plaintiv claimeth that the defendan accuseth him of houlding hem by the throt hallf an oure or tharabout and all most throtelled hem. The corte finds for the plat that the defendat shall give publick satisfac or pay 20 shilling.[166]*

I read on, discovering various other changes that year that surely affected Grand-Mary's life and added that data to her story:

According to Peter Ross's *History of Long Island*, by 1660, the town meeting gave the school teacher the added responsibility of acting as town clerk.[167] At the same meeting they voted allegiance to Connecticut, elected deputies to the General Court at Hartford, and chose Mr. Strickland, Jonas Wood, and Thomas Benedict as Magistrates.[168]

The town fathers made and repaired highways. They ordered fences built to keep cattle and hogs from wandering. They impounded stray cattle, sold them at auction, and added the proceeds to the town general funds. They administered their ideas of justice in criminal as well as civil cases, fixed legal fees, and fined without mercy. They established laws to insure proper conduct.

When the nine o'clock bell rang, the elected constables walked their rounds to see good order kept and to take up loose people. They built stocks wherewith to detain and punish offenders.[169] [170]

Thom Scudder could not serve in any of these offices. By law, he could hold no public office, for he was not a full-fledged member of the church.

Slow though it might be, progress and civilization was wending its way across Long Island.

During my Internet search, I also found an obscure note suggesting that Reverend William Leverich may have sailed to Holland that year, 1660, to train as a physician under the auspices of the Dutch governor at New Amsterdam. His family did not accompany him.[171]

ꙮ

Dinnertime. I took a quick shower, slapped on some lip-gloss, and went out for dinner with Ken. Until his family had moved to Canada in the 20th century, they had remained in England, Tories to the end. My mind was so filled with events of the 1600s, I could hardly carry on a conversation about current day happenings. Ken had heard quite enough about the 1600s and Grand-Mary. It was a quiet meal.

Back at home, I went straight to my office and finished the transcription, with a few additions. Suddenly, goose-flesh rippled on my arm, and I knew Grand-Mary was back.

Rosy-faced, she seemed as eager as I to continue her story.

"I almost forgot to tell thee the good news. My little sister Abbie and Mara's brother, Samuel King, were wed in October 1660. The two of them first met at Southampton when Thom and I married, and though Samuel inherited property in Salem, they chose to live in Southold. It pleased me to know that Abbie had made a good marriage."

Grand-Mary glanced then at the transcription of her story on the computer monitor. "I see you found the court records," she said with a nod of approval. The beginning of a smile tipped the corners of her mouth, and she raised a soft, vein-corded hand to my cheek as if I were a small child. "I beseech thee, do not judge the reporter as uneducated," she said kindly. "It was difficult to spell words consistently when there were no rules."

My face warmed, pink with embarrassment. "Tell me," I said, changing the subject. "Did Reverend Leverich truly leave the Huntington church to go to England?"

"Holland, it was. But let me tell you how that came to be." For a moment her face clouded as she recalled a bitter memory.

Anno Dom 1660
Huntington, Long Island

I was visiting my dear friend Ellen one day when there came a gentle knock at her door. A man introduced himself and asked if he and the two women with him could have audience with the Reverend William Leverich.

At his study door, when Ellen told her husband he had callers, he took one look at the three guests and snapped, "Vagabond Quakers! I've heard they were in the area."

I could see that this was not one of the minister's better days. The grooves between his eyebrows had deepened, and his eyes mirrored pain. I'm sure they had heard his harsh comment, but the man said kindly, "Sir, if we could have one moment of your time..."

Although the Reverend's tone was grudging, he invited them to take seats in his office and then closed the door.

Eleazer and Caleb had not yet finished their morning drinks, and while their mother filled cups for her husband's guests and carried them into the office, the Leverich boys invited me to sit with them and have a cup of my own. Ellen returned to join us, but ere we had taken half a dozen sips, loud voices burst from the office and the guests poured out, followed by an irate Reverend Leverich. "There is no revelation from God in these days," he shouted.

The man turned to him. "From what, then, do you minister in yourself, and to what?"

"From the Spirit of the Lord, to the souls of the people," he answered, "but I deny revelation, except through the written word of the Lord."

One of the women entered the fray. "Priest Leverich," she said softly, "if you deny revelation, how then do your words profit the people?"

For a moment, words seemed to fail the usually forthcoming Leverich. I watched him as he looked this way and that, and then lowered his gaze.

Suddenly he tilted his head upward and with chin extended, said, "I fear my words profit them as much as the Quakers, which," he said, "is nothing at all." With that, he chased his challengers into the courtyard in full view of the neighbors.

Fully disturbed by the fracas, his family and I followed. To our wonderment, the Quakers knelt on the ground, and one of the women began praying.

Beside himself at this action, Reverend Leverich ran upon her, and grabbed her arm.

His sons, Caleb and Eleazer, had watched wide eyed, but seeing their father in so unseemly an action, they could no longer stand quietly by.

"Father, stop this brutishness," Caleb cried as the two of them ran to pull him off the woman.

That day, the madness and folly of Reverend Leverich was hereby made manifest to the people.[172]

To my surprise, Goody Leverich[173] insisted that I come back inside the dwelling with her family. "Here, dear friend," she said, "finish your drink. We all need to quiet ourselves." Then, as if I were not present, she turned to her husband.

"For shame, William!"

"For shame yourself, woman," he said, his breath coming in raspy wheezes. "Don't they know what we do with dissenters in these settlements? We banish them. Dost they not know what banishment can mean in a land of snow and savages?" With that, he retreated to his study.

On Sabbath next, a contrite minister climbed to the pulpit, opened the Bible, and read a most apt scripture:

Do not spread false reports. Do not help a wicked man by being a malicious witness. Do not follow the crowd in doing wrong. When you give testimony in a lawsuit, do not pervert justice by siding with the crowd, and do not show favoritism to a poor man in his lawsuit. If you come across your enemy's ox or donkey wandering off, be sure to take it back to him. If you see the donkey of someone who hates you fallen down under its load, do not leave it there; be sure you help him with it. Do not deny justice to your poor people in their lawsuits. Have nothing to do with a false charge and do not put an innocent or honest person to death, for I will not acquit the guilty.[174]

Reverend Leverich closed the Bible and looked at the congregation — left and right — before he spoke.

"Lately," he said, "I have been dealt a mind of intense and volatile temper. The devil hath given me a ride most evil, filled with jagged pain. Even though I search the scriptures, just as the cobbler's feet go bare, so am I unable to heal myself. Finding no Godly revelation for relief of my suffering, I have turned to some of the ancient men in medicine — Hippocrates, Aristotle, and Galen. They advise drilling a hole in the skull to release evil spirits lurking within."

Our dear minister's announcement brought dread to my heart and tears to my eyes. I retrieved a handkerchief from my pocket, and in so doing, I saw that others in the congregation were also weeping. Never before had those in the pews been so attentive or filled with empathy.

Reverend Leverich paused and cleared his throat. "Therefore," he said, "I soon shall sail on the ship *Spotted Cow* from New Amsterdam to Holland[175] to become better versed in the art of physic as I search for healing.

"Ye all know that lately I have complained somewhat bitterly of the people having failed to pay me according to contract, and I have threatened to preach no more in Huntington. But after a year or so of study in Holland, if you would have me here, I will then return to serve in the capacity of your physician as well as your minister.[176]

"My wife and two sons will remain here in Huntington while I am gone. Please treat them with Christian love, and when I return, ye must decide if ye would yet have me serve as minister. Until then, may the Lord prosper your endeavors and water them with his abundant blessing in Jesus Christ.[177] May He keep you in his care while we are absent, one from the other."

Anno Dom 1661-1663
Huntington, Long Island

We sorely missed the eloquence of Reverend Leverich after he left for Holland. On some Sabbath days, we had a layman or a traveling preacher who stood in for him, but in spite of my many points of disagreement with the Old Testament sermons of Reverend Leverich, seldom did a visitor bring as much light to my understanding.

One guest speaker was Elder James, a sickly-looking man much enamored with worldly fashions that seemed not at all suitable for the pulpit. Even the tithing man could hardly hold back his laughter when Elder James' periwig went awry. The hapless preacher seemed not to notice, but carefully adjusted the curly hairpiece, saying,

"Excuse me please, but in so draughty a building, I must keep my head covered ere I catch a chill."

'Twas most unkind of us to find another's discomfort so amusing, especially on the Lord's Day, but in truth, his garb was of such distraction that I know not what he said in the sermon.

On another Sabbath Day, Uncle Robert Fordham came to preach, bringing with him my dear Aunt Alice, most like a mother to me. They brought us welcome news of my Southampton cousins. Molly and young Edward Howell now had three children, and expected another soon. My cousin Gideon, with whom I had argued so, had graduated from Harvard and settled in Hempstead as minister. Like his father, he seemed to have an inclination for business and trade as well as the ministry, and was doing well. Cousin Hannah and her husband, Sam Clark, had moved to Plymouth Colony. Young Joseph and his dainty little bride were living in Southampton near his parents. On family days, the Fordham house was bursting with grandchildren, which greatly pleased Aunt Alice.

How wonderful it was to receive the bread and the wine from Uncle Robert's hand and to hear him preach again from the New Testament! *By this shall all men know that ye are my disciples, if ye have love one to another.*[178] His words were like water to a thirsty soul.

Perhaps the absence of a minister was God's test. Through our daily devotions and reading of the Word, Thom and I drew even closer. So many questions we shared! Not many husbands allowed their wives to discuss issues as equals with them, and this knowledge made my appreciation for Thom doubly strong. One evening, we read Matt. 25—*Come, ye blessed of my Father,*

inherit the kingdom prepared for you, for I was an hungred,
and ye gave me meat.... We then began considering the
implications of the final judgment. Were God's people
saved by works or by faith? What did it mean to walk in
his way? How could we know if we were one of God's
elect?

Thom reached for my hand and said to me, "Every
night I thank God for bringing you into my life. Yet how
can He bless me so by giving me one of his elect if I am
not among them?"

"You are His child, Thom," I said as I stroked a dark
strand of hair off his brow. "He created you for a purpose."

"What might my purpose be," he asked, "but to work
the land and build a home for my family? When have I
ever seen my Lord hungry or in need?"

I stroked his hand—a hand rough and hard with cal-
luses from daily toil. "Did you not loan my brother Luddie the tools to work his land? Were you not a good
neighbor to the Whitney family when they were ill? Did
you not help harvest barley for Jedidah Higbee when her
husband was lost?"

Thom raised a quizzical eyebrow and then shook his
head. "Is God's purpose for me to serve in such small
and simple ways? Never have I taken part in great un-
dertakings or in things over hard for me." His voice was
soft with regret. "Surely the Lord demands more of me."

"You heard the scripture Uncle Robert read," I answered. "Doth not your work show love for those in
need?"

The yearning look in his eyes deepened. "Faith comes
so easy to you, Mary."

Though snow was falling from the skies, his sigh reminded me of a warm swish of wind through new leaves.

On her trundle bed, little Elizabeth roused from her sleep, then murmured softly and closed her eyes again. Thom stood and placed the devotion book and Bible on the shelf above the table, then raised me to my feet. "How blessed I am," he whispered, "to have a mate with whom I can share doubts and questions without fear of rejection."

At the hearth, I banked the fire and hung the morning pot of porridge over the warm coals. The air was fragrant with the lingering scent of bayberry as Thom blew out the light.

"Come, Aphrodite." He pulled me down onto our bed and then closed the curtains around us. The smell of his clean hair and the musk of his body was all round him. His chest was a lion's pelt, strong and mighty, and in the glow of the fire, he beckoned me unto him.

ॐ

A deep sorrow we had not expected came in April 1661 when Thom's brother Henry, not yet 35, sickened and died, leaving his wife Catherine with four children under the age of five—Jonathan, Rebecca, Moses, and little Miriam, barely walking. I could hardly imagine Catherine's plight and her heavy load of grief. The big house her father, Jeffrey Este, had willed his grandson Jonathan Scudder a scant four years ago, was once more devoid of a man in the house. Neighbors gathered to do the spring planting on Henry's fields, and we were all there to help Catherine in any way we could. I worried though, for she seemed more ill than grieved. Food agreed not with her though the good wives of the town brought in tasty morsels and meats from their storehouse. "Don't worry, Mary," she finally said to me. "I'm oft unable to eat much during the first few months." She burst into tears, and between sniffles said, "Henry so wanted another boy."

I, too, was with child again, but this time I suffered no sickness as I had before. When Thom suggested that we might keep Jonathan for a while to take some of the burden from Catherine—at least until the new year when her baby was delivered, I was delighted with the idea.

Three-year-old Elizabeth held a special affinity for her cousin Jonathan and followed in his steps like a small waddling duck, but he never seemed to mind.

"Do you suppose she'll be as patient with her little brother as Jonathan is with her?" Thom asked.

"Her little brother? You are sure it's a boy?"

"Of course it's a boy."

Thom's certain hope seemed to give him renewed energy, and the presence of Henry's son brightened his days while also easing his grief over the loss of his brother. When we asked Jonathan why he insisted on wearing a leather strap across his chest, he said, "It's a bandolier like my Papa's. See all the vials of gunpowder it holds? Papa's gone now, so I'll take his turn standing guard."

Thom gathered the small boy in his arms, and said, "Your papa was my brother, you know, so I'll help you stand guard."

After that, Jonathan seemed to be happiest when he could be outside following in his Uncle Thom's footsteps.

"Reminds me of the way Henry used to tag along with me when he was Jonathan's age," Thom said, smiling as he recalled those days. "The boy's really quite strong for a four-year-old and good with the animals. He says his papa always told him he could trade in his skirts for breeches when he was five. I've never seen a child so eager." Thom started laughing. "Do you know," he said, "that Jonathan knows what a gliff is? He can say the one my father taught me years ago, and with scarcely a twist in his tongue. He rattled it off to me just yesterday — Dick drunk drink in a dish; where's the dish Dick drunk drink in?[179] — and then he laughed till he was rolling on the grass."

I saw a moment of sadness in Thom's eyes, but then the twinkle was back.

"Thinking of Henry when he was that age brought tears to my eyes," he said, "but soon I was laughing with Jonathan. He says his papa taught it to him. Seems as if he hath inherited his papa's sense of humor too. I remember Henry laughing like that. No one could resist joining in."

ஐ

In September, Thom and the neighbors made the first cider of the year, some of which we drank fresh and shared with Henry's widow Catherine. The rest we stored, a potent brew, in barrels purchased from the new cooper in town. Later in September, Catherine's neighbors, including Thom and the Leverich boys, Caleb and Eleazer, gathered corn for her, and as the weather got colder, they chopped and stacked wood to last her family through the winter months.

In the harbor, the landing and piers required sinking of piles and building stone foundations.[180] Thom joined other townsmen to break and haul stones for roads and walls. They worked early to late in autumn's glowing light—the glimmering yellow and gold leaves of the tulip trees, the purple and scarlet of the pepperidge trees, and the fragrant red and orange mitten-shaped leaves of sassafras.

For families maintaining farms, tools were the big expense—cider presses, knives and candle molds, looms and spinning wheels, wooden plows and heavy iron hoes, harnesses and harrows, sickles, scythes, and hickory flails.[181] Craftsmen could charge a goodly price for many of these, and some tools had to be imported or at the very least shipped from other colonies.

Winter arrived. Time to slaughter sheep, hogs, and cattle for food; thresh the oats and wheat; and to prepare our new crop of flax for spinning.[182] Now, instead of purchasing cloth from England, Huntington women made almost all the linen and woolen fabric for clothing as well as for the table and bed linen for the household. A woman had to be a fuller, a tailor, and a seamstress. Hosiery was wholly handmade, and girls as young as four learned to knit mittens and hosiery. Although I could not do some of the usual woman's work, Anna Wing was always there to help me, and it was she who first placed the knitting needles in Elizabeth's hands and helped her make her cousin Jonathan a pair of red woolen mittens that winter. He wore them proudly, especially when Thom's workday made it possible for the small boy to go with him.

Perhaps God used the difficulties I had suffered at childbirth to teach me skills to help other women once they were on the birthing bed, and oft, I was called for in such a time. Of course, this was also an occasion for the community of women to gather, offering advice and sharing skills in difficult births and then rejoicing when the child was finally brought forth from the womb, kicking and squalling.

Catherine's baby came easily on a warm winter day, January 1, 1662. Anna Wing and I stopped in to see Catherine early that morning and found her in labor. "Anna," I said, "please go get Goody Leverich to preside at the delivery, and then hurry back so you can take charge of Elizabeth and Jonathan and the other little Scudders."

When Ellen knocked, I waddled to the door to let her in.

Ellen came in and with a glance at me, standing with my hands pressed against the small of my back, she said, "When do you expect to need me for your baby's birthing?"

"Three weeks, about. I can hardly wait."

I was disappointed when she shook her head at me and said, "I think you are not the one to bring forth Catherine's child today, my dear Mary, lest your own labor pains begin."

Obviously, she could see the disappointment on my face, for she put her hand on my shoulder. "Don't worry, dear," she said. "Other neighbor women will soon arrive to help."

She was right. Soon the house was bustling with chattering housewives come to share in the birthing and offer advice.

I stood back, but then rejoiced when Ellen handed the babe to me to wash and wrap in swaddling clothes. Peace surrounded me, and I realized the terrible fear I had suffered when Elizabeth was a baby had finally lifted. I laid the baby next to Catherine and hurried to find my own child, suddenly yearning to hold her, to make up for all the joys I had missed when she was a baby. But Elizabeth was engrossed in a game with her little cousins and had no time for me.

&

When the next visiting preacher arrived, Thom and I walked with our sister-in-law Catherine to the meeting house. Jonathan, proudly dressed in breeches now, held Thom's hand and Thom held the baby in his other arm as he had carried our baby nigh on four years ago when she was baptized. Catherine walked beside me, and to my delight, on my other side, my darling little Elizabeth put her tiny hand in mine. The rest of Henry and Catherine's little ones followed — Rebecca, Moses, and Miriam — under the care of Anna Wing. In the meeting house, when the pastor asked the baby's name, Catherine spoke out with certainty. "His name shall be as his dear father chose. The baby's name is David."

It was barely a month until our own baby arrived, Feb 3, 1662. Another girl. Maria, we named her. If Thom was disappointed, he showed it not. He rejoiced in my quick recovery, and especially in my good spirits and ability to care for a newborn — with only a bit of coaching from Anna Wing.

Elizabeth, not at all jealous of her baby sister, set about playing little mother to her. Snuggling close to me, she learned to sing Bye Baby Bunting as I nursed and rocked the baby. Elizabeth begged to hold her sister, brought me clean bands for the baby after her bath, and oft tucked her in again after I finished nursing and put Maria down to sleep. "Rest in God's love, Maria," I would whisper to her, and soon I heard Elizabeth whispering my words of blessing. "Rest in God's love, little sister."

It was not long before Catherine married again and took Jonathan, now almost seven years old, home to live with her, his four brothers and sisters, and their new stepfather.

"Don't worry, 'lizabeth, I won't live far away and I'll come see you," Jonathan said when he saw the tears in his cousin's eyes. "Unless I need to help in the fields, every day when my lessons are finished, I'll come teach you to read."

Elizabeth, shy for once, handed him a new pair of mittens she had knitted. Bright blue this time, blue as Jonathan's eyes and large enough to fit him when winter snows blew in again.

I do not know which of our family missed Jonathan most—Thom, Elizabeth, or me.

ဆ

To welcome Reverend Leverich back to the pulpit when he returned from Holland, the people voted at town meeting to authorize the purchase of a house and land for a new parsonage with an office room suitable for a man schooled in the art of physic as well as a diviner of the scriptures. They constructed shelves for his large collection of books and a large cupboard where he might store herbs and medicines. In hopeful expectation, the next month they voted to grant him the use of all of the meadow about Cow Harbor on both sides of the creek, as long as he should remain their minister. [183]

The minister's homecoming, a time of thanksgiving, gained reason to celebrate with his younger son's announcement. In the minister's absence, Eleazer, now 22, had proposed marriage to Rebecca, the 18-year-old niece of Reverend Leverich's old friend Peter Wright of Oyster Bay. Townsfolk accepted the calm manner their minister displayed as proof that he had indeed regained his health — for everyone knew the bride-to-be was a Quaker, a cousin of Mary Wright, the girl who had sailed home with us from Boston after challenging the authorities who hanged Mary Dyer.

Soon after the Leverich family moved into their new parsonage, Reverend Leverich received a shipment of medicines from Holland addressed to "English Clergyman, versed in the art of physic, and willing to serve in the capacity of physician."[184] He stored his medical instrument, a lancet, in the office cabinet along with bottles of healing concoctions either sent from Holland or prepared with herbs he gathered and hung to dry in the loft of the parsonage.

The townsfolk had confidence in their physician. If the patient recovered, people were prone to be prompt with taxes they paid for his "spiritual prescriptions" as minister. If a patient died, it must have been the will of the Lord.[185]

England was once more under the rule of a King, for Charles II had been crowned King of England and Ireland on April 23, 1661. This seemed to make little difference in the town of Huntington. Through town meetings, residents ran things for themselves. Their religion and their government were as one, and as such, extended to moral conduct. Their rule was based on their conscience as well as on the laws of Moses. They taxed themselves to care for the poor — the widows and orphans of their own members. [186]

Reverend Leverich headed a committee that examined the character and credentials of every applicant for admission into Huntington. A newcomer could not simply sail across Long Island Sound and settle into Huntington. The committee stringently tested the applicant with a series of questions: "Do you have skills required by the town? Will you abide by the faith and the rules of the community?" A troublesome person in his previous community, was not welcome.[187]

No one interfered with the town meeting's edicts. It was a law unto itself; its verdict was supreme, and there did not seem to be any idea of an appeal from its decision to a higher court."[188]

In the spring of 1663, the Huntington town meeting ordered that *"all fenses that are in generall either about felldes or hom lotes are to be sofisently mended within 3 days after this meeting ... or the ownar shall pay 5 shilling fine."*

Apparently, the cows, goats, and sheep of one settler had broken into the land of another and ruined his crops. Thom and my brother Luddie were among the men selected to determine whether fences were in proper condition. Though important, this was certainly a less prestigious job than Thom could wish for: He still claimed no conversion experience, and therefore could climb no higher on the official rung of Huntington's ladder.

Before long, the owners of livestock set aside a common pasturage at Cow Harbor, and then hired a boy to watch over their collective herd of cattle.[189]

Anno Dom 1664-1665
Huntington, Long Island

In 1664, a frightening event took place in a town near us, serving as a forewarning lest any should need it. You might recall the Goody Garlick trial of 1657, held in Connecticut, but *this* Witchcraft trial, held only 16 miles east of our home in Huntington by boat, was the only one ever held in New York State: the trial of Ralph Hall and his goodwife, Mary Hall.

George Wood, Setauket landowner and innkeeper, had been at odds with Goody Hall for some time, and near the end of December 1663, the innkeeper sickened and died. Soon after, his infant son followed him to the grave.[190]

In connection with the death of the Woods, the Halls were indicted on charges of witchcraft and sorcery. The majority of damaging depositions had come from Goody Smith whose husband, Richard Smith, had himself at Boston experienced imprisonment and banishment for Quakerly behavior, but was now a man of note in his region.[191] Goody Smith had had many run-ins with Mary Hall and said she had heard Goody Hall oft make complaints about the unruly behavior of one of George Wood's sons.

The court records from the Court of Azzises, New York City, state the charge:

"Ralph Hall thou standest here indicted, for that having not the feare of God before thine eyes, thou did'st upon the 25th day of December, and as is suspected, at sev'all other times since did maliciously and feloniously practice and exercise, witchcraft and sorcery upon the bodyes of George Wood and his Infant Childe.

"What dost thou say for thyselle, art thou guilty, or not guilty?"

The Halls pled not guilty. They were both found innocent.[192]

The weather was frigid that winter, especially in February, but as all good Puritans did, on the Lord's Day we bundled six-year-old Elizabeth and two-year-old Maria in their sealskin boots and woolen coats. Carrying heated bricks wrapped as foot warmers, we walked to the tavern that served, on the Lord's Day, as our meeting house. The wind howled fiercely around the building, seeping in every available chink in the walls. Thom took his place in a seat on the right, and our daughters huddled close to me as we sat on the hard benches on the left side of the room. Such well-behaved children they were with nary a whimper or whisper during the long service. Midway in the sermon, when I took Maria out to nurse, Elizabeth slipped quietly over to her papa, snuggled up on his lap, and went to sleep. Maria, too, was sound asleep by the time I returned to my seat, and her warm body against my breast was quite comforting.

The minister's eyes were dark with warning as he said, "Forget ye not the evils of the world from which we came." Shaking his head, he continued. "In England, the growth of trade is still yielding handsome profits for merchants and large landowners. But, alas, as the rich are getting richer, the poor are getting poorer. King Charles continues to withdraw from the treasury beyond that which Parliament hath granted him. He demands more monies from poor farmers and laborers to furnish his extravagant hobbies and arm his soldiers for further conquests. Taxes, taxes, taxes. Poll tax, land tax, hearth tax. All create ever-greater hardships upon the lower classes. Now, in appreciation of the assistance certain nobles gave him in gaining the throne, he hath given the area we know as Carolina to these rich noblemen, calling them Proprietors. Are we next?" The minister raised his voice, and his eyes blazed with the fire of conviction. "To whom will he award *our* land, *our* island? His Catholic brother James?"

Reverend Leverich paused, and then resumed the sermon in a voice of contrition and regret. "On my travels to the old country," he said, "in the streets I saw vagrants and beggars who had lost everything and given up hope. There is still tremendous tension there between Catholics and Anglicans and Presbyterians. The country needs change, I say. Change from excessive profits that are nothing more than thievery. Change in wage and price controls to ensure fair profits from goods and services. Change toward moral certainty. Change toward spiritual consolation. Here in the colonies we can lead the way," he said, pointing his finger emphatically to enforce his message of change, "but we must be ever vigilant. In our quest for purity, we must cling to our Mosaic laws and look not to the frivolous designs of new and misdirected thoughts."

I glanced Thom's way and saw the straight firm line of his mouth, as if his teeth might be clenched.

In spite of our icy nose and toes, the message Reverend Leverich brought to us that particular Sabbath day inspired much discussion that week, particularly between Thom and me at morning devotions. Thom was unusually restrained as we discussed the sermon.

"It seems to me," he said, "that striving to restore some period of the past may be a mistake. If God is a living God, then He is with us just as much now and will be with us just as much in the future as He was in the past, although I can't think of a scripture to support that idea."

"I agree," I said to him. "But you have only to look in the New Testament to find our hope in something new."

I turned in our Geneva Bible to I John 2:7-8. "Look, Thom, here it is:

A new commandment I write unto you, which thing is true in him and in you: because the darkness is past, and the true light now shineth.

"The study notes say that the doctrine indeed is old, but it is in a way new, both in respect to Christ, and also to us: in whom He through the gospel engraves his law, not in tables of stone, but in our minds."

Thom took the Bible from me and reread the verse I had shown him, then raised his eyebrows. "So, what vision is God giving us now?" he said as he pulled a book based on the writings of Calvin from the shelves. Finding the words he was searching for, he read them aloud:

God, in his infinite mercy, will spare a small number of "elect" individuals from the fate of eternal hellfire. That elect group of "saints" will be blessed, at some point in their lives, by a profound sense of inner assurance that they possess God's saving grace. This dawning of hope, the experience of conversion, might come upon individuals suddenly or gradually, in their earliest youth or even in the moments before death. God hath decided who will be saved or damned before the beginning of human history, and no good actions on the part of men and women can alter their preordained fates.[193]

"Why dost thou sigh so, Aphrodite?" Thom asked.

"I fear I am becoming ever more Quakerly," I said, "for I believe the Spirit within us gives glimpses of a better future, and then invites us to create that future. And if I understand them rightly, the heart of the Quakers hath always been on the future. I've read that Quakers are a 'people of the sunrise,' not of the setting sun."

Thom returned the book to the shelf and shook his head. "Why have I never, in all my life, had the experience of Paul's conversion on the Damascus Road? Does this mean that I am not chosen? In advancing my own family's profit and the community's well-being, am I not also furthering God's plans? Surely He does not draw lines of distinction between the secular and religious spheres. Is not all of life an expression of the divine will? If that is not enough to be chosen by God, why do I remain hopeful? Why do I not sink into despair — or decide to wallow in the world's pleasures, if I can do nothing to affect eternity?"

I shrugged, wishing to cast off Calvin's restrictions. "I have oft heard Reverend Leverich refer to predestination as a comfortable doctrine that affords great solace and security in times of uncertainty," I said, "but I know not where either the Scriptures or the Spirit within says, 'Trust in John Calvin.'"

Thom smiled, but I saw the confusion in his eyes and took his hand in mine and said to him, "Christ himself saith, *Whosoever believeth in me shall never die but have everlasting life.*"

Thom's eyes were cheerless. "Long have I believed as you do," he said, "but my faith is not so strong as yours."

For a very long time, Thom sat with his head bowed nearly to his chest.

I waited, in silence.

Suddenly an immense smile crept over his face, and when he looked up at me, his eyes shone like stars. "Oh, Mary," he said. "The most strange and marvelous experience! As if a warm and gentle rain were poured over me, trickling down over my whole being!"

"Sweet!" I said.

He began laughing. "Sweet, indeed. The sweet assurance of God's favor. I see it now!" He grabbed me round my waist and twirled me around the room. "Blessed assurance!" The words rang out, resonating as if from the very depth of his soul.[194]

ℰↄ

In Hartford on 12 May 1664, along with a list of 20 other men of Huntington, the Court's scribe recorded these words: "... and Thomas Scudder, accepted to be made free, and the Commissioners of Huntington are to administer the oath of freedom to them."

As directed, the Commissioners of Huntington gave Thomas Scudder of Huntington, Long Island, the "Oath of a Freeman," the first document to be written as a pledge of allegiance to the Commonwealth, giving the right to vote. They had to be male, churchgoing and have had a transforming religious experience.[195] Under the first Massachusetts charter, only "freemen" had the right to hold public office or vote in town meetings. Indentured and bonded servants were not eligible. Thom's acceptance as freeman meant he was a full citizen.[196]

Feeling more of a kinship with other English settlers than with the New Amsterdam at their west, Huntington town meetings had voted in 1660 to place itself under the jurisdiction of Connecticut to gain some protection from the Dutch. In 1664, at some distance from the direct involvement of Connecticut leaders, the residents of Huntington were quite satisfied to run things for themselves through actions of the town meetings.[197]

But Governor Winthrop's Massachusetts Bay Colony leaders had watchful eyes on both Connecticut and Long

Island. "We cannot permit lax controls," said the Bay Colony Governor. "If we should change from a mixed aristocracy to mere democracy, we should have no warrant in scripture for it. There was no such government in Israel. A democracy is, amongst civil nations, accounted the meanest and worst of all forms of government. To allow it would be a manifest breach of the 5th Commandment."[198]

The Dutch had settled New Netherlands, the area to the west of Long Island, and they longed to control the whole of Long Island, so they formed an alliance with the French against the English.

Realizing likelihood of war, Thom, who had built the first tanning mill in Huntington town, poured his energy into increasing the production of his tannery. After leather was cured at the tannery, he sent it by wagon three miles down Rogues Path, a trail lined with the shacks of disreputable people, to a drum factory at the end of the trail. There the leather was transformed into drums for military use.[199] From there, both the *Scudder Schooner* and the *Sea Hawk* oft sailed to far away ports, delivering the drums for infantry battalions.

In response to the Dutch and French alliance, in March of 1664, King Charles II formally annexed New Netherland as a British province and granted it to his brother James, Duke of York, as Lord Proprietor. Soon, the Duke sent a fleet under the command of an English soldier named Sir Richard Nicolls to seize the colony.

In August that year, Nicolls sailed his warship into the deep water off the western Long Island shoreline, dropped anchor, and ordered the Dutch to leave their small community on Manhattan island. It took only a few days for the Dutch to comply.

In September, the Dutch Director General Pieter Stuyvesant surrendered Fort Amsterdam and on 24 September 1664, Fort Orange capitulated. Both the city of New
Amsterdam and the entire colony were renamed New
York, after the English patron James, the Duke of York.

On 28 Feb. 1665, the Duke's laws were imposed. With
Richard Nicolls appointed as his deputy Governor, he
placed Long Island under English Rule.

Thom and the other men of Huntington were aghast.
They called a town meeting to air their grievances and
consider their possible recourse.

"Are we not capable of governing ourselves as we have
been doing for years?"

"Do we not care for our widows and orphans as God
demands?"

"Do we not guard our village so that only the most fit,
the most lawful, are permitted to live here?"

"How can the King hundreds of miles away simply declare that he has taken the land we purchased from the
Indians and given it to his brother, the Duke? This does
not sit well with me, to say the least," one of the townsmen protested.

"New York is a long way off," another said. "From that
distance, how can the Duke's governor know what is best
for us?"

"To have a governor and judges to answer to, and a
new set of laws drawn up with no consideration for our
needs — Tarnation! It is a thorn in my side!"

Thom mourned these changes with the other townsmen. "I fear all our work is lost, along with our freedoms,
he said. "The Duke has a reputation of being a selfish ty-
rant."

When Thom reported to me what had gone on at the meeting, his sun-bronzed face creased in lines of worry. "Mary," he said, "your husband may soon be penniless. The property I have worked hard to purchase—the meadow and cattle, the farmland with its fields of grain, the tannery—will at the very least be heavily taxed by the Royals. I cannot be sure it will not be confiscated entirely."

The Duke, an autocratic despot, had no interest in listening to the opinions of the people, nor did he care for their good will. When the townsmen claimed the right to assemble and present their grievances to the authorities, their actions infuriated the Duke. He ordered his governors to levy taxes to the maximum possible.[200]

Hoping to sell the Duke's Laws to his new subjects, Governor Nicolls held, in the tiny hamlet of Hempstead, a political convention—a first for Long Island. Nicolls summoned the most elite males from every English town on the Island. The representatives were required to bring with them evidence of title to their land and to receive new grants affirming that title. Much to their chagrin, the upshot of the convention was new orders against which they had no remedy. Representatives Jonas Wood and John Ketcham returned home to Huntington with copies of the Duke's Laws.[201, 202]

Long Island, Staten Island and Westchester were formed into an entity called Yorkshire, which was divided into three "ridings," as land was divided in England. Suffolk County, including Huntington, became part of the East Riding.[203]

The Duke's Laws regulated virtually every area of life—how arrests were to be carried out, how juries were to be picked, how much bounty was to be paid for dead wolves. Loosely based on English common law, the Duke's Laws allowed no representative assembly and made no provision for town meetings, an elected assembly, or for public schools. All shipping trade was required to flow through the port of New York. This generated much resentment amongst the settlers.

Bowing to the Dutch who had permitted religious dissidents such as Quakers, the Duke allowed for religious tolerance—unheard-of in the church-dominated government of Huntington. The laws set out rules by which a person could be arrested—on any day but the Sabbath. Jurors were to be paid three shillings six pence per diem.[204]

The laws also covered what Indians could and could not do. For example, Indians were required to fence in their cornfields and were specifically barred from practicing their own religion. One section of the laws said, "No Indian whatsoever shall at any time be suffered to powaw or performe outward worship to the Devil in any Towne within this Government."

In patents issued by three different governors-general, residents were given official title to the land. But another edict reads: "All persons who have any Grants or Patents of Townships, Lands or Houses, shall bring those Patents or Grants to the Governor and shall have them renewed, and shall pay two pounds for every 200 acres." That was the first town-wide tax. The Duke recognized the Magistrates that had been previously chosen in Huntington.

One of the Duke's Laws read: "A piece of ground shall be layed out whereupon shall be built a Town House and Prison. Pounds and Stocks shall be provided."

Another section regulated the value of foreign coins in circulation. Also, "If any man shall rob an orchard or garden or shall steal linen, woolen or other goods, he shall be whipped or pay double. . . If any man be found guilty of hog-stealing, he shall have one of his ears cut off . . . If any person shall express any but the true God, he shall be put to death." Death penalties were imposed for any of the following acts: For murder; Any child over 16 who shall strike a parent; For 2nd offence of stealing, and many other crimes. [205]

Another of the laws decreed that every 15th gallon of oil from whales cast upon the shore was the king's. It also said, "All Huntington cattle shall have the town mark of an E, that they may be recognized. All marked as such shall be taxed at 2 pounds per head."

Our life went on as if there were no threat hanging over us. It was spring planting season. There were fields to prepare, new animals to tend, leather to send to the drum factory and ship on to markets far and near.

Thom, now fifty years old, and still without a son and heir, took his place as captain of the *Sea Hawk* for one of the shipments, and because of this, our lives were forever changed.

At New York Harbor, as he turned to board the *Hawk* to return home, a small boy, quite ragged and dirty, came bursting up out of the sloop, tripped, and went sprawling at Thom's feet. The small pack of his belongings scattered across the wet planks of the dock. Thom grabbed his arm to help him up, but the boy struggled and fought to get away.

"Mary, he had such a look of terror in his eyes," Thom told me later. "My heart went out to him. When the boy found that I was not inclined to loose him, he suddenly changed and became the soul of submission.

"'Please, Sir, forgive my awkwardness.' The boy glanced about me and began picking up his meager belongings. I stooped to help, and to my amazement, found that one of the boy's trinkets was the Red Hawk amulet, surely the same as the one you lost last year when we were in Boston. So, here you are, Mary," Thom said as he handed it to me. "The totem is yours again."

"Wherever did the child find it?" I asked, as I clutched the treasure to my breast.

"Well, when I demanded to know the answer to that question, the boy stuttered and trembled as if he were sure of a terrible punishment to be meted out to him.

"'I-I f-found it t-tucked neath the ropes of the anchor,' he told me." 'Please, Sir, but I was hungry and was only looking for a scrap to eat. One of the sailors bade me come aboard and gave me bread.'"

Thom smiled a wry smile and shook his head. "The boy said he had been a stowaway on a ship from England. His parents died last fall, he told me, and the overseer of their land was such a cruel taskmaster that the boy escaped and slipped aboard one of the ships bound for New York where he might find his fortune." Thom's smile widened. "Such a dreamer the boy is, yet he is most wiry and strong — and also has the biggest hands and feet I've ever seen on a ten-year-old." Thom sobered and added, "Truthful, too, I believe. Through the rips in his shirt, I could see the stripes of the overseer's whip." My husband paused and looked at me with pleading eyes. "Oh, Mary, you should have heard his proposition to me, such as a grown man might make.

"'Sir,' he said, 'Do you keep animals? If you would have me as your indentured servant, I would serve you for seven years. I assure you, I am good with animals.'

"And what about planting and harvesting?" I asked. "For a moment the boy looked disheartened, but only for a moment.

"'Please, Sir, I am a quick learner. Would you show me the ways of a yeoman, for I would set my sights on reaching that goal by the time I am of age.'" A grin spread across Thom's face as he told me of the boy's lofty ambition.

"Does this boy have a name?" I said.

"He does indeed, a big name for a small boy. Walter Noakes, it is."

Suddenly, I felt the movement of the baby inside me for the first time and my breath quickened. "Thom Scudder, I believe you already love this Walter Noakes. But what will happen when your own son is born come December? Will you still have room in your heart for him?"

I could hardly hold back my laughter at the blank look that appeared on Thom's face.

"In December? This December?" His voice was joyous. "Oh, yes, I have more than enough room!" Thom was speechless for scarcely an instant. Then, in his usual way, he was bubbling over with plans. "Our house may become a little crowded. We'll push out the walls on either side of the fireplace and build a room for Anna Wing on one side next to the kitchen, and a room for Walter on the other." He paused to catch his breath. "A baby, you say? A little boy?"

I could but smile. "Or another girl," I said, flashing a teasing look at Thom. "I think we should name this one Sarah."

Until the Duke imposed his laws, the Huntington tavern had served our village well as an inn, town hall, courtroom, and Lord's Day meeting house. The Huntington church, formed twelve years before, had been an independent, self-governing body. Now, unhappily, the Duke had stolen away that independence.

Reverend Leverich's inclination was still to follow in the footsteps of John Calvin, but whatever his discomfort with having to live under the Duke's authority, the preacher was surely pleased with one part of the new mandate: Any town not already having a church had to immediately build one large enough to hold 200 people — proof that we were a theocracy.[206] The Duke's Laws required Reverend Leverich, as well as all other ministers under the new rule, to present his credentials to the government to prove he was not an ignorant pretender to the ministry. To abide by the Duke's Laws, he was obliged to preach every Lord's Day and must pray for the King, the Queen, the Duke of York and the Royal Family.[207,208]

The new laws provided specific directions for the building of a church, and Huntington followed them to the letter. We accomplished the raising of the meeting house with an air of community celebration. The women exhibited their cooking skills, bringing baskets filled with roasts, sallats,[209] pies and cakes — their finest recipes — to spread out on linen-covered planks set up for the noon meal. Each male supplied nails, logs, and lumber, labor, the use of horses, and a barrel of rum. In fact, the corner posts were baptized in rum!

In spite of the air of celebration, the meeting house was built with no frills, no vain or extravagant show. A dry, woody smell pervaded the area. With few windows in the structure, the light was dim, and the air close. In winter, it was sunless, frigid, drab. In summer, it turned into a seething, glaring, pine-smelling hothouse.

The only objects of beauty were the webs of spiders that hung from every rafter like grey funeral garlands — unless you consider the furry black bats that hung from the ceiling, occasionally darting from one corner to another, barely missing the preacher's head. Or the red squirrels that leapt through the loft, attracted by the corn stored there. Or, when the door was left open to coax a bit of a breeze inside, the dark blue plumage of the swallows that flitted in and out.

Of course, the Duke believed in divine right, so his specifications for the order of seating had no effect on the Puritan concept of determining the placement of pews according to social status. For the safety of the congregation, soldiers sat near the doors.

As decreed by the Duke, on the green near the meeting house, workmen erected stocks, whipping posts, pillory, and cage.

The drum signaled people to worship. We had no bell at this time in Huntington.

According to the decree, we walked to church in decent order, Thom and I walking first, Elizabeth and Walter following in quiet procession. Anna Wing walked beside me carrying Maria until she was old enough to walk with her sister. Walter chose to sit with Thom, though other boys, clad in knee breeches and homespun coats, dragged along and took their places at the back of the church where they fidgeted, squirmed, and ducked the judicious raps of the tithing man.[210] Except for the new building, nothing much had changed at the meeting house.

Although Reverend Leverich sometimes addressed social issues, usually he preached on a theological topic, a rational exposition supported by quotations from scripture and drawing on his own library of Bible commentaries.

One Sunday a month was Communion Sunday, a time for the congregation to share the Lord's Supper following the command of Jesus to "do this in remembrance of me."

On other Lord's Days, a baptism might follow the afternoon sermon, ending with public announcements — banns of marriage or the governor's proclamation of a day of public fast or thanksgiving.

On weekdays, instead of meeting at the tavern next door for town meetings and other civic events, the community gathered at the new meeting house, and then, after the meeting, they adjourned to the tavern for a sociable drink or two.

&)

In June that year, at Mecox Bay, Papa died of a hectic fever, and though we had not oft been together since my marriage, my sun turned black. Only my dear family and the thought that Papa had gone to be with Mama carried me through. Yet from that tree of sorrow came the fruits of joy when my dear sister Abbie, her husband, Samuel King, and their two small children from Southold joined us all in Southampton for our father's funeral and the reading of his will.

Papa's will, the first ever recorded in the City of New York under the British, gave clear evidence of his earthly success — cattle, housing, business property, goods, monies, and lands, and I felt a flush of pride as my brother Hal, whom Papa had appointed executor, read the document to us:

The Last Will and Testament of William Ludlam, Sr.: I commend my soul to God, and my Estate I bestow as followeth:

Imprimus:

My Will is that my sonn William shall have a Cow.

I do give unto my daughter Grace one Cow.

I do give unto my daughter Mary one Cow.

I do give unto my daughter Frances one Cow.

I do give unto my sonn Anthony all my Housing and Land at the old Ground and fifty Pound comming to him and his heirs forever. Provided that my sonn Henry shall have a third part of ye said Land for the Terme of seven years after the date hereof.

I do give unto my sonn Joseph my dwelling House with two acres of Land adjoing to the Mill and Mill Pond on the east side of the Mill and with fifty pound comming to him and his Heirs forever.

I do give unto ye eldest Childe of my sonn William fifty shillings and my sonn Henry's Childe fifty shillings and my Daughter Mary's eldest chile fifty shillings.

That whereas there is a covenant made between me and Sam Davis, the said Samuell Davis is to enjy the Cowes and ye Benefitt of the House and Land specified in said covenant from the date hereof until the fourth of March next ensuing.

9thly and Lastly. I do will that my sonn Henry bee my Executor and to pay or cause to be Paid all my Debts and also all the above mentioned Legacyes and also to build up the Mill that now is sufficiently, vizt., halfe at his own proper charge and the other halffe out of my estate, and my sonn Henry to have halfe of the said Mill to him and his Heires forever, [211] *and my sonn Joseph the other halfe to him and his Heires forever. Also I do give unto my sonn Henry fifity Pound comming with and belonging to the Land he hath now in possesson as it standeth upon Record. Also I do give unto the said Henry Thirty-six acres of Land lying and being at ye Mill Pond head with all my household Goods, Cattle or Cattles whatsoever, to him and his heires forever. Witness my hand the day and year above written*

Signed: William Ludlam [212]

Our Ludlam family's time together seemed all too short—a time to mourn, a time to embrace, then time to say goodbye. There was work to do at home. Harvest time was upon us.

Thom was in an unusually pensive mood on the way home. "So, your father has left you a cow," he said with a gentle smile. "Perhaps, if I am to have only daughters to inherit my wealth, instead of land, I should buy cows."

"Perhaps you should," I said. "At least you have Walter."

The boy, though a bit awkward, was, as he had promised, a quick learner. At first, he started in the barn, working with the animals and milking the cows.

Late the first night after we'd returned home, I watched through the window as Walter, practically strutting with success, carried the bucket of milk to the house. As he entered the door, he held the bucket toward Thom to show his accomplishment. "Look, Sir—"

Suddenly Walter tripped and sprawled in the threshold. The milk went everywhere, splashing across the floor and onto Thom's shoes. Thom jumped up and lunged toward Walter, aiming to steady him as he got up. With a fearful look, Walter flinched as Thom moved toward him, then with a dash, he turned and fled the barn.

Later, Thom told me he'd found Walter hiding in the hay, trembling. "After assuring him that I'd oft spilt milk and worse when I was a boy, Walter arose, wiped his nose with his sleeve, squared his shoulders, and swore his allegiance.

" 'Sir, Not since my parents died have I been treated with such kindness,' the boy said."

Walter liked caring for the cattle, and when Elizabeth asked him why, I heard him say, "Because in the quietness of the meadows, I like to listen." He closed his eyes for a moment and then said, "My own Pa told me that the life of God is within all things if we would but listen."

Elizabeth looked at him with adoring eyes. "But Walter, if God is in everything, must you always do your listening in the meadow? Can't you hear Him when you're working in the field?"

"For such a small girl, you ask remarkable questions," he said. "Can you read?"

"Oh, yes. Mama is teaching me. But I'd rather cook and clean with Anna Wing, or help Mama with Maria. Someday I will be a mother."

"I want to be a kind yeoman like your Papa," he answered. "But a yeoman needs to read and do numbers. One day perhaps I will have my own field. I have no parents to teach me to read, and no father to leave me a cow or land, but I will work hard."

At the end of the first day of using the sickle, Walter came in from the field covered with sweat and grime. After he'd washed up, Elizabeth touched his hand and asked him to play London Bridge with her.

I saw the surprise and disappointment in her eyes when he jerked his hand away, but she was quicker than I to see what was wrong.

"Look, Mama, look at Walter's hands. He needs some ointment from your special cupboard."

On his palms and fingers were rows of red open sores—blisters broken from working with unaccustomed tools. When Thom asked to see and then insisted that the boy's hands be bandaged, Walter protested.

"I must do my chores! Bossy is waiting for me."

"You've done the work of a man, today, Walter," Thom said as he clapped the boy on his shoulder. "I'll do the milking tonight."

🕉

The summer and fall of 1665 passed quickly. Elizabeth was almost eight, and Maria, almost four. Walter, who said he, like Thom, was born on the 5th of November, would be eleven. Walter endeared himself to us daily. He and Anna Wing were as much a part of us as kin would be.

Walter said he had celebrated Bonfire Day in England, and to please him we cooked meat on a spit outside and sat on cold benches in the November dusk, telling stories to celebrate.

"Papa, tell us about the Fox," Maria begged as she snuggled on Thom's lap.

"The fox?" Thom asked with a grin. "Oh, might you mean Guy Fawkes? Well, Fawkes was in a group of religious conspirators who wanted to blow up King James and his family as well as the House of Lords...."

Maria yawned, and before he had gone further, she was fast asleep. The sky had darkened and storm clouds moving in had hidden the stars and moon, turning the sky from deep blue to ebony.

"I'm shivering, Mama," Elizabeth said. "Let's go in to bed."

We all arose to help Anna Wing gather up our leftover foodstuffs and trenchers, and headed inside. My legs were so stiff from sitting on the cold bench I could hardly walk, and the child within me was also protesting with kicks that took my breath away.

On 16 December, the baby arrived. Ironically, though it was my easiest birth, the whole community of Huntington women was there to assist Goody Leverich with the delivery. Anna Wing ran back and forth from kitchen, to parlor, to birthing room, gathering towels and water at Ellen Leverich's request, then brought in cakes and drinks for the women—their usual birthing celebration, then back to the kitchen to care for Elizabeth and Maria.

Poor Thom, excluded from the birthing process, took refuge in the barn with only Walter at his side. 'Twas there Anna Wing found him waiting.

"You can come in now, Goodman Scudder. Come in and see your new daughter."

Twenty

&

Anno Dom 1666-1668
Huntington, Long Island, New York

Our town of Huntington grew and in 1666, when Governor Nicolls issued a patent defining its territory and boundaries, we had 57 freeholders and heads of families living within our boundaries. The patent records:

> *Whereas there is a certain Town within this government called and known by the name of Huntington, now in the tenure and occupation of several Freeholders and Inhabitants, the same is confirmed to Jonas Wood, Wm. Leveridge, Robert Seeley, John Ketcham, Thomas Skidmore, Isaac Platt, Thomas Jones and Thomas Weeks, in behalf of themselves and associates.*

That was the autumn when Thom's mother died. On her tombstone next to her husband's inscription, they engraved these words:

Here lies ye Body of ye
Dearly Beloved and Godly Wife and Mother,
Mrs. Elizabeth Scudder
who Fell Asleep in Jesus
September ye 9th Anno Dom 1666 in ye 75th year of her age.

Before we left the Scudder home in Salem, Thom's sister, Elizabeth Bartholomew, brought forth gifts that her mother had asked her to give to her 13 granddaughters when the time came.

Sarah and Maria were too young to appreciate the careful stitches and time their grandmother had applied to their samplers, but Elizabeth could not have been more blessed.

Together, Elizabeth and I read the words her grandmother had stitched:

Proverbs 31
Who can find a virtuous woman?
For her price is far above rubies.
She seeketh wool, and flax,
and worketh willingly with her hands.
She stretcheth out her hand to the poor;
she reacheth forth to the needy.
Strength and honour are her clothing;
and she shall rejoice in time to come.
She looketh well to the ways of her household,
and eateth not the bread of idleness.
Her children rise up, and call her blessed;
her husband also, and he praiseth her.

Elizabeth age 9 1600

My daughter's eyes were wide as we read the last line. "Mama, Grandmother's name was the same as mine, and she was my age when she embroidered the words—the duties of a good wife. Just look at her beautiful flowers!"

Bright silk threads of copper, cream, blues, greens, magenta, pinks, and gold meandered in a floral border around her linen sampler. Cross-stitches, Algerian eyes, chain stitches in lovely hues created by twisting together strands of two different colors.

After his mother's death, Thom worked harder than ever, perhaps to quell his sorrow. Often leaving hired overseers in charge of the tannery and farmland, he loaded one boat or the other to ship a load of various products to market in New York. And then, Thomas was chosen Town Constable. Even when he was home, I was lonely, for we seldom stopped for morning devotions, and at night, he oft fell asleep before our usual discussions and prayers.

In late fall, the weather was unusually cold and snowy, but by then the harvest was in, the herbs and fruits were gathered and dried, and the meats butchered and cured and hung in the keeping room. When Thom was home, he and Walter spent time in the house, sometimes working on a new trundle bed for the girls, paneling the rooms added for Anna Wing and Walter with smooth pine boards, or repairing the chinks in the other walls to keep out the cold. Thom worked in silence, and though Walter's attempts to carry on a conversation were rebuffed, the boy seemed to understand. Two orphans, they worked side by side.

On the rare occasions when the baby was fussy, Walter surprised me by the tenderness he displayed when he rocked Sarah's cradle to comfort her. He had a gift for making up rhymes and funny little ditties, and when Sarah was falling to sleep, he sang to her:

The love and affection of heaven be to you,
The love and affection of the saints be to you,
The love and affection of the angels be to you,
The love and affection of the sun be to you,

The love and affection of the moon be to you,
each day and each night of your life,
To keep you from haters, to keep you from harmers,
to keep you from oppressors.

"Where did you learn that song, Walter?" I asked.

He hesitated as if listening for the answer. "So long ago it was," he said. Finally he spoke again. "I think it is my mother's voice I am hearing."

Although Elizabeth was happiest when helping Anna Wing knead the bread or do the knitting, I found great joy in teaching her to read and write. To hold her interest in learning the ABCs, I helped her embroider the letters on a sampler—careful cross-stitches on a square of linen. When Walter, with Thom's help, fashioned a frame for the sampler and hung it on the wall next to the table, Elizabeth was delighted. However, when Walter asked her to teach him the letters, she said without a trace of curiosity, "I do not know the meaning. I only stitched the pattern Mama drew for me."

I am sure she caught the flicker of disappointment in Walter's eyes, for after he had gone to the barn to care for the animals, Elizabeth whispered to me, as if he might be listening, "Mama, show me the letters that spell Walter Noakes."

Together, as Elizabeth learned the alphabet, we marked a new linen square. Each morning and evening when Walter was outside, she slipped her needlework out of the basket and added more details, then quickly put it away whenever she heard him coming.

When she had embroidered his name and birth date, around the border she cross-stitched the alphabet and then asked me to show her letters that spelled her own name and age. Above the lower border, she signed her work.

"Look, Mama, there's a big blank spot in the middle. Show me how to write Walter's song," she said.

I printed the letters for her to use as a guide, and in the blank spot, she marked a pattern of tiny stitches to form the words.

"Walter likes blue, Mama. Do we have blue thread?"

I dug into my sewing basket and found a skein of bright blue.

On November 5, 1666, she removed her first sampler from the frame and replaced it with her latest handiwork.

"When Papa and Walter come in for breakfast, may Walter sit here across from the sampler?" she asked.

I nodded and smiled as she traced the letters with her finger, reading the words she had stitched.

WALTER NOAKES
born November 5th 1654
The love and affection of heaven be to you
each day and each night of your life

ELIZABETH SCUDDER age 8

It was not until Walter raised his head after bowing for Thom's blessing that he saw the sampler. Shyly, Elizabeth ducked her head, but I watched with enjoyment as his face and ears turned pink, and a smile bloomed across his face. "You made this for me, Elizabeth?"

Their eyes met, and quickly Walter looked away, swiping at his eyes before the tears could fall.

"Working in the barn or fields, I hear words that I must say though I cannot speak them aloud." Walter paused and looked up at me with solemn eyes. "When I am not needed in the fields, Mother Scudder, would you please teach me the letters?" Softly then, he added, "I wish to write on paper what God writes on my heart."

Once, at day's end when lessons were over, while nursing Sarah, I seemed to hear the voice of my own mother telling a story that I had nearly forgotten. The children gathered around me, and I told it to them—the parts I could recall, making up the rest as I went along. "Once, there was a young boy," I began... "umm, Sekáon he was called. He had no father or mother for they had long been lost to him. Deep in the mine of a great mountain, he worked for a cruel taskmaster. Digging, digging, always digging. His pay was little, sometimes only a crust of bread.

"'That's all there is,' growled the cruel taskmaster. 'Who do you think I am? Midas? Don't you understand that the King demands a huge share of my diggings? There is hardly enough left to fill my own belly.'

"One day when Sekáon was digging in the dark, subterranean caves of the mountain, when he stood to wipe the sweat from his brow, he tripped over his shovel and fell sprawling in the dirt. Arising, he made an error in judgment and took a different turn. Far ahead stretching into the distance, he could see a golden gleam, a thread of light. He continued in that direction, digging as he went, for he would not shirk his job no matter how cruel his master might be. To his wondering eyes, he discovered an ugly old woman with golden hair sitting on a rock ahead of him, knitting a long thread of light. With every beat of her heart, the thread pulsed and shimmered like a firefly in the darkness.

"'Young man, are you lost?' the old woman asked in a faint voice.

"'Perhaps I am, but once I eat this crust of bread, I think I will have the strength to find my way back.' Sekáon paused and said, 'Mother, are you hungry? Here, let me share my bread with you.'

"The old woman was pleased, and took a piece of the bread that Sekáon offered. 'Here,' she said, handing the boy a small length of the thread of light she had knitted. 'Take this with you to guide your way. If you should lose your grasp, simply listen and it will call to you, and you shall once again take it in your hand. It will surely lead you home.'

"'Where is my home?' Sekáon asked. 'Where will it lead?'

"But the old woman had disappeared."

"And did he find his way, Mama?"

Walter nodded. "I think he did, Elizabeth." In a soft voice he added, "For a time, he may have lost hold of the thread of light, but I think he found it again when he went sprawling at your Papa's feet on the *Sea Hawk*." Shyly, he looked up at me. "But you are mistaken, Mother Scudder, about the woman who first gave Sekáon the thread," he said. "She is quite beautiful, and not ugly or old at all."

That winter, ice blocked the waterways between Huntington and New York, and Thom found work enough to do at the tannery and the barn, bedding the animals down with fresh hay from the autumn crops. How good it was to have him close, although the child within me kicked and moved about so impatiently that neither Thom nor I slept well once we were finally together again in our own bed.

On January 7, 1668, when my time for delivery came, Thom sent Walter to get Goody Leverich. Before others could arrive to aid with the birthing, the child made an appearance. As soon as the cord was snipped, Ellen Leverich wrapped the babe in a blanket, then throwing open the curtains around my bed, she welcomed Thom to hold his newborn babe. I watched as he took the mewling infant from her, and folded back the blanket that he might see this child of his loins. The baby, unimpressed by the entire ruckus, stretched, stiffened, and urinated in a clear spouting geyser, raining over the crags of Thom's cheeks and chin.

Thom began laughing, his shoulders shaking, his knees sagging until he could no longer stand. He plopped into his armed chair, holding the baby with one hand and wiping his face with the other. "My son, my little lamb," he said as he cuddled the child to the warmth of his chest. "I think you have it backwards, young Benjamin Scudder. It is I who should baptize you."

ഌ

I had thought that with the birth of Benjamin, his first living son, Thom would put an additional burden of work on his laborers that he might spend more time at home. In fact, the opposite happened. Thom seemed compelled to work ever harder. With Walter by his side, Thom spent extra hours at the tannery, saw to the loading of the leather to be sent to the drum factory, and then took the helm of one or another of his ships, sailing the goods to market through New York. When his ships returned to Huntington Harbor, there was always farm work to oversee. I must admit Walter was receiving a good education at Thom's side, but I missed the young man who every week seemed to grow in wisdom and stature. It amused me to see him with pen and paper in hand, scheduling tasks of the coming days. So like his mentor. I could not but admire Thom for his dedication to his tasks, but also could not help feeling disappointment that he found it necessary to work such long hours.

Of course, even with the ever-faithful Anna Wing to help me, my days were filled dawn to dusk with a medley of household sounds and duties created by three small daughters and a new baby. Actually, there were few chores that ten-year-old Elizabeth could not handle competently. She taught Maria how to feed the calves and chickens and gather eggs, and how to gather wood to feed the fireplace. With the arrival of planting season, the girls helped me seed and water the garden and later tend it, hoeing weeds, and cultivating the soil around the plants. Joyfully we watched tender green leaves put forth blossoms that turned into tiny pods of peas and beans. Huge golden blooms soon became small globes that would grow and ripen into squash and pumpkins.

Before bedtime, as I nursed Benjamin, I read to the children from the Psalms and the love chapters of John and Galatians, adding an occasional fairy tale told by heart. Sarah and Maria were most attentive, but Elizabeth oft appeared to be daydreaming rather than listening.

When Benjamin finished nursing, Anna Wing took him and tucked him into his cradle beside her bed. "Time for bed for you too, my daughters," I said. We prayed together, asking God to take care of Walter and Papa while they were away, and that He watch over us through the night.

Because Elizabeth was the oldest, I allowed her to stay up for a while. By candlelight, she had begun embroidering blocks for a quilt. A bride's quilt, she told me, like her cousin Liza Bartholomew, who pined for the handsome John Pilgrim of Salem.

"Liza told me her father will not give her a dowry until the quilt is finished," my daughter said.

She completed a petal stitch, then looked up for a moment. "Cousin Liza fears she will be an old maiden ere that happens. But she dallies, and besides, I can stitch much faster than she can." She paused to thread a golden strand on her needle, then with eyes honest and clear as spring water, she said, "Do you think Papa will give me a dowry?"

Softly clearing my throat, I tried to hide my growing amusement. "He loves you very much, Elizabeth. The young man who asks for your hand will have to be very special."

"Of course," she said. "A man like Papa."

"And who do you think that might be?" I asked.

Elizabeth looked up at me, eyes round with surprise. "Prithee, Mama, don't you know? It will be Walter, of course."

I watched my daughter with a great, overflowing affection. Surely, it would be many years before Walter came a-wooing.

Elizabeth put away her broidery, stood and stretched. "Goodnight, Mama. It's good to have someone to talk to. I'll see you in the morning."

Yes, it was good to talk, but right then I sorely missed my husband. When we could again have the intimate discussions we used to have after the children were in bed. Surely, it was time.

In the hush of the room, I heard Benjamin cry out, and then the gentle rocking of his cradle quieting him. Dear Anna Wing. Whatever would I do without her?

I returned the Bible to the shelf, slipped into my own linen night shift, and stretched out on the bed Thom shared with me when he was home. In the stillness, I could hear the September music of the night. Owls. Tree frogs. The night bird calling across the grey mist rolling in from the bay. Far away in the dark region of the green conifers, the faint "Kree-eee-ar" of the Red-Tailed Hawk.

That summer, no sooner had my brother Luddie sold his mill to Goodman Meggs than talk began that the fever spreading in the area may have been caused by the stagnating waste that the mill poured into the bay.

℘

On the first Lord's Day in September, our baby, four and a half month-old Benjamin, awoke me with piteous crying. The child was burning with fever. Feebly, he tried to nurse but could not keep the milk down. By Monday, his skin and eyes had tinges of yellow, and neither the fever nor his listless crying had abated, yet I could find no relief for him. We spooned feverfew into the baby's mouth and when he heaved it forth, we tried willow bark tea, to no avail. Praying without ceasing for answers to my son's affliction, I scoured my memory for the herbal remedies Nowedanah had taught me long ago. Finally, Anna Wing took Benjamin in her arms, and said, "My mother made cinquefoil tea to cool the blood. Roots must be dug only in full moon at midnight," she insisted.

I remembered seeing wild cinquefoil plants in a nearby field, but I could not wait for midnight. I handed Maria the basin of cool water and the cloth that she might soothe the baby while Anna Wing held him. "Elizabeth," I said, "prithee make sure there is boiling water enough for tea, and then feed Sarah. She has not eaten this morn."

Picking up a digging tool from the kitchen shelf, I rushed to a nearby field along the road to the Leverich house. I was digging and pulling at the plant when Ellen Leverich called to me.

As I worked, I explained why we had missed the Lord's Day service, and then listened as she told me her frightening news. Young John Ludlam, my nephew, had come rapping at their door on Saturday, she said, asking that Reverend Leverich come to the Ludlam home, not only for prayer but also for his skills as a physician. His papa, John told him, had fallen gravely ill with chills and fever. Luddie was vomiting and tinged with yellow like baby Benjamin, suffering with a terrible headache and back pains.

When I asked what physic Reverend Leverich had prescribed, Ellen said, "Cinquefoil tea."

God had surely heard my prayers. Both Benjamin and his Uncle Luddie would soon be well again.

I hurried home with the root of the cinquefoil. "Here, Elizabeth," I said. "Cut a chunk of the root and pound it to a pulp in the pestle we use to make flour, then let the pith of the root steep in boiling water." I handed her the plant, then hurried to feel the baby's forehead and chest.

ဆာ

That afternoon, Thom finally returned from a long trip to Boston and back, his eyes rimmed with exhaustion. He found me frantically applying cooling cloths to wee Benjamin's face and body and trying to coax him to suck on my finger after dipping it in sugar and the cinquefoil tea.

Seeing the baby, Thom's eyes wild in a look of grief and terror, he took Benjamin into his arms and sat rocking his precious son all through the third dreadful night of illness. I knew Thom could feel the heat of Benjamin's fever and his rapid breathing and heartbeat. With every pitiable cry of the baby, my dear husband's face told me he, too, was suffering.

Though exhausted to the peak of my endurance, I could not sleep. I knelt by my bed, praying, then rose every few hours to prepare a new batch of cinquefoil tea and cool cloths to ease the fever. I think I had nearly dozed off when Thom, still holding our son, called and asked me to read to him. "The scripture in Exodus about the iniquity of the fathers, prithee," he said.

"Would you not prefer the promises of the New Testament?" I asked.

"No," he said softly. "I see now that my ill-chosen devotion to earthly treasures has been like a snake curled up in the grass, waiting, and now it has struck, catching me off guard. I have been too busy for the devotion I owe to God and my family."[213]

And so I sat at the table and read the scripture that speaks of visiting the iniquity of the fathers upon the children and upon the children's children unto the third and to the fourth generation.

Thom arose and handed the baby to me. He turned then, and I could hardly bear the sound of anguish in his voice as he cried out, "Father, forgive me. Do not desert me now, though in my iniquity I have forgotten to put Thee first. But, Lord, this Child of the Promise, while slow in coming to us, was conceived and born through your miraculous creative power. Do not take him from us. A son should not die before his father. Take me instead."

Thom's knees buckled and he fell, face down on our bed, asleep. Quietly, I moved into Thom's chair with Benjamin. Though sleeping, Thom moved restlessly, struggling as if he were wrestling with the demons of hell.

Dawn came—the morning after the third day. Benjamin's symptoms had receded, the fever was gone, and as I held him, he nosed against my breast, rooting and grunting with pleasure like a piglet at his mother's teat. Elation and joy flooded every fiber of my being.

Immediately Thom roused, sat up, and looked toward Benjamin with wonder and amazement. Within his eyes, though, I saw the strangest expression. Uncertainty and doubt, mixed with a wonderful anticipation and optimism.

"Whilst you feed our little one, Mary, I must tell you of the incredible vision that came to me in my sleep. A vision of Abraham with his son on the altar, ready for sacrifice. My heart went out to him that he surely must lose his only son."

Thom looked at me as if for confirmation that he was really voicing such an inconceivable story or yet dreaming. I nodded expectantly, and he continued.

"Then I heard a voice saying, Hear Me now, Thomas Scudder. Your lamb is not the sacrifice I demand." Thom took a big breath and went on. "Then the voice said, Beloved—he called me beloved!—there is nothing amiss in the love you feel for your spouse and children or in the blessings earned by the sweat of your brow as long as you do not crowd me out of your life.

"Mary, the words are written on the tablets of my heart for I may read them still: *Go forth,* the voice said and not in the words of our Geneva Bible, but in the words of our own day. *Use fully all of the talents and abilities I have given you, but not for your own glory. And to you I make an everlasting promise: I will be your God and the God of your descendants.*"

Who can understand the way of the Lord? Our son returned to us healthy and whole. My brother Luddie did not. Though Luddie's symptoms receded after the third day, they returned with a vengeance, bleeding into the skin and extreme prostration. By week's end, he lapsed into delirium and coma, and died.

Fit, sick, dead in one week's space. Engrave the remembrance of death on thy heart; when, as thou dost see, how swiftly hours depart.

My brother Luddie left five children between the ages of one and ten.

Why, God? Why? I cannot understand.

21st Century
Memory Catchers' Office

The Sony card was full and the switch clicked off. Grand-Mary sat quietly, as if still mourning her brother Luddie.

When she raised her head, I was ready with questions.

"What happened to Luddie's wife and children?"

"Well," she said, "his wife married Nehemiah Smith soon after Luddie died, and they moved with the children to the western end of Long Island. Within a few years the area was given the name of Queens, for Catherine of Braganza, the Catholic wife of King Charles II.

"And the mill?"

"Well, you might say Luddie, good man that he was, left his mark on the town. The canal that conveyed water to the mill wheel could be traced for years.

"However, when the new owner, Mark Meggs, sold the mill to the town, they tore it down, and drained the pond.[214] Goodman Meggs and his wife moved across the sound to Connecticut, and I heard tell that he and his wife both died shortly after of another outbreak of yellow fever."

I glanced down at my notes, but when I raised my head to ask another question, Grand-Mary had faded from view. I switched on the Sony, turned to my computer, and began transcribing the latest chapter of Grand-Mary's story.

It was not until the fourth of July that Grand-Mary reappeared in my office, sitting in her usual chair.

"Such a noisome day it is!" she said, holding her hands over her ears. "Reminds me of the sounds of the militia practicing their drills in Huntington, but I see no guns in evidence. Is this a protest? Or a celebration of victory against taxation? I thought that problem was finally settled. In my day, I recall, the demands of Francis Lovelace, proclaimed governor of New York by King Charles II himself, created much worry." Grand-Mary shook her head, remembering how distressed Thom had been in 1670.

"When Governor Lovelace demanded money to repair the fort at New York, nearly all of the English towns voted to refuse to obey the order. And why should they not refuse? They had no one to speak for them. The King's subjects in England at least had Parliament.

"I clearly recall my husband's passionate dislike of the governor." Grand-Mary laughed then. "Once Thom suggested that we would all be better off if Francis Lovelace had become a poet like his philandering brother Richard."

Grand-Mary straightened her shoulders and seemed to sit a bit taller.

"I was so proud of Thom and the other men of Huntington," she said, "for the emphatic stand they took in a document they sent to the governor:

We of the town of Huntington can not see cause to contribute anything toward the Repair of the forte for these following reasons: First, because we conceive we are deprived of the liberties of Englishmen; secondly, we conceive we have little or no benefits of the Law; thirdly, we can not conceive of any benefit or safety we can expect from the fort; fourthly, we find ourselves so much disenabled by manifold troubles when we thought ourselves in peace that we can not imparte with any such disbursement.

"When Lovelace received a copy of their refusal, 'twas said he went into a rage. 'Scandalous!' he shouted. 'Illegal and seditious! Burn the document!'

"Perhaps you know not, my dear granddaughter, that Huntington never bowed to the governor's demands. And though it was a long time coming, this spirited protest, one of the earliest defiances against taxation without representation, accomplished its purpose."[215] Grand-Mary raised an eyebrow, perhaps testing my knowledge of American History. "Was this not the resistance that led, a hundred years later, to the Revolution? [216] Is this not why you celebrate Independence Day?"

She stood and ran her finger over the names in the sprawling family tree hanging on my office wall. "Look," she said. "Just look at all my descendants who fought for independence in that war. I am so proud of them all!"

Again, she took her seat beside me. "My time here is nearing the end. My purpose is nearly fulfilled. Thank you, Granddaughter."

I nodded and turned on the Sony, but my usual feeling of accomplishment was mixed with regret.

A glimmer of sadness in her eyes quickly changed to joy. Poised and eager, she said, "Now, shall we get on with my story? I have miles to go."

Twenty-one

 ࣾ

Luddie's death left a hollow spot in my heart, and I regretted that we had not spent more time together in recent months. To compound the loneliness for Luddie, my good friend Ellen Leverich, her sons and husband, Caleb, Eleazer, and Reverend Leverich, soon moved away to Newtown.

Having grown up in the home of my Aunt Alice and Uncle Robert Fordham, a minister, and then living most of my married life under the ministry of Reverend Will Leverich, I missed hearing the words brought to us each Lord's Day.

When no traveling preacher was available, oft a respected town father of Huntington Village would lead the meeting, sometimes bringing a helpful homily but more often than not, a disappointing rant. In Reverend Leverich's absence, the town belatedly admitted to the good he had done and the gratitude they owed him.

The next years passed in relative tranquility. Thom, in one of our evening discussions, said to me, "I believe I have a better idea now what it is God wants me to do. I see things that I had missed before." With that revelation, he revised his priorities.

"Mary, I'm going to sell our ships. Taxes are too heavy to allow the profit of a few years ago. And they take me away from other loves — you, and the children, and the land."

It was sad to think of the *Sea Hawk* in a stranger's possession, but the memories would linger — the voyage from Boston Harbor to Southampton when I was nine and a newcomer to the New World. The lovely days after our marriage as we sailed to Babylon. The journey around the island from Southampton to Southold to our new home in Huntington. Ah, such memories.

Thom sold the schooner, and not only received a good price for it, but better yet, he sold it to cousins from Barnstable, sea faring people, even the women of the family. With the profit from the schooner, Thom bought cattle and more land, southeast into the hills of Huntington. The Barnstable cousins offered a good price for the *Sea Hawk* if Thom should decide to sell.

With God in first place, his notion of love toward his family shifted from a continual drive for material success in business to a determination to be a constant presence in our home. No doubt this explains the timely increase of children in our home.

In 1669, in the eleventh year of our marriage, when Benjamin was just learning to scamper around the house into one thing and then the other, our daughter Mercy was born.

Scarcely nine months later, much to the delight of my husband, I delivered another son. We named him Timothy.

By the winter of baby Timothy's weaning, no matter how cold the wind blew, I seemed to be spending both day and night fanning myself and wiping the sweat from my brow. God had seen fit to visit the ending cycle of Eve's curse upon me, and forsooth, at this time it seemed more blessing than blight.

My days marched in hurried steps, one busy day blurring into another. Indeed, I cannot say whether it was Benjamin or Timothy who was born in such an ice storm that the midwives had trouble making their way to the birthing. And was it Sarah or Mercy whose first words were, "Papa, hold me?" Trying to recall those childbearing years is like looking back into a foggy mirror, with only a few clear-cut scenes reflected in vivid color.

While I was enduring the ending cycle of the curse, my daughter Elizabeth, now thirteen years old, was just beginning. In our time together, after the young ones were fast asleep and Walter and Thom were still out tending the animals, I tried to do my duty, telling her about God's plan for love, and families, and how nature worked.

Perhaps she was more observant than I thought, for in response, she would blush and say, "Oh, Mama, I know," and quickly change the subject.

My lovely daughter Elizabeth had grown into a fine, healthy young woman — thoughtful, industrious, and quite contented with her lot. A Martha, not a Mary. There were very few housewifely duties she could not accomplish. Gardening, cooking, sewing, caring for her younger siblings. She persuaded her papa to buy a spinning wheel, and then took lessons from a neighbor skilled in the art. The thread she spun from flax we grew was carried to a weaver who turned it into fine cloth, some dyed and some bleached pure white, then sent it to us, ready to be stitched into garments, always saving — Elizabeth insisted on this — the white fabric for her bride's quilt blocks.

Walter, as well as Maria and Sarah, surpassed Elizabeth in reading skills, but she was content as long as she could share in our daily scripture readings. Actually, that was as much as girls were expected to learn in my day. Elizabeth excelled in other skills. Quilt making became her joy! The only book I remember her reading was one her papa brought her when he returned from a marketing trip. *How to Stitch Broderie de Marseille.* Detailing the art of quilts created in a French nunnery, it explained how to plan the composition, transfer the design to the fabric, stitch the narrow channels, and finally, how to use a long needle to draw yarn through the channels and motifs to raise the design and realize the pattern.

During the year of the quilt, Elizabeth gave up her place working beside Anna Wing to her younger sisters and me. She spent hours far into the night turning white squares of linen into blocks of carefully stitched symbols of love and fidelity, symbols she found in the Songs of Solomon — pomegranates and apples and doves.

Elizabeth's eyes shone when, after completing the last embroidered block, she stitched the entire thing together, one block to another until it grew large enough to make a full coverlet. "Come see, Mama. My bride's quilt is nearly finished. I have spread it over my bed in the loft. Come see!"

I climbed to the loft as she requested. One glance at her coverlet astounded me, so lovely it was. "Glory be, Elizabeth. Glory, glory!" She let me put my arms around her, and I gave my remarkable daughter a hug. "What lovely work you have done, my darling. But why is the center block empty?"

"It's a bride's quilt, Mama. That square is for my initials and those of my husband, dost thou not know?"

Thirteen, she was, and already preparing for a wedding. Tears came to my eyes but I quickly wiped them away as I realized the changes that were soon coming. With one hand on each of her shoulders, I leaned back slightly to view this wonderful work of God's own hand. "Oh, my little Elizabeth," I said. "While I was not looking, you have become a young woman." A lump in my throat arose. "My dear, the work you have done on the quilt is as exquisite as any full-grown woman could possibly do. You are indeed an artist."

Elizabeth ducked her head, but I felt the lift of her shoulders and witnessed the glow of her eyes.

"Prithee, Mama," she said, "can you help me attach a silk backing and fill it with down?"

Her request touched me deeply. The scars of rejection I had inflicted when she was a tiny baby had healed years ago, but there was still a shadow of distance between us. It would break my heart to say no to her request, yet I could not hold a needle without my fingers soon becoming useless claws. Suddenly, I knew what we could do.

"Elizabeth, prithee, come with me to the Women's Bible Study on the morrow. The women quilt while they read, and they could quickly stitch the backing to your lovely work and add a bit of down to make it softer yet.

"Thank you, Mama," she said. "I dream of having all kinds of pretty things in my home after I marry. But with all the chores to be done, I will have little time for making pretty things."

Once the bride's quilt was complete, Elizabeth packed it away in a trunk with other pieces she had made. Instead of beginning a new project or returning to her work in the house, she began following Walter to the barn to help him tend to the milking, gather eggs, feed the chickens and other animals, and then pitch clean hay from the loft as bedding for the flocks.

I do not remember giggling when I was thirteen, but perhaps that's because of a faulty memory. Nevertheless, I oft heard Walter say something to her and then watched as she leaned toward him, whispered her reply, and giggled. Thom, too, noticed their closeness, and after finding them in the barn—her bonnet askew and Walter's ears bright red—Thom determined something had to be done. "I'll talk to Walter. You can talk to Elizabeth," he said.

After the smaller children were asleep that night, long after dark, Thom came in from his talk with Walter. Jaws tense, he sat me down at the table.

"Apparently, Walter thinks he's quite grown up, now. Sixteen, he is." A gruff laugh exploded from Thom's throat. "Huh! What does he know of a man's responsibilities? He's but a boy." Thom's words poured forth, tripping over each other in his haste. "He told me that he has looked inside himself and knows where he is going. Not that his goals are not without problems, he admits, but he has a plan for reaching them. What a piece of work he is, admirable in action.[217] Not a lazy bone in his body. He reminded me that his indenture is up next year, and he wants to buy a bit of land and a few animals with the money I pay him. Moreover, he wants to continue working for me."

Thom drew a deep breath. "After telling me all that, can you imagine what the boy asked? He wants to take our Elizabeth as his bride. Says they love each other." Thom scowled and shook his head. Looking down at his hands as if an answer could be found within them, he said slowly, "Perhaps...perhaps I should send him away—I hear the Scudder Schooner needs a new hand, and on its next voyage they will be gone for months."

In the near darkness, he had not noticed my pale face and swollen eyes.

I put my hand on his arm. "Thom," I said softly, "Elizabeth is with child."

"My Elizabeth? My child?" Thom's eyes opened wide, and then, as their expression changed from shock to dismay, he shook his head. "Ah, how green in judgment children are when in their salad days." He straightened his shoulders, and swallowed hard. "Well," he said slowly, "once the acorn's open, you cannot stop the oak."

Slowly, the beginnings of a smile transformed the stern line of Thom's mouth and then changed into a quiet but joyous laugh. "Mary, we're going to be grandparents!"

For the next three weeks, wedding banns were posted on the meeting house door. Thom agreed with Walter that the best place for the Noakes cabin would be on the north shore of Crab Meadow.

"That's where you most often send me to work." Walter said, "so it seems only logical to build there. I'll be close to Elizabeth if she should need me when I'm at work."

So it was that the neighbors joined our men folk in a house raising for Walter and Elizabeth on Thom's Crab Meadow property.

During that time, Anna Wing and I and a few of our friends planned and prepared a wedding feast the town would long remember. While we worked, Elizabeth, a gentle smile on her face, sat quietly dreaming, most unlike her usual scurrying about. Then inspiration empowered her. She created a bride's dress, and after that, embroidered ES and WN in the center block of the wedding quilt. Underneath the initials, she stitched the date of her approaching wedding—7 August 1671.

Soon after her 14th birthday, on April 23, 1672, Elizabeth—surrounded by a multitude of community midwives—brought forth her firstborn child. They named him John Noakes.

∞

If anything was yet lacking in the bond between my Elizabeth and me, little John Noakes completed the tie.

I was the first to rock him to sleep, making up my own version of the old nursery rhyme about King John of Gaunt.

Diddle, diddle, dumpling, Grandson John,
Went to bed with his britches on;
One shoe off, and one shoe on,
Diddle, diddle, dumpling, Grandson John!

In 1674, Thom and I were blessed with our seventh child in sixteen years. Knowing that my time of conception was nearly over, I named her Clemence after my mother and prayed she would be our last.

I'll never forget the day Little John Noakes came to visit, and showing his adoration of his new Aunt Clemence, poked her in the eye with the chicken bone he chewed while cutting teeth. Elizabeth, whose second child was due in time for Little John's second birthday, was not as nimble and quick as Anna Wing, who grabbed baby Clemence from her cradle. Startled, Little John started crying but was comforted when Anna Wing handed the bone back to him. "Wait till the baby has teeth," she said gently. "She'll need your gift then."

In March 1675, Elizabeth and Walter presented us with *our* special gift, our second grandson—Thomas Noakes.

℘

Though Long Island enjoyed years of peace with the Indians, war did break out again between England and the Dutch, who recaptured New York. The next year, the English regained control.

Then, in 1675, someone murdered John Sassamon, an Indian who served as liaison between the colonists and savages. His death led to King Philip's war between Indians and colonists. It took some time for us to receive the reports of the first bloody battle, led by the Wampanoag leader Metacomet, or King Philip as the colonists called him. Hostilities spread from the Mt. Hope peninsula in Rhode Island to the outermost colonial settlement of Northfield, Massachusetts.

Rumors flew. The report Thom read to me asked, "Is the war the fault of the colonists hunger for land and their heavy-handed treatment of the Indians, or are the savages to blame? Has not the hand of God wrought disease and destruction upon the savages that the way might be prepared for His chosen people?"

Though King Philip's War raged no more than a dozen miles to the north of the old Scudder home in Salem, for the most part, we were isolated from the terrors of this conflict. Yet it was a stern reminder of our need to be ever vigilant.

Anna Wing, an Indian who long ago had become a Christian, was unusually somber when she first heard of the fighting, but when Thom read aloud the article that called Metacomet braves "savages," she broke away from the bonds of her usual stoic self.

"Savages? How can Puritans who profess to be God's people participate in such barbarous carnage? I am a descendant of the people who first came to this land. Does that make me a savage? Matinecock is not a tribe. We took the description of the land as our name — people of the flat land, people of the dawn, people of the hill country — 'Matinecock.' We came here that we might share the goodness of the land, not possess it.

"Goodman Scudder, you have sworn to protect *your* people, *your* island. Why should the Sachem Metacomet do less?"

Anna Wing's indignation abated, but she was not finished. "Your Puritan leaders claim to be Christian, but they seem to follow the patterns of attack and capture and conquer only — the way of the Old Testament God. I do not understand this God of yours. Where is the God of love, your Jesus, in all of this?" she asked. "Even the praying towns of Indian converts have been decimated by your people."

The town of Huntington, taking a lesson from the English and Dutch conflicts as well as from King Philip's

War, renewed their vigilance and declared that they would defend themselves and their property from any aggression.

And at last, in 1676, by a vote of the town meeting, Huntington hired a new minister, the Reverend Eliphalet Jones.[218]

Spring, Anno Dom 1677
Long Island to Salem and Back

Thom and I decided that before we sold the *Sea Hawk*, we should invite our offspring on one last trip on the ship—children, in-laws, and grandchildren. I think the sea air was good for my oldest daughter, Elizabeth, who was looking pale and thin. The stress of her busy life had taken its toll. Walter and Elizabeth had three young sons by then, John, Thomas, and the baby, Walter II, and to lighten the load for her sister Elizabeth, Sarah, now eleven years old, had moved to the Noakes home for a brief time when little Walter was born.

On the deck of the *Sea Hawk*, our youngest daughter, Clemence, not yet three, toddled after her two slighter-older Noakes nephews. Watching these little ones filled my soul with sweet music. Not so sweet, though, were the sounds coming from our sons, Benjamin, now nine, and Timothy, seven. The swaying motion of the ship sent them to the rails—an inherited bent for seasickness from Great-Grandfather Scudder. They were much happier once we landed in Boston, and happier still to be back home in Huntington studying their lessons and working with their papa in field and meadow.

In early April, John and Pricilla Arthur's son Robert who had been courting Maria, came to ask Thom for our daughter's hand in marriage. We were friends of the Arthur family, and were pleased with Maria's choice. As soon as the banns had been announced the required three Sundays, the couple was wed.

"I, Robert Arthur, take thee, Maria Scudder...."

By year's end, we had another reason to celebrate with them—the arrival of our first granddaughter, precious little Sarah Arthur. I think her Aunt Elizabeth was a wee bit jealous, for she longed for a daughter, and had only sons.

၈၅

In late summer 1677, Lydia, young sister of the Mary Wright who had demonstrated against the hanging of Mary Dyer 17 years before, decided she, too, must make a stand for her belief. She and other Quaker women accompanied Margaret Brewster who entered a Puritan Church in Boston dressed as a penitent—barefooted, head uncovered, and clad in sackcloth and ashes.

When I heard that all of the women involved had been arrested and were to appear in court, I knew I wanted to be at the trial.

Thom was hesitant. "What can you do, Mary? If you protest, you will be standing trial next, and what will that accomplish?"

"Oh, my darling, I know I cannot speak for Lydia in court, but I can be there to show my support."

We sailed to Boston to hear her testimony—Thom's gift to me. The voyage would remain as bittersweet in my memory as raw Spanish chocolate, for it was our last trip on the *Sea Hawk*.

What poise young Lydia Wright showed as she stood trial.[219] When Gov. John Leverett began questioning her, he asked, "Did you come to our house of worship to hear the word of God?"

In her place, I'm sure I would have trembled, but she answered in a calm voice. "If the word of God was there, I was ready to hear it."

Magistrate Juggins sat with clenched jaw, and when he spoke, his words were caustic as lye. "You, young woman, are led by the spirit of the devil, to ramble up and down the country like a whore cater-wauling."

Lydia turned pale, but she flinched not. "Such words become not those who call themselves Christians," she said. "If you worshipped the God of Abraham, Isaac and Jacob, the same God that Daniel worshipped, as we do, you would not persecute his people."

The judge's face flushed an angry red and the gavel came down with his terrible pronouncement. "Take her away."

"Thom," I whispered. "What if Lydia were one of our daughters? Isn't there anything we can do?"

Thom shook his head. His eyes were sad as he said, "Once we prayed that God would stop the hangings, and He moved the King to forbid them. Let us pray that soon there will be laws forbidding such maltreatment."

I turned away while they stripped Margaret Brewster to the waist, but I could hear every one of the twenty lashes that came down upon her back. Lydia and the rest of the women were not whipped, but all were tied to the back of a cart to be drawn through town. Banished.

We boarded the ship, reeling with emotions. Guilt. Sorrow. And a sense of awe that one so young as Lydia could dare to stand for her faith in spite of perilous consequences. Finally, a sense of renewed courage and purpose came to me, and my lips formed a prayer that in some way, someone might see within me the inner light and strength I saw in Lydia.

Difficult it was to erase the punishment Thom and I had witnessed, but finally the *Sea Hawk* quieted our souls with its rhythmic rocking.

Suddenly Thom noticed that I was wearing the ring he had given me at our marriage. I saw the surprised look on his face.

"Mary?"

"Times are changing, my dear husband. As I grow older, I seem to care less what other people think. I even question myself less. Seems as if I've earned the right to be wrong, and the right to be forgiven, as well. I shall wear the ring and no longer be in bondage to the rigid rules that make no sense to me." Thom slipped the ring from my finger, a plain gold band that had first belonged to his grandmother, and read the inscription within. "*Amorem Nostrum In* — Our love for eternity."

He smiled and slipped the ring back on my finger. Touching my ear lightly with his lips, he repeated the vow. "Our love for eternity, my sweet Aphrodite." Wrapped in the arms of love, we slept. What better way to say goodbye to the *Sea Hawk*.

&

In early winter, 1680, our nephew, Jonathan Scudder, invited us to attend his wedding to the lovely Sarah, daughter of Francis and Martha Brown. I could not help feeling a measure of pride as this dear young man stood beside his bride, tall, strong, and smiling — yet the image in my heart was that of a small boy laughing and playing with my own children. It hardly seemed possible that Jonathan could have so soon reached the age of twenty-five. Seemed like only yesterday that his father, Henry, had died, and for a while afterward, Jonathan lived with us. Such a lovable little boy he was.

'Twas the very next day that an enormous comet appeared in the heavens with a long golden tail so bright it could be seen in the daytime, not just at night. I shiver to think of it. Surely a warning from God of great calamities to come, a brilliant and fearful aspect.

> Eight things there be a Comet brings,
> When it on high doth horrid range:
> Wind, Famine, Plague, and Death to Kings,
> War, Earthquakes, Floods, and Direful Change.[220]

Within a week, Martha Brown was dead, turning the happiness of the newlyweds inside out.

After the funeral, I overheard one old man say to his neighbor. "Ah, I well remember the comet of 1652. It appeared when the great John Cotton drew near his end, and then went out soon after the preacher's death."

The comet of 1680 continued to blaze through the sky — a beautiful yet awful omen. Most people feared that the end of all things was at hand, and in Huntington, the town fathers declared a day of fasting and humiliation in order that the wrath of God might be assuaged.

Visible over New England until mid-February, this blazing comet prompted the Reverend Increase Mather to provide the Puritans of Boston with a theological explanation. A neighbor who had attended meeting house at Boston that month came home to tell of the sermon the Reverend Mather brought to the congregation.

"Repent your sins and pay heed to this sign from an angry God," he had said. "The day of judgment is evidently approaching." He explained away the words of Jeremiah — *Be not dismayed at signs in the heavens* — and showed that comets have been forerunners of nearly every form of evil. At last, rising to a fearful height, he cried out: "Do we see the sword blazing over us? Let it cry unto God that the judgment be diverted and not return upon us again so speedily."

&

Our family had its own problems. On a gloomy winter day in 1681, Elizabeth, now in her twenty-third year, sat at my table and began pouring out her anguish: "Mama, I am unwell." She hardly needed to tell me that, for I could see by her eyes, dark and circled, that she was either ill or exhausted beyond endurance.

Elizabeth sighed, a long and heavy sigh. "How did you do it, Mama? From sunup to sundown and after, even with my sister lending a hand, there is more work than I can do. Cleaning and cooking, drying apples and salting beef, making sweetmeats and sausage, spinning and sewing, washing and ironing. I am almost out of soap — the suet and ashes are still waiting to be boiled, and our supply of candles is dwindling." She pushed a limp strand of hair off her forehead, and I saw how her hand shook.

Slowly, as if she could hardly make the effort, she continued. "Walter's decision to buy horses and export them to the West Indies for sugar and molasses failed when the animals took sick and died, and now we cannot pay our creditors. When I want to talk to Walter about it, he goes to the tavern and returns soused in rum."

I put my arms around her. "Of course, you're tired, Elizabeth, with three young boys barely in breeches, little Isaac still in his gown, and baby Sara at your breast. Any woman would be weary."

She ducked her head, holding her lower lip between her teeth for a moment until the quavering stopped. "I cannot sleep at night when Walter is gone. My heart is in constant fear of the comet's warning," she said softly. "It seems I hear a woman wailing, 'Oh my children, what shall I do?' It prays upon my vitals like horseleeches, and I am almost wearied to death." In a hopeless gesture, Elizabeth put her hand to her breast. "My milk has gone sour and disagrees with the baby when she nurses. Oh, I am so afraid!"

"Afraid of what, my darling?"

"If Sara cannot nurse, I will surely be with child again within the year, and that not only makes me afraid but also angry," she said. "Walter expects me to have more sons for him, and I can not bear the thought. Yet he is the head of our house, so what am I to do?" She paused for a moment. "I know the book of Ephesians says I am to submit myself to my husband, and also that I should make melody in my heart, but, alas, I am sadly out of tune."

She smoothed her apron over a nearly flat belly. Blushing as if in shame, she whispered, "I've heard that mixing ground acacia tree bark and honey together into a paste may stop conception. Would that be evil of me?"

I had not known of her desperation, and when I was not forthcoming with my answer, she pinched her lips together and looked down at her feet. With only a brief pause, she deliberately changed the subject, and began speaking in a bright, forced tone.

"Mama," she said, looking up at me again, "did you hear of the family of vagabonds that Walter caught stealing milk from our cow? They had been sleeping in our barn, and when Walter saw the stripes on the man's bare back, he was sure they were the people whom the Salem officials had lately whipped out of town at the cart's tail. Walter took pity on the man and gave him bread and cheese to eat, along with the milk. Walter's a good man, though we have our troubles."

I patted my daughter's hand. "Walter *is* a good man, Elizabeth. He has a tender heart, though it may not always show."

"Yes, but I'll never understand his decisions. I had invited some of my friends to come to our house, but Walter would not let me have a turkey to roast for supper, and I am so ashamed that I feel I may never get over it." Elizabeth shook her head and again changed the subject. A weak smile appeared.

"Oh, Mama," she said as she reached for my hand. "I am such a selfish child. I have not asked how you are enduring. Does the comet make you hurt and ache like other storms do?"

"Bless you, Elizabeth, but think naught of it. My workload is lighter now, with only four nearly grown children at home, and I have learned to ignore small twinges. Oh, did your papa tell you? He has bought another 60 acres at Crab Meadow. Half plowed field and half meadow. I think he intends to lease it to Walter."

The next time I decided to take the five-mile trip to visit Elizabeth, my daughter Mercy, now fourteen, packed a bag and drove me to Crab Meadow. The road to Eliza-

beth and Walter's house at the shore—at first no more
than a narrow Indian trail—had been widened and
smoothed somewhat over the years. Still, as I neared my
25th year of marriage, every bump seemed to jar my in-
wards, and I liked not to travel, but I could not ignore my
troubled daughter. Pleased I was to hear Elizabeth
greeted us with a lilt of happiness in her voice, and when
Mercy told her sister she had come to help with the children, I could see Elizabeth's burdened shoulders lighten.

Baby Sara, now two, was stirring in her cradle and
making whimpering sounds, so Mercy went to tend her
needs. "Sounds as if you're getting hungry, sweetie. Do
you want your Aunt Mercy to change you and then take
you to your mother to nurse?"

That finished, she turned her attention to her nephews.
"Look at you, Isaac, in breeches already. Why, you're almost as tall as Wally. You boys want to show me how to
milk the cow? 'Bout time I learned, don't you think?"

The boys grinned, and when Wally picked up the milk
bucket, Mercy and Isaac followed him out the door.

Except for my granddaughter Sara's contented sucking
sounds as she pressed her mouth to her mother's breast,
the house was quiet.

"Oh, Mama," Elizabeth said, "everything is going to be
all right. Sit down and let me tell you."

She pointed me to a seat beside her and took my hand.
"Please forgive me for not telling you the whole of it before, but I did not want you to worry," she said.

I raised an eyebrow and peered at her lovely face. "Is it
not a mother's duty to worry?"

"What I did not tell you was that at the time Walter
gave the vagabond family cheese and bread, we were

ourselves short of food." She lowered her eyes, obviously embarrassed to tell me how bad it was.

"I'm sure you know, Mama, that the government has passed a law requiring people to keep their free ranging hogs confined. Anyone finding a stray hog can kill it, keep a third of the meat, and give the rest to the town.[221] Well..." Elizabeth paused, and in her eyes I saw approval and renewed respect. "Walter found a stray hog that could have saved us from going hungry," she said, "but he was sure the pig came from the Conklin farm. It was not an easy decision, but he and the three boys, little Walter and Thomas and John—so proud they are when they can help their pa—returned the hog to Goodman John Conklin."

The look of pride in my daughter's face, brought tears to my eyes.

Elizabeth smiled and nodded. "The old man was so pleased that he rewarded each of the boys with a piglet," she said. "Now Walter wants to begin our own herd of hogs. He says the comet is a sign from God." She looked up at me with amazement in her eyes. "Oh, Mama, Walter is a changed man. He has sworn off the rum and spends most evenings at home with our family and me. Isn't it wonderful?"

A year later, in August, 1682, a lesser comet appeared, and Reverend Mather followed this with a sermon saying, "...wherein is showed that the voice of God in signal providences, especially when repeated and iterated, ought to be hearkened unto.... Many things that may happen according to the course of Nature are portentous

signs of Divine anger and prognostics of great evils hastening upon the world." He then recalled the eclipse of
August, 1672, and added: "That year the college was sor-
rowed by the death of the learned president there, worthy Mr. Chauncey, and two colonies—namely, Massachusetts and Plymouth—by the death of two governors,
who died within a twelvemonth after.... Shall, then, such
mighty works of God as comets be insignificant
things?"[222]

How I would like to have been sitting in Reverend
Mather's meeting house that day in '82 when the second
comet appeared, for when he made his pronouncement,
my spirit would have cried out: "Reverend Mather, I
mean no disrespect, but the Spirit within me says that
many of the mighty works are not at the hands of an angry God, but are glorious signs of His watchful care."

Anno Dom 1684-1685
Huntington, Long Island

Such a spate of fortunate happenings there was in the
next two years. First, our daughter Elizabeth and Walter
Noakes' last child, Rachel, was born in February 1684;
and in the same year, our daughter Sarah wed young
John Conklin, son of Captain John Conklin of Huntington, and grandson of John Conckelyne Sr., brother of
Anaias—the glassmakers who made the beautiful window for our Babylon house so many years before. Surprisingly, when young John's grandfather died, he left a
will that stated in part: "I do give to Walter Noakes three
pounds and all my wearing cloathes except my best
coat."

The following year, 1685, our nephew Jonathan and his
wife Sarah gave birth to their second daughter. They

named her Abigail and asked us to stand with them at her baptism. Timothy and Benjamin, now 15 and 17, joined us, while Mercy, our 16-year-old daughter, sat with her sister Clemence, five years younger, together in the Scudder pew.

In the course of time, Thom acquired some one thousand acres of land — some that he had purchased the year we lived in Babylon, much of it along the Huntington Bay waterside, some extending south into the hills from the Huntington Bay, and other acres four and five miles eastward to Cow Harbor and on to Crab Meadow. [223]

As Huntington prospered and grew, people moved to fill the outlying areas. In addition to the many farms that were established in remote as well as central portions of the town, the town included a school, a church, flour-mills, saw mills, brickyards, tanneries, a town dock, and a fort.

Huntington's fine harbor meant that shipping became an important part of the economy. The harbor was a busy place, with vessels traveling not only to and from other ports along the Sound but also as far as the West Indies. Ship making and related nautical businesses prospered, since water was for many years by far the most efficient way to transport both goods and people.

Alas, our gladness turned to mourning shortly after the baptism of our grandniece, Abigail, for in that same year, 1685, we received the news that King Charles II had died, and James, the Duke of York, inherited the crown. All the colonies of North American became his subjects. The arrogant King James II determined to rule the colonies by his instructions alone. "It is my prerogative," he said. "The people have no liberties, either civil or religious, for

God has decreed that I should wear the crown." His governors imitated him in their contempt of the people. Such bigotry, such greed for power!

Anno Dom 1686
New England

On 3 June 1686, in order to enforce the Navigation Acts and retain control of the colonies, King James II created the Dominion of New England. By September, the Dominion included the Colonies of Connecticut, Massachusetts Bay including Maine, New Plymouth, Rhode Island and New York. [224]

The King himself appointed Edmund Andros the Dominion Governor. Andros began promoting the Church of England, banning town meetings, and challenging land titles. The titles issued by Puritan governments before 1686 had to be reissued. Puritan colonists had to pay new title fees as well as quitrents, an annual land tax. To make matters worse, a court with no jury was set up in Boston to enforce Navigation Acts that forbade both importing and exporting any goods to or from the British colonies unless in English or colonial ships. It forbade the shipping of tobacco, sugar, cotton, and wool to any country except to England or some English plantation. Even when shipped to England, heavy duties were collected. When the court found at least six merchant ships guilty of violating the Acts, they seized the ships. Merchants started avoiding the port of Boston, further deepening the poverty of the colonies.

Over the forts and royal offices, a new flag waved, bearing a St. George's cross on a white field, and a crown embroidered in gold in the center.[225] Corn Laws forbade the shipping of grain raised in the colonies, so they began manufacturing. Then England forbade manufacturing in the colonies.

The election of deputies stopped in Massachusetts, but in other colonies, no changes whatever took place.

New Englanders continued tilling the soil, going to church, and gathering in town meetings as they had done for half a century.

Twenty-two

❦

DECEMBER ANNO DOM 1686
HUNTINGTON, LONG ISLAND, NEW YORK

One winter night in December, Thom seemed particularly pensive after we had blown out the candle and sought the warm comfort of our bed.

"Mary," he finally said with a faint wryness, "I should write a will. Although my father has been dead for only eight years, I am past three score years now. God only knows how much time I have left, and once I am in the grave, I vow you shall have your share of our wealth."

I put my fingers across his lips. "Hush, my husband. Must we talk of death and separation?"

But he would not be stilled. "I must look to the future, Mary. I must leave business matters in competent hands." He paused then, and it seemed that memories of his father must be playing through his mind. "You know, I never expected my father to die. Isn't that odd? And living without him has been like going on a journey without a map to guide me. Did ye ever think of that yourself Mary, having lost your mother?"

"Yes." I buried my face in his chest, my voice muffled in the folds of his shirt. "I used to — when I was younger."

Tenderly, Thom touched the smooth skin of my neck and traced his way down to cup my breast with his hand. "Mary, are we old?"

In the firelight, he could not see me smile, but I am sure he heard it in my reply. "Old as the hills, my darling."

"Then why, my dearest, do I feel this old familiar stirring in my loins?"

To tease him, I pushed his hand away and pulled the quilt up to my neck, then giggled and turned it back down. "I love you, old man. But whatever are you doing in bed with such a sweet young thing as I?"

I was quiet, waiting for his laughter, and then realized that his only response was a gentle snoring. I cupped my body around the curve of his back, and soon, I, too, slept.

The next morning, true to his pledge, Thom sat at the table with inkpot, quill, and paper, and wrote in his own hand:

WILL OF THOMAS SCUDDER II. Dated 2 December 1686

In ye name of God, Amen. I, Thomas Scudder of Huntington upon Long Island in ye County of Suffolk & Province of N. York in America, being in a competency of health & having my perfect memory, have made this my last Will & Testament in manner & form following:

I give & bequeath my soul to God my maker & Redeemer & my body to ye earth from whence I was taken to be laid in decency according to the discretion of my Executors, Mary Scudder my wife & Benjamin Scudder my son.

Item--I give & bequeath to my son Timothy Scudder my farm at Crab Meadow both upland & meadow with all its rights & privileges after Walter Noakes seven years expiration which began in 1685--And that lot at ye Harbor on ye South of Capt. Fleet, also that piece of Meadow that lyeth on ye north side of Jonathan Rogers--Also a bed which is to be at ye disposal of his mother—

Item--I give & bequeath to my daughter Elizabeth Noakes a cow—

I give & bequeath to my daughter Mary Arthur a cow—

Item--I give & bequeath to my daughter Sarah Concklyn twenty pounds —

Item--I give & bequeath to my daughter Clemence twenty pounds —

Item--I give & bequeath to my daughter [Mercy] twenty pounds —

All the rest of my lands goods & chattels not given & bequeathed I give & bequeath to my loving wife Mary Scudder & to my son Benjamin Scudder Equally to be divided between them and after the natural life of my wife both land & meadow housing & orchards to return to my son Benjamin and what goods & moveables my wife possesseth at her death to be at her disposal

And thos that I have committed my trust to see the performance of this my last Will & Testamt is my loving wife & my son Benjamin whom I make my full & whole Executrix & Executor of this my Will & Testament to see all things done & performed according to the just intent there of.

In Witness Whereof I have subscribed my hand & set to my seal ye seventh day of December in ye 2d year of the reign of James II & in ye year of our Lord 1686.

Satisfied with the document, he sent for his friends, Thomas Powell and Joseph Bayley, to witness his signature, and in their presence, he added his name to the end of the testament.

Sprinkling sand over their signatures to dry the ink, he thanked the men and then put the document away for safekeeping.

Twenty-three

❧

ANNO DOM 1688
HUNTINGTON AND THE DOMINION OF NEW ENGLAND

It was but ten months later that the English Governor Andros came to Connecticut to take away the charter and the colonists' legal rights.

On May 7, 1688, the Provinces of New York and East and West Jersey were added to the Dominion of New England—eight colonies in all now. Puritan citizens of the colonies formerly known as New England were angry and despairing. They had little power to represent themselves to Parliament, and no hope of subverting the Dominion.

Thom was in mourning. "Mary, I fear for the future of our grandchildren and grandnieces and nephews. You and I have made great strides, but it looks as if the good times are over."

Suddenly I realized that my husband, slumped in his chair, fingering his sagging chin, was growing old. Sixty years he was. Where had the time gone? Now, he seemed to think the liberty we enjoyed, our way of life, was ending.

"Is it that bad?" I asked.

"Oh, yes. The king has demanded a hefty tax of the East End towns of Long Island. Needs more money for his wars, I suppose. Of course, the East End objected, so he has ordered the arrest of the leaders of the communities." Thom became more agitated, and his voice grew testy. "How long will it be before James makes the same demands on Huntington? Those East End landowners are expected to purchase their land a second time! Who can stand such a heavy burden?"

Thom shook his head. "If that happens, our children and grandchildren will end up on a bare plot of ground in a crowded log cabin."

Suddenly, Thom drove his fist into the other palm. "Such gall the king has! Oh, Mary, this is the stuff of revolution."

With a determined grimace, he heaved himself up from the chair. "We cannot submit to such unconscionable demands! Perhaps it's time to begin selecting men from our trainbands to form a fighting unit." Slowly he turned to me. "Don't wait up for me, Mary." His voice was gentle but resolute, his lips bloodless. "I'm going to the tavern. There must be others who agree." [226]

I drew in breath, suddenly afraid. "Careful, my husband. Your words could get you hanged for treason."

ANNO DOM 1689
REVOLUTION IN BOSTON

In May, Thom received a missive from Henry Bartholomew, his sister Elizabeth's husband. He opened it and read it aloud.

Salem, April 25, 1689.
Dear Brother-in-law,

I write you now to share the glorious news, though by the time you receive this missive, I am sure you will have heard. Who could have guessed that the young king who had enslaved us would soon be overthrown?

As I understand it, when the queen gave birth to a son and potential Catholic heir last year, Parliament, not waiting for the King's next unconscionable action, invited Protestant Holland's William of Orange to invade England and force James II off the throne.[227]

He agreed, so in November last, William was welcomed in London, and James II fled to France.

When the news of this Glorious Revolution first reached Salem, we were afraid to believe it. But once the good news was confirmed this month, Boston rebelled against the Royal Governor in their city.

I heard this directly from Samuel Prince, my friend in Boston who himself witnessed the rebellion. Forgive me, please, the length of this missive, but I know, dear Thom, feeling as strongly as you do, you would want to know all.

My friend Samuel told me that he knew nothing of what was intended until it was begun, but at the north end of Boston town, only a few miles from our Salem properties, he saw boys running along the street with clubs in their hands, yelling encouragement to one another. Hurrying toward the town dock, he saw men running for their arms.

Oh, Thom, how I wish you and I had been there to hear the drums begin to beat, drums your own tannery must have had a hand in making!

According to Samuel, all the companies rallied together at the Town House, and about four of clock in the afternoon, orders were given to go and demand the Fort. When the governor refused to surrender, they told him that if he did not, he

must expect to be delivered up to the rage of the people. Curs-
ing, he capitulated.

Had the Royals within the Fort been determined to fight to
the death, they might have killed an hundred colonists at once,
but God in His mercy prevented it.

Thom, I fear whether settling things under a new govern-
ment may not prove far more difficult than the getting from
under the power of the former, except the Lord calm and quiet
the disturbed spirits of people.[228]

Farewell, dear brother-in-law. Your sister Elizabeth sends
her affectionate regards.

Yours in peace and celebration,
Henry Bartholomew

The news put a light back in Thom's eyes. For three
decades, after the Duke's Laws had taken away local control, Thom had railed against these capricious laws.[229]
Now, with Catholic James ousted and a new King in his
place, everything changed.

New charters gave Huntington and other towns the
powers of town corporations. Though the colonies of
New England remained royal colonies rather than privately owned colonies, they had preserved their independence. Their lawmakers were popularly elected.
Their courts were local. Their laws were valid.

Twenty-four

ANNO DOM 1690
HUNTINGTON, LONG ISLAND

Early in the spring of 1690, Thom's breathing grew labored, and he burned with ague. There were times when he seemed quite out of his wits with the illness, rambling and making no sense at all. Friendly neighbors believed we should bleed the fever from him, but I had seen too many die after such remedy. Instead, Clemence and I fed him all the potions we could concoct, then laid cold compresses on his body that it might bring him relief and comfort.

The morning he asked for the Bible that he might read it himself, I wept, for I knew he was on the mend.

His lips moved as he read, and after closing the Holy book, I watched in awe as this beloved husband of mine smiled with that ironic twist to his mouth. Then in all solemnity, he got to his knees, trembling though they were, and bowed his head. When he tried to stand, I put my hands under his arms and lifted him up as he struggled to reach his chair.

When Thom was settled, I was astonished to see that his face was crimson and his eyes blazing.

In spite of his breathlessness, his words came bubbling forth. "Didn't He promise that the days of our years should be three score and ten, and by reason of strength be fourscore, yet my strength and labor is too soon cut off, and I will fly away."

He paused to catch his breath, and I saw his rage abate.

"Mary," he said in a hoarse, gravelly voice, "How do I cope with my brevity of days without demanding of God what his hurry is? Surely I am more useful to him right here on earth than in my grave. I cannot fathom God's will."

Thom seemed to be at least in a right mind, but at the slightest exertion, he huffed and puffed like the big bad wolf of the old nursery tale.

Our sons took over Thom's usual labors, and he spent the summer sitting by the fireplace, stoking the embers.

Clemence was sixteen that summer, and after helping Anna Wing tend to the housework, she spent her time close to her papa, knitting a blanket for his lap that he might not shiver so. I moved the writing desk closer to him, reading when he asked, writing during our quiet times. The days, instead of flying by, now oozed slowly away.

"What doest thou write, Mary?" Thom asked one morning after Clemence had slipped outside to do barnyard chores.

I was glad that for once my journal was not filled with worry and gloom. "A list. A long list."

"Of plans for the day?"

He breathed with a dry rattle, and I opened the window across from him to let in the warm breeze. Perhaps that would give him relief today.

"It's been a long time since *I* have compiled such a list," he said as he shook his head, disbelieving, and when he looked up, I saw his eyes were moist.

My list, a poem, was complete. Perhaps the words would bring him cheer. I lay down the quill.

"You're finished?" he said.

"It's for thee," I said. "But I cannot read it to thee. Thou must do that for thyself."

He took my list, and though he paused and closed his eyes between stanzas, he read it to the end, and a growing joy gradually replaced the sadness in his eyes.

In Praise of My Loving Husband

Since long ago you pulled me from the sea
Ne'er did I love another willingly.
I love you, for in crippling cramps of storm,
Without complaint, you held me, kept me warm.
When I in childbirth screamed God's name in vain,
Twas you he sent, delivered me from pain,
And in my arms such sweet contentment laid,
Fruit of your loins. Oh, I was amply paid
With living likeness of your face and bone,
That should you leave, I'd never be alone.
Though women had no rights, you set me free —
You listened well, and shared your thoughts with me.
My carping words did oft protest, and yet
You listened best, and soothed my every fret,
When I'd not hold my tongue, could not agree
With magistrates who launched their dread decree

You stilled me not, though worried you might be,
Concerned that I'd be next on hanging tree.
I know God loves thee more, who gave thee breath,
But my love too will span the final death.

Finally, Thom whispered, "Oh, my Aphrodite, you must keep writing. Promise me you will tell thy story. God hath given thee a gift for it."

"A gift? Do not you write as well?"

"Most of my writings have been lists from my head, not from my heart." He smiled, his eyes crinkling in the old familiar way. "Remember the parable of the master who gave talents to every man according to his abilities? When the talents were multiplied, the Lord's joy was doubled and the servant's joy fulfilled."

"And you think God's intention for me is as easy as that? Can blessings come from writing about my life? I'm just an ordinary woman."

"Not so ordinary a woman, me thinks. Your faithfulness shines through like the sun in spite of all your doubts. That light could show the way for others, if they only knew. Write your story, Mary. Do you not hear the voice of God calling you to that purpose?"

He paused for breath. "We've had a good life together haven't we?" He lifted his drinking glass and peered deep inside.

"There may be dregs at the bottom," he said, "but there is a lot of good wine left! From now on, every morning of my life I shall wake up with joy instead of anger and bitterness. The sweet wine of praise shall fill my mouth. And at night I shall go to bed with thanksgiving in my heart."

"Now who is wearing the laurel crown of the Scudder castle?" I said, smiling. "You, my dear, are my poet laureate. And if wine will accomplish such beauty, I will fill our glasses full each morning."

From that day, I kept a bayberry candle lit while I read to him, combining two senses — hearing and smelling — our hearts a partnership of praise. I often opened the Bible to the Song of Solomon, and when I paused midway through a verse, Thom remembered where it led and finished the lines for me.

Kiss me with the kisses of thy mouth--

"...for thy love is better than wine," Thom answered.

A bundle of myrrh is my well beloved to me; he shall —

... lie all night between my breasts.

He brought me to the--

...banqueting house, and —

...his banner over me was love.

Stay me with flagons —

...comfort me with apples: for I am sick with love.

His left hand is under my head, and his right hand doth —

I paused and there was no reply. My beloved began snoring lightly — a lovely sound to my ears. *Stir not, nor awake my love, till you please.*

Sixty-five years old on November 5, Thom Scudder — ancient by some measures — tottered across the great room, cane in hand. As if docking the *Sea Hawk* aft backwards, he navigated his backside toward his beloved wingback chair next to the fireplace. Grasping the arms of the chair, he hovered for a moment before plopping into the seat. The effort left him gasping and set off a racking cough. Afterwards, he laid his head back against the chair and closed his eyes. "Mary… remember our moonlit sail through the bay to Brother John's house at Newtown?"

I blushed, and Thom's laughter sent him into a coughing fit. Again he leaned back and rested for a moment, eyes closed.

"John's dead now." He sighed—a wheezing rasping sound. "Henry, too." He paused. "So why am I still here?"

"Perhaps…" The lump in my throat made speaking difficult. I leaned toward him and whispered in his ear. "Perhaps because I need you."

Thom's weary eyes twinkled. "There's nothing better than a beautiful woman and a bit of moonlight."

"And finally, God's blessing of healthy daughters and the strong sons you longed for."

Thom nodded. "Twelve years of marriage and only daughters…then at last, a son, Benjamin. And in a few more years, our daughters Mercy and Clemence, and a son between them to carry on the Scudder name. Timothy Scudder." Even now, there was awe in his voice. "Two sons." Every breath was labored. "God willing, they'll give us grandsons…." He pressed blue-tinged fingers to his chest as a terrifying cough left him gasping for air.

Trembling, I touched a linen cloth to the corner of his mouth. "Thom, would you like me to ask Rev. Edwards to come and pray for you?"

He shook his head. "Never had much use for him. Poor substitute for our old friend, Will Leverich."

With a quivering, wrinkled hand, Thom reached to touch my cheek. "So soft." He paused. "We've been good for each other, haven't we?" He smiled, and then his expression changed. "No, not Edwards." Thom's words came in a breathy whisper. "It's been thy prayers that have kept me in God's hands all these years. *You* pray."

The children apparently heard their papa's request, having just come in from the barn with the dog bounding in after them.

"Quiet, Shep," Clemence commanded as they tiptoed into the room. Benjamin set the milk bucket down quietly, and they came and stood round Thom's chair next to me, joined hands and bowed their heads. Even the dog found a place on the rug, tucking his nose between his beloved master's feet.

Except for Thom's raspy breathing, it seemed the room itself was holding its breath.

Taking my husband's hand in mine, I struggled to shape fitting words of prayer.

Thy will be done? No! How could I let him go?

High in the evening sky, I heard a lone hawk take flight, its scream echoing the piercing cry of my heart. "Kree-eee-ar!"

Through the open window, together we watched the last rim of the late autumn-red sun slip down below the horizon.

Thom smiled and his voice took on new strength. "The storm is ending, my beloved ones. Everything will be different in the morning."

He settled back in his chair and closed his eyes. "Ah, it's true," he said. "Red sky at night...sailor's delight."

Strength drained from my limbs, and I fell to my knees beside his chair. With trembling fingers I caressed the celestial smile that had settled on my husband's face.

Thom Scudder had sailed away for the last time.

Twenty-five

ANNO DOM 1690
HUNTINGTON, LONG ISLAND, NEW YORK

The whole town of Huntington turned out for Thom's funeral, yet in that entire crowd, I have ne'er felt more alone. The sun of those wintery days was a cold, pale yellow. I wished only to crawl under our covers and sleep away whatever might remain of my life. Yet, once twilight was past, I could not sleep. Oft I flung my arm across Thom's space in our bed, expecting to feel the warmth of his strong body and the beating of his heart. My hand found only emptiness. My heart filled to the bursting with tears, yet I could not cry. Our 34 years together seemed to have flown by in the span of a day, yet after Thom's passing, each day seemed a year.

With a heart burdened with grief, I sought comfort; tried to talk to God; but oft the prayer turned into a conversation with Thom.

"Good news, my husband. This winter, our son Benjamin and Thomas Smith gained permission at the town meeting to build a gristmill at Stony Brook if they can procure funds for the dam. You would be so pleased to see how hard they have worked. You would be pleased, too, to know that our grandchildren are growing daily in both wisdom and stature.

"Still, I mourn. I remember you saying, dear Thom, that broken hearts are what give us strength and understanding and compassion.

Yet today I find it difficult to reach out to others. My strength fails me."

Later I began a poem to Thom, to tell him how I felt—all my grief, my questions, my anguish, as well as my brief joys—the ink poured forth.

April 23, 1691
Poem to my dear husband

> My dearest, how I miss you now
> That spring hath come again.
> The fields and trees are clad in green
> And skies give forth the rain.
> But though you willed me plenteous goods,
> Still one thing do I lack:
> When I have all these questions, you're
> Not here to answer back.
> Will Isaac be a tiny babe
> When him in heav'n I see?
> Will Papa and my brothers there
> Be older still than me?
> And when I walk those golden streets,
> Will you walk by my side?
> How could a love as strong as ours
> In heaven be denied?
> How will you recognize me, dear?
> And how will I know you
> When our decaying bodies He
> Hath changed to something new?
> Too soon, my dear, death slipped our bonds,
> The knot that made us one.
> These April days seem long and dark.
> Without you, where's the sun?
> My doubting dulls a flick'ring faith
> That soon I'll be with you.

And though a voice within me says,
"His promises are true,"
I'm plagued by fears of fruitless trust:
Mere trickery or ruse?
Still hope abides within my bones,
Assurance of God's truth.
In heav'n God says there'll be no tears,
No sorrow, fear, or pain.
If everything is perfect there,
No chance of loss or gain,
Without the labours we've enjoyed,
Will you have naught to list?
If praise and singing lasts all day,
Won't challenges be missed?
In dreams, I feel you near to me,
Your arm around my waist,
And, darling, if I knew the way,
I'd come to you in haste.

The words stopped as suddenly as they had begun. Grief o'ertook me, and my ink ran dry.

I heard the voice I had heard before: *Heed my call, Mary. I have empowered thee to build bridges, past and future, bringing joy and fulfillment to your descendants forever. Awake, for this is your epiphany.*

Slowly, for a second time words began to flow, the end of Thom's poem:

Belov'd I'll fill your last request
And will my story tell.
If that's the plan God hath for me,
Pray that I do it well.
And if His way of love and life
Shows 'tween the lines I've lived,
In spite of all my doubts and fears,
What better could I give?

Far past the place my dreams leave off
and 'magination ends,
Here, saith First Corinthians 2,
The love of God begins:
Hearts can't conceive nor hath eyes seen
The grace of God above
For those who follow in His steps
And imitate his love.

I wiped the quill clean and put it away with the ink and paper, then laid my head down on my arms as I sat at the table. I covered my face with my hands, but I could not release my tears.

Again the voice spoke, louder than before. *Mary!*

I put my hands over my ears. "Why must I write when the pain is so fresh? Who will listen? I am an ordinary woman," I said. "Not the daughter of a governor or king."

Do not protest so, Mary. Can you not read and write? Do you not think and question? Who gave you those gifts? My child, I have allowed your struggles to bring you wisdom and understanding. Your forgiving spirit and loving actions have led you to walk in the way. Because you have learned the truth of the narrow way, you must tell your story.

In my dreams, I oft heard a voice call my name:

Mary, didst thou not promise to write your story? Is it not time to shatter the silence that shames thee? To offer encouragement to those who follow in thy steps? To bolster the courage of those who would speak out against persecution?

"Is that thy voice, Thom? — or is it the Spirit within me? Whichever it is will not let me go. It seems that to hold my tongue now, to neglect my quill, would make my struggles senseless. I well remember my fearful silence. I could not speak out for my sisters-in-faith even when they were arrested, whipped, and banished. I could do nothing for them. But there will be others yet to come. Perhaps even my own daughters. My granddaughters. Must each forever hold her tongue as I have done?"

With a fresh understanding and determination, and with a lightened heart, I slept. The new dawn found my pillow drenched with the dew of tardy tears. A blessed release.

From that day on, the children and I read from the scriptures each morn, just as we had when Thom was with us. After praying that we might all put into action our better impulses, while they went about the day's work, I sat with quill and ink. First, I addressed a letter to Thom. It was almost like having him there beside me, sharing questions and thoughts and plans for the day. Then I began my life story — about Mama's death and burial at St Giles church in Matlock, England, when I was seven; about the terrible punishment I received for running away; about the trip to the colonies on the ship Triall. Whatever Mnemosyne brought to my mind.

15 June 1691
My dearest Thom,

Even though you are gone, do you know my heart? Are you pleased that in this year of loneliness, I have gained a newfound freedom to make decisions without being overruled by either father or husband? I have managed family wealth, business, and estate. I have learned that though I can see only a little way in front of me, step by step I can make the journey.

I wish I could see the day when government will be limited by law from impinging on individual freedoms, but I cannot see so far. Will humankind ever see universal suffrage?

31 August 1691
Dearest One,

Oh, how our town is growing. Nearing 500 souls in Huntington now. Another flourmill is set up and running, and a tannery. A new man in town is building a brickyard.[230]

Benjamin tells me the town fathers are talking about building a highway beginning at the head of the wigwam swamp, and there is talk of banning unauthorized tree cutting on the common land.
[231]

21 September 1691
My dear husband,

Last night I had a dreadful dream wherein were blood and dark water, and the pages of my life floating away on dark waves. I heard children weeping and the cries of the hawk circling and diving overhead. "Kree-eee-ar." I reached for you but found only an empty pillow beside me.

Like a premonition, I saw terrible trials coming for women, worse than those we have known. I saw lightning strike a tree on Gallows Hill, rendering it the shape of a broom. Moreover, I heard a deep voice prophesying: 'Innocent blood will be shed, souls scoured for even the faintest stains.'

High above, the red-tailed hawk called to me, "Mary, thou must soon 'scape the cruel bonds of earth. Yet wilt thee find the steps that lead thee to thy purpose, the joining of past and future, bringing strength to all thy descendants forever.

24 October 1691
My dearest Thom,

Tuesday, two days ago, Benjamin and I executed your estate as the law commands. I am so proud of your fair distribution of the property and the freedom you gave me to act in this matter. I am glad, too, that you permitted our oldest son to share as executor for I have passed the peak of my energies in such matters.

I lived a full life with you, Thom. I know you must be proud of our seven children, eleven much-loved grandchildren and, yes, still counting. Sarah and her husband John have a new little daughter—Rachel.

The October days are beautiful this year. Remember the twin tree stumps where we oft sat in the soft hours of twilight? The glorious colors entice. Tomorrow I shall take a walk down the harbor path, and there I shall write.

That lovely Thursday, carrying my Geneva Bible, quill, ink, and paper, I found my way through tall grasses to the water's edge,

then to the twin tree stumps. There I rested, enjoying the soothing, rhythmic sounds of water lapping against the edge of the
cove, birds skittering across the harbor, and the faint voices of
children's laughter. After taking ink and quill from my pocket,
from the back of my Bible I removed the memoirs and poems I
had previously written, and a few blank sheets of paper. I finished the poem and put it with the others.

That done, I began writing a missive to my most reliable
daughter.

25 October 1691
My Dearest Sarah,

My memoir is that of an ordinary life, the restricted existence of a woman in the New World of the 17th century.
This story is my legacy to you and your siblings, and to all
your children and your children's children. When the time
is right and there is no longer fear of prosecution for heresy,
please share the legacy with them.

When I am gone, prithee lay my body beside thy father's,
and if it please ye, carve a headstone that says,
Mary Ludlam Scudder,
wife of Thomas Scudder, II.
She was a tender, honest woman
who lived a purpose-filled life
and died in the Lord

I paused to watch as the late afternoon sun painted the sky
with strokes of red. An east wind began whipping the water
into a white-capped splendor tinged with gold and scarlet.
Soon I should be getting back home, so I turned my attention
to finishing Sarah's missive.

You'll find the pages I have written tucked away in the – "

Suddenly, a short distance away, I heard a child
screaming.

"Aunt Mary! Aunt Mary!"

I looked up to see Jonathan Scudder's six-year-old Abigail floundering in the cold water of the harbor. Quickly, I cast aside my writing tools, papers, and Bible. Pages of my precious writing scattered in the rising wind, but there was no time to chase after them. I jumped into the bay and started swimming to the spot where I had last seen Abbie struggling. Tiring quickly, I began treading water, hoping for new-found strength. By the time I reached Abbie and grabbed her, my legs and arms had developed severe spasms. Abbie clung to me, trembling. About all I could do was to hold her head out of the water and call for help. We had nearly reached the bank when a passerby heard us. He grasped the child and pulled her from my hands and onto dry land.

My arms knotted in excruciating pain, and for an interminable moment, I could no longer battle the cold waves. Throat burning, yearning for a gulp of air, I fought to reach the surface.

The cry of a red-tailed hawk shattered an unearthly stillness. "Kree-eee-ar. Kree-eee-ar." A sound ominous, yet beautiful. As if in a dream, I saw the hawk swoop down to carry me away on its dark wings. Again, it dipped, loosed his talons, and released me.

In blessed exhaustion, I drifted down, down beneath the dark waters of Huntington Harbor. Once the pain was gone, drowning was as alluring as a long-awaited sleep, floating down through soft pillows of beguiling darkness, a passionate seeking for the loving arms of peace and consolation.

In one last flicker of perception, I heard the cry of the hawk and felt myself rising from darkness to light.

The disarray of my sopping red tresses mingled with seaweed and the tangled strands fell over my shoulders, hiding the clinging fabric of my bodice. I heard laughter and a familiar masculine voice:

"Well, if it isn't Aphrodite, my bride, rising from the sea. Welcome home, beloved."

Endnotes

CHAPTER ONE

1 The 17th century was a time of change in the English language. In the early part of the century, verbs and pronouns (thou, thee, thy, thine, and ye and verb forms, eg. "thou takest," the singular counterpart to the plural pronoun ye, and "he taketh," the third person singular ending,) were standardized by the King James Bible. By the mid part of the century, many of these verbs and pronouns were dropping the King James standard, changing to the modern English more familiar in the 21st century. Spelling rules were non-existent during Grand-Mary's time. The same word repeated in any document might very well have been spelled differently each time it was written.

2 "Goody" was the common term of address for an ordinary woman of that day. Men were called "Goodman."

3 Uncle Arthur Ludlam's real name was Anthony, but to avoid confusion with other Anthonys, here he is called Arthur.

4 From the Matlock [Derbyshire, England] Register, the entire list of Ludlams as baptized and buried from beginning of the Register, 29,Sept. 1637, to the end of the seventeenth century, extracted by Dr. Walter D. Ludlum, The book [register] begins " A true Regester of all the Christian Mariages and Burialls in the Par of Matlock since 1637 September 29. Hank E. Smith: Rector; Henry Knowles and Robert Oates: Church wardens. Included— Burialls: 1646 Clemence uxor William Ludlam Junior sepult August 21st. I have taken the license to move her death and burial date to the week of Joseph's birth rather than two weeks after.

5 Accessed 11/15/2008. From

http://www.andrewspages.dial.pipex.com/matlock/reg/index.htm

6 Accessed 11/15/2008. From

http://www.andrewspages.dial.pipex.com/matlock/rectors.htm

7 The Bay Psalm Book, compiled by John Hardwick and John Cotton.

CHAPTER TWO

8 1627: WILLIAM LUDLAM loans 40s to "ayd his Majesty, King Charles I." Many in Derby-
	shire, like other counties at the time, considered it illegal for Charles I to raise a levy (or
	"loan") in 1627 without the consent of Parliament. "Persuasions, threats and force were
	used throughout the country to extort the loan". This roll covered the hundred of Apple-
	tree and Wapentake of Wirksworth, listing the names of all people who "agreed" to lend
	money to His Majesty, collected by Robert WILLYMOTT of Chaddesden, appointed Col-
	lector. Accessed 11/15/2008. From
	http://www.andrewspages.dial.pipex.com/matlock/c17thlists.htm.

9 Accessed 11/15/2008. From
	www.channel4.com/history/microsites/H/history/guide17/part04.html

10 Winthrop Papers 4:460: Hank Walton to John Winthrop: "...Mr. Fowrdams plantacion hath
	too lately suffered haueinge too much treated those unfaithfull heathen, three men haue
	been cutt of at their worke and one of goodman Carmas children almost Masachred and
	Another carried away and yet to him they pretended greatest friendship. Flatlands in
	New Netherlands, the 4th Mo. 1644. (Hempstead, New York.)

CHAPTER THREE

11 Maury's "The Physical Geography of the Sea and Its Meteorology"

12 "1590: the first recorded knowledge of an approximate position of the Gulf Stream." The
	influence of the Gulf Stream in the colonization of North America was great. In 1606 the
	English divided their claimed land into two parts, northern and southern territories pre-
	scribed by the routes the ships had to take to reach their destinations.

13 Edward Howell is Phyllis Rowland's 13th great-grandfather, through Dorothy Howell12,
	Jemima Woodhull11, Jemima Halsey10, Abiah Rowe9, Lemuel Scudder8, etc.

14 McGrave, Jeff. Hampton Bays Online. The early settlers purchased the Southampton area
	from the Shinnecock Indians for sixteen coats, three score bushels of Indian corn and the
	protection from raiding Indian tribes from New England and in return the Indians taught
	the colonists how to plant corn and beans, to use fish for fertilizer, the use of succotash,

shellfish, wild plants and techniques of whaling in canoes off the south coast of the town. Whales were plentiful off the coast at the time and in 1644 people were posted to watch for beached whales. Equipment for killing the whales and furnaces for processing were started behind the dunes along the beach. Accessed 11/15/2008. From http://www.hamptonbaysonline.com/history.php

15 Genesis 31: 49.

CHAPTER FOUR

16 Bradstreet, Ann Dudley.

17 Cotton Mather, "Diary" I 535-536, quoted in The Puritan Family, Edmund S. Morgan.

18 Christopher Marlowe, "The Passionate Shepherd to His Love."

19 http://www.nationaljousting.com/history/medieval.htm

20 Snell, Melissa. "How to Joust." Medieval History. Accessed 11/15/2008. From http://historymedren.about.com/cs/knighthood/ht/joust.

21 Warren, Patricia Nell. Joan of Arc, Champion Jouster, Sexually Ambigious, She Remains a Heroine. Accessed 11/15/2008. From http://outsports.com/history/joanofarc1.htm

22 Marlowe's Translation of Ovid's Elegia 5: Corinnae concubitus.

23 "Book Rags Biography on ." 19 August 2005. From http://www.bookrags.com/biography/john-cotton/ John Cotton, the leading clergy-man of New England's first generation, a leader in civil and religious affairs, and a persuasive writer on the theory and practice of Congregationalism, was born in Derbyshire, but left when he was thirteen (William Ludlam, Sr. was 23 then) to begin his studies at Cambridge. His father was an ardent Puritan.

24 Adapted from Meditation May 13, 1657, by Ann Dudley Bradstreet.

CHAPTER FIVE

25 Per the NEHGR, Thomas immigrated to Boston from Lime Tree Farm, Matlock, England, in about 1648 with son John and daughter Dorothy. Also Encyclopedia of Quaker Genealogy, 1750–1930, vol. III, "New York Monthly Meeting", p. 43.

26 Volo, James M. and Dorothy Denneen Volo. Family Life in 17th and 18th -Century America, 2006, p. 17. Large numbers of Royalists and Catholics migrated to Virginia and Maryland

to avoid Puritan repression during the English Civil Wars (1642-1649). By 1660, 45,000 of these people had been reduced to half by disease, starvation, and Indian attacks.

27 Sirach 6:33, a book of the Apocrypha included in the Geneva Bible, 1559, as well as in early editions of the King James Bible.

28 The North Sea harbor on Peconic Bay is the sight of the landing of the first English immigrants from Massachusetts, in 1640. From there, the Shinnecocks led the Colonists down to the south coast of Long Island in 1648 where they established Olde Towne. The rich hunting and fishing grounds, the fertile soil and the grassy grazing pastures were all the new colonists dreamed of. The Shinnecocks taught the new settlers about local foods, craft traditions and whaling. Email: hismusdir@hamptons.com

29 The Great Hurricane of 1635. Accessed 11/15/2008. From http://www.islandnet.com/~see/weather/events/gh1635.htm., also from the diary of Rev. Richard Mather, a passenger aboard the *James*.

CHAPTER SIX

30 Halsey, Abigail. "In Old Southampton." Columbia University Press, 1940, p. 22-23. "By 1648, the Olde Towne settlement of Southampton had grown too large, and in a town meeting, they decided to move to a tract of land they called "the Great Playne," with room for "incomers." The long Main Street of Southampton today, winding from the ocean to the woods, follows the general plan of Towne Street of 1648. Besides his home lot of three acres, on which he might build but one dwelling, each householder had twelve acres for his farm and about thirty-four acres of meadow and upland with a certain number of shares in the undivided commonage or common land. A stranger coming into town owned only what he bought and had no share in the undivided lands."

31 Winthrop Papers, 4:460, tells briefly of the attack on the Fordham plantation.

32 Purchase recorded in full in New York Deed Book, iii, 100. This purchase included 100 miles of sandy loam, rich in woods, streams, harbors and long beaches, with offshore island and 1,500 acres of barren heath.

33 Winthrop Papers. In a letter to Governor John Winthrop of "4th 4th Mo. 1644" Hank Walton of Flatlands in New Netherland described an Indian assault on "Mr. Fowrdam's plantation" (Hempstead) in which "three men have been cut off at their work and one of Goodman Carman's children almost massacred and another carried away."

34 Quoted directly from Doc. Hist., iv, 105, Annals of Hempstead, Hank Onderdonk Jr.; Ja-
      maica, L.I.; June 188?.

35 Col. His., i, 186, Annals of Hempstead, Hank Onderdonk Jr.; Jamaica, L.I.; June 188?.

36 Description adapted from the writing of Daniel Denton regarding Long Island, 1670.

37 Southampton: A History of Long Island: from its earliest settlement to the present time, by
      Peter Ross, New York: Lewis Pub. Co. , 1902, transcribed by Coralynn Brown: "South-
      ampton was a Christian, democratic town, but by no means a theocracy. Its reasons for
      formally annexing itself in 1644 to Hartford rather than to New Haven was that, under
      the laws of the last named commonwealth, church membership was an essential to the
      full rights of citizenship, to the right to speak and vote at town meetings. The best and
      most influential townsmen welcomed 'the well-beloved servant of the Lord, Mr. Ford-
      ham,' as they expressed it, in April, 1649, in their contract with him as their minister. So,
      with Fordham's ministry, the town of Southampton entered upon a different order of
      things, as well as upon a new era of prosperity, which has continued until the present
      day. Under Mr. Fordham a new church building was erected in 1651. This church stood
      until 1707, when a third structure was erected, which was occupied by the congregation
      until 1845, when it was replaced by a more commodious structure.' Mr. Fordham contin-
      ued to act as minister until his death in 1674, and long before that he enjoyed the reputa-
      tion of being the wealthiest man in Southampton. Yet his stipend never seems to have ex-
      ceeded 80 lb., so he must have largely engaged in mercantile affairs and been a good
      business man."

38 History and Vital Records of Christ's First Presbyterian Church of Hempstead, Long Island,
      New York, Contributed by John Dean Fish, who tells us that the Rev. Richard Denton
      was the first minister of Hempstead. The Town books on March 4, 1658, list the payment
      of his salary at the rate of f174os. per quarter. In 1660, Jonah [Gideon] Fordham, a young
      man, son of Robert Fordham, whose name heads the list of grantees in the Kieft patent,
      became the second minister to be installed in Hempstead. The Rev. Jonah [Gideon] had
      spent some of his boyhood days in Hempstead. He was graduated at Harvard College in
      1658, and was settled in Hempstead as minister in 1660. His ministry was uneventful, if
      we may judge from the Town Records. Like his father, he seems to have had an inclina-
      tion for practical affairs, for business and trade. He remained in Hempstead until the
      death of his father in Southampton in 1674, when he removed there, becoming his fa-

ther's successor as the minister of the Southampton Church, and also the inheritor of his father's considerable worldly possessions.

39 Halsey, Abigail. "In Old Southampton." Columbia University Press, 1940, p. 19. "Newcomers were admitted only with the approbation of the original company, and great care was taken not to admit those who might be undesirable neighbors. To those who were admitted, parcels of land were usually sold, but sometimes they were given in return for definite service to the town." As a miller, William Ludlam was supplying a definite service.

40 Elizabeth's father, John Smith, had been killed by Indians at the 1643 uprising at Mespath, Queens Co, NY

41 Halsey, Abigail. "In Old Southampton." Columbia University Press, 1940, p. 20.

42 _____ Pierson was greatly revered as "a man of strong faith and leadership who helped the little colony through those early years. His oldest son became the first president of Yale College," [after our William Leverich rejected the offer.]

43 See note 38.

44 Tithing man employed to keep order during the service.

45 Thomas and Phebe Wheeler Halsey were the 12th great-grandparents of Phyllis Rowland. They were the great-grandparents of Abiah Rowe who married Grand-Mary's grandson, Jacob Scudder in 1731.

46 Although the facts about the Halseys are historically accurate, their friendship with the Ludlam family is a logical supposition.

47 Southampton, NY – Court Records, Source Material: "Celebration of the Two Hundred and Seventy-fifth Anniversary of the Founding of the Town of Southampton, NY," written in 1915; The General Court. [This is in reference to the murder of the wife of Thomas Halsey, Sr.] Magistrate and citizens in the market place. Enter Wyandanch, chief of the Montauks, with Indian prisoner. Wyandanch speaks: "We bring this man to you. He killed one of your squaws. Deal with him according to the white man's law. He is not of our tribe, but a Pequot from across the water.

48 The Bay Psalm Book, compiled by John Hardwick and John Cotton

49 Gardiner, Lion, 1599–1663, English colonist in America. Under contract with patentees of Connecticut, Gardiner designed and erected (1635–36) the blockhouse at Saybrook, which he defended in the Pequot War (1636–37). He purchased (1639) Gardiner's Island from Native Americans and founded there the first English colony in present-day New

York. The Columbia Electronic Encyclopedia, 6th ed. Copyright © 2005, Columbia University Press.

50 Lion Gardiner, Narrative of the Pequot War, Part 3, Gardiner's Narrative 145, 1660.

51 Town of Southampton, supervisor Patrick A. Heaney. Accessed 11/15/2008. From http://town.southampton.ny.us/comprehensive.ihtml?mode=detailandid=36

52 Halsey, Abigail. "In Old Southampton." Columbia University Press, 1940, p. 19. "On March 7, 1644, 'it was voted and consented unto by the Generall Court trhat the Towne of Southampton shall enter into Combination with the jurisdiction of Connecticute.'"

CHAPTER SEVEN

53 Richard Mills, a schoolmaster, was made freeman in Southampton on Oct. 7, 1650, and was secretary register and town clerk there between 1650 and 1652. He was given the old meeting-house in April 1651 in order to keep the "ordinary," (i.e., to lodge strangers,) which he agreed to do for four years. It was also decreed that only he would be allowed to sell liquor in the town. [Southampton Town Records. Book A: 1640-1660. Manuscript. Town Hall, Southampton, Long Island: pp. 73, 81, 92, 95, 109.].

54 Accessed 11/15/2008. From http://www.newsday.com/community/guide/lihistory/ny-history-hs504a,0,6436799.story by Katti Grey, staff writer.

55 Halsey, Abigail. . "In Old Southampton." Columbia University Press, 1940, p. 36. The Fordham Manse was about 4 miles south of the North Sea wigwam of Nowedanah, and approximately 4.5 miles south east of the Shinnecock village at Sebonac (now Shinnecock Hills National Golf Club, about 3 miles east of Canoe Place. Quogue was the winter home of the Shinnecocks, and Canoe Place was an Indian camping ground. Perhaps the tree Joshua climbed was a 2 mile walk from the Fordham home, and then he walked another 2 miles down the Indian path to reach the Shinnecock village.

56 Idea from the text of the Commencement address by Steve Jobs, CEO of Apple Computer and of Pixar Animation Studios, delivered on June 12, 2005.

57 "Invisible People of Suffolk, Nassau, Queens and Kings Counties, New York State (and extended families): The African and Native Americans Genealogies."

58 Halsey, Abigail. "In Old Southampton." Columbia University Press, 1940, p. 12. Nowedanah, sister of Wyandanch of the Montauks was head of the Shinnecock at one time.

She was married to Kockenoe, who helped John Eliot translate the Bible into the Algonquin language.

59 "Invisible People of Suffolk, Nassau, Queens and Kings Counties, New York State (and extended families): The African and Native Americans Genealogies."

60 Adapted from sermons of John Calvin and Jonathan Edwards' "Sinners at the Hand of an Angry God."

61 Rath, Richard Cullen. How Early America Sounded. (From letter to Increase Mather from Samuel Arnold, 1666), p. 1.

62 "East Hampton in the 17th Century." Lecture by John Murrin, Ph.D. 30 May 1998. Tells of Foulke's arrest and trial but not his death.

63 Accessed 11/15/2008. From http://www.newsday.com/community/guide/lihistory/ny-history-hs202b,0,5453755.story?coll=ny-lihistory-navigation, by Steve Wick, staff writer. Found in description by Dutch minister Jasper Danckaerts, early 1600s.

64 Samp is porridge made from coarsely ground corn.

65 From the writing of Daniel Denton, 17th century Long Islander.

66 Accessed 11/15/2008. From www.parabola.org/magazine/forum/2404evil.php4.

CHAPTER EIGHT

67 Jonah [Gideon] Fordham was graduated at Harvard College in 1658, and became the minister of Hempstead in 1660. Like his father, he seems to have had an inclination for practical affairs, for business and trade. He remained in Hempstead until the death of his father in Southampton in 1674, when he moved there, becoming his father's successor as the minister of the Southampton Church. He is not mentioned his father's will.

68 Proverbs 25: 8

69 John Carman was my 8th great-grandfather. The family line is Phyllis Wilson11, Beulah Heath10, George Heath9, Deidamia Mcdonald8, Jacob McDonald7, Mary Larue6, Jacob LaRue5, Phebe Carman4, James Carman3, Caleb Carman2 [brother of Joshua], John W.Carman1.

70 "John Carman," William Frost and McDonald-Shehi family tree records.

71 The Rev. John Hardwick's Record of Church Members, Roxbury, Mass. Transcribed by William B. Trask, Esq., of Boston. William and Mary Heath, first Heaths to immigrate, were also charter members at the Roxbury church.

72 "Being recorded and accepted as a member of the church congregation had a significant distinction. Only church members could be made freemen. It was not enough to have taken the oath of fidelity and have been voted to admittance as a resident of the town. A "freeman" had to have all these plus ownership requirements." http://www.carman.net/roxbury.htm.

73 Demos, John. The Redeemed Captive, 1994, p. 3.

74 Richard M. Bayles, Sketches of Suffolk County, Friedman, Port Washington, 1873, copy 1962, p. 235.

75 George R. Howell, The Early History of Southampton, Yankee Peddler, Southampton, 1887, p. 170.

76 "The Goody Garlic Witch Craft Case." Official reports of testimony taken from East Hampton records of the 1600's, copied mostly by Joseph S. Osborne, verbatim et literatim.

77 "Thou shalt have no other gods before thee," Exodus 20:3.

78 Leviticus 20·:27

CHAPTER NINE

79 "The Goody Garlic Witch Craft Case." Official reports of testimony taken from East Hampton records of the 1600's, copied mostly by Joseph S. Osborne, verbatim et literatim.

80 Edward Howell was my 10th great-grandfather: Phyllis Carrol Wilson13, Beulah Lillian Heath12, George Milton Heath11, John SylvesterHeath10, Jane C. Scudder9, Lemuel Scudder8 Richard Scudder7 Lemuel Scudder6 Abiah Rowe5, Jemima Halsey4, Jemima Woodhull3, Dorothy Howell2, Edward Howell1.

81 On April 7, 1661,Caleb Carmen and his older brother John and his brother-in-law, Benjamin Coe, (husband of Abigail Carmen) petitioned the government at New Amsterdam that John Hicks, who married their mother, be made to render an account of her estate. From "Caleb Carman, Whaler, Millwright and Miller: Builder of the first Mill in Cape May County." By H. Clifford Campin, Jr. The Cape May County Magazine of History and Genealogy, June 1945 pp. 283-290.

82 Joshua Carman's brother John's will of 14 September 1684 ordered two of his sons "to take my brother Joshua Carman's estate into their hands and to provide for him, if he wishes" [NYGBR 65:115].

CHAPTER TEN

83 Adapted from Isa. 43:19.

84 Accessed 11/15/2008. From

http://www.birds.cornell.edu/programs/AllAboutBirds/BirdGuide/Red-tailed_Hawk.html.

85 From http://www.birds.cornell.edu/programs/AllAboutBirds/BirdGuide/Red-tailed_Hawk.html

86 Ideas for the sermon are derived from "Celebrating Our Life in Christ" readings compiled by Garee Geist, including thoughts from the works of Thomas Merton and from The Ragamuffin Gospel, by Brennan Manning, as well as from selected verses of the Geneva Study Bible of 1599.

87 Bradstreet, Anne. Adapted from Tenth Muse Lately Sprung Up in America (1650).

88 Burke, Helen Newbury. Foods from Our Founding Fathers, p. 238.

CHAPTER ELEVEN

89 By 1659 Richard Gildersleeve had acquired "Mr. Carman's right at Merocke" in Hempstead [HempTR 1:115, 455]

90 Now called Flushing, New York.

91 Conklin, Lawrence H. John Conklin (1598-1684) From "glasseman" to mineralogist in 400 years. http://www.lhconklin.com/bio/genealogy.htm. In late April 1650, John and Ananias Conklin and Thomas Scudder, moved to Southold, Long Island. Conklin brothers were glassmakers whose Salem business had not paid off, and they were eager to move elsewhere. Their brother Cornelius stayed in Salem. In about 1657, John moved to Huntington. Years later, his grandson, John Conklin III, married Sarah Scudder, Mary and Thom's third daughter.

CHAPTER TWELVE

92 Hank Bartholomew. Accessed 11/15/2008. From

http://etext.virginia.edu/salem/witchcraft/Perley/vol1/images/p1-315.html.

93 Perley, Sidney. The History of Salem, Vol. I, p. 322. Accessed 11/15/2008. From

http://etext.virginia.edu/salem/witchcraft/Perley/vol1/images/p1-311.html

94 Accessed 11/15/2008. From

   http://www.firstchurchinsalem.org/history.htm#Succession%20of%20Ministers, First
   Church of Salem, Archives and History, Succession of Ministers.

95 Scudder, Henry. The Christian's Daily Walke in Holy Securitie and Peace. London, 1628.

96 Catch-colt: From the unsupervised breeding of horses in unfrequented fields. Old-field colt
   is one of several old-fashioned regional euphemisms for a child born out of wedlock.
   (Now obsolete) The term is native to the Virginia Piedmont. Old-field is the Southern
   term for an over cultivated field allowed to lie fallow. Being isolated and usually undis-
   turbed, these fields provided a place for unplanned breeding of horses and, figuratively,
   of children. The term is sometimes shortened to field colt. A related Southern expression
   is woods colt. The Western U.S. equivalent is catch colt. Accessed 11/15/2008. From
   http://education.yahoo.com/reference/dictionary/entry/old-field%20colt.

97 ___. pp. 94, 96.

CHAPTER THIRTEEN

98 Accessed 11/15/2008. From http://www.crystalinks.com/caulveil.html: "A caul or veil
   (Latin: Caput galeatum) is a thin, filmy membrane, the remnants of the amniotic sac, that
   covers or partly covers the newborn mammal immediately after birth." Diviners say a
   reddish caul brings good luck, but if the membrane is lead-colored, the infant will have
   misfortunes.

CHAPTER FOURTEEN

99 A jumble of imagery from Revelation 17.

100 According to the Visitations of Kent, Taken in the Years 1574 and 1592 published by The
   Harleian Society, London, 1924, this was the crest of Scudder of Northcray, England.
   "Scudder" or "skudder" is an old English term denoting a person employed in the tanning trade in the treatment of hides. The name could also be nautical in nature, as "scud"
   is a nautical term. The word "schutter" means archer or bowman in Dutch or Flemish. It
   could also mean a shooter, which could be why the family arms include cannon balls.
   Family members of today in the Darenth Valley, Kent, are of the opinion that the name is

of Dutch or Flemish origin. And, since many of the inhabitants of that part of England came from that part of the continent, there could be some credibility to that theory.

101 Cinquefoil was an ingredient in many spells in the Middle Ages, and was particularly used as a magic herb in love divinations. It was one of the ingredients of a special bait for fishing nets, which was held to ensure a heavy catch. This concoction consisted of corn boiled in thyme and marjoram water, mixed with nettles, cinquefoil and the juice of houseleek.

102 Documents Relating to the Colonial Hist. of N.Y., V 2, P180-- "16 July 1660. Jan Gerritsen, seaman, late of the Prins Mauris (pd) fl. 11.00.00." Jacob Alrichs, First Director of New Amstel, gave a full report on the incident to the authorities back in Amsterdam saying, in part: "...The Lord God not vouchsafing, this through the ignorance of the skipper, pilot and others of the ship's officers, about eleven o'clock on the night of the 8th of March after we had sailed that day in 26, 18 and 16 fathoms of water, although the skipper, pursuant to my customary warning, had promised not an hour before to take good care and spare the lead, and that he should quickly cast anchor and then come into the cabin to report or communicate the matter, yet the men unexpectedly called out eight and nine fathoms. Wishing thereupon, to tack, and the ship refusing, she immediately struck, and so shaved, which she afterwards continued to do harder and harder, so that we were not a moment certain whether we should leave there alive or perish. After passing through most of the darkness of that night in the greatest anxiety and fear, we found ourselves, at day-break, about a gunshot from the shore, but being between the shores and the strand in such a bad position, and ignorant whether this place was south or north of the Manhattes, it was unanimously resolved, first to save our lives and then to exert every nerve to save as much as we possibly could.

" Accordingly on Friday, the 9th of March, in severe, bitter and freezing weather, with drifting ice, after great trouble, dangerous breaks in a very leaky boat, with considerable water in it, we succeeded in reaching the shore on a broken split of foreland, on which neither bush nor grass grew, nor was any tree or fire-wood to be found. On Sunday morning, the third day we, for the first time, saw and spoke to some Indians, who informed us that it was the foreland of Long Island, and that the place was called Secoutagh. Meantime, the ship getting nearer the shore, we from time to time unloaded and saved all the dry articles. Having met and experienced this misfortune, I sent an Indian, with advice thereof, to General Stuyvesant, who immediately sent us a small sloop and came, himself, on the second day after, to us at the above place mentioned, which lies about twenty leagues north of the Manhattes. On the other, or land, side of said place a small opening or inlet to a river has been discovered, which a small sloop can enter…"

See also http://fourkings.freeyellow.com/Swearingen.html

103 Matthew 12: 11

104 Matthew 22:31-32.

CHAPTER FIFTEEN

105 Geneva Study Bible, 1599.

1061657: Mary and Thomas Scudder settled "by the waterside" of Huntington Bay, possibly on the site of the "Old House at the Inlet" near the junction of present New York and Park avenues, Huntington.

CHAPTER SIXTEEN

107 Adapted from "Wickham Wakened; or, the Quakers Madrigall in Rime Dogerell," published in Ebsworth's "Choyce Drollery." The Rhymster tells how the Quaker is settling down to "great thrift," his period of "tipling being done," i.e., his days of ranting being over, and those who come into competition with him wish him back in the ranting stage. Also found in Autobiography of George Fox.

108 Rebecca Wright, Peter's niece, married Eleazar Leverich in 1662, and divorced him sometime before 1673 because he gave her no children.

109 Dejected - affected or marked by low spirits.

110 Leverich agreed to run the mill at Huntington, and in payment, five years later the town voted to give him most of the land around Cow Harbor.

111 Leverich, Susan M. "The Reverend William Leveridge." Compiled circa 1902.

110 Town records of Huntington, Suffolk county Long Island, v. I, page 7, presented in the "Essex Antiquarian."

113Hammond, John. "The Early Settlement of Oyster Bay." The Oyster Bay Historical Society: The Freeholder: Magazine Online. http://www.oysterbayhistory.org/freejh1.html. Leverich, Mayo, and Wright purchased Scituate upon Oyster Bay, bounded by Oyster River to the east side, and Papaguatunk River on the west side and southward to a point of trees called Canteaiug. Besides that, they bought a tract six miles square at Huntington. All that land for such a small price—coats and stockings, kettles and bottles, hatchets, awl-blades, and shovels, and as much wampum as would make £4 sterling. This was signed by the mark of Assiapum the Sachem; and immediately the three purchasers gave a paper admitting the rest of the Company to an equal share in these lands. The Settlement filled up rapidly, many coming from Sandwich, fleeing from persecution by those falling away from the church. By 1663, there were fifty land-holders living in the area.

114 Leverich, Susan M. "The Reverend William Leveridge," Compiled circa 1902.

115 A 1939 article in the New York Genealogical and Biographical Record, describes the events.

116 Morris, Tom. "Huntington Village: It Struggled but Endured," Newsday. Accessed 11/15/2008. From http://www.newsday.com/community/guide/lihistory/ny-historytown-hist0061,0,7179593.story?coll=ny_community_guide_lihistory_promo.

117 Letter to fellow missionary John Wilson, dated Sandwich, this 22nd of the 7th, 1651, and signed by William Leverich. Probably in the archives of Society for the Propagation of the Gospel in New England, as reported by Tom Leverich. Accessed 11/15/2008. From http://longislandgenealogy.com/WILLIAMLEVERICH.htm.

118 Leverich, Susan M. "The Reverend William Leveridge," Compiled circa 1902.

119 Wikipedia.

120 Where Charles Street now runs.

121 Northport Chamber of Commerce.

122 Little, Bob. The Many Names of Northport. Northport History. Northport Historical Society.

123 Ulrich, Laurel Thatcher. Good Wives, Alfred A. Knofp, publisher, 1980, pp 19-20.

124 This actually occurred in March 1658. Booth, Antonia. "A Brief Account of Southold's History. Accessed 11/15/2008. From http://southoldtown.northfork.net/History.htm. Also, Thompson, Benjamin Franklin. The History of Long Island, from It's Discovery to the Present. 1843, p. 380, includes detailed description of the testimony and trial.

125 Antinomianism is the polar opposite of legalism—the notion that obedience to a code of religious law is necessary for salvation.

126 Romans 3:20, 28; Ephesians 2:9; 2 Timothy 2:9; and Titus 3:5 could easily be interpreted as a claim of freedom from all obligation to obey the moral law. Thus, righteous persons might well hold such a doctrine and behave in an exemplary way, not from compulsion

but from a devotion higher than the law. Gross and vicious persons, however, might well interpret the exemption from obligation as positive permission to disregard the moral law in determining their conduct.

127 Near the junction of what is now New York Avenue and Park Avenue, Northport, Long Island. The original house was torn down in 1875.

128 The Thom and Mary Scudder house "by the waterside," Huntington Inlet as it looked in the mid-19th century. Several generations of Scudders lived in this house. Compiled by D.B. Scudder, from Scudder Association Newsletter.

129 Ross, Peter. "The History of Long Island, from its earliest settlement to the present time." NY Lewis Pub. Co. 1902,[transcribed by Coralynn Brown]

130 Bliss, William Root. Side Glimpses from the Colonial Meeting House. Boston, 1896.

131 Robert Saal, Commack History, 1653-1953. Accessed 11/15/2008. From http://www.commackhistory.com/history.html

132 'Tiddler' is a British term for youngster.

133 Bliss, William Root. Side Glimpses from the Colonial Meeting House. Chapter VIII. "The Disturbers of Public Worship."

134 Bliss, William Root. Side Glimpses from the Colonial Meeting House. Chapter VIII. "The Disturbers of Public Worship."

135 Genesis 3,17-19.

136 From Scudder Association Bulletin, XVII, October 1957. "The Original settlers were Independents or Presbyterians who recognized no other church officers than Pastor, Elder and Deacon. They followed the laws of Plymouth Colony and were very strict as to Sunday observance and as to dress. Women's dresses must cover their shoe buckles, no short sleeves, no ribbons and ruffs. The town records contain a confession by Moses Scudder, son of Henry [Thom's brother], dated June 3, 1683. 'We last winter travelled from Huntington to Hempstead on the Lord's Day for which we are sorry tht we have sinned against God and offended our neighbors for which we desire God to forgive us and hope we shall never offend God nor man in like manner.' Signed Moses Scudder, Thomas and Edward Higby."

137 See Karlsen, Carol. The Devil in the Shape of a Woman, and Lyle Kohler, A Search for Power: The "Weaker Sex" in Seventeenth-Century New England, for more on this topic.

138 Fuller's soap (Heb. borith mekabbeshim, i.e., "alkali of those treading cloth"). Mention is made (Prov. 25:20; Jer. 2:22) of nitre and also (Mal. 3:2) of soap (Heb. borith) used by the fuller in his operations. Nitre is found in Syria, and vegetable alkali was obtained from the ashes of certain plants.

139 Malachi 3: 2-3. Geneva Bible.

140I Corinthians 13: 2-5. Adapted from Mary's Geneva Bible and it's commentary. Here I have substituted the word "Love," for the Geneva Bible's "Charity."

141 Foods: Accessed 11/15/2008. From

http://etext.virginia.edu/salem/witchcraft/Perley/vol1/images/p1-329.html.

142 This interesting relic of Dr. Leverich exists in the town clerk's office at Newtown (now Elmhurst), New York. It is a volume of six or seven hundred pages, about one hundred of which are occupied by a running commentary on the first 14 books of the Old Testament, written by his hand but in part copies from the commentary of the learned Piscator. The book seems to have been originally intended by Mr. Leverich as an index to the subjects he should meet with in course of study, the pages being numbered and headed with a great variety of subjects, written in Latin and arranged alphabetically, but the design was never carried out, and after his decease the book was given to the town for public records that were kept on the back side of his notes.

143 Piscator arranged to have the Jewish writings in Aramaic, "The Talmud," placed in University Libraries to help scholars with their Old Testament studies.

144 Much of Grand-Mary's history lesson is taken from quotations of Ellen Leverich, Accessed 11/15/2008. From http://www.animatedatlas.com/ecolonies/ecoloniesglossframe.html

145 Letter from Davenport to Winthrop, Nov. 22, 1655. Oyster Bay and Huntington, ([London] 1778).

146 Words taken from a letter to fellow missionary John Wilson regarding Leverich's missionary endeavors, dated Sandwich, this 22nd of the 7th, 1651", and signed by William Leverich.

CHAPTER SEVENTEEN

147Levy, Barry. The Quakers and the American Family. Oxford University Press, NY (1988).

148 Harris, S.B. The Skeptic. vol 1. no 2. 1992. In Italy, in the 1400s, newborn babies who failed to breath spontaneously were given mouth-to-mouth resuscitation by midwives. With

the coming of the "germ theory," mouth-to-mouth resuscitation was abandoned in the 18th century- with a move to the use of bellows to force air into the lungs.

149 Afterburden: afterbirth. The word "placenta" was not in use until after 1677.

150 Direct quotation from Rev. William Leverich

151 Stevenson, Kenneth. "The Mystery of Baptism in the Anglican Tradition," Canterbury Press, 1998. From The teachings of Richard Hooker (1554-1600).

152 Calamy, Edmund. Condensed from A Practical Discourse Concerning Vows: with a special Reference to Baptism and the Lord's Supper, London, 1697. Accessed 11/15/2008. http://www.apuritansmind.com/Baptism/CalamyPracticalDiscourseConcerningVowsBaptism.htm

153 Evil as defined by St. Thomas Aquinas.

154 George Fox, the founder of the Quaker religion.

155 Thom Scudder's version of Lord Thomas of Winesberry's folk song, "As I Look'd over the Castle Wall."

156 Records of the Quarterly Courts for Essex County, volume 2, page 54.

157 Acts of the Apostles 9:3-19a

158 VanSpanckeren, Kathryn. *An Outline of American Literature: Early American and Colonial Period to 1776:The colonial period in New England.* Accessed 06/22/2008. http://www.let.rug.nl/usa/LIT/ch1_p3.htm. The Scudders are Puritans, but they didn't come to the colonies for religious reasons. They are entrepreneurs, land owners, whalers, husbandry men. Moreover, the concept of stewardship encouraged success. The Puritans interpreted all things and events as symbols with deeper spiritual meanings, and felt that in advancing their own profit and their community's well-being, they were also furthering God's plans. They did not draw lines of distinction between the secular and religious spheres: All of life was an expression of the divine will.

159 The fifth Book of Moses, Deuteronomy 13.

160 Their differences were finally settled, a copy of which is furnished by James Riker of Waverly, New York from the original yet preserved by one of the descendants of Rev. Leverich.

161 Shakespeare, William. *The Tragicall Historie of Hamlet, Prince of Denmark.* London, 1603.

162 Huntington Court Records 1659-1700, pp. 28-30. These records are preserved at the Huntington Town Archives at Town Hall, Huntington, Long Island, New York.

CHAPTER EIGHTEEN

163 Higby, Clinton David. Edward Higby and his Descendants, 1927. Also spelled "Higbee."

164 Puritans believed children were born into sin and that midwives were often in league with Satan. In such cases, the baby might be born with horns or scales, feet or head like a monster. They believed in the existence of witches. On the other hand, Indians danced and laughed at the time of a birth, capable of joy that was rare among Puritans who insisted behavior must be orderly and respectful.

165 Online publication - Ancestry.com. OneWorldTree [database on-line]. Provo, UT, USA: MyFamily.com, Inc. .Patience Higbee, born in 1660, was the last of Edward and Jedidah Skidmore Higbee's six children.

CHAPTER NINETEEN

166 Accessed 11/15/2008. From http://higpic.com/genealogy/genealogy.htm.

167 Ross, Peter. "The History of Long Island, from its earliest settlement to the present time." NY Lewis Pub. Co. 1902,[transcribed by Coralynn Brown]

168 From http://www.longislandgenealogy.com/dukelaws/1.htm

169 Ross, Peter. "The History of Long Island, from its earliest settlement to the present time." NY Lewis Pub. Co. 1902,[transcribed by Coralynn Brown]

170 Accessed 11/15/2008. From http://town.huntington.ny.us/town_history.cfm.

171 Accessed 11/15/2008. From http://www.ristenbatt.com/genealogy/dutch_dr.htm

172 New England Journal G. Although identification of this journal is uncertain, many of these words are quoted directly from the Journal report.

173 "Goody" was the common term of address for an ordinary woman of that day. Men were called "Goodman."

174 Exodus 23:1-8.

175 Compiled by Tom Leverich. Rev. William Leverich (1603-1677), Progenitor of the Leverich Family in the United States of America: An Historical Biography, with information from Leverich, Susan M, "The Rev. William Leverich", photocopy of a handwritten account of his life, 14 pages, signed "Susan M. Leverich, Bridgeport, Connecticut", undated; copy courtesy of Mrs. Edna Charles (widow of Charles H. Leveridge [713]) of Ft. Lauderdale, Florida, 1975.

176 Register of New Netherlands 1626-1674.

177 Words of blessing adapted from a letter written by William Leverich to Reverend John Wilson.

178 John 13:35, Geneva Study Bible.

179 A gliffe from the 17th century. A gliffe is a tongue twister, a word game played by Puritan children. Accessed 11/15/2008. From

http://www.erasofelegance.com/history/baroquelife.html.

180Shillingburg, Patricia. The Provisioning Plantation: 1652-1693: Slavery as the Economic Engine. Accessed 11/15/2008. From http://www.shelter-island.org/slavery.html.

181 Shillingburg, Patricia. "The Settlers of the East End." 2003. quotation from speech by Henry P. Hedges, a lawyer and East Hampton historian, on the subject of agriculture in 1866. Accessed 11/15/2008. From http://www.shelter-island.org/settlers.html

182 These are some of the farming activities listed in Ebenezer Miller's diary out in Suffolk County, between 1762 and 1768.

183 Accessed 11/15/2008. From http://pages.zoom.co.uk/leveridge/leverich1.html

184 Leverich, Susan M. The Reverend William Leveridge, compiled circa 1902. This edition prepared in 1999 by Richard Mervyn Leveridge from a typescript version at the Sandwich Archives and Historical Centre, 145 Main Street, Sandwich MA 02563. Document received 1980-07-15. This article contains significant inaccuracies and should be treated as a period item of historical interest, rather than as authenticated history. The editors' notations appear in square brackets. According to the author, ['William Leverich was doubtless familiar with the medical teaching of that day for nothing was more common among the university educated Theologues, than to attend the lectures of the medical professors, and "walk the hospital" as it was termed, which was connected with nearly all the universities.] In Herbert's old book, The Country Parson, we are told that a parson may become qualified to treat the ills that flesh is heir to by 'Seeing one anatomy, reading one book of physic, and having one herbal by him.' This was the extent of an education in physic which the poor parsons of New England possessed."

185 Bliss, William Root, Side Glimpses from the Colonial Meeting-house.

186Shillingburg, Patricia. "The Settlers of the East End." 2003. Accessed 11/15/2008. From http://www.shelter-island.org/settlers.html.

187 Only members of the church were voting members of the community. This remained true until 1789 when the United States Constitution became the law of the land and churches were separated from government. From

http://pages.zoom.co.uk/leveridge/susanlev.html.

188 Ross, Peter. "The History of Long Island, from its earliest settlement to the present time." NY Lewis Pub. Co. 1902,[transcribed by Coralynn Brown].

189 27 April 1663, Huntington Town Records.

190 "Witchcraft Trials in New York (1665)." Accessed 11/15/2008.From

(http://homepages.rootsweb.ancestry.com/~tmetrvlr/hd10.html.

191 (Bishop, New England Judged, ed. of 1703, p. 11; Howell, Early History of Southampton, L. I., second ed., Albany, 1887, p. 448; Early Long Island Wills, New York, 1897, p. 78 ff.)

192 Records, Town of Brookhaven, Patchogue, NY 1880.

193 Heyrman, Christine Leigh. "Puritanism and Predestination." Divining America, TeacherServe©. National Humanities Center. Accessed 6/23/2008.

<http://nationalhumanitiescenter.org/tserve/eighteen/ekeyinfo/puritan.htm>

194 Campbell, Donna M. "Puritanism in New England." Literary Movements. 05/21/2007. Accessed 06/22/2008. <http://www.wsu.edu/~campbelld//purdef.htm>. "The Covenant of Redemption was assumed to be preexistent to the Covenant of Grace. It held that Christ, who freely chose to sacrifice himself for fallen man, bound God to accept him as man's representative. Having accepted this pact, God is then committed to carrying out the Covenant of Grace. According to Perry Miller, as one contemporary source put it, "God covenanted with Christ that if he would pay the full price for the redemption of believers, they should be discharged. Christ hath paid the price, God must be unjust, or else hee must set thee free from all iniquitie" (New England Mind 406)."

195 Campbell, Donna M. "Puritanism in New England." Literary Movements. 05/21/2007. Accessed 06/22/2008. From <http://www.wsu.edu/~campbelld//purdef.htm>. "Since citizenship was tied to church membership, the motivation for experiencing conversion was secular and civil as well as religious in nature. God's covenant that bound church members to him had to be renewed and accepted by each individual believer, although this could be seen as a dilution of the covenant binding God and his chosen people."

196 Hoadly and J. H. Trumbull, eds., Public Records of the Colony of Connecticut, 1636-1776, 15 vols. (Hartford, Conn.: Brown and Parsons, 1850-1890), 2:292 (1676).

197 Accessed 11/15/2008. Accessed 11/15/2008. From

   http://town.huntington.ny.us/town_history.cfm.

198 Perry, Bliss. The American Spirit in Literature, A Chronicle of Great Interpreters. "Chapter

   II. The First Colonial Literature." Public domain, Project Gutenberg. This page created by

   Philipp Lenssen.

199 Thom Scudder's tanning mills faced the water in the area now called Tanyard Lane. From

   there, leather was sent to a drum factory on Rogues Path, to be made into drums for mili-

   tary use all over the world. In 1690, the year of his death, he is referred to as a farmer and

   tanner.

200 Accessed 11/15/2008. From http://www.shelter-island.org/settlers.html.

201 Ross, Peter. The History of Long Island, from its earliest settlement to the present time. NY

   Lewis Pub. Co. 1902,[transcribed by Coralynn Brown]

202 Huntington's delegates, Jonas Wood and John Ketcham, returned from the meeting with

   that now famous document of the Duke's Laws. It is locked in a safe, housed in a vault,

   and is well protected under the care of the town historian.

203 With some modifications, including the abolition of "Yorkshire" and "ridings," this was the

   form that the government of New York retained until the Revolution.

204 Newsday.com. "Legacy: The Duke's Laws." Steve Wick, Staff Writer. Accessed 11/15/2008.

   From <www.newsday.com/community/guide/lihistory/ny-history-

   hs320a,0,5781435.story>

205 LI Forum 1970 No Copyright Information Data Found

206 Old First Presbyterian Church founded 1658, present building 1784 at 125 Main Street (NW

   corner of Main St. & Sabbath Day Path), Huntington.

207 ____

208 O'Callaghan, E.B. The Documentary History of the State of New York, (Albany, N.Y., 1849-

   51). 3:52-63; E.H. O'Callaghan. The register of New Netherland, 1626 to 1674, (Albany,

   1865), 127.

209 17th century word for 'salad'

210 Earle, Alice Morse. Sabbath in Puritan New England. Accessed 11/15/2008.From

   http://www.fullbooks.com/Sabbath-in-Puritan-New-England1.html.

211 Grand-Mary's brother Hal (Henry) Ludlam b. 1635 at Matlock, Derbyshire, England mar-

   ried Jane Shaw of Southampton Long Island New York. He inherited the mill of Southampton and this family were the Puritan hereditary millers and Millwrights of South-ampton.

212 Abstracts of Wills Vol I 1665-1707. Will of William Ludlam (1600/05 - 1665) of New York. (Copy of the First Will on Record in the City of New York, April 27th, 1665.)

213 Newell, J. Philip. Listening for the Heartbeat of God. Paulist Press, 1997.

214 Huntington Town Records, 1667, June 13.

215 Ross, Peter. The History of Long Island, from its earliest settlement to the present time. New York: Lewis Pub. Co., 1902. Accessed 11/15/2008. From http://freepages.genealogy.rootsweb.com/~jdevlin/newyork/huntington_hist.htm

216 Taken from Civil, Political, Professional and Ecclesiastical History and Commercial and Industrial Record of the County of Kings and The City of Brooklyn, N.Y.; from 1683 to 1884. by Henry R. Stiles, A.M., M.D., Editor-in-Chief. Vol. I; pgs. 27-29. Accessed 06/22/2008. From http://www.rootsweb.ancestry.com/~nynassa2/convention.htm.

CHAPTER TWENTY-ONE

217 In the17th century, the phrase 'a real piece of work' was a compliment, almost exactly the opposite of the 21st century meaning.

218Reverend Eliphalet Jones ministered in Huntington for the next 55 years, until his death at the age of 93.

219 Beese, Joseph. A Collection of the Sufferings of the People Called Quakers. 1753.

220 From an old German poem.

221 Accessed 11/15/2008. From http//www.easthamptonlibrary.org/lic/lectures/johnstronglecture.htm. Accessed 11/15/2008.

222 Accessed 11/15/2008. From http://www.infidels.org/library/historical/andrew_white/Chapter4.html#II.

223 Scudder Searches, 1989, Vol. 1. No. 2.

224"Dominion of New England" Encyclopedia Britannica. 2008. Encyclopedia Britannica Online. 30 Oct. 2008. Accessed 11/15/2008. From <http://www.britannica.com/EBchecked/topic/411429/Dominion-of-New-England.

CHAPTER TWENTY-TWO

225 "The Dominion of New England; or, the Puritan Revolution." Accessed 11/15/2008. From
    http://thehistoricpresent.wordpress.com/2008/05/19/ the-dominion-of-new-england-
    or-the-puritan-revolution.

CHAPTER TWENTY-THREE

226 Shillingburg, Patricia. "The Settlers of the East End."
    Accessed 11/15/2008. From http://www.shelter-island.org/settlers.html.
227 William was conveniently married to Mary Stuart, the daughter of Charles I.
228 Andrews, Charles M. Narratives of the Insurrections. 1675-1690 (New York, 1915), 186-90.
229 Accessed 11/15/2008. From http://www.newsday.com/community/guide/lihistory/ny-
    historytown-hist006l,0,7179593.story.

CHAPTER TWENTY-FIVE

230 Street, Charles R. introduction to the 1888 publication of the Huntington Town Records.
231 DeWan, George. "In Charge at Town Hall." Newsday. Accessed 11/25/2008: From
    http://www.baltimoresun.com/topic/ny-history-hs339a,0,6017687.story.

Made in the USA
Middletown, DE
24 June 2019